FOR THE LOVE AND MUSIC

For the Love and Music

LEAZA NORMAN

Purple Stone Books
Purplestonebooks.com

PURPLE STONE
Books

Publication date: 8/15/2022
ISBN: 978-1-958758-03-8
Cover Design by: Leaza Norman
Printed in the United States of America

This book is dedicated to everyone that has ever believed in me and to my new fans. Thank you everyone for your support and dedication for my passion of writing.

New to the Neighborhood

I couldn't believe I was up before my alarm went off. What the hell was that loud sound outside anyway? Slowly, I rolled over and peered outside my window where a large moving truck was idling in the neighbor's driveway.

I glanced over at my clock that read five-fifteen am. My eyes rolled as I tried to muffle the loud sounds with my pillows, but it didn't do me any justice. I let out a frustrated yell and sat up. Guess my day was starting three hours earlier than it was supposed to. Thank goodness it was Friday. I guess.

Down in the kitchen I made my tea and sat in the dining room still frustrated and bored as hell. Why did people have to be so inconsiderate of others? If you're going to be here for a while, shut the Goddamn truck off.

I walked out of the dining room and glanced over in my fitness room. I stared at it for a while contemplating if today would be the day I used my dusty equipment. Nope. I kept moving to the living room trying to run from the loud engine outside. It didn't make a difference.

Usually, I liked my mornings nice and quiet. Could do some meditation, plan out my day… But with this, I couldn't even hear myself think too well.

The tv turned on and I continued to watch the show I had been binge watching for the last two weeks. I sunk down in my couch, pulled the covers up to my neck, and started it.

A few hours had gone by, and I hadn't even realized it. So caught up in the drama. The last episode ended, and I quickly began to get ready to go to a place I hated going to. Work.

On my way out, I grabbed my keys, opened the door and was greeted by an unfamiliar, yet handsome face at my steps. I jumped back startled as he began to speak.

"Good morning. Sorry to startle you. My name is Jamal. I'm moving in next door and wanted to formally introduce myself."

"So you're the one that woke me up three hours ahead of time?" I said in a half joking manner.

"Yea… sorry about that. This is the only free time I have to move in."

"My name is Cadence. It's nice to meet you as well. Welcome to the neighborhood." I said walking out and locking the door.

"Thank you. Thank you. Well, I won't hold you up too long. And again, I apologize about the noise."

"Just turn the truck off and you'll be fine."

"Will do. Catch you later."

I shook my head as I started my car and pulled out of my driveway. As I drove off, I glanced in the rear-view mirror and caught him smirking. I couldn't help but to smile and blush a bit as well.

Fridays were always the busiest days at my job, and it was the day that you didn't really want to do much. I was just happy it was over, and I could go home and relax. There was a bottle of wine waiting for me in the fridge for me to indulge in and I couldn't wait to get my hands on it.

As I pulled into my driveway, my phone began to go off.

"Hello?"

"Cadence, are you free tonight? Janelle and I are going out to the new lounge that just opened up on Front Street. We wanted to know if you wanted to join us."

"At what time?"

"We're trying to get there by nine, but you know she is, so more or less around ten, ten-thirty."

"That works for me. I probably won't stay too long. I've had a long day."

"You always say that and you're always the one that doesn't want to leave." she teased. "See you later."

My head rested back on the seat. I wanted to go out, yes, but I much preferred it to be on a Saturday. Yes, I was picky about my days and liked to stick to my schedule whenever possible. An exception was made here and there, and I guess tonight was one of those nights.

I gathered my energy to get out of the car and headed to the house. On my way up, loud music could be heard playing from the new neighbor's house. I just hoped it wasn't going to be something I had to deal with on a regular basis.

The wine bottle was taken out of the fridge and poured into my favorite wine cup where it was slowly sipped on as I began to pick an outfit for tonight. My long, relaxing Friday night bath was taken as I exfoliated my skin and shaved in preparation.

This lounge was no ordinary lounge, so I heard. Its grand opening was broadcasted for months on tv, social media and the radio. Supposedly some famous rapper owned the place, and it was supposed to be one of the nicest places to go to. I had to mentally prepare myself for the large crowd of people. The only good thing was, Janelle knew a few people that could probably get us in without having to stand in line.

One more hour until we were supposed to meet, and I began to beat my face. On an average night, I wouldn't take the time to apply a full face of makeup, but tonight, I wasn't sure who was going to be there, and I wanted to look my absolute best. Cuz ya girl is definitely single and is definitely ready to mingle.

My dress slid down my body, jewelry was put on as well as my heels to match. The phone vibrated again, and I picked it up.

"Hey, what's up girl?"

"Are you ready? We're outside."

"Be out in a minute."

I hung up, grabbed my keys and headed out the door to the car.

All the girls yelled and clapped as I came down the driveway. The loudest of course was Janelle. She was always the loudest and liveliest of the group and I absolutely loved her for that. Her energy always rubbed off on me allowing me to be loud and rowdy right along with her.

"Hurry up sexy Mama! You're holding us up."

"God damnit Char, I'm coming." I yelled as I made my way to the car and got in.

"Damn girl, you look hella cute tonight. Trynna get you some dick huh?" Janelle teased.

"Can y'all just let me be great in peace. How far is this place anyway?"

"About twenty minutes away. Not too far. Jay is going to be up there to let us in so, you're welcome ladies."

"Janelle with the win again!"

"Yes, yes, I try."

The music was put on blast as we sped down the highway to our destination.

Friday Night

The place was crowded just like I figured it would be. I was so glad we didn't have to stand in the line. It was about sixty people deep and wrapped around the block with anxious people waiting to get in.

The car parked and we all got out and made our way to the front where we were met by Jay. He gave Janelle a quick kiss on the cheek before he let us in. My first stop was the bar and the ladies all followed me over to get our drinks. Soft music was playing in the dimly lit space as we looked around and sipped.

"How do you guys feel about it?" Charmaine asked.

"I like it so far. It has a nice atmosphere." I replied.

"I hope it gets lit later. I'm trynna turn up in this bitch." Janelle added.

More and more people flocked in as the time went on. I was on my second drink and was definitely feeling it along with the vibe. The music was getting more intense, and people were starting to get loose.

I felt a tap on my shoulder and turned around. "Hey, what's up Khalil, how have you been?"

"I'm doing good. Doing good. See you ladies are enjoying yourselves, glad you could make it out."

"Absolutely. Are you performing tonight?"

"Nah, not tonight. Just here to enjoy the show. You guys want anything else to drink?"

"Hi Khalil." Janelle said over my shoulder. She had the biggest crush on this man but was too shy to ask him out. Which was actually quite strange coming from her.

He smirked. "Hi Janelle." He had a small crush on her too. I just wished they would fuck already and get it over with so I wouldn't be caught in the middle hearing about their 'what if' stories.

"Hey hey, my girl Cadence. What's up with you ma? Haven't seen you in a hot minute."

"Hey Brad. How have you been?" I asked giving him a big hug.

"I've been doing alright. How about yourself with your fine ass?"

"I've been good. Just working for the most part."

"You guys want another drink?"

"Khalil beat you to it, but thanks."

"The night is still young, if you want one come holla at me."

"I definitely will. Thank you."

A cup was soon placed in my hand by Khalil before he disappeared into the crowd. Janelle's eyes watched him as he walked away.

"Why don't you just go ask him out already?"

"Girl, what do I look like? I'm not desperate."

"Who said you had to be desperate? You know what? Imma leave it be. You're gonna let him slip between your fingertips."

"Ugg, whatever Cay. Come and dance with me." she yelled, pulling my arm and leading me to the dance floor. Charmaine came with us too and we all danced. With each other at first, but as time went on, men were dancing with us too.

The man behind me suddenly stopped dancing and spoke. "Oh, What's up Mal? Didn't think you could make it with the move and all."

"You know I had to come out and show my people's some love." A familiar voice responded back. I turned around to fulfill my peeking curiosity. "Oh shit, hey neighbor."

I stood there shocked and tried to fix myself. I wasn't expecting to see my new neighbor standing right in front of me as I was acting a tad bit... promiscuous. I smiled a nervous smile. "Hey... neighbor."

"And I thought you didn't like loud noises." he teased and made a face.

"Not at five o'clock in the morning I don't."

"Look man, Imma catch you later. Enjoy, she's a wild one."

I felt myself blush hard as the man I was just dancing with called me out and left. Jamal didn't seem to mind. He just smiled.

"Are you here alone?"

"No. My friends are around here somewhere. What about you?"

"Mine are about to perform soon. Can I get you a drink or anything?"

"No, I'm alright. Thanks though." After I spoke, someone came and whispered in his ear.

"I gotta catch you later. Hope you enjoy the show." He smiled and followed the guy.

"Who was that?"

"He was cute as hell."

The ladies asked.

"He's... my neighbor."

"Holy shit, are you serious? Since when?"

"This morning." I said, nodding my head in disbelief. "Where the hell is Khalil? I could use that drink now."

"He went that way." Janelle said pointing.

All I could do was giggle. "Of course you would know where he went. Come on, let's get your lover boy."

We made our way to the bar and were greeted by warm embraces from Khalil and his crew again. I tried my hardest not to laugh when Janelle held on longer than a simple 'hello' hug.

7

"What's up Ma, you ready for that drink now?"

"Yes! Two pineapple vodkas and a dirty martini. Please."

"I got you Luv." He chuckled and repeated my order to the bartender before turning back to me. "You aren't mixing drinks again are you?"

"No sir I am not."

"Good, cuz I don't want another repeat of the last time you did."

"We're not gonna talk about that here." I replied sarcastically. Janelle was close behind me and I could tell she wanted to say something. So being the good friend that I was, I opened the door for her.

"Janelle has to ask you something." I said and moved out the way with mine and Charmaine's drink. She gave me a dirty look before looking back at the chocolate man.

"What is she doing?" Charmaine asked.

I took a sip out of my drink. "Hopefully shooting her shot." The both of us laughed just before the DJ came on the loudspeaker.

"Alright, alright. How are y'all doing tonight? We have some live entertainment for you that I think you'll all enjoy. Give it up for Mally Boy!"

"Yoo... What's up Philly? I got some new shit for you tonight. Hope you like it. Let's get it."

My eyes grew big as Jamal walked out on stage and the crowd went wild. I had never even heard of him, but it seemed like he was a big deal.

"Is that your fuckin neighbor up there?"

I nodded my head. "Yup."

"Did you know...?"

"Nope."

"Are you going to..."

Absolutely not." I quickly responded to Charmaine's questions. I already knew what she was going to ask before the words left her mouth.

The both of us sat there and watched his entire performance which, actually wasn't that bad. Hell, it got me vibin to the beat and flowing with the lyrics. When his time in the limelight was done, he jumped off stage and into the crowd where he was swarmed by groupies. I was not a part of them.

"Cay, can I speak to you for a minute?" Khalil asked out of nowhere.

"Yea, sure. Char, I'll be right back." I said leaving her side as Janelle walked up next to her. He brought me over to a somewhat excluded spot. "What's up?"

"Your home girl just asked me on a date."

"Ok... and? What did you say?"

"I said yea."

"So what's the problem then?"

"Nothing. It came out of nowhere. I'm surprised she did. I'm glad she did. I didn't even know she liked me like that."

"Listen. Y'all been flirtin around this shit for a minute now. Go on a date, feel her out and take it from there. You're over analyzing this shit. Y'all make me sick." I joked.

"You right, you right. Iight. Imma give it a shot."

I smirked reading his emotions. "Are you shy or something?"

"What? Hell Nah."

"Aww Lil actin a lil shy shy."

"Shut up Cadence. You play too damn much."

"Go dance with her. Stop being shy." I teased again.

"I'm about to."

"Yo Lil." someone yelled above us. We both looked up and who was it? No other than Jamal.

"What's up bro?"

"You think you can check something out for me right quick?"

"Yea, yea, I got you. Give me a minute."

"How do you know him?"

"We work in the studio together sometimes. You know him?"

"Not on a personal level. Go handle what you gotta handle and you better ask her when you're done."

"I will gees Ma." He gave me a hug before he left, and I made my way back to the girls.

"Did he tell you?" Janelle asked anxiously. I smiled.

"He told me."

"What do you think?"

"Oh God, now we have to listen to this shit all night. Cadence, why did you do that?"

"We'll talk about it later. Right now, I wanna dance." I said leading them both to the dance floor to continue dancing.

Getting to Know You

"Last call for alcohol." The DJ announced over the mic. Khalil knew me too well and came up to us holding drinks in his hands.

"Thank you, thank you." I said, grabbing my cup from him.

His eyes glanced over at Janelle before he pulled her away to the dance floor. Finally, Charmaine and I danced with some guys behind us and just let the beat and the liquor take control. I looked up briefly and saw Jamal staring at me from where he was standing.

He was surrounded by females, yet all his attention seemed to be on me. Me being the person that I was, gave him a little show and began to grind on the guy I was dancing with harder while looking him in the eyes as I did it. Jamal smirked flirtatiously before focusing back on his small crowd.

"Damn Baby, what you doing after this?" the guy asked.

"Going home by myself and going to bed." I snarked and left his side.

At the bar, I could see my girl Char getting it in with some guy. Janelle and Khalil were in their own little world. "I see Lil finally talked to Janelle." Brad said from behind me.

I turned around to face him. "About damn time. They look like they're enjoying themselves."

"Yea, they do. Did you enjoy yourself?"

"I did very much so. How about you?"

"I'd enjoy it better if you danced with me quick fast."

I smiled before taking his hand and going back on the floor. Our dance, however, wasn't that long before the lights came on and the music was turned down.

"When Imma see you again?"

"I'll be around."

"I better witchyo fine ass." A kiss was placed on my cheek before he left my side.

Charmaine came up to me followed by a very drunk and very happy Janelle and Khalil. "Y'all bout ready to head out?" Janelle asked.

"Yea, it's about that time. Come on."

"I'll walk y'all to your car." Khalil added and followed.

Everyone seemed to be dispersing at the same time for there was a literal line to get out the building. Once outside, the two new love birds kissed before we got in the car.

"Good night ladies. Get home safe. Let me know when you get there."

"Will do Lil. Good night."

The entire ride back was filled with excitement from Janelle talking about her night with Khalil. The girl was over the moon that she actually danced with him and was bold enough to ask him out. Half of it, I'm assuming, was all the liquor she drank throughout the night, but I was happy that she was happy.

We pulled up to my house and I got out of the car yelling at the girls to let me know when they got home. On my way up the driveway, I heard a voice off in the distance.

"Hey neighbor." he startled me once again.

"What the fuck. You scared me to death. Hi. What are you doing out here?"

"Just enjoying the summer night. How did you like the show?"

"What?" I yelled back. I could barely hear him.

Soon, footsteps came closer, and his figure appeared under the moonlight. "I asked you how did you enjoy the show?"

"It was alright I guess." I teased and he chuckled.

"Just alright? I saw you vibin to it."

"Just a little bit." I giggled. "No, it was good. I really did enjoy it. How long have you been performing?" I asked taking my heels off.

"About a year. I love the rush of getting the crowd hyped up."

"You did a good job at that."

"Thank you. I don't want to hold you up though. I'll see you around." He began to walk away.

"See you." I replied. As I went to turn around and walk away, I ran smack into my car causing a loud thudding sound. I laughed at my stupidity and clumsiness.

"Are you alright?" he asked, rushing back to my side.

"I'm good. I'm alright."

He grabbed my arm gently and walked me up the steps to my door. "Make sure you sleep that shit off. I won't be loud in the morning so you can get some rest." he joked.

"Thank you. It would be greatly appreciated."

He walked back to his house before I opened and walked through my door. My shoes were tossed to the side before I made my way up the steps and nosedived into the bed. Before falling asleep, I texted Khalil and let him know I was home safe. But, instead of just responding with a simple 'ok' message, he decided to call.

"Hello?"

"Cay, what are you doing?"

"About to go to bed. What's up? Did you make it home safe?"

"Uhh... Not really. No"

"What do you mean not really no? Where are you?"

"On my way to Janelle's crib."

"Say what now?"

"She invited me over."

"Really Lil? If you don't take your drunk ass to bed."

"I can't, my night isn't over like yours is."

"Ha, ha, funny. Don't do anything stupid."

"I can't promise you that. You know what time it is."

"Lil. Khalil." he hung up.

Oh gah, what was this girl thinking? I couldn't with her, but hey, they're both grown adults. Enjoy it while you can. Me on the other hand, I was about to be passed out. I guess it would have been nice to get some action tonight or be snuggled up with someone. Ugg. What the fuck ever. My day would come. Right?

Another Long Night

Most of my Saturday was spent sleeping and recuperating from last night. After that, I cleaned up the house and just watched tv for the rest of the day. It was a quiet day, just how I liked it. Nothing to do, nowhere to go, no one shouting at you telling you what to do... just, nice and quiet. For now.

My phone rang with Janelle on the other end.

"Cay?"

"Hey Babes, what's up?"

"We did it!" she squealed.

"Did what?"

"We fucked last night. Oh my God, it was amazing!"

"Nelle, ewl. I don't want to hear about my two friends fuckin."

"I know, I know, I just had to tell you. I'm so glad you talked me into talking to him last night. We really hit it off."

"Don't you think you're moving a bit too fast?"

"What? Hell no. I've been wanting him inside me for the longest now."

"Yup. Alright I'm hanging up now."

"Wait, wait no..."

"Did you at least use protection? I'm not ready to be a God Mom yet."

"Yes, yes, we did."

"Does Char know?"

"I'm about to call her next. Byee."

Well, at least one of us was getting some dick. I played my show and watched a good fifteen minutes of it before my phone rang again.

"What do you want with my life?" I teased.

"We fucked." Khalil said.

"Really? Do I have to know all this?"

"I just had to let you know."

"But why though? I don't need to know where your dick has been. I'm sitting here watching my show."

"What are you watching?"

"Lil, really?"

"It was mad good Cay. It was like…"

"Imma stop you there. You know I love you, but I don't need to know every excruciating detail."

"Why not? I always tell you."

"This is different. Both of y'all are my friends and I don't need to see images of y'all fuckin flashing in my mind when I'm trying to sleep. Is that all you called for?"

He was laughing hard in the background before he responded. "Nah, nah, just checking in on you. See how you feelin after last night."

"You sure you ain't mean to call Janelle about the question."

"You funny as shit yo. You got that one."

"I'm doing alright darling. I really am. Just trynna watch my damn show."

"I'll let you go then. One."

My phone immediately lit up again with Charmaine on the other end. "Hello?"

"They fucked!"

16

"I know."

"Wait, how do you know?"

"Both of them called me and told me. I fuckin can't."

"Well, it's about damn time. Anyway. What are you doing?"

"Trying to watch tv."

"Call me later then."

"Bye."

It was like this all the time in this group. You couldn't do anything without someone saying something about it happening. The one thing I did like, was that it never got out to anyone else outside of the group. And, if one of us said not to tell the others yet, no one told anyone else until they got the ok to do so.

My stomach yelled at me angrily to feed it. As I looked in the fridge, there wasn't anything I had a taste for. I closed the door and rolled my eyes before getting dressed to go get something.

As I was leaving the house, a car pulled into the neighbor's driveway and a young woman got out and headed to the door. She knocked on it and Jamal opened it up. Our eyes met briefly before he rushed the woman inside. I must have dick repellent on cuz everyone was getting some but me.

Back at home I sulked on the couch for a while until my eyes burned. My phone was dry as hell and I was up, bored. I looked at the time and the night was still young. I texted the girls to see if they wanted to go out to our favorite spot, but they both declined.

That wasn't going to stop me though. I got dressed and headed out the door. Although I didn't have much energy to dance, I could still have a few drinks and enjoy myself.

The parking lot was rather full as I made my way to the front of the line where my friend Danny let me in. There were a few people that I knew there, but I really didn't want to stick around and chat it up, so I said hello and kept it moving to my favorite spot to sit.

Some food was ordered, and several drinks were sent my way and before I knew it, I was full, tipsy and relaxed. I swayed gently to the music that played and watched everyone enjoy themselves. That was enough entertainment for me. When I had had enough of people watching, I gathered my things and headed back home.

As I pulled up to my house, Jamal was pulling up to his. Both of us got out at the same time but I didn't know what to say to him. But I didn't have to. He spoke first.

"Another late night I see."

"Something like that."

"Did you enjoy your evening?"

"You know I can't hear you way over there."

I heard him laugh before his footsteps came closer. "I asked if you enjoyed your evening."

"For the most part, yea. Did you enjoy yours?"

"Yea. Had another performance at the lounge tonight. Were you there?"

"No. I went somewhere else tonight."

"With your friends?"

"No. Just me."

I walked over to my porch and sat down on one of the steps. He followed. "Are you feeling alright? You seem a little down tonight."

"Why do you say that?"

"Your posture, your energy… Seems like something is on your mind." he replied.

"I'm alright I guess. It's just been a long day is all."

"Anything I can do to make your day better?"

I snickered. "No. There's nothing you can do to make it better."

"Not even talk?" he asked, sitting down next to me.

"About what?"

"Anything. Anything that's on your mind. How long have you been here?"

"About three years."

"You like it?"

"I like it. It seems quite enough. No one really causes problems, and most people stay to themselves. What made you decide to move here?"

"It's quiet and close to the city without being in the city. I came to really start my career. Heard Philly was a great place to start."

"Where were you before you moved?"

"I'm originally from Newark, but I lived in Neptune for most of my life. Not too many ways to get your name out, out there."

"You seem to have a really big following so far."

He scratched his head. "Yea, I know, but it's not enough. Mostly, people know me from my online music, but I'm trying to be more."

"But why Philly? Why not New York or Atlanta or something?"

"Honestly, I'm not a big fan of the city. Don't mind going there to visit, but to live? That's not my thing."

"I understand. So how did the show go tonight?"

"It was great. I think better than last night."

"You write your songs?"

"Yea. And make the beats."

I nodded in approval. "You did a good job."

"Thank you. Much appreciated. So how do you know Lil? I saw y'all chattin it up the other night."

"He's one of my good friends actually."

"Word? He's been helping me in the studio and what not. Showing me around, introducing me to people."

"Yea, that sounds like something he would do." I giggled. "So when's your next show?"

"I'm not sure. Won't know until later on in the week. But until then, I'll be in the studio making more."

I yawned. "I feel you."

"Oh my bad, am I boring you?" he asked sarcastically.

I laughed. "No, no. Like I said, it's been a long day."

"Alright Miss Cadence. I won't hold you up any longer." He stood to his feet and helped me to mine before guiding me up to my door. "You have a good night."

"You as well." I said with a smile and watched him walk back to his house.

Inside, I took a brief shower and headed right to bed. Mad that I had drank a little too much and now my head was spinning a bit. Before I fully closed my eyes, I tossed and turned and tried to get comfortable, and for some reason, I had Jamal on my mind. His handsome face and his lovely smile. His kind demeanor that was nothing like his music. I shrugged it off before falling asleep.

The Summer Evening

The next morning, I awoke to a loud car engine that was idling outside followed by a man yelling.

"Man, turn that loud ass car off."

A woman's voice responded. "My bad Mal. I'm so glad to see you."

The car door closed, and it was quiet once again. But it was too late. I was already up. I sighed before heading into the bathroom, then the kitchen to make some tea. Nothing else around the house needed to be done, so I lounged around and watched tv. For the most part, I enjoyed the show, but I wanted to get out of the house and do something today. Unfortunately, I had waited too long to decide this for mostly everything by now was probably closed.

I picked up my phone and called Janelle. No answer. Next I called Charmaine.

"Hello?"

"Hey Babes, what are you doing?"

"Making dinner. Shrimp linguine."

"And you didn't invite me over?" I laughed.

"I would have but I'm making it for my date."

"Your date? Who?"

"Shawn. We met a few weeks ago."

"I remember him. Alright then, I'll let you go."

"Are you alright? What are you doing?"

"Nothing much, just lounging around. Wanted to know if I could come chill, but obviously, I can't. So I'll just be bored."

"I'll call you after he leaves and let you know how it went."

"I'll be waiting! Bye."

I sighed before grabbing my bottle of wine and going on my deck in the back to enjoy the summer evening. It was so peaceful outside. The crickets chirped, the lightning bugs were out, and the sun was starting to set leaving the sky in bright colors.

About an hour had gone by and I heard the loud car start up again and pull off. Soon after, another car pulled up and I heard a different woman's voice speak out. I didn't pay attention to her words. Was just happy that it was quiet again until...

Loud music started playing in his backyard and they both came out and sat on the deck. She was loud and rowdy as she came out the door and I glanced over and met eyes with Jamal who was shocked to see me out there. He waved and headed over to my surprise.

"Is the music too loud for you?"

"A little bit, but it's cool. I was just about to head inside." I said standing up.

"I'll turn it down for you, it's no problem. You want anything to drink? I have some Moscato if you want it."

He must have noticed my empty bottle I held in my hands. "It's quite alright."

"You sure? I have a few extra bottles."

I smiled. "Sure. I'll take some."

"Mal, what the hell are you doing over there with that bitch?" the woman yelled from across the yard.

He held his head down in annoyance. "I'll be right back. I gotta go check her right fast."

I sat in shock as he stormed over to her and literally cussed her out and told her to leave. Finally, she did unwillingly though, and he came back with two big bottles of Moscato.

"Sorry about that. She won't be back."

"I see you like 'em rowdy." I teased.

"Rowdy, but not disrespectful. Have a good night Cadence."

"Wait," I yelled as he walked off the deck. He turned around, but I didn't even know why I had called him back. "Uhh, you wanna drink with me? If you're not busy that is."

"I'll drink with you. Let me go close the door and grab my phone. I'll be right back."

As he went to his house, I went into mine and grabbed an extra cup and some ice and set it on the table. In no time, he came back and joined me on my deck.

"How was your day?"

"Boring, but it was alright. How was yours?" I asked, struggling to get the top off the bottle.

He laughed. "All you gotta do is pull the tab." The bottle was taken from my hands and opened with ease before it was handed back.

I blushed and poured our cups. "Thank you."

"No problem." He leaned back in his chair and relaxed. "It's so peaceful out here. So quiet."

"I know. I love it."

"My fault for disrupting your peace."

"It's alright. You're entitled to your own enjoyment as well."

"So what's up? What did you do today?"

"Lounged around for the most part. Watched tv."

"You ain't chill with your man today?"

"Who the hell said I had a man?" I sipped from my cup. "That sounded like a prying question." I called him out and sipped again.

"Yea, you got me. I was prying. So you're single then?"

"Very much so."

"How's the single life treating you?"

23

"Like shit, but it's cool. Not trynna rush anything."

"I feel you."

"So… are you single as well?"

"Yea, I am. Kinda hard to lock down something serious when you're always on the go or in the studio. Especially now. I'm in a new area and barely know anyone."

I laughed. "Doesn't seem like you're having a hard time finding people though."

He laughed back. "Ya mean, they ain't nothing I would want to be serious with. They come and go."

"So I've seen. Better be careful out there. These chicks are crazy."

He scratched his head. "Yea, I know. But they throw themselves at me."

"Doesn't mean you have to bite the lure every time."

"You right. I don't. But I can't say no sometimes."

I laughed. "If you say so."

Another sip from our drinks were taken before he spoke. "Yo, you mad cool. I didn't think you would be."

"Why is that?"

"I don't know, you just seemed like you were gonna be a pain in the ass, boring neighbor when I first met you."

"Gee, thanks."

"Dead ass. But your vibe is iight. I like it."

"I like yours too. You seem like a laid-back person."

"I really am. Most people can't believe it when we chill cuz of my music."

"Yea, your music is completely different than your demeanor."

"Gotta give the crowd what they like."

"Do you like writing that type of music?"

"Yes and no. Like I said, that's what our people like and if I wanna get my name out there, that's what I have to put out."

"Well, what kind of music would you prefer to make?"

"Some slow jams, RnB type shit. But I don't know if anyone would listen to it. I wrote a whole bunch, and I always write those, but I only put out what you hear."

"Ever thought of putting it out under a pen name and see how it goes?"

"You know, I never thought about it. What would my name be though? Smooth Mal."

I giggled. "I don't think that would go over well. I'm sure people would put two and two together and realize it was you."

"Well, what name would you give me?"

I thought for a moment as I finished my drink. It was quickly replenished at Jamal's hands. "I think the name Antonne or Damien would fit you well. Something sexy and manly. Or even Darius."

"Ooo, I like Darius."

"Me too. You should give it a try and see how it goes."

"I think I will do that then. Thank you. Do you have any hidden talents? Can you sing or rap?"

"Everyone can sing. Question is, can they sing well?"

"Are you one of those that can sing well?" he asked after laughing.

"I sing around the house sometimes, but that's about it. I write poetry here and there…"

"You do?"

"Yea."

"I would love to hear some of your writings."

"I'm afraid they're not good."

"Have you ever put it out there?"

"Hell no. It's just a few things I write when it comes to my mind. I'm not an entertainer like you are."

"What do you do anyway?"

"I'm an accountant at an accounting firm."

"So you're good with numbers then?"

"Accounting deals with more than numbers. It mainly deals with money." I giggled.

"So like… budgeting and balancing checkbooks?"

I laughed again. "That's one aspect of it. There's bookkeepers, cost accounting, accounts receivable and payable, managerial accounting…"

"Damn. So what do you do then? What part?"

"Bookkeeping and the CPA finalizes it all. I just make sure the books are balanced and that the money is being allocated to the correct accounts."

"I like that. I may need your help soon."

"Why is that?"

"Things are starting to pick up and I'm getting a bit more money, but I need help staying on track with all these damn bills."

"Professional or personal?"

"Uhh… there's a difference?"

"Absolutely! Do you have a brand?"

"I am the brand."

"Are you trademarked?"

"No. Didn't think I had to be."

"Oh man. So you only have one account for all your business and personal expenses?"

"Yea."

"Oh gees." I sighed.

"How much would you charge to help me?"

"I will have to get back to you on the price, but I don't have a problem helping out."

"Definitely. Sort that out and get back to me,"

"Well, are your songs copyrighted at least?"

There was silence. "My manager handles that."

"That's not what I asked you." I replied sternly.

"I have to check and see."

I shook my head and finished off my drink. "That's more important than this other stuff. That's your money, that's your work. If someone stole your music and claimed it as theirs, how would you show that it's yours in court? Now someone else is making money off your hard work."

He pulled out his phone after filling both of our cups up. "Hold up, I'm about to check that out now." He began to text away and soon got a response and looked back at me. "He said the guy he told to do it did most of them."

"The guy he got to do it? What is that even supposed to mean? You hired him to do it right?"

"Yea, I did."

"You need to get on that ASAP. Better yet, do it yourself."

"I don't know how to do that shit man. That's why I hired him."

"Learn how to do it."

"That's why I'm asking for your help. Wait, how do you know about this stuff anyway?"

"I had a few businesses I tried to start but couldn't get the marketing down for it, so I stopped."

"What did you start?"

"Clothing line."

"You have anything I can see?"

I pulled out my phone and flipped through my picture gallery and showed them to him. "That's just some of the designs I have."

"Oh shit. That's dope. You created these yourself?" he asked, grabbing the phone and swiping through the designs.

"Most of them, yea."

"Here, Khalil is calling you." he said, handing me the phone back and I answered.

"Hello?"

"Yo, what are you doing?"

"Drinking outside with Jamal."

"Jamal? Who the hell is Jamal?"

"Mally Boy."

"What the hell? I don't believe you, put him on speaker."

"Are you serious right now Lil?"

"Yea, put his ass on speaker."

The phone was placed down on the table and put on speaker. "You're on speaker."

"Ayo, Mally Boy?"

"What's good Lil?"

"What you doing at Cay's house?"

"She's my new neighbor. We just having a few drinks chattin it up. What's up with you?"

"Nothing man, nothing. I didn't believe her when she said you were there. You better treat her right, you feel me?"

"Nah, nah, it's nothing like that bro. Not at all. We talking business over here."

"What business?"

"Lil, what the hell did you call me for?" I interrupted.

"I was gonna ask you something about Nelle, but I'll ask you later. Enjoy ya drinks Ma."

"I'll call you later then."

"'Iight. One."

"Who's Nelle?"

"Janelle. She's one of my friends and they recently uhh... started talking."

"Oh, ok. I see."

"But anyway. I have all those designs and just don't know how to market them."

"You can make custom shit? Cuz what I saw was dope."

"I can. You really liked it?"

"Hell yea. So Imma propose something to you." He took a drink from his cup and sat forward.

"What's up?"

"You help me get this shit on track and I'll help promote ya gear."

I sat back and thought for a minute while taking another sip from my cup. "I think we can do that. I'll write something up and get back to you."

He clasped his hands together. "Yes! Thank you. You have a website for it? I'll buy some shit now."

I giggled. "Are you serious?"

"Hell yea. I saw a few of 'em that caught my eye."

"What's your number? I'll text you the link."

He grabbed my phone and put his number in and dialed. Afterwards, I sent him the link to my poorly put together site.

"I need to work on the site, but you can still order what you want."

"I see that. That may be one of the problems with why your sales aren't great."

"You have a website?"

"Just sent you the link."

As I scrolled through, I was utterly amazed. It was vibrant and straight to the point. I was impressed. "Did you set this up?"

"Me and my boys did."

"How much would you charge to fix mine like this?"

"Help me get my copyrights and trademark and I'll call it even."

I smirked. "You have a deal then."

He looked up from his phone. "Are you forreal?"

"Yes, I'm forreal."

A smile spread on his face. "I'll get in touch with them and start on it tonight."

"I will do the same and write up something for doing your books."

"You work tomorrow right?"

"Unfortunately."

"Just do it when you can then. Don't want to overload you."

"Well, it's something that will keep me preoccupied for the time being."

"No doubt, no doubt. Just let me know when it's ready. You have my number, and you know where I live." He joked and stood up. "Imma head on out so you can get some rest."

I stood up with him and began cleaning up a bit. "Alright, I'll be talking to you soon."

"You need help with that?"

"No, I got it. Thanks though. Enjoy your night."

"You as well Cadence."

I smiled to myself as I was putting everything away and washing dishes. Excited about possibly getting my work out there and with a fan base like his, I could be making easy sales. This would also be the first time I would be working on someone else's books for profit. Usually, I only worked in an office setting, where I could ask for advice or have someone double check my work.

New adventures all around but it would definitely keep me busy during my boring evenings. Plus, I knew what I was doing and had confidence in myself to do it the correct way.

On my computer, I began doing more research on trademarks, and copyrights. It wasn't that complicated to get everything done, so I had no problem doing it. During my research, I was curious and decided to do some digging through the copyright records. I wanted to see if or what was copyrighted by him, so I searched his name up. Nothing.

I did some research on the internet to find a few names of the songs he had written. He had a few thousand subscribers and most of his videos were in the high thousands for views. Back at the copyright website, I put in the name of his song. His name didn't pop up, but someone named Thomas Brown did. Song after song I put into the database and the same name popped up. Thomas Brown. Something was definitely wrong here.

I picked up the phone and called Jamal. He answered. "Hello? I thought you'd be sleep by now."

"No, not yet. Hey, what is your manager's name?"

"Tom. Why?"

"Thomas Brown?"

"Yea, how did you know that?"

I exhaled deeply. "We may have a problem."

The Scam

There was a moment of silence on the other end before he spoke. "Problem? What problem?"

"Uhh... I don't know how to tell you this, but... all of your songs are copyrighted under your manager's name."

"What?"

"...Yea. There aren't any songs under your name in the database."

"So what does that mean?"

"It means we have a serious ass problem. According to the law, none of the songs are yours and if he wanted, he could sue you for infringement."

"Are you fucking kidding me right now? Every fuckin song?"

"I don't know about every song, but the ones on your social media accounts are under his name."

"This fuckin asshole. What the fuck can I do?"

"I don't know yet. I'm sure there's something, but I have to figure out what. You have all your songs that you wrote on your computer or something? Did you email them?"

"I write my shit on paper. I'm gonna kill that bastard."

"Hey! Relax. It's no time to get mad. You can't think when you're mad."

"I'm about to cuss his ass out."

"No!"

"What?"

"Don't let him know you know. Get your ducks in a row before you say or do anything."

"But what the hell am I supposed to do Cadence? I worked my ass off for that shit. Does it mean he's making money off my shit?"

"He can if he decides to sell the songs to someone. They can sue you for any revenue you've made off the music, plus fines and fees. Let me do some more research and I'll get back to you."

"Fuck!" he yelled. "Alright."

"Hey, don't do no dumb shit."

"I won't, I promise."

"Good. Call you back."

After another hour of research, I came up with a solution and called him back. He still sounded furious as he answered.

"Hello?"

"Hey…"

"Please tell me you found a way to fix this shit."

"Please tell me you have the original copies of all your work."

"It's all on my computer."

"Where's your computer?"

"Right next to me."

"You have the programs that you used to create the songs and all of the tracks stored on there?"

"All the recent and hot ones, yea."

"You may be able to prove to the court that you are the original owner of the work and that he was hired to copyright everything, and he stole your stuff. As long as you show them where you created it on your computer. But you may want to hire a lawyer for it though. That's out of my profession."

"Thanks Cadence…"

"Don't tell anyone this is going on, so no one brings it to his attention that you've caught on to him. We have to keep the cards in our hands."

"I won't say shit to no one. Imma call around for a lawyer in the morning."

"Do you have the contract between you and your manager?"

"Yea."

"Did you read it before you signed it?"

"I should have, right?"

"What? Of course you should have. Read everything you sign. I want to see that contract if possible or bring it to your lawyer to look at it."

"I pulled it up now. Want me to bring it to you?"

"If you want."

"Be over in a second."

Quickly, I jumped up to get dressed and threw some leggings on and a loose-fitting shirt. A few minutes later, there was a knock at my door and Jamal was standing there with his laptop and papers in his hand. I invited him and we sat down on the couch to get to the bottom of it.

I skimmed through the long ass contract trying to find something that had to do with the copyrights or something that could possibly be of use. As I did that, he was checking to make sure that all his files were there and untouched.

"Did you find anything yet?"

"Not really, but you gave him a lot of power over your shit."

"What do you mean?"

"He's in charge of your finances, bookings, most of your royalties..." I sighed. "Why didn't you read this shit before you signed?"

"Is there a way I can get out of it? I don't want his sneaky ass working for me anymore."

"I have to look and see. You signed a five-year contract with him. Where did you find this guy?"

"One of my boys referred him to me."

I read through the contract some more and saw a new name on it. "Who is… Robert Daniels?"

"My boy that referred him."

I handed him the page. "It seems like they set you up to rip you off."

As he read the document, he got even more upset. "How the hell is he getting fifteen percent of my earnings?"

"Do you check your accounts?"

"No. My fucking manager does all the shit."

"I can guarantee you they're taking more than what they're supposed to. Not to get too personal, but how much do you get paid to do gigs?"

"It depends on the spot. Some places pay one grand, while others pay like three."

"Are you sure about that? Or is that what he's been telling you?"

"You think they've been paying more?"

"I don't know. That's what I'm trying to figure out. Did you see any receipts or anything that was signed at the bookings?"

"Nah."

"You might want to get those and compare what they paid less your expenses and see if it adds up."

"Expenses?" He looked at me a bit confused.

"What it costs you to pay for everything. Lighting, your manager, whatever."

The papers in his hands fell to his lap. "I can't believe this shit is happening right now. I'm finally making traction and getting noticed and this shit happens?"

"It's just a good thing you caught it before you really blew up. Or else, you would be in some deeper shit then you are now. I'm going to see if anyone knows a good lawyer tomorrow. A lot of people at my job know people. I'll ask around. But, no matter who you get, be sure to do a background check on them first before you sign anything or hand over your money."

"Thanks Cadence. This really means a lot. It's just… a lot."

"One situation at a time. You can get through this. Just take it as a lesson learned."

My eyes scanned through the papers again trying to see how he could get out of this terrible contract without repercussions.

"Question. What does this manager really do for you?"

"He's supposed to book gigs, get me in front of new eyes, set up studio time… things along that line."

"Does he do that?"

"I do most of the work. I booked the last few gigs, and he just went to finalize the paperwork. I get myself into the studio. I market myself. He basically doesn't do shit but finalize the paperwork."

I rested back on the couch in relief. "That may be your way to get out of the contract. He's not doing what you hired him for. But most definitely run that through a lawyer and get the rights to your music back."

He hung his head low. I couldn't figure out if he was happy or sad. Or maybe a mix of both? My hands rubbed his back gently trying to comfort him a bit and he looked up at me with sad eyes.

"What's wrong?"

"I just can't believe this is happening. I appreciate you taking the time to go over this with me."

"No problems at all. It will all get cleared up. Don't worry."

He stood up. "I think I've bothered you enough for one night. I'm gonna head out. I appreciate your help, and we'll be in contact about everything else."

"Most definitely." I said walking him out but not before he gave me a big hug which caught me off guard.

"Have a good night."

"You as well."

The door closed and I rested back on the couch and thought about what they were about to put him through. I really hoped he could get all this shit cleared up and out of the way. My phone rang with Charmaine on the other line.

"Hey Babes."

"Hey yourself. How was your drinking time with Mally Boy?"

"Khalil told you?"

"Of course he did. So, did y'all fuck yet?"

"What the hell? No. We just hung out a bit and talked. I'm not wild like y'all are."

"And that's why the Cay store is bone ass dry. You gotta let go sometimes."

"I can't with you Char. But it wasn't even like that. We were talking business."

"Mmm hmm. Tell me anything."

"ANYWAY. How was your date with Shawn?"

"It was alright. When we talk on the phone, the conversation is great, but in person, it's not. Even the sex was bad."

I laughed hysterically. "You gave up them cheeks already?"

"First and last time. Ehh. It was so bad, I want to block his ass."

"Well damn. I'm sorry to hear that."

"Anyway, just calling to tell you that. I'm about to go to bed and finish myself off."

"He didn't even make you cum?"

"It was fast as fuck. I don't know if he hadn't had any in a while or what. It was literally two strokes and done. I get more pleasure from my damn tampon." I burst out laughing. "Cay, it's not funny." She whined then laughed soon after too.

"Well go ahead and take care of that. I'll talk to you in the morning… Oh. Do you know any lawyers for musicians?"

"The hell do you need that for?"

"Will you just tell me yes or no."

"I may know a few. I can ask around and see if anyone knows one. How soon do you need one?"

"Like, yesterday."

"I can ask. Janelle probably knows a few."

"I'll ask her then. Have you spoken to her today?"

"No. I know Lil was over there earlier. He probably put her ass to sleep. Lucky bitch. I'm going now. Bye. I'll ask around."

"Please do. Good night."

I looked at the time. I had forgotten I was supposed to call Khalil back, but it was too late at night to do so. He would just have to wait until the morning. I'm sure he would understand. I took a big stretch before walking to my room, turning everything off on my way and taking my ass to bed.

Do it on Your Own

Another long day at work down in the history books. The only upside of this day was that I was able to get a few lawyers' numbers that I could relay to my neighbor. Hopefully they would be able to help him if he hadn't found one yet. I didn't know if he did or not, for I hadn't heard from him all day.

As I pulled up to my driveway, he was standing outside on his porch with some new female friend. When he saw me, he quickly left her side and met me at my car. His female friend wasn't too thrilled about it and sped off.

"Hey, did you have any luck today?" I asked anxiously.

"Someone referred a few lawyers to me, but I looked them up and they didn't have the best reviews. But I kept looking and found one that I liked. I wanted you to take a look before I contacted him."

"Why do you want me to take a look?"

"I just want a second opinion. Plus, I trust yours."

"Yea, I'll take a look for you." I said walking up my steps, but he didn't follow. I turned around and stared at him. "Are you coming?"

"I didn't know you wanted me to follow. My bad."

"Well, I damn for sure am not standing in that heat." I teased and closed the door behind us. "Let's see what you have."

"His name is James Rosenbaum." he said, handing me his phone with the website pulled up. "He has great reviews and works specifically on cases like this."

I scrolled through the website for a while then handed his phone back before taking my shoes off. "He looks like a good candidate. You should give him a call and see what he says."

"The office is closed now. I have to wait til the morning."

"It wouldn't hurt to call and leave a message. You want more of that Moscato?"

"Hell yea, I'll take some of that."

He stood by the door nervously and I couldn't help but to laugh. "You can have a seat and relax. You don't have to be all shy."

"I'm not shy, just didn't know if I should or not."

"I'm not gonna bite you." I joked as I let my hair down out of my tight bun and washed my hands before getting the cups out and the drinks. Everything was brought into the living room where he was sitting, and I could feel his eyes on me. I looked up. "What?"

"Nothing. Nothing at all… is that all yours?"

I smiled as I sat next to him. "My hair? Yea, it's all mine." Our cups were poured, and I took a swig, but he kept staring. "What is wrong with you? You're making me feel mad awkward.

"My fault. How was your day?" He took a drink too.

"It was alright. Some of my co-workers gave me a few numbers if you wanted to check them out."

"You asked around?" He sounded shocked.

"Why wouldn't I? I told you I was going to."

"Yea, I'll take a look at them, but I'm leaning towards this guy."

I dug in my purse and pulled out the numbers I had collected, and he did some research on them as we sat in the quiet room.

"You see any you like?"

"Yea, this guy does the same thing." he said pointing. "I might just call them both."

"You should. It never hurts to have a few options."

He dialed both of the numbers and left two different messages. He looked a bit nervous as he did so.

"So how was your day?" I asked, trying to distract his mind away from the situation a bit.

"It was alright. That dick called and said there weren't any gigs open this weekend, so I had to make a few calls myself."

"You didn't tell him anything right?"

"Nah, I didn't say anything."

"Were you able to book anything?"

"My whole weekend is full. From Friday night to Sunday evening."

My eyes grew wide. "Wow."

"Everyone wants me to perform at their spots. I don't know what the hell he's talking about."

"So you see you are more than capable of doing it yourself."

"Yea, I see that. Guess what else I did."

"What else did you do?"

"I started a few social media accounts for Darius."

"Are you serious? You did?"

"I just haven't figured out how I'm going to post the songs up yet or market myself without showing my face."

"A mask? Or just show the neck down?"

"That could be a possibility. I'm going into the studio later tonight to record better versions of the RnB songs."

"That sounds exciting."

"When they're done, do you think you could show me how to get them copyrighted?"

"Of course. What name are you going to put them under? Shit, I was supposed to do your trademark. Hold on." I said leaving to grab my computer. When I came back, both of our drinks were replenished.

The laptop opened and we began to do the process together. "I was thinking of just copyrighting them under the name Mally Boy."

I paused and looked at him. "Where do you see yourself in five years?"

He looked at me confused before he responded. "A very famous rapper or singer."

"Do you see yourself being signed to a label or do you want to start your own label?"

"Being signed. I would just want to focus on making music and performing. Nothing else. But then again, I don't want to get burned like I just did. What are you getting at?"

"Creating your own label so you don't have to go through this shit again. I was doing research at work and artists that sign, sign over their copyrights and only get a small percentage of what they earn. If you have your own label, you could keep what's yours plus sign other artists under you. It would be harder to do, but the benefits would be better."

"I'd have to think about that. Definitely would have to think about that. Will that stop us from doing what we need to do now?"

"No. I don't think so. I just saw the option of DBA and the thought popped in my head. You have a logo or anything?"

"It's on my website. Can I get that trademarked too?"

"Yea." I replied as my phone rang. "What's up Lil?"

"Why didn't you call me back last night?"

"It was too late to call you, can I call you right back though? I'm in the middle of something."

"What you in the middle of?"

"Eww, mind your business." I joked.

"Better not be given up them cheeks."

"I know the fuck you're not talking."

He laughed. "You right, you right. You with Mally Boy again aren't you?"

"Once again. Mind your business."

"Iight. I see you Cay. Make sure you call me back man."

"I will. I promise." I looked back at Jamal. "My bad."

"Nah, it's all good. My logo is on my computer though. Should I go get it?"

"Yea. You should fill out the application on yours anyway. We can do it together."

"Iight bet. I'll be back."

He was back in no time and his computer was opened and we got straight to work. During the process, he decided to start his own label and put everything under it. By the end of the night, his name, slogan and logo was trademarked, his LLC and state forms were filed and set up and he officially had his own record label. The only thing he had to do now was to get a separate business account for it all.

I yawned and sat back, taking my cup with me and sipping from it. "Yo Cadence. On some real shit, I really appreciate the help. Anything you need, just holla at me and I gotchyu."

"Only thing I need for you to do is stay focused and handle your own shit. Don't give anyone enough power of your shit to where you don't know what the fuck is going on."

"Bet. Imma do that Love. Word up. Imma head out though cuz I gotta go to the studio. I'll let you know what happens with the lawyers tomorrow."

The door was opened, and a hug was given before he walked back to his house. I stretched and felt relieved that I could help him. And even though we barely knew each other, I really enjoyed his company and the vibe he brought. Just wished he wasn't so naïve to everything.

The clock read nine o'clock before I called Khalil back.

"Hello?"

"Hey Ma. What's up?"

"Nothing, tired. What are you up to?"

"He wore that ass out didn't he?"

"We didn't have sex. Like I said, it's not like that." I snapped.

"Iight, iight, damn. Mah fault."

"So what's going on? How's you and Janelle?"

"Everything is great actually. I just wanted to know some things that she liked so I could get her something nice the next time I saw her."

"That would be cheating sir."

"Cheating?"

"Yes. You find out what she likes through getting to know her better. Not asking her friend what she likes."

"Damnit Cay, can you just point me in the right direction? I don't wanna fuck shit up."

"Her favorite color is green. Figure something out with that."

"Are you serious right now sis?"

"She likes taking scenic walks."

"Thank you. Damn. It's like pulling teeth with y'all sometimes." He paused. "Cay, I'll talk to you later, she's calling me now."

"Talk to you later then."

I stretched one last time before making my way into the kitchen. I still hadn't gone grocery shopping and still, nothing in the fridge looked appetizing to me at the moment. It was too late to eat anything this late at night anyway, so I would just call it a day.

The Contract

"Hello?"

"Cadence?"

"What's up Jamal? I'm at work."

"Sorry to bother you, just wanted to let you know that I hired a lawyer who's going to help me out with the copyright. I'm so hype right now. I couldn't wait to tell you."

"Who did you go with?"

"Rosenbaum. I liked his energy and the price too."

"Glad you found someone to help. We'll talk about it more when I get off."

"Iight, bet. Have a good day."

"You too."

"Cadence. Can I speak with you for a minute?" my boss asked from behind me.

"Uhh, yea, sure. Is everything alright?"

"Let's talk in my office."

Fuck. What did I do now? I could never get a break in this damn place. It was always something new. Some new bullshit I had to deal with. The door closed behind me, and I took a seat in the chair across from his. He sat down, sat back and glared at me.

"I just got the report you sent over to Joleen and your numbers are way off."

"What do you mean way off? I got my numbers directly from the report Kenneth sent me."

"Cadence. The numbers on account one-nine-five-nine were off by one-hundred thousand dollars."

"What?"

"This is the third time this month this has happened. I'm putting you on an unpaid suspension til Monday. I don't know what is going on with you, but you need to pull it together."

"Until Monday? Can I see the report you are referring to?"

A piece of paper was handed to me, and I glanced over the numbers, but they weren't what I put in. "This isn't the report I submitted." I replied confidently.

"Joleen said this was the one you sent over to her. When she ran the numbers, it was off."

"That's not the report I sent to her this morning." I handed the papers back.

"Can you go forward me the report you sent?"

I stood up quietly and went to my desk and forwarded the email to him before I went back in and sat down. His eyes scanned the screen briefly before he picked up the phone and dialed an extension. "Joleen, can I please see you in my office please. Thank you."

A few minutes went by before the arrogant woman came in the door and sat down next to me. But not before sneering her nose up at me.

"When did Cadence send you this report?"

"I believe she sent it around eleven-thirty."

"I'm looking at the one she forwarded to me, and it is balanced."

"She must have not sent the correct one to me."

"I'm looking at the email now and she sent it at nine-ten this morning."

"I'm not sure which email you're referring to. I didn't get one from her at that time."

He clenched his jaw and looked at me. "You're dismissed. You can stay the rest of the week."

"Thank you." I said standing and leaving.

Was this snobby ass bitch trying to set me up? Even though I wasn't fond of this job, I needed it and I knew what the hell I was doing. I wonder if the other times she said the numbers were off, was it her doing as well. Was it on accident, or on purpose? So glad I didn't let him let me go without seeing the documents myself.

I sat at my desk and continued to work, thinking about what Jamal had proposed to me the other night. What would I charge him to do his books? What happened if my little business took off and gave me steady income to where I didn't have to work in this place again? That would be too great of a reality. But could it really be happening in the near future? Only time would tell I guess.

My work was done early today and as I sat there at my desk bored, I decided to write up a contract and get shit moving. I was going to take a leap of faith here and trust my abilities to lead the way. I just hoped it would all work out in the end.

As I pulled into my driveway, I half expected to see Jamal waiting for me. The only thing I noticed were a few new, luxury vehicles in his driveway. Gah I hope they weren't his and he just had a few people over.

Inside, I removed my shoes and took my bun out and began typing my written contract up for him. It didn't take that long, but before I could finish, there was a knock at my door.

"Why didn't you tell me you were home? I would have come right over."

"My bad." I responded in a low tone moving to the side to let him in.

"You good? What's wrong?"

"Some bullshit at work today is all. I'm almost done writing the contract up. You want to see it?"

"No, I trust you." I glared at him, and he changed his mind. "You're right, I'll look at it."

The document was printed and handed to him, and he began to glance over it. I did, however, have a test for him. As he finished reading, I printed the final copy and gave it to him.

"What do you think?"

"It looks good. I think this will work out great. Let me read this one."

I handed him the new copy. "If everything looks good, we can both sign it, and I will begin working. Is there anything you want to change?"

"Why do you need access to all my financial information?"

"I'm dealing with your money. I need to know what income you get, what expenses you incurred so I can put them in the right accounts. Plus, I have to go back a year and move things around and differentiate what was personal and what was for business."

He nodded his head and laughed slightly. "Uhh, don't judge me by what you find in there."

"No judgments over here." I giggled back.

"You have a pen?"

I handed him a pen and he began to sign it when I slammed my hand down on the contract. He looked at me oddly. "You didn't read the new one thoroughly did you?"

"What do you mean? It's the same thing from before."

"No, it's not." I pointed to a new line that I added.

"Oh shit."

"Gotta pay attention. Read everything you sign."

"Damn." he began to laugh at what I wrote. "I owe you a Twix every day though?"

I laughed too as I went to print the correct contract. "Yes. I love Twix."

"I can still do that for you, you know."

"Oh God no. I'm gonna get bigger than I already am."

"You not big. Stop it. You're perfect. Not too skinny, got some meat on them bones..."

"Ok, you need to stop it. Here, here's the correct one."

"Damn, can't even give you compliments?"

"Jamal!"

"Iight, iight, Imma read it."

It took him a while to get through some of it and he had to ask me what some of it meant, but we got through and he signed. I signed right after him. This was going to be something big for the both of us. A copy was made, and I handed it to him.

"Make sure you keep that in a safe place."

"I will. You're gonna start tomorrow right?"

"Yes sir, so I need all your information by tomorrow so I can see what I need to do and set up all of your accounts correctly."

"I will definitely get it to you."

"So... Tell me what happened today!"

"Is there any Moscato left?"

"Yea, you want some?"

"You know what, I think I want something stronger tonight."

"I don't have anything stronger."

"I do. I'll be back. You gonna drink it with me?"

"What is it?"

"Henny."

"I don't drink dark liquor."

"You don't? Why not?"

"I get a little umm... agitated and a lot bit angry, so I stay away from it."

"I have some clear rum too, would you prefer that?"

"I would much rather prefer that."

"I gotchyu."

"Hurry back, I wanna hear some good news."

My heart fluttered a bit as I looked at the signed document. This was really happening. My first, official client. I had set up a business for it a while ago and never did anything for it, but now, I finally had something. And it could benefit the both of us greatly.

"You got ice? It's not cold."

"I have ice."

"And a chaser? Unless you trynna do shots with me."

"If I didn't have work in the morning, I wouldn't mind shots." I walked over to the fridge. "I have cranberry, orange juice or pineapple juice."

"Pineapple."

"That's my favorite!"

"Mine too."

The cups were grabbed and were filled with ice. The rum was poured in before the juice was. Everything was stirred up and we headed into the living room.

"Damn, this shit is good. I see you Miss Bartender."

"Stop beating around the bush Mal. What happened today with the lawyer?"

"So, he told me basically the same thing that you did. When I wrote and created the songs, they were already copyrighted and legally, he can't copyright the songs. So we have to go to court so they can change some shit and put it in my name. Also, due to this, the contract between Tom and I will be voided, and he has to pay me fines and fees and anything he earned from the sale of the songs. I'm so glad I had all that stuff on my computer."

"Yes! I'm so excited! I told you it was all going to work itself out!"

"And, if I get the receipts for how much I was paid out for the gigs, do the math and see that he undercut me, I get that money back too."

"I hope he didn't do that to you. It should be easy to get the receipts though. And the deposits will show in your account. I'll get that ready for you, so you'll have it."

"And one more thing!" he said, moving and sitting next to me with his laptop. He opened it and went to a website with very familiar pictures on it. As soon as I realized what it was, my eyes lit up.

"Is that my website?"

"Yea. It's just the first draft of the front-page layout though. You still have to add the products and stuff to it, and we have to connect it to your domain name. You like it?"

My eyes teared up a bit. "I love it. Thank you."

"Aww Love, don't cry."

"I'm sorry. I never fuckin cry but this looks so amazing."

"I'm glad you like it. Was this the vibe you were going for or was it something more subtle?"

"No. This is it right here. It's perfect. It matches the edginess of the designs."

"You know when I start wearing this shit, your sales are gonna go up tremendously. How are you going to fulfill everything?"

"All the orders are automated. That won't be a problem. Plus, you'll be getting a percentage of that too."

"Yea, I saw that in the contract. Thanks for adding that."

"Absolutely."

"So, you wanna finish up tonight?"

"What do you need from me?"

"You gotta change the domain over to this site and add any plugins you use to automate everything. It's on the same platform so it should be the same ones you used before. I'll add some other ones in there to upsell if you want. People can add it to their wish lists, sign in, everything. It will be ready to go."

"Uhh. I can't thank you enough for this."

"I can't thank you enough for what you did. I say we'll call it even."

A smile spread across my face before I wrapped him up in a hug. I held my glass in the air. "We'll call it even then." He tapped his on mine and we both took a drink.

"Shit, what time is it?"

"Seven-thirty. Why?"

"I gotta get to the studio." He sprang up and headed for the door. "I'll text you later Cadence." He was gone.

I sat back in my chair realizing how productive of a day this was. With the thought of everything that had just happened, I got giddy and excited all over again. My phone rang causing me to snap out of it.

"Hello?"

"Is Mally Boy with you?"

"No, he just left not too long ago."

"Damn Cay, you holding him up for work."

"I didn't know he had to be at the studio tonight."

"Every day on the first three days out the week. "

"Ok. I got it. I won't let it happen again."

"What was y'all doing?"

"Bye Khalil."

After I hung up, I went to update my accounting software in preparation for getting his accounts in order. It had been years since I even looked at this stuff, so it took me until midnight to get everything in order and get recertified to run the books. But, nonetheless, it was done, and I was ready for business.

Don't judge

Another long day at work and to my surprise, Joleen wasn't there. Her desk had been cleared off and cleared out and it looked like she no longer worked there. I guess she really did try to set me up to get fired. But why? Whatever, she was someone else's problem now.

The two luxury cars were gone and were replaced with yet another new car that had some new female in it rolling out the driveway as I rolled into mine. Soon after I walked in the door and got into comfortable clothes, a knock came at my door.

"I might as well leave it unlocked at this point." I joked.

"I'm about to send you over all my information so you can get started. Is it cool if I work on your site in here?" he asked, pointing to the dining room table.

"Yea, that's fine. I'll bring mine over there too. We drinking?"

"Of course. I can't drink too much though. I was fuckin up in the studio last night."

"Yea, about that. You almost got me in trouble with Khalil."

"He barked at me when I got there. You aren't the only one."

"Now I know your schedule, so that won't happen again right?"

He chuckled. "It won't happen again."

I put my laptop on the table along with the drinks and chaser.

"How long do you usually stay in the studio?"

"About four hours. Maybe more. Why?"

"Just wondering is all. Did you make any more hits?"

"Hell yea! Did some of Darius' music too. They liked it."

"I thought you had some recorded already."

"I do, but I didn't record them with the guys. I did it when I was in Neptune."

"Got ya. See, aren't you glad you tried it?"

"Yea, they definitely liked it and liked the idea of doing it under a different pen name."

"Good."

"I just sent over my credentials. You get it yet?"

"Yea, just got it. Let's see what we're working with here."

"Please don't judge." He chuckled.

"Gees, what's in here?"

"You'll find out. I almost don't want you to see it."

"Ok, now, I'm nervous."

"It's nothing bad. Just embarrassing for you, of all people to see."

"Why me of all people?"

He shook his head and focused on his laptop. "Nothing."

"Did you ever open a business account?"

"Yea, I did." He dug around in his computer bag. "Here. There's the info for that too. I'm just waiting for the card to come."

As I looked through his bank information, I could see what he was talking about and why he didn't want me to see everything. All types of sex toys and condom receipts were scattered throughout his statements. I glanced over at him.

"I told you don't judge." he said, nudging my shoulder.

I took a sip from my cup. "I'm not judging but it is a bit excessive don't you think?"

"It is, but I gotta stay safe."

"Mal…"

"Shit, I'm single, and they throw it at me. What can I say?"

53

"Think of all the other things you could be using this money for towards your career. That's all I'm going to say about it."

"You right, you right." He took a nervous drink from his cup. "I need your credentials for your hosting platform."

I took out a pen and wrote the information down on a piece of paper. "Don't you lose that paper." I teased.

He chuckled. I'm not gonna lose the paper Cadence."

While he went to work on my website, I went to work on setting up his chart of accounts. Before we knew it, it was time for him to leave. Honestly, I was a little upset he had to go because I really did enjoy his company. I kept working for another few hours before I decided to call it a night. Most of the personal and business accounts were created and the only thing left to do was to create rules and sync the financial accounts to the program and he would be set.

My phone rang. Janelle finally called me back after how many days. "Hello?"

"Hey girly, how are you?"

"I've been good. How are you? You disappeared on me."

"I know, I'm sorry. Got caught up with work, school and Lil."

"How is that going?"

"Oh my goodness. Yesterday, we went on a nice walk on the waterfront. It was absolutely perfect."

"I'm glad y'all are feeling each other. About damn time y'all broke the ice."

"Well, the ice was broken thanks to you, but I'm glad you did."

"So how are you and Mally Boy doing?"

"What are you talking about?"

"Rumor has it that y'all have been seeing each other a lot lately."

"Ain't no rumor has it. Lil told you didn't he?"

"Maybe." she said giggling.

"It's not what you think, Nelle."

"Then what is it Cay? Heard you made him late last night and he's never late."

"It's about business."

"Mmm hmm. I bet he's handling yours."

"Oh my God, I can't with the both of y'all. It's not at all like that."

"Ok, ok. So what is this business that y'all be talkin bout?"

"Can't say just yet, but it's in the works and I'm super excited about it!"

"I can't wait to hear what it is! But anyway, I'm about to go to bed. I just wanted to check on you and see how you were doing."

"Alright Nelle, I'll talk to you later then."

Once again, another productive day in the bag. Shit, I was on a roll. Wish this could keep going for a long time.

Takin Shit Too Far

Different cars parked in the driveway of his. Nothing out of the ordinary there. I didn't even bother closing the door behind me when I walked in, and soon enough, he was there in my dining room hard at work on my website. My laptop was on the way across from his along with our cups of rum.

"No studio today right?"

"Nah, not today. I can stay as long as you allow me to." he said a bit flirtatiously. "Your site is almost done. I had my boy add some shit to it to increase the speed and the SEO."

"The what?"

"Search engine optimization." he chuckled. "Glad I can teach you a thing or two. I feel like such a dummy over here."

"No one said you were a dummy."

"I feel like it sometimes talking to you. You're so damn smart."

"I just do the research that I need to get shit done is all. We gon' get you there. I'm almost done with your accounts too. All I have to do is set some rules and sync and you'll be up and running."

"Hey, you think you could help me budget too?"

"I can give you some pointers on what you can do. The rest will be up to you. Did you have a goal in mind or something you wanted to save up for?"

"Some studio equipment for the basement. Set it up real nice down there so I don't have to keep spending money on going to the studio. Plus, if I want to sign artists in the future, they'll have somewhere to record."

"We can do that. Does the basement need to be renovated?"

"Not really. It's already a full basement. I just have to get equipment and decorate."

"How much is the equipment?"

"About fifteen stacks."

"Fifteen?"

He laughed. "And that's on the cheap side."

"Shit. Are you sure you want people to come to your crib to record?"

"It's just a starting point. As I get more income, I'll get a building." I nodded my head before he continued. "So, besides the obvious, what would you suggest?"

"You have a few things you could sacrifice in order to reduce your expenses on the personal side. Stop eating out as much, stop buying so much expensive jewelry and clothes..."

"That's just to keep up appearances though. Most of that stuff I use for gigs and shit."

"Didn't know that. I have to make some adjustments then. Those could be considered business related if you wear them to shows or events only."

"What's the purpose of a business account anyway?"

"It's mainly for tax purposes and to see where your money is going and coming from and to monitor the growth and health of your business. You can get special tax exemptions by using your business card. For business only though."

"Anything else?"

I began to scan through the documents when a knock came at my door. It startled me a bit, for I wasn't expecting anymore company. The door opened and in came my group. Janelle, Charmaine and Khalil.

"What the hell are you guys doing here?" I asked giving them all a hug.

"We came to see what you were up to. We were about to head to Buffalo Kings and wanted to know if you wanted to come. It's been a minute since we all hung out." Charmaine said.

"What's up Mally Boy? What you up to bro?" Khalil said, giving Jamal dap.

"Oh my goodness. Y'all are really chillin together." Janelle said. "What are you guys doing?"

We all headed into the dining room. "I told you, we're working on business."

"What the hell? You were serious. I didn't believe you."

"So you had to come see for yourself huh?"

"Something like that." Char giggled.

"Do you guys want to come and eat with us?"

I looked at Jamal who had a perplexed look on his face. There was an awkward silence before he responded. "Sure, what the hell, why not?"

"We won't keep y'all long. We know y'all busy doing… whatever it is y'all are doing." Khalil said.

"Let me go get dressed right quick and I'll be ready." I said shutting down my computer.

"I'm ready when she is." Jamal shut his down too.

I disappeared in my room and changed my clothes quickly into something chic yet relaxed. Jamal stared at me when I came from around the corner like he had seen someone new reappear. I blushed and smiled which caused him to smile.

"You guys ready?" I asked, grabbing my keys.

"Hell yea, let's go. I'm hungry as hell."

"Hungry for what?" Janelle flirted with Lil.

All of us piled into Khalil's big ass SUV and headed to the restaurant. Most of the conversation in the vehicle consisted of the two people in the front flirting with one another. Charmaine was too busy on her phone and Jamal and I sat awkwardly in the back exchanging glances at one another.

At the restaurant, we all ordered our meals and a few drinks and just caught up with one another. A lot of the conversation, however, was to pry information on what Jamal and I had been working on and why we were spending so much time together lately.

"Come on Cay, you can't even give us a little hint?" Charmaine begged.

"Nope, sorry. You guys just have to wait and see."

"You guys are no fun. I'm not telling you shit else."

"So Jamal, how are you liking the neighborhood so far?"

"I like it a lot. It's very peaceful and quiet and close to the city."

"I'm sure a certain neighbor has welcomed you warmly."

"Nelle!" I yelled.

"What? I'm just asking a question."

They were really starting to piss me off and usually, it took a lot for me to get to that point. "Why must you go there?" I snapped. "Why is it so hard to understand that nothing is going on between the two of us?"

"Look at the way the both of you look at each other. Something is definitely there even if you don't see it for yourselves."

"I gotta admit, y'all have been spending a lot of time together. Something could definitely be starting. He even talks about you at the studio."

"Damn Lil." Jamal said angrily after being thrown under the bus. I stared at him in shock.

"You talk about me?"

"Not in a bad way Cay, relax."

"In what way Lil?"

"Khalil, don't."

"He's even singing these love songs. I think one of them…"

"Yo Bro… Chill." Jamal interrupted him loudly. Silence fell about in our group and the surrounding tables. He angrily stood up and walked out of the restaurant. I immediately followed.

"Hey, what's going on?" I asked trying to calm him down.

"Shit just really irks me yo. He be doing too damn much."

"He's probably just drunk. You know how he can get."

"I know, but still. Then you sitting there getting frustrated and shit, it only makes me frustrated. I don't like seeing you like that."

"It's ok. Just calm down alright. We can just eat our food and try to ignore them. They're only messing with us."

"They takin shit too far."

"Mally Boy." Khalil's voice rang out from behind us. "I'm sorry Cay. Can you give us a minute?"

I stepped back and rubbed Jamal's back gently. "Yea, sure."

Back in the restaurant, Janelle and Charmaine watched me sit down with apologetic eyes.

"We're sorry Cay."

"We didn't mean to make y'all upset. We were only teasing."

"Sometimes y'all take it too far."

"We won't bring it up again. We promise."

"Is Jamal alright?"

"He's pissed, but he should be alright. What was Khalil talking about though?"

The two looked at each other before coming in close. "We weren't supposed to say anything to you, but he's been writing and singing a lot of RnB songs in the studio lately. Under some new name Darius."

"We thought it was because of you."

"I know about that. That's nothing new. I'm the one that gave him the pen name after he told me he was afraid of what people would think of his slower music."

"Oh shit, are you forreal?"

60

"Yea, I'm forreal. Y'all are really thinking too hard into this situation. When we chill or he comes over, we discuss business. If you must know, I'm his new accountant."

They both covered their mouths. "Oh shit. So there's like nothing at ALL between y'all. No hugging, rubbing, feeling, touching?"

"Nothing at all."

"But he does look at you a certain way."

"I noticed it too. You do the same."

"And what way would that be?" I asked.

"I don't know. Maybe we are thinking too hard on it. We were just excited that you may have met someone. We know how you feel about being single."

"We're just friends. Like me and Lil."

They threw their hands up in defeat as the guys walked back in and sat down. Jamal looked a little better, but I think he was putting up a front. The food was served shortly after, and Jamal and I pretty much ate in silence while the rest of the group chatted amongst themselves. They didn't say another word about our possible relationship for the rest of the night, but I was curious to know what was said about me in that studio.

What's Next?

The ride home was a quiet one for the most part. We said our simple goodbyes and walked back into my house where more liquor was poured in our cups and drank down rather hastily. Nonetheless, another round was needed as we continued to work quietly on our respective projects.

I looked up from my computer and his eyes darted past his and met with mine. I quickly looked away blushing, then back again before speaking.

"How are you feeling?"

"I'm feeling alright. A bit more relaxed. How about you?"

"Same. I had to tell them about me being your accountant so they would get off our case."

"It's cool. I don't mind. How's it looking over there?"

"Just waiting for everything to finish re-syncing and I'll be done. How's it looking on your end?"

I'm almost done over here too. Just finishing up the plugins and apps so they match the brand." His voice lacked enthusiasm as he spoke. His vibe was off a bit, and it bothered me.

"Are you sure you're alright? You seem a bit off."

"Just a bit tired is all and I'm planning out what I need to do tomorrow in my head."

"What do you have to do?"

"I have to go do dry rehearsals at a few of the spots I'm going to be doing gigs at this weekend."

"Are they at clubs and lounges and stuff?"

"Most of them are but there are two that are kind of like a festival type thing." Talking about his career brought spark back to his voice.

"You'll be alright, you got it."

"You wanna come to one of the festivals this weekend? It's down on the riverfront. On the Philly side though. Harbor Park I think it's called."

"I'll go and show my support. What time do you perform?"

"I perform at one, but I'll be there at eleven."

"What time do you want me to be there then?"

He chuckled. "Whatever time you wanna be there, just don't miss the show."

"I won't miss it. Will you be performing the same songs or new ones?"

"Until I get this copyright shit situated, it will be the older songs."

"Is Tom gonna be there?"

"Most likely, but I hope not. I'm gonna finalize everything when I go tomorrow so there won't be any problems."

"Ok, good."

His computer spun around to face me, and I glanced at the screen. It looked even better than it did a few days ago. "Is it done?" I asked scrolling through the page.

"It's done. You're ready to launch it."

I clicked through the different pages and the collections and product pages as well before asking, "How do I launch it?"

He smirked and came beside me. Patiently, he talked me through how to launch the site and when I did, I felt a sense of joy and excitement flow through my body.

"Thank you. Thank you. Thank you." I repeated as I held on to him tightly. He laughed and hugged me back.

"You're welcome, Love."

"I think yours is done as well!" I said looking at my screen while he went back and sat down.

We both took a few more sips out of our cups before we shut down and closed our laptops.

"So what's next?" he asked.

"I don't know. Wanna watch a movie or or do you have to go?"

"I don't have to. We can watch a movie. What kind you like?"

"End of the world type movies. There's a new one that just came out called The Hunted. It looks so good. Wanna watch it with me? Do you like those kinds of movies?"

"Yea, I like em. I saw the trailer for that too."

I stood up and he followed my lead into the living room with our drinks in our hands. The tv turned on, the lights dimmed, and we sat on the couch to watch the movie. Unfortunately, I didn't make it to the end and passed out halfway through.

"Cadence." I heard him say to me softly. When I opened my eyes, I realized my head was resting on his shoulder and he was looking down at me with caring eyes. I quickly sat up.

"I'm sorry."

He chuckled. "You're good. Go ahead and go to bed. I'll catch you tomorrow."

I stood up slowly and watched as he cleaned up everything. I felt like I was in a daze as I stood there, still fucked up from the liquor.

"Sweetheart, what are you doing?"

"Nothing, I'm still drunk." I giggled.

Gently, he grabbed me by the arm and led me into my room where he tucked me in and kissed my forehead gently. He stroked my hair and stared at me for a while before he spoke.

"Get some rest alright. Is your alarm set?" I nodded my head. "Alright. I'll talk to you tomorrow."

"Ok." I replied in a groggy voice. "Have a good night."

"You as well." was the last thing I heard before I drifted off.

Glad You Made It

It had been a whole day and I barely talked to Jamal, let alone saw him. He was too busy getting ready for his shows and performing as well. I wanted to call him and ask him how everything was going, but I didn't want to be a bother. For some reason, I was missing his company and I kinda wished he would stop by and at least say hi. We had spent so much time together setting up the businesses and I truly did miss it. Now that they were set up, was that really it?

Today was the day of the festival and I was getting ready to leave. I had asked the girls if they wanted to go with me, but they both declined complaining that it was going to be too hot. Whatever. I had no problem going places by myself, but I definitely wish they did come.

Ever since that dinner night, they had been a little standoffish. Most of the time, I was the only one that called them, and if they did pick up, the conversation felt rushed and unwelcomed. Eventually, I would just stop calling and let them get over whatever was crawling up their asses.

When I arrived at the festival, the place was overly crowded. My car was parked in the garage, and I made my way over to the outdoor festival. My vibrant, tunic shirt fluttered in the wind along with my straightened hair. My shades were on, and I was going to enjoy this day even if I had to do it alone.

I had gotten there a little bit early so I could shop around a bit and see what other festivities and events they had going on. Most things had long lines and I was not a fan of lines, so I watched from afar before moving on.

It was a half hour before the show was to start so I made my way over to the already crowded arena. I ate something light and drank plenty of water as I sat in the third row and waited.

The closer it got to show time, the more packed it got, and everyone waited in anticipation just as I did. Soon enough, the announcer came out and introduced the first artist. He was a local and people seemed to enjoy his music. Me? Not so much. I wasn't a fan of the N word being thrown into the song every five seconds. To me, it showed a lack of creativity. But hey, who was I to judge?

The next artist came out and then the next, and then then next. Finally, they called Mally Boy's name and the crowd erupted and stood to their feet taking me quite by surprise. I looked closely at his attire and realized it was one of my designs. I was overly ecstatic just by seeing him perform with it on. Matter of fact, his whole crew had a design on.

As he performed, his eyes were searching through the crowd. A big smile came on his face when his eyes met mine and he pointed to me from the stage. I felt myself blush and the people on either side of me glanced down and gassed me up a bit for the simple, yet very noticeable shout out. Little did I know, something bigger was about to happen.

Three songs were performed by him and his crew and at the end, he wanted to say something very special.

"I wanted to give a big shout out to my shirt designer Cadence. I see you Love. Be sure to check out her gear at Cay City dot com. If you want more info, check it out on my website. Y'all know where to find me! We out!"

He dropped the mic and exited the stage as the crowd went wild. The performance he gave was absolutely amazing and very entertaining. I could see why he had a strong fan base.

For some reason, I wanted to run up to him and give him a big congratulatory hug for a job well done. But I kept my composure. I didn't want to seem like one of his groupies or anything. I knew he had enough of those. Instead, I sat patiently in the audience while everyone, well, mostly everyone, dispersed out of the arena.

From my seat, I spotted him backstage signing autographs for his fans and taking selfies for social media bragging rights. Each shot he took, it seemed like he not only showcased the fan, but also the shirt.

Out of nowhere, my phone started vibrating like crazy, but it wasn't a phone call or messages. It was shirt sales. An even bigger smile grew on my face as I continued to watch him until no one else, but the crew and I were left.

When he had a chance, he ran out from behind backstage towards me. I stood up in anticipation but wasn't ready for the greeting that he gave me. Instead of a simple hug, he lifted me off my feet and spun me around.

"I'm so glad you made it."

"Why wouldn't I come? You did an amazing job out there and…" I looked him up and down, "Nice gear."

"You know I had to stunt on 'em a lil bit, feel me. Did you eat anything yet? You thirsty?"

"I'm a little hungry. Are you?"

"Yea, a little bit. Wanna go grab something right quick?"

"Are you done?"

"Yea, yea, I'm done. Come on." he said, grabbing my hand and pulling me along. "What do you have a taste for?"

"I don't know, pizza?"

"We can do pizza." He looked around for a bit before changing directions. "You came here by yourself?"

"I asked the girls to come, but they said it was going to be too hot for their liking. So yea, I'm here by myself."

"It is type hot out here, but I'm so glad you made it."

"Were you looking for me in the crowd?" I asked as we stood in line.

"Ha, yea, I was. Was it that obvious?"

"Just a little bit."

"Oh damn."

"I really appreciate the shoutout, my phone has been blowing the fuck up since like, fifteen minutes after the show."

"How many orders did you get?"

"Let me check." I said checking the phone. He slightly pushed me up when the line moved. "Two-hundred and fifty-seven orders. Holy shit. We just made five grand!"

"We? That's all you Love."

"Couldn't have done it without your help."

"Mally Boy!" a fan noticed him. Once one did, the rest of them did too and they all flocked to him taking us both off guard. I was basically pushed off to the side as everyone gathered around and took pictures of him, with him and got signed autographs from him. Every now and then, when he got the chance, he would look up and make sure I was still there and that I was alright.

The crowd stayed around him for a good fifteen minutes before it slowly began to dissipate. When mostly everyone was gone, he came back and grabbed my hand and we got back in line to get our food. As he went to pay, the owner of the food truck gave us the slices for free in exchange for a selfie with him.

We found a semi-secluded area in the shade and sat down to eat after washing our hands. "I'm sorry about that."

I giggled. "It's not your fault. No need to apologize. How's your pizza?"

"It's really good. How's yours?"

"Good." I replied, taking another small bite.

69

"You know damn well that's not how you eat. If you don't stop trynna be cute."

"What are you talking about? This is how I eat."

"Yea, whatever Cadence. You ain't foolin nobody. Who you trynna look cute for?"

"Stop it. Nobody." I said bashfully.

"What are you doing after this?"

"Nothing. Go home and relax I guess. What about yourself?"

"I have to get ready for the next gig coming up tonight."

"Where is it?"

"Fantasy Lounge down on Broad Street. You wanna come?"

"That place is always so crowded. I don't think I've ever been there."

"Perks of being a friend of an entertainer, you won't have to stand in line, and you can get in free."

"More like a mini celebrity."

"I wouldn't go that far now."

"Shit, I would. People love you."

"For now." he said, finishing his food.

"Why do you say that?"

"All good things must come to an end."

"But you're just getting started."

"I know, but..."

"Mally Boy!" another fan yelled out and instinctively, I moved away from him so he could entertain the crowd.

"What time do you have to go?" I asked after we were alone again.

He looked at his watch. "I got about a half hour left. You never answered my question though." he said, posting up against a rail.

"And what question might that be?" I asked standing in front of him.

"Are you coming to the show tonight? You look cute by the way."

"Oh, thank you. Yea, I'll come. What time does it start?"

"Twelve, but get there early so I can make sure you get in. And be sure to text me when you're on your way."

"I will do that."

He looked at the time once again. "Alright Love, let me walk you to your car. I gotta head out soon."

He gently nudged me back away from him and grabbed my hand as we walked to the garage. At my car, he gave me a big hug and a small peck on the cheek. "See you later on tonight. Hopefully, your friends will come with you too." he said before walking away from me.

Perfect Moment

The day seemed to drag as I anxiously waited to get to the lounge. Not only because it was my first time going there, but I got to see Jamal as well. Usually, due to the line and the price to get into that lounge, I wouldn't have even considered it as a destination even though I've been wanting to go for a very long time.

My heart fluttered in my chest as I started getting ready. Initially, I was going to put on a full face of makeup, but then decided on just a smokey eye and lipstick. My tight-fitting dress was put on along with my jewelry and matching shoes.

Once again, I was going by myself because Charmaine declined my offer to go, and Janelle and Khalil flat out didn't answer my calls, even though this was a place they wanted to go to just as bad as I did. I didn't know what to make out of this whole situation, but tomorrow, I was going to find out. Tonight, I was going to enjoy my little self.

I started my car up and made my way to Broad Street after I let Jamal know I was on the way. I didn't leave until he responded back and told me he was able to get me in. I wasn't about to waste my time if I couldn't.

As I got out of the car, it felt like my knees were weak and were about to buckle. It felt like my chest was about to cave in, and my palms were sweating like crazy. Before I could even get to the door, I got a message asking if I was there yet. I replied yes, and when I got to the entrance, Jamal was waiting for me.

Everyone in the line was pissed, but they began to yell once they saw his face come out. He grabbed my hand and escorted me into a VIP section where I was surrounded by people I didn't know. Most of which were his friends where he introduced me.

"Hey everybody, this is Cadence. She's a good friend so treat her like one of us." They all nodded, smiled and waved before talking amongst themselves again. He took my hands in his. "You want something to drink Love? You look a little nervous."

"I just wasn't expecting all this."

"All of what? To meet everyone?" I nodded my head. "They're all mad cool. No worries. You want rum and pineapple juice?"

"Yes please."

"I gotchyu. Maybe you'll loosen up when you get some alcohol in your system." he teased before turning to the waitress and giving her my order. "I want you to meet someone though. She's been wanting to meet you too." He led me to a beautiful, thin, dark-skinned woman who smiled as we walked up to her.

"Hi, I'm Nia. I'm Jamal's sister." she said, extending her hand out.

I took it and shook it before responding back. "Hi, I'm Cadence. It's nice to meet you."

"I know who you are. This guy talks about you all the time."

A shocked look appeared on my face. "He does?"

"You're his neighbor right? The one who helped him?"

"Yes. That would be me."

"Even prettier than he described."

"Alright, alright. Thank you Nia." he interrupted pulling me away. "Damn she's annoying."

I giggled. "She only said a few words."

"She wasn't supposed to say all that extra shit."

The waitress came up to me and handed me my drink of which I basically slurped down thanks to my nerves. It helped me relax a little bit, but it still wasn't enough. "Can I get another one?"

"I gotchyu." he replied and ordered another one for me as he drank more of what was in his cup.

"What are you drinking?"

"Henny. I'm trynna pace myself unlike you."

"Hey," I said, tapping his shoulder. "All this is new to me. I can't help it if I'm a bit nervous."

"Well don't be. Go be your usual self and talk to people. Make some new friends, enjoy the vibe. I have to head down soon to get ready."

"I know. Are you ready? Are you excited?"

"I'm hella excited. I can't wait to get up there and do what I love."

"I'm excited for you. I know you'll do an amazing job."

"Thank you."

The waitress came back and handed me my second drink and I sipped on it slowly while Jamal took me around to talk to everyone. As I talked to them, it was as if they already knew me, and they welcomed me warmly. As time went on, I found myself enjoying the conversation and even adding to the jokes.

Jamal ordered me another drink before he was called to go backstage and get ready. Before he left, he gave me a big hug and a kiss on my forehead. When I turned back to the group, Nia was staring at me and eventually waved me over to sit down next to her.

"How are you enjoying yourself this evening?"

"I'm having a great time. How about yourself?"

"I'm having a great time too. Can't wait to see Mally. I haven't seen him perform on stage before."

"He is amazing. The first time I saw him, it shocked me."

"So how long have you known each other? You seemed to appear out of nowhere."

"We've only known each other for... a week now? I met him when he first moved in."

She nodded in understanding. "He seems to have become quite fond of you. I heard you were his accountant now?"

"Yes. We were talking about business one day and he asked for help. Actually, it was kind of a mutual agreement where he would help me if I helped him."

"The shirts, right?"

I giggled. "Yea."

"He showed them to me. They're really dope."

"Thank you. That means a lot. So are you older or younger than him?"

"I'm younger by two years. I just turned 23."

"Aww, happy belated birthday!"

"Thank you!"

"Hey Nia and Cadence, we're going down to dance. Wanna come?"

"Wanna go dance?" she asked with bright eyes.

"Absolutely!"

She grabbed my hand and the small group of six went to the dance floor and began to dance. A few songs had gone by, and my cup was empty. I made my way to the bar, and someone offered to buy me a drink. Of course he wanted at least a dance after that, so I gave him a song's worth. Honestly, it felt kind of awkward to be dancing with a guy at this point in time, so I left his side and went back to the group.

A few more songs played before the DJ introduced Jamal on stage and the crowd went wild. Nia held my hand anxiously as her brother came on stage and performed. No surprise here, but the crowd got hyped as he entertained them like a professional. At the end, he gave me and my brand a shout out as well as a happy belated birthday to his sister.

"Oh my God, he is so good!" Nia exclaimed in my ear.

"I told you he was. He knows how to hype the crowd up."

75

"Oh my God, yes! They fuckin love him!"

Before I could respond, I felt a set of hands on my waist and a body was pressed up against mine. I turned to the left and his head rested on my shoulder.

"Did you like it?"

"I loved it. You did an amazing job once again."

"Aww, you guys are too cute together." Nia admired.

"It's not like that sis, chill."

"Yea, whatever you say."

He let me go and went over to her and gave her a big hug. "You did such an amazing job! I'm so proud of you."

"Thank you. You enjoying yourself?"

"Yes, big brother, I'm enjoying myself."

"Good. Y'all want another drink?"

"Hell yea." she exclaimed.

"I'll take another one."

He grabbed us both by the hands and led us to the bar where we ordered. While we waited, people swarmed us all and took pictures. One girl even grabbed his dick, and he couldn't resist to go and dance with her.

Our drinks were handed to us, and we went on the floor to dance. For some reason, I was feeling some type of way as I watched the woman grind on him. Then he moved to the next.

"Are you alright?" Nia asked, coming up beside me.

"Yea, I'm fine. Are you?"

She looked at me oddly, then at her brother's actions and shook her head. "I don't know why he acts a fool like that. Stupid."

"Why do you say that? Seems like he's enjoying himself."

"He's gonna miss out on something great chasing the right now."

I was confused at her words, but I didn't get a chance to ask further because she was whisked away by someone who wanted to dance with her. I sat at the bar lonely, sad and miserable and I couldn't put my finger on as to why. Usually, I would be right out there dancing my ass off and having a great time especially with all this liquor in my system. But not tonight. I sighed and sipped my drink slowly as I watched everyone else around me.

Soon, I felt a familiar embrace and heard a familiar voice behind me. "What you doing here Lovely?"

I turned around and was greeted by an old fling from years ago. We ended on mutual terms and there were no hard feelings, but we fell out of touch throughout the years. His presence here actually surprised me for he was never the club kind of guy.

I turned around and gave him a hug. "Hey Booski, how are you? How have you been?"

"I've been alright, no complaints, how about yourself?"

"I'm good, I'm good. Was not expecting to see you here."

"Yea, me either. What brings you out here?"

"Showing support for a friend that performed tonight."

"Oh yea? Who?"

"Mally Boy."

"Oh word? That's what's up. You mind if I dance with you? You lookin hella good tonight."

"No, not at all and thank you." I said taking his lead to the floor where we danced.

A few songs in, I felt eyes on me and as I looked up, Jamal was staring at me. All his attention was on me even though a woman was provocatively dancing on him.

"You ain't tell me you guys were talking." Marcus said from behind me noticing I had stopped dancing too.

"We aren't talking. We're just friends." I said, but my eyes never left Jamal.

"That's not a just friends look." He kissed my cheek and let me go. "It was good seeing you again Candy. Hit me up sometime."

Once I was alone, he began to come to where I was standing. A few women tried to dance with him on his way over and he harshly refused them. His eyes were glued on mine as he approached, and I couldn't take mine off him either.

My heart fluttered as he got closer until he was finally standing directly in front of me. I looked away with shyness, but he brought my face back up to him and rested his forehead on mine. My arms wrapped around his neck and his around my waist as we slowly swayed to the music.

If I was to be asked of the feeling I felt in that moment, I wouldn't be able to describe it. It was almost an instant realization of what everyone around us had been telling us. My hands caressed his face and ran through his beard. It was like I was seeing him in a different light with different eyes. It could have been the liquor. It could have been the atmosphere. But what I do know is, it was perfect.

Someone tapped his shoulder pulling him out of our trance. He pulled away and listened to what the man said before turning back to me. "I have to go handle something backstage right quick. I'll be right back." He gently tapped under my chin before disappearing into the sea of people leaving me alone once again. But not for too long. Nia came to my side and started dancing with me.

Song after song played and we danced to each and every one of them happily until we both got worn out and went back to the VIP section to rest our feet.

"Oh my Gah, I haven't had this much fun in a long time! I need to get out more."

"Do you live around here?"

"No. I live out in Neptune, but I wouldn't mind coming down for the weekends to do this!" She glanced at me with a smile. "Are you feeling better?"

"A little bit, yea. I'm so tired, I can't wait to go to bed."

"Me either girl. The people out here party harder than what I'm used to."

"Are you driving back tonight?"

She shook her head. "No. I'm staying with Mally for the weekend even though he told me he won't be home most of the time."

"I'm right next door if you want some company."

"Aww, thanks! I'm probably gonna be sleep most of the day anyway. Are you going to his show tomorrow at the festival?"

"I hadn't planned on it. I went earlier today. I'll go with you if you want to go."

"Are you sure? You don't have to go twice."

"Makes no difference to me. I love a good show."

She giggled. "I feel you on that one. Yes, please come, it would mean a lot to him."

"I'll be there then."

"What's your number so we can link up."

She handed me her phone and I put my number in before calling my phone. "Call me anytime." I stood up and walked over to the small bar in the section. "You want any more to drink?"

"I'll have some juice or something. I'm already a lil fucked up."

I laughed. "What juice do you want?"

"Is there orange juice over there?"

"Yea, I got you." I replied, pouring her some and handing it to her before going to mix mine.

We sat and chatted for a while and got to know each other a little better. A few of the people from the group slowly started returning and we all conversed a bit more. The DJ called for last drinks at the bar, and I knew this night was almost over. I was a bit sad that it would be because I was truly enjoying myself. Even got to know some really dope people and made a few new friends.

Twenty minutes later, Jamal came up and everyone clapped and congratulated him on a job well done. He sat between Nia and I and joined in the conversation. Soon enough, the lights turned on, and the music stopped playing. People began to leave, but we were one of the last to exit.

"It was so nice to meet you Cadence. I hope we can chill again sometime."

"It was nice to meet you all too and most definitely!" I replied to the group that was heading in the opposite direction to their car.

Jamal walked closest to the street with my hand in his and my other hand in his sister's as we headed to my car.

"Are you sure you're good to drive Cadence?"

"Yes, I'll be fine. Are you good to drive?"

"I'm good. Let me know when you get home."

"Will do. Talk to you later."

My car door closed, and they walked away before I started my engine and made my way home. I was so damn exhausted from dancing, but I would do it all over again in a heartbeat.

I sat in my driveway for a while when I got back trying to muster the strength to get up and go inside. I grabbed my heels that I had kicked off a while ago and stepped out the car locking it before heading to my house.

Car lights came from down the street and pulled into the driveway next to mine. Chatter could be heard as the two people got out and began to walk to the house.

"I made it safe." I yelled in a humorous tone.

The front door of the house opened and closed, and footsteps came my way. Soon, a figure appeared right in front of me.

"I'm glad you made it home safely." His voice was deep and sexy. Nothing like I had heard before.

"I'm glad you guys made it safely too." There was an awkward pause. "So, what are you about to do?"

"Probably just go to bed. I have to be up again in the morning."

I nodded my head. "Well, good night then." I simply said and began to walk away.

"Cadence."

I stopped and turned back around and found him standing there with his arms extended towards me. Slowly, I made my way back to him and accepted his invite for a hug. It wasn't our regular hug though. It was something deeper than that.

He kissed the top of my head and let go. "Have a good night."

"You as well Mally Boy."

The Set Up

The next morning, I woke up with a serious hangover and a terrible headache. I took some pain meds and went to make some ginger tea to calm my stomach a bit and it helped. I looked at my phone and it was just as dry as my mouth was. I sighed. Initially, I was going to call the girls and see how their night went, but I didn't want to feel the pain of rejection. Not this early in the day anyway.

I watched a little tv before I decided to start getting ready to go. Half of me wanted to stay in and lounge around all day, and the other half wanted to go to the festival. Of course the festival half won, especially when I got a text from Nia asking what time I was leaving. I asked if she needed a ride, and she told me she had ridden over with her brother. I responded that I would be on my way in the next half hour.

I showered, brushed my teeth and got dressed before heading out the door. The trip there didn't seem as long as it was yesterday, but there were just as many cars if not more in the parking lot. I picked up my phone and called her.

"Hello?"

"Hey, are you here?"

"I'm walking up to it now. Where are you?"

"I'm actually backstage at the arena. Hold on." There was a brief pause before a male's voice was in my ear.

"Cadence?"

"Hey! How are you?"

"I'm good, getting ready for the show. What are you up to?"

"I'm heading over to the arena."

"Wait, you're here?"

"…Yea. Nia didn't tell you I was coming?"

"No." he laughed.

"Surprise!" she yelled in the background.

"I can't with you man." he said to her before talking to me again. "Where are you? You wanna come backstage with us?"

"Am I allowed to be back there?"

"Yea. Come to the top of the arena, I'll meet you there."

"Ok, see you in a few."

I hung up the phone and made my way to the meeting spot. As I stood at the top, I could see him walking up to where I was. He wrapped his arms around me and held me tight.

"I'm so glad you're here. I had no idea you were coming." He grabbed my hand and helped me down the steps.

"It seems like your sister set the both of us up."

"She definitely did. How was your night though? Did you get enough rest?"

"I should be asking you that. You have to perform in a few hours."

"I did and this is nothing. I'm probably going to be passed out after this event though."

"Yea, I bet. Is it the same as yesterday?"

"Exactly the same. I need to come up with something new for next week. Maybe you could help."

"Me? Why me?"

"Can't it just be because I like spending time with you?"

I blushed as Nia ran up to us. "Glad you could make it!"

"Did you set us up?"

"Maybe. But look at both of your faces."

"Alright y'all, I gotta get back to work. Hang out, chill, whatever. Drinks are over here if you want any."

"Ughh, I don't wanna hear the word drinks for at least a week." I complained.

"Me either. I woke up with the worst hangover ever."

"Oh my God, me too." I looked around at my surroundings. "I don't think I've ever been backstage before. Not at something like this anyway."

"Me either. New experiences all around. I didn't realize my brother had such a huge following until last night."

"Yea, his videos average fifty thousand views. It's probably gone up since then."

"Damn. I'm so proud of him. He's really worked his ass off for this. Everyone told him not to do it and that he would fail. He even started to doubt himself for a while, but his love of music wouldn't let him. And now look at him. I don't think I've ever seen him this happy." She began to tear up and I rubbed her back.

"Don't cry. Aww."

"Just watching how far he's gotten really makes me happy for him, you know. Not a lot of people can say they get to do what they love. And he's touched so many people with his words. That's all he ever wanted. For his story to be heard."

"Well they are listening now, and his story is far from over." Just listening to what she told me made me tear up and I never even watched the steps he took to get to this point.

She waved her face. "I don't even know why I'm crying right now."

"Cuz you're happy for him. Happy that you get to see it all for yourself."

Jamal walked past us and looked at us like we were crazy. "Are y'all crying? What are y'all crying for?"

"Nothing Mally, go finish what you're doing and leave us be. We're having a moment over here." she snarked.

He shook his head and kept working while the both of us laughed it off. "Can I get a hug?" she asked.

"Of course."

"I swear you are the sweetest person. He hardly ever lets me meet his girlfriends."

"Uhh, we're not…"

"Friend girls. Sorry. He usually keeps his relations under wraps. So when he told me about you, it completely caught me off guard."

"So… what did he say?"

She laughed again. "Just how you were smart and had a cool ass vibe and you were easy to get along with. I asked how if you've only chilled a few times. He said, when you know, you know. Whatever the hell that means. But I think you guys look cute together. Even if you're just 'friends'."

Jamal walked up behind Nia and gave her a look. "Why you tellin all my secrets yo? Damn." he teased. "The show is about to start though. You wanna sit out there or watch it from here?"

"What do you think Cadence?"

"I think you'll get the best experience out there. You can feel the energy and the love the crowd has for him."

"We'll sit out there then. How do we get there?"

"Follow me." he said, leading the way once again.

The arena was already starting to get packed when we found a spot to sit and watch from the audience. We waited about another twenty minutes before the first performers came out and did their thing. It was the same that was seen yesterday, but it was all entertaining, nonetheless.

The announcer called Jamal's name and the crowd erupted. Nia looked around in shock at everyone's reaction to her brother before she too began clapping and cheering for him. He performed another great show, and it was as if I was watching it for the first time.

Nia cried when he mentioned both of our names afterwards in disbelief and shock that this was really happening. That his dream was finally coming true. Once he left the stage, he took more pictures and signed more autographs for his fans. Old and new. This time, more people wanted to take pictures and he made sure to take them with every single person.

The show had been over for at least an hour before he finally was finished entertaining everyone. Nia and I sat patiently and talked small talk as we waited. When she saw him coming up to us, she sprang to her feet and held him tight.

"You did such an amazing job. I fuckin loved it!"

"Thank you. You guys ready to head out? I'm fuckin beat."

"Yes! I'm hungry too." I added.

"Y'all wanna go out and eat somewhere?"

"I'm ready to go back to the house. I've had enough excitement for one day. Maybe we can order in. That cool?" she suggested.

I shrugged my shoulders. "That works for me."

"Iight bet. We can do that. Come on, let's get outta here."

All of us walked to our cars and pulled off headed in the same direction and pulled up to our houses at the same time. I told them I would meet them in a half because I had to get out of my sticky clothes and freshen up. They agreed cuz they had to do the same.

I don't think I ever took a shower as fast as I did. I was so eager to get back and enjoy the rest of my day with the both of them. I absolutely loved their vibe and the conversations that we had. Even though I was dressed and ready, I still waited at least forty-five minutes, so I didn't seem so eager.

"Cadence, are you done yet? What the hell is taking you so long?" Jamal called and asked. It was good to know the feeling was mutual.

"Yes, hurry up and come back!" Nia whined.

"I'll be over in a minute then." I said hanging up.

My shoes slipped on my feet, and I headed to the next house over and knocked on the door. I stood there nervously, for it was my first time actually being at his house instead of mine. The door opened and I walked in.

The inside of the house was not what I expected a bachelor's house to be. It was decorated beautifully and elegantly, and it was very, very clean.

"You've never been here before?" Nia asked.

"No, he usually comes over to my place. It looks nice in here."

"Thank you." he said, greeting me with a hug. "So what do you have a taste for? I was thinking Caribbean or Spanish food."

"Ooo, that sounds good. I have a taste for oxtails, peas and rice."

"Oh, that does sound good! Mally, hurry up and order. I want that too." she nudged.

He laughed as he put our orders in. While he did that, I pulled out enough to cover my order. He looked down at the cash in my hand. "What the fuck is this for?"

"… My food. Is it not enough? I can pay for y'alls too if you want."

"Cadence, put that shit away. You know I gotchyu."

My face got flush as I put what I had in my hand back in its place. His sister simply smiled at me before going into the dining room pulling me along.

"You know how to play Uno?" she asked.

"Of course. It's been a while, but I love that game."

Jamal placed the cards on the table. "Wanna play then?"

"Tuh, hell yea! I'm a beast."

"Yea, you say that now. You ain't ever played against me before."

"Well don't you sound cocky." we flirted.

Round after round was played for a few hours. The only time we stopped was to eat and even that was rushed or we ate as we played. Spades was next, and before I knew it, it was already twelve at night. My eyes began to grow heavy, and I yawned.

"Oh shit, you got work in the morning."

"Yea, I do, don't remind me."

"Come on then, let's get you home. Don't want you cranky at work."

He stood up and helped me to my feet. Although I was ready to go to bed, I really didn't want to leave because we were truly having such a great time.

"When are you leaving?" I asked Nia giving her a hug.

"Tomorrow morning. I have work in the afternoon."

"It was great meeting you. I hope we do this again sometime."

"I have your number. You'll be hearing from me."

I walked out of the house and began to pull the door closed when it stopped. "What are you doing?" Jamal asked following behind me.

"What are you doing?"

"I'm walking you home."

"I live right there."

"And?"

"I'm sure I can manage walking fifteen feet away."

"I wouldn't let you walk one foot in the dark alone." I shook my head, smiled and began to walk away with my hand in his. "Did you enjoy yourself today?"

"I really did. From the show to the Uno. It was a great day. Did you enjoy it?"

"Every second of it. You know you can come over anytime you want."

"Tuh, you sure about that?"

He rolled his eyes and smiled. "I'm sure about that."

I couldn't help but to smile. "I'll be sure to call first."

He laughed. "Whatever floats your boat Cadence."

We stopped at my door, and I really didn't want him to leave. I guess my face showed what my mind was thinking because he asked, "What's wrong?"

"Nothing. I just, really had a good time and I don't want it to end."

"We'll have more times like these, no worries. Now go get some rest."

"Ok." I said gently before I was pulled in for a hug and quickly released before he quickly left.

His actions were strange, but I had the feeling, he didn't want to leave either. My door opened and I walked inside and went straight to bed.

Mean It

The day seemed to pass by so slowly as I tried to force myself to stay up at work all day. I was so exhausted, and my body was punishing me for not letting it get enough rest. Finally, five o'clock came around and as I made my way home, it was like I got a second wind. I was wide the fuck awake.

To my surprise, there was only one car in my neighbor's driveway, and that was his. I think it was the first time I had ever seen just his car there. Especially on a weekday when he had more free time. A smile fell on my face when I saw him sitting on the front porch with his notebook and laptop out working on new material. When he saw I was home, he smiled too and put his things down to greet me.

"Hey you. How was your day?" he asked after letting me go from his hug.

"Long as hell. I hate it there." I pouted. "How was your day?"

"Productive. I wrote a few more songs that I'm going to record tonight. I also heard back from my lawyer. We have court in two weeks with a positive outlook."

"Oh that is good news! Well, don't let me distract you from making your music."

"Is that an excuse to leave me alone?"

"What? No. You seemed like you were in the zone over there."

"Wanna come see what I have so far?"

"Yea, let me put my stuff down and I'll be right over."

"Iight, cool. See you in a few."

As I went to put my things down, he made his way back to his porch. I also went to change into something more comfortable. I always found that the stretchy material from my leggings offered me this comfort.

"Hey." I said walking to his porch, but he didn't hear me because of his headphones. He was vibin hard to something and I startled him when I touched his arm.

"Oh shit. Didn't even see you walk up."

"What are you listening to?"

"A new beat. Here."

His headphones were handed to me, and I held them up to my ears. Soon I was vibin just as hard as he was. "You made this?"

"Yea, a few minutes ago. You like it?"

"Hell yea, it's hard. You write any lyrics to it yet?"

"I'm about to do it now. Just trynna figure out what to write."

"I'm sure it will come to you." I said sitting next to him on the outside couch quietly so as to not distract him.

"Why are you so quiet?"

"I don't want to distract you."

He laughed. "You're good Love. When you listen to the beat, what do you think of?"

I thought for a minute before responding with, "Triumph."

"Triumph? Really?"

"It sounds like your story. What it took you to get where you are now."

He nodded his head. "I can go with that."

His pen hit the paper and it never seemed to stop. For twenty minutes straight, he wrote and came up with two pages worth of lyrics. His eyes met with mine and he smiled. "What?"

"Wanna hear it?"

"Now?"

"It's just a rough draft."

"Alright, let's hear it."

The headphones unplugged from the computer and the beat played. As it played, he rapped to it with the lyrics he had just written. My eyes grew big at the amazing talent this guy had. The rhyme and the flow of the song came together as one in no time, and I had faith it would be another song people would love.

"What you think?"

"What do I think? I think people are going to love it!"

"I think it's missing something."

"Umm… like what?"

"I don't know." He ran through the song again. "Do me a favor and sing this part."

"Say what now?"

"Just sing the damn lyrics Cadence."

My heart began to beat faster in my chest not sure of what he would think of my voice, and I didn't want to embarrass myself. I glanced at the words on the page and sang it in my head. "Jamal, I can't sing this."

He laughed. "Just sing it Cay."

"Ok, but don't laugh."

"I won't laugh. Ready?"

"Ready." The music started up and I very shyly and very quietly sang the chorus of the song.

I looked at him waiting for his critique or for him to laugh at my voice, but he didn't. He smiled and asked, "You wanna be on the track?"

"What? Me? No."

"Why not? Your voice matched perfectly with what it was missing."

"So why not get a professional vocalist then?"

"Cuz I want you. You helped inspire it, why not sing on it?"

"Jamal…"

"Cadence…" I scrunched my face up at him. "What do you have to lose?"

"I don't want to fuck up your song."

"You have a good voice. Just need to be confident with yourself. Come on Cay, please."

"Ugg, fine." I buried my hands in my face being bashful.

"You'll do fine."

"Wait, so does that mean I have to go to the studio with you?"

"Yup."

"And I have to sing in front of other people?"

"Yup."

"Damn it Mal."

"You'll do fine."

My stomach churned and balled up in knots at just the thought of singing in front of him, let alone in a studio in front of people I didn't even know.

"What makes you nervous?"

"I don't want people to laugh and say I can't sing. I don't wanna fuckin embarrass myself."

He flipped to a blank page and wrote the chorus down and handed the paper to me. "I guess you better practice then."

"Are you serious?"

"Yup."

The music began to play again, and he went through his verse. When it was my time to go, he pointed to me and led me in.

"Louder. Mean it." he said and started it over.

For a good hour, we sat on his porch rehearsing the song. As time went on, I began to feel a lot more comfortable with it and sang it as if it were my own words from the heart.

"I think you got it. Keep that same energy tonight. You hungry?"

"I could eat. I have some chicken I need to cook before it goes bad."

"What are you making with it?"

"Baked BBQ with some vegetables. What time do I have to be at the studio?"

"Eight."

I looked at my watch. "I have time to make it. Wanna come over?"

"Hell yea. It's been a minute since I had a home cooked meal."

I giggled. "Come on then."

After gathering his things, we headed over to my house where I started cooking. As he waited, he started working on another beat. I sat there quietly as he showed me how he created it all and I actually was surprised at how fast he could make one.

When the food was done, it was plated and brought over to the table where we ate together. "Is it good?" I asked noticing that he was tearing it up.

"Very." Was all he said before he finished it off. "So how are your shirt sales going?"

"Very, very well. Another two- hundred were sold today. I guess I have you to thank for that."

"How many have you sold all together?"

"About five hundred."

"Keep making designs. Always put out fresh material on a regular basis and put the new shit on the front page."

"I have to mess with the site a bit to figure out how to do that."

"It's easy. I'll show you when you get there." He looked at the time. "You bout ready to head out?"

I laughed nervously and stood up grabbing our plates. "Tuh, no. I'm nervous."

"Don't be nervous, you'll be fine. Want me to wash those?"

"I got it, it's alright. Thank you though. Is what I have on alright?"

"No. The guys are gonna be staring at your ass all night." I turned around quickly and made a face at him. "What? I'm being honest."

"Is it only going to be guys in there?"

"There's one female that floats in sometimes, but she's barely in the studio. Don't worry, I gotchyu. Nobody's gonna fuck with you. Plus, Khalil might be up there."

"Oh gees. He's gonna be hella surprised when I walk in there with you."

He chuckled. "I know right. But come on, we gotta go. Go get changed. I'll finish cleaning up."

"Alright, alright. I'm going."

Truth is, I had no idea what to put on as I glanced around in my closet. Some jeans and a nice shirt I guess. I quickly threw it on and headed out to the living room to where he was.

"You look nice." he said with a smile. But not even his gorgeous smile could calm the nerves that were plaguing me at the moment.

"Thank you. Am I riding with you?"

"Of course. You ready?"

"No."

Studio Time

If I thought I was nervous earlier, that wasn't nothing compared to what I was feeling as we walked through the doors of the studio. My hands were sweating, my breathing was deep and my heart, my poor heart was working overtime.

"Hey, what's up Mally?"

"Hey, what's good bro? How you feelin?"

"I'm doin iight. You know we don't allow groupies in here bro."

"She's not a groupie, this is Cadence."

"Oh shit. What's up Ma? How you doin?"

I was taken aback at the warm greeting this strange man was giving me. "I'm doing alright. How are you?"

"I've heard nothing but good things about you."

"You have?"

"Iight, iight, can we head back now?"

"Yea, yea, you know where to go."

"Iight man, see you in a few."

A slight nudge was placed on the small of my back before we headed into another part of the building down the hall. As we got closer to our destination, male voices could be heard from inside.

Jamal opened the door for me and we both walked in. The chattering stopped, and everyone looked at me like I was lost. All except for Khalil, who couldn't believe his eyes.

"What's up Cay? What the hell are you doing here?" he asked, giving me a hug. "You coming to show support?"

"She's gonna be on the new track."

"Word? You got this. You'll be great. I didn't even know you could sing."

"She's actually not that bad."

"What's up Mally Boy? How you doin bro? You ready to get to work?" Lil switched his attention off me.

"Ayo, who is shawty?" another guy asked, looking me up and down like he wanted me.

"Yo chill bro, this is Cadence." Jamal protected.

"So this is Cadence." The tall, slender man came up to me and shook my hand. "It's nice to finally meet you. We hear about you all the time from these two."

"Well, this is news to me."

"You want anything to drink?"

"Please. I'm so nervous."

"No need to be nervous. We're all family here."

Jamal and Khalil went to get me a drink. It was like they were battling to see who could get there first. Khalil ended up getting it for me and he knew exactly what I wanted.

"Thank you Lil."

"No problem Ma."

"So Mally Boy, what did you bring for us today?" yet another man asked as I took my seat. Having Khalil here, a familiar face, definitely helped calm my nerves a bit.

"I got some new shit that I wrote today. Check it out." His laptop came on and was hooked up to the speakers before the beat played. Everyone bobbed their heads along to it.

"Ahh shit, we gotta another banger. Come on, let's get this shit started."

Just in front of us, there was a recording booth that Jamal entered into. Headphones went over his head and the mic in front of him was adjusted. The music played and he began to let his words flow. All too soon, he was done and stepped out to where we were.

"That sounded good bro. Real good." the tall man responded. I gulped down what was in my cup realizing my time was almost up. "Why you ain't rap the chorus though?"

Jamal pointed to me. "That's her domain."

"Iight, iight. You ready Ma?"

I took a deep breath and stood up. "Want me to go in there with you?" Jamal asked.

"Please." I pleaded.

"No doubt, come on." Inside the booth, he helped me gear up and adjusted the mic for me. "Just pretend we're on the porch vibin out. Sing it like you mean it. You got this." he said tapping my shoulder and stepping back.

The music in my headphones began to play with his voice on the track and I waited for my queue to start as I held the paper in my hand nervously. When I heard the beat change, I started. In my mind, I just envisioned us being on the porch practicing together and tuned everything else out. When the chorus was over, the music stopped.

"Run that shit one more time Cadence." the man in my ear said.

The music started up again and I sang my part. This time, I felt a little more confident and relaxed and let the beat take control. The music stopped again. "We got it. Good shit!"

"That's it?" I was surprised.

"That's it. You did good." Jamal said, helping me take the headphones off before grabbing my hand and leading me out the booth. "Let her hear it Boogie."

The track played with my voice on top and I was shocked at how well it sounded. Jamal, along with everyone else was nodding their heads as the entire song played.

"It's still missing something, Mally." one guy said.

"I know. She might have to go and do some background vocals."

"I think that's what it is."

My hand was grabbed again and I was led back into the booth. "What's going on?" I asked as the headphones were replaced on my head.

"On your part, add some background vocals."

"What the hell is that?"

He took the headphones from me. "Play her part Boogie." he demanded and demonstrated what he wanted me to do. "You think you could do something like that?"

"I think I can do that."

"Just go with the flow and don't force anything." he said putting the headphones back over my ears.

The music played and I listened to my words. Each spot I felt it needed something extra, I added more vocals to it.

"Do it one more time using different vocals for the second chorus." The man in my ears said before the track played again and I sang.

"We got it!"

I looked over at Jamal with a smile and was greeted with one too. "Let's go see how it sounds." he said, helping me with the headphones.

When we stepped out of the booth, the track played again with the ad libs. "There it go. Much better! What you think Mal?"

"I think it sounds great. Can't wait to hear the finished product."

"You wanna record anything else tonight?" Boogie asked. "Maybe some RnB tracks. What you gonna do with those anyway?"

"I'm not sure yet, but yea, we can record a few of those."

"You got one in mind?"

Jamal looked through his computer before playing a slow beat that reminded me of a love song. I guess that's why it was an RnB doing right.

"I like that. You got lyrics for it already?"

"Hold up, I gotta pull 'em up right quick." He went through his phone briefly and stood up. "Alright, y'all ready?"

"Do ya thing man." they replied, and he stepped into the booth and got ready.

"How you feeling Cay, you good?" Khalil asked.

"I'm feeling good. Enjoying my time. What the hell have you been up to? I tried to call you."

"I know, my bad. We'll talk about it later. Promise. You want another drink?"

"Please?" He stood up and poured a drink for me before returning briefly. "Thank you."

I sipped on it slowly while Jamal performed. Even though I couldn't hear what the lyrics were, the reactions of the guys let me know it was something good. If his singing was anything like his rap, I could understand why.

"Damn Mal. Good shit." Boogie exclaimed in the mic. "You want her to come in now?"

My ears perked up, and my nerves began to run wild once again as Jamal nodded his head, and Boogie turned to look at me.

"He wanna ask you something Cadence."

I slowly stood to my feet and made my way into the booth. "What's up?"

"You feel like recording another song with me?"

"Now?"

"No, tomorrow." he replied sarcastically. "Yes now. Right now."

"What's it about?"

"Being in love with someone you can't have. Initially, I was gonna sing the whole thing, but since you're here, I was thinking about a duet."

My throat constricted, and I took a nervous sip from my cup. "Can I hear what you have so far?"

He handed me the headphones and I put them on. The song played and as I listened to it, my eyes teared up. The lyrics and the melody were great, but his voice is what did it for me.

"What's wrong?"

"It's beautiful. I've never heard you sing before."

"Forreal, you like it?"

"I do."

"Enough to do a duet with me?"

"I don't wanna fuck it up."

"Oh mah gah, here you go. You'll be fine, look. This is the part I need you to sing, and some of the chorus as well. Can you at least give it a try?"

I took the phone in my hands and read the lyrics and tried to sing it in my mind. I sighed. "I'll try it, but don't laugh if I fuck it up."

"You're not gonna fuck it up."

The headphones were adjusted on my ears by his hands, and he put another set of headphones on before he queued the music to play. Next, he queued me to start. The first take wasn't that great, but he gave me some advice and it progressed.

Five takes later, a voice came out from my headphones. "We got it. How you want the chorus to go?"

"Play it back right quick from the beginning."

The music played, and I could see him calculating how he wanted everything to sound. I stood there and listened as everything started to fall into place.

"Iight, I got it. Hold up." He turned to me and pointed. "You're gonna sing this part after I'm done this part. Then you'll come in after me again with this part and we'll sing the last bars together."

I nodded my head and the music started again. More queues were given when it was my time to sing. As we sang the last bars, the harmony came together and it sounded beautiful. The guys in the other room started clapping and getting hyped at how it sounded.

Jamaal looked over at me with a smile before we heard, "Damn y'all sounded good. Do it one more time for the second chorus."

The track played again and we sang our respective parts. This time, there was more intensity and more passion in our notes.

"The chemistry right now is on fire. Y'all wanna ad-lib?"

"Let's do it!" I replied enthusiastically.

The track ran through one more time as were added our extras and then, "We got it! Y'all gotta come hear this shit."

We took off our headphones and headed into the other room where the song was played. I instantly melted when I heard the full thing play out.

"Damn Cay. I ain't know you could blow like that. You need to come up here more often." Khalil complimented.

"Absolutely, y'all gotta do something with this shit."

Jamal gave me a high five before I finished off my drink amazed at what the outcome of the song was.

"You done for the night, or you got something else up your sleeve?"

"I'm done for the night. I gotta get Cadence home. It's getting late."

I looked at the time and it was already past eleven-thirty. "Damn. I didn't realize how late it was."

"Time flies by right?"

"Iight Mally Boy. We'll see you tomorrow then. Give me a few days to master these and I'll have 'em to you." Boogie said, giving Jamal dap, then grabbing my hands. "Miss Cadence, it was a pleasure working with you. We hope you come up here again. And keep this man outta trouble."

"I will try and it was a pleasure working with you too." I turned to Khalil. "You better call me tomorrow. "

All the guys ooo'd him before he responded. "I will, I will. I promise."

"See y'all tomorrow." Jamal said, grabbing my hands and holding the door for me.

I couldn't hold in my excitement as we walked out to the car. "You liked it huh?" he asked, opening my door.

"What? It was awesome!" I replied when he got in. "Oh my goodness, that song! I loved it."

"I'm glad you liked it. We sounded good. I can't wait til he masters it."

"What are you going to do with it?"

"I'm not sure yet, but Imma definitely think of something."

"I had such a good time. I'm so glad you pulled me out here."

He laughed and grabbed my hands. "Maybe next time you'll be more willing."

I yawned. "Most definitely."

"Aww, I'm sorry sweetheart. I didn't mean to keep you out this late."

"Well don't let it happen again!" I teased.

He laughed slightly and brought the back of my hand to his lips and kissed it gently. Chills ran through my body at his actions, but I didn't say a word. Just enjoyed the feeling and affection. My fingers intertwined with his the whole ride home.

When we got back to the house, he pulled into his driveway, and walked me home hand in hand. On my front porch we held each other tight for a long while, not saying much of anything, just enjoying the energy and the chemistry flowing between us. He finally pulled away, even though he didn't want to, gave me a kiss on the cheek and walked back to his house.

Unbelievable

As I pulled into my driveway after work, I noticed a new car was in his. Usually, it didn't bother me, but it made me feel some type of way today. I got out of my car just as he and his female friend were coming out lip locking one another. I just stood there watching as anger and a hint of jealousy began to build up inside.

His eyes met mine and he stopped. I slammed my car door and walked briskly into my house slamming that door too. Not too long after the car left, there was a knock on my door. I honestly had no desire to open it until he began yelling my name

"Cadence!"

"Go away Jamal." I yelled back.

"Can you please open the door?"

The door was snatched open, and I looked up at him with an irritated face. "What?"

He didn't say anything for a while. Just stared down at me, but I could hardly look him in the face. "Why are you upset?"

"No reason. What do you want?"

"Tell me, what's wrong?"

"I just had a long day is all. I'm tired and I want to go to bed."

"You're full of shit. What's wrong?"

"If you really can't figure it out, then I don't know what to tell you."

"It's never bothered you before, I don't understand."

"Then stay oblivious to the situation."

He sighed. "Damn. I didn't mean to hurt you. I didn't know."

"Didn't know what?" I shook my head in disbelief. "I should have known. It's my fault. Can you just... get out of here." I said pushing him back and closing the door.

"Cadence!"

"Go away!" I hollered once more and then there was silence.

I should have fuckin known. He showed it from the beginning and here I was stupidly slowly growing feelings for this guy. Ugg. I hadn't really paid it any attention until last Saturday, but I couldn't deny it. I really was beginning to like him.

On my couch I sulked. Half of me wanted him to be here and half of me said to hell with it. It's not like it wasn't a mutual feeling. I know he felt it too. Or did he? I was so fuckin foolish, and now, I felt like I looked dumb. What the fuck ever.

My phone rang with Khalil on the other end. I didn't even want to answer, but I did.

"Hello?"

"Hey Cay, what's up?"

"Nothing, sitting here tired. What about you?"

"Yea, you definitely sound tired. Nothing much though. Just seeing how you were doing."

"Where the hell have you been? Where the hell have you all been? It feels like everyone is ignoring me or doesn't want to be bothered by me anymore. I call and invite you guys places and you always turn me down. What the hell?" I exploded.

"We saw you were getting close to Jamal and things didn't end so well the last time we went out. We thought we needed to give you space."

"How is it that you think I need space when I'm reaching out to you guys? That doesn't even make sense."

"What else is bothering you? I know you're not just mad at that only."

"Nothing Lil. I'm just tired and you know how I get."

"I'll talk to the girls and see if we can't meet up and do something together this weekend. How does that sound."

"It's whatever. I don't even feel like being bothered at this point."

"Damn Cay, don't say that."

"Shit hurts man. Your best friends don't wanna chill with you or simply ignore you and you don't know why. I just don't care anymore. Have a great day Lil." I yelled and hung up.

As soon as my phone was set down, my eyes welled up with tears. I usually didn't cry and let things slide, but this was really a rough day. I really did want my friends to talk to me and cheer me up like they usually do, but I'm not about to beg anyone for attention. Not even them.

I took a deep breath and tried to settle my mind. Tried to calm my nerves. I made my way to my Zen room and played soft relaxing music to help me relax and to meditate. It had been a while since I simply just took it slow and focused on me for a while. Took time to clear my mind and ease my restless thoughts.

It helped tremendously and I came out of the room feeling refreshed. Having a drink or two would have been even better, but I didn't have any. So, I put some clothes on, grabbed my keys and headed out the door almost tripping over something as I made my way out.

A small bouquet of flowers, a bottle of Moscato and a flash drive. I picked everything up and looked at my neighbor's house. No one was there. Inside, I opened the bottle and read the card that was attached to the flowers.

Cadence,
I really am sorry for what you saw. I didn't know the feeling was mutual and that something else had evolved. I wrote you something. I hope you enjoy the song.
Jamal

I didn't bother pouring the liquid contents of the bottle in a glass this time. I chugged it right from the bottle as I put the flash drive into my computer and pressed play. It was a slow song and it described how a man could do something stupid and lose something he's been looking for his entire life. It was beautiful, but I was still pissed.

I turned it off and drank more of the Moscato until my vision blurred and my mind had settled down again. One last thing I knew would help me relax was a nice hot bubble bath by candlelight. As I sat there waiting for it to fill up, Jamal kept flashing in my mind. All the times we spent together, the conversations and laughs we enjoyed together. Was I crazy for thinking about this so soon when we had only met a few weeks ago? Why were these emotions so strong, and I had only realized them a few days ago?

Needless to say, my bubble bath wasn't that relaxing so it soon concluded and I went to watch tv. A half hour into the show, Khalil called me again.

"Hello?"

"Yo, what the hell happened today?"

"Umm… what do you mean?"

"Mally Boy ain't on his shit today."

"And how is that my fault?"

"Ever since he's known you, he's been on his game and tonight, he ain't on it."

"Once again, how is that my fault?"

"I know something happened, so what?"

"I don't know. Ask him."

"You're a real piece of fuckin work Cay."

"Nothing new. Bye." I said and hung up before continuing my show. At least I tried before he called again.

"What Khalil?"

"Cadence, it's Mal."

"Err. What do you want? And why are you calling me from his phone?"

"He damn near begged me to."

"Why?"

"Cuz I'm not on my shit and he thinks you can help me. Did you get what I left for you?"

"I did. Thank you. But I can't help you. Not tonight."

"I'm not expecting you to." he simply said.

"I guess I'll talk to you later then."

"Wait!"

"What?"

"Damn it. I know I fucked up. I'm sorry. I honestly didn't know you liked me the same way I like you."

"How could you not tell?"

"We never spoke about it."

"Look. It's no hard feelings. I already know how you are and it's my fault for catching feelings." I took a sad, deep breath trying to hold in my sorrow and not show this man just how upset I really was. "I'll talk to you later." I said and quickly hung up.

Ugg… why the hell was I feeling like this? I think it was more or less that I already knew what was up and let it get this far in the first place. Or maybe it was because I had gotten my hopes up and for what?

My phone rang again, and I declined the call before turning it off completely. Slowly, I made my way to the bed and fell asleep wanting to get this day over with. It would be better in the morning right?

Spittin Game

Well, morning came and went, and I still felt like shit. The only thing that kept my mind off things was being busy at work. When I got home, no new cars were in the driveway. His wasn't even there. I guess he went to a hotel and did his dirty work.

Why was I even thinking like this? Like we were together, and he cheated on me or some shit. I dismissed the thoughts of everything we had done these past few weeks and went back to my normal schedule. A wine glass in my hand and my ass planted on the couch watching tv. No one called and I didn't bother to call no one.

It stayed that way for a while until I got an unexpected call from Nia.

"Hello?"

"Hey, it's Nia. How are you doing?"

"I've had better days. How are you?"

"I'm just a bit concerned about my brother is all. When I spoke to him, he said y'all weren't talking and he sounded really down. What did he do?"

"Why do you think he did something?"

"We both know how he is. Of course he did something."

"It was nothing that I should have been mad about, but it still upset me, so I had to fall back."

"God he's so stupid. He can't even see what he has chasing all these dumb ass hoes. It was a girl right?"

I paused. "Yea."

"I figured. He wouldn't tell much, but I knew what it was. Ever since he's been getting big, these broads throw themselves at him and he can't say no."

"So I've noticed. I was so stupid to actually start catching feelings for him."

"He does like you, you know. I think he has for a little minute now. I don't think he thought you felt the same."

"We never really talked about it. I didn't even realize until we were at Fantasy Lounge."

"I know. To be honest with you... God, I shouldn't even be telling you this stuff." There was a pause. "I don't know if he's going to change Cadence. I honest to God hope he does to keep a woman like you, but I don't know. Maybe I can talk some sense into his simple little head."

"Don't worry about it Nia. If he wanted to change, he would have. But we don't even know each other like that."

"I know, but he really, really does like you. He talks about you all the time and when he does, his face lights up."

"I didn't know that."

"It's just a shock that he's still doing this stupid shit. I just hope he didn't hurt you too badly."

"It does hurt, I'm not gonna lie, but like I said, it's not like we've known each other that long or even spoke about the feelings we had towards one another. I've been through worse. I can get over this too."

She sighed. "Alright then. I just hope both of y'all come to your senses and realize something great could have been there. Don't be a stranger though, I still like you."

I laughed slightly. "I won't be. Have a good night."

"You too."

My mind began to wander, but I wouldn't let it as I pressed play and continued watching my show.

I awoke to soft knocks at my door, and it was only then I had realized I had fallen asleep on the couch. I checked the time, and it was only eleven, but still, who the hell could be it? I only had one guess, and I was right.

"Hey Cadence." His voice was low, and I wasn't used to seeing or hearing him this way. He was always so vibrant and full of life, but not tonight.

"Hey." I simply replied.

We stood there at my door for a minute before I stepped aside and let him in. The both of us sat down awkwardly on the couch and could barely make eye contact.

"How are you? How was your day?" he asked, breaking the ice.

"I'm doing alright. My day was... regular. How was yours?"

"Not too good."

"Why not?"

He glared at me. "I think you already know the answer to that."

I held my head down. "A few people are worried about you. What's been going on?"

"I feel like shit. Cadence, I really am sorry. Like I said, I didn't know you liked me like that. I thought you just wanted to be friends."

"I've grown fond of you over time. It really hit me when we were at the Fantasy Lounge. I got upset when I saw you dancing with those other girls..."

"I got upset when I saw you dancing with that guy. That's why I came over. And we had that moment. I think we realized it at the same time."

"That's what I thought too. That's why it kind of caught me off guard to see you..." I began to get choked up. "But it's whatever. It's not like I didn't know all of this before. I just feel stupid for catching feelings."

"Why?"

"Because I know how you are. It's not like it's something new. You have a new chick over damn near every day. It's probably going to be more as you grow. How can I expect you to change for me?"

"I want to." he said gently. His words were almost sincere.

"Why?"

"You're something different. I love spending time with you. Love your vibe. I don't want that to stop."

"Me either. But I think, for now, we should just be friends."

"Damn, you really just friend zoned me?" he joked a bit. "I do want more from you though?"

"Like what?"

"Something serious."

"We haven't even known each other for a month. How can you possibly know you want something serious with me? I can't see you as being serious with me."

"No one in a long time has made me want to be serious with them except for you. Women come and go, but rarely do I feel this way about someone. I mean look at me. I'm a fuckin mess cuz you were mad at me."

"I can't trust you Mal. I can't trust that if we were to be something more, that if the right woman came along, you wouldn't just go and be with her for the night."

"Can I prove it to you?"

I sat back on the couch. "I don't know how you could."

"Can we at least take it day by day and see where it goes? I really don't want to lose you Cay. Not even as a friend. Or a business partner or..."

"Ok, I get it." I said, trying to calm him down a bit. "We can take it day by day. I'm not making any promises though."

"That's all I'm asking for is a chance."

"Are you even ready for a relationship? You're just now getting out there and these chicks are going to be throwing themselves at you. Why now?"

"I didn't have any intentions on it. I told you it was hard to have anything serious because I'm always at the studio on the go. Most of the females I used to talk to didn't understand the grind, but you do. And I'm not gonna be happy with sleeping around with different females all the time. I want one rock to hold me down. Pussy is pussy, but a real connection with someone is priceless and can never be replaced."

"It sounds like you spittin game to me right now." I teased.

"I know, it does, but I'm being dead ass. I really like you woman."

"I like you too man."

I looked at him with soft eyes before he came closer and sat down next to me wrapping me up in a hug. "I missed your energy man."

After some time, I hugged him back. "I missed yours too."

"So we cool now? We good?"

I smiled a bit. "We're good."

"What were you watching?"

"More or less, it was watching me. Some show I've been binge watching."

"You were sleep?"

"Yea, I fell asleep on the couch."

"Damn. I'm sorry I woke you up."

"It's all good. I'm glad you did actually, cuz I would have overslept in the morning without my alarm."

He stood up. "I'll let you go back to bed then. I'll see you tomorrow?"

"I'll see you tomorrow." I reassured.

Before he left, he gave me one last hug and a kiss on my forehead. "Have a good night Cadence."

"You as well Jamal."

Honestly, I didn't know how to feel at this moment. Elated that we were on good terms again. Confused as to what I should do moving forward. Keep the same energy we had before? Or be a little standoffish because I was pretty sure he wouldn't change his ways.

I sighed as I laid in the bed, in the dark room with my thoughts. Something was needed to distract my wandering mind. Soft music was played and that helped a little until sleep took over me once again.

Please Stay

The next day at work was much better than the last. I wasn't thinking so negatively about things, but I was still indeed still thinking. Around three-thirty, I got a message from Jamal with an attachment. Unfortunately, I was caught up in meetings for the rest of the day, so I wasn't able to listen to what he sent until I got in the car.

By the time I was able to read it, there were a total of two attachments. The first one was opened, and I listened to it. I realized it was the song we had recorded the other day. This was the first one, and it sounded so much better and so much clearer than it did in the studio.

I covered my mouth as I listened to it in its entirety. When it ended, I played the second one recorded and by far, it was my absolute favorite. You could definitely hear the chemistry in our voices, and it was as if the song was something we were both dealing with. Like it was a heavy problem and there was nothing we could do than watch the one we loved walk out of our lives.

The song played over and over again in the car until I got home where I was happily greeted by Mal. The both of us were a little standoffish and held back a little still trying to feel each other out. It was as if we had reverted back to the second time we saw each other. No, not even that. It just felt off.

"Hey. How was your day?" he asked, helping me out of the car.

"It was good. I loved the songs. They sounded great."

"They really do. I just don't know what to do with them yet. I'm thinking of performing a few new songs I recorded last week."

"When is that?"

"I booked a club for both Friday and Saturday night."

"The same club?"

"Yea, it's in south Philly though. I gotta talk to my crew and see if they're ready to perform it."

"Have you been practicing?"

"Not as much as I should have. Had a shit kind of week."

"I feel you. Are you hungry? I have to cook some salmon tonight."

"What else are you making with it?"

"Some rice. Maybe some vegetables to go along with it."

"Yea, I could eat."

"Come on then."

When I entered the door, my phone began to ring. I looked down to see who it was and surprisingly, it was my cousin. "Hello?"

"Cadence…"

"Yea?"

"Granny passed away."

"No. No, no. Please tell me you're lying." My heart sank.

"She passed away this morning."

"How? She was doing just fine."

"She fell a few days ago and when they took her to the doctor, they thought she was fine. But this morning when Jenae went to visit her… She found her dead. We don't know if the fall was the problem though. Not yet anyway."

I rested my back on the wall in disbelief and sat down on the floor. Jamal looked at me precariously before he joined me rubbing my shoulder. "How's Janae holding up?"

"She's not doing too good. You know she was closest to her."

"I know."

"Do you think you're gonna come to the funeral? I know how you are about them."

"I'm not sure, most likely not, I don't want to see her like that. When is it? Do you know?"

"Don't know yet, but I'll let you know when I find something out. Hopefully you come, but if not, I understand. I gotta make a few more calls, I'll hit you up later."

"I'll be waiting."

After I hung up, I buried my face in my hands. I was completely shocked, I didn't know what to make out of it.

"What happened?"

"My Grandmother passed away out of nowhere."

"Damn Love, I'm sorry. Come on, let's go sit on the couch." he said, helping me to my feet. "Where y'all close?"

"Yea. We were. I used to live with her for about a year before I moved here." I grew quiet thinking about that time. None of it really hit me yet. I was still in shock from the news I just heard.

"What was her name and when's the funeral?"

"Elsie and they don't know yet. I most likely won't go. I hate funerals."

"I think you should go when you find out. Being around family could help."

I shook my head. "I'm like the black sheep of the family. No one invites me to shit or calls on birthdays. Or even calls to say hey in general. Eventually, I stopped reaching out."

"Well, I still think you should go. You need some time alone?"

"No. Please stay. Preoccupy my mind. Please. I don't want to think about it right now." I stood up and went into the kitchen like nothing had just happened. Like the news was never delivered to me. Ingredients were grabbed to cook with, and I began cutting up the vegetables but my mind was a hot mess.

The knife I held in my hand was taken from me and placed gently on the counter and I was led to the dining room table to have a seat.

"I'll cook for you Love, just relax. You have any of the Moscato left?"

"I drank it all on the first night."

"You drank that big ass bottle?"

"Yea." I simply said with no emotion.

"You want me to go get you more?"

"I think I'm going to need something stronger than that tonight." I stared blankly at the wall in front of me as I spoke.

"Stay right here. I'll go get you something. I'll be right back ok?"

"Ok." I uttered and he left, leaving me alone with my thoughts once again.

He was back in no time and poured the both of us a cup and mixed it with my favorite mixer. I guzzled it down rather quickly and he made me another one. This one had a tad bit less alcohol, but I didn't say anything about it.

I watched as he cut the vegetables, cut and seasoned the salmon and prepared the rice for us to eat. I didn't even know the man could cook, but he seemed like a seasoned pro at it. Soon everything was served, and I simply looked at the plate that was in front of me.

"It doesn't look good?"

"It looks delicious, I just don't have much of an appetite."

"Take a few bites. You have to eat something with all the alcohol. Plus, I cooked it for you, so you better at least try it." he joked trying to raise my spirits.

A meek smile spread on my face as I picked up my fork and took a few bites and then some more and then some more.

"You like it?"

"It's delicious. I didn't know you could cook like this."

"I have a few secrets up my sleeve. I'm glad you enjoy it."

"Talk to me about something."

"Like what?"

"Something. Anything."

"Uhh… Have you created any new designs yet?"

"Not yet. I need to, right?"

"Yea, you do. How are your sales?"

"Steadily growing."

"You have to keep their attention now that people are looking at you."

I glanced at him and smiled again. "You sound like me over there."

"I guess you rubbed off on me. But definitely work on that. I'm here if you need some help or inspiration."

"You wanted me to make you a custom design right? What was the design?"

"My logo. I wanted to know if you could help design my own merch."

"I can do that. We can work on it… some time. How does tomorrow sound?"

"I'm in no rush Love."

"It would be perfect timing though. You're gonna be releasing new songs, you can also advertise your new line. Did you want a higher royalty payout for it?"

"No. We stick to the agreement."

"But it's your line."

"Cadence." he said sternly.

"Fine. We stick to the agreement. How many designs did you want?"

"How many can you make in a day?"

"Ten. Most likely. And I can add more. Are you going to put them on your site?"

"I was thinking of putting a link on there that links to a collection on your page."

I nodded my head and took a sip. "That could work."

"Should I postpone the new song?"

"Why would you do that?"

"I don't think we're ready to perform it."

"Have you advertised the release of it?"

"Nah. Not yet. Just figured I needed to switch things up. I've been doing the same show for three weeks straight. It would be different if I was on tour or something traveling to different places, but it's in the same general vicinity."

"How confident are you in performing it?"

"It's not me I'm worried about. It's the guys I'm performing with. Every time we go to practice, they bullshit around."

"So let them go. Do it on your own."

"Do it on my own?"

"If they don't want to take shit seriously, then fuck 'em. How long have you known them for?"

"A few months. Tom referred them to me."

I glared at him. "Do you think it's a coincidence they wanna bullshit around now?"

In his mind, I could see him putting two and two together. "Yea, they might have to go. But would it be the same without them?"

"When you're on stage, do you think people are really paying them any mind, or are they mainly looking at you? Are they cheering them on? Or are they cheering for you?"

"You right. You're completely right. We're supposed to have rehearsal in a few, but Imma tell 'em don't even show up."

"Do it only if you feel it's right. Not because I said something."

"Nah, I don't need no slackers on my shit. I'm not trynna have them do something stupid and fuck shit up."

"Do you need help copyrighting the songs?"

"You already know I do. Can we do it before I perform it?"

"We absolutely can."

I took another rather large sip from my cup. "How you holding up over there?"

"I'm doing alright. It hasn't really hit me yet that she's gone. I'm still in shock."

119

"I understand." His phone began to vibrate and he answered it. As he spoke, I began to clear the dishes off the table and wash them. When he was done with his call, I felt his warm embrace around me from behind.

"Cadence baby, I hate to do this to you, but I have to head out. They are about to start rehearsal soon. If you need anything, you call me alright?"

I nodded my head before he let me go and left. The kitchen was fully cleaned, and I made my way to the living room with the entire bottle of rum in my hand. I made myself nice and comfy and poured me a strong ass cup before turning my show on. It helped in the meantime, but I knew the storm was about to come soon.

On My Way

Once again I had fallen asleep on the couch, but this time I was awakened by a terrible nightmare. I couldn't remember what it was in its entirety, but it terrified me to death, and it also brought me to tears.

The emotions finally hit, and I let it all out as I cried alone on my couch gulping down the rest of the bottle to try and calm my brain. Happy thoughts of the time spent with my grandmother. Even thoughts of when she would be pissed at me but had her own special way of showing that she still cared and loved me.

For a good hour I laid there and cried until I finally calmed myself down. I was so caught up in the emotions, I hadn't even noticed that my phone had three missed calls from Jamal. I looked at the current time and the time he had called. It wasn't too long ago, so I decided to text him back.

Instead of responding with a text, he called.

"Hello?"

"Hey. I was just checking on you to see how you were doing."

"Not too good Mal." I said softly.

"Why not? What's wrong?"

I practically broke down with him right there on the phone. "Where are you?" I asked finally coming to.

"I'm on my way home from the rehearsal."

"Can you come over?" I asked through my tears.

"Of course. I'm about fifteen minutes away. You want me to pick something up for you while I'm out?"

"No. I just need a hug."

"I'm on my way Baby. I'll see you when I get there."

I hung up the phone. I didn't want him to hear me cry. Didn't know why I had even asked him to come over in the first place. I didn't want him to see me like this.

Ten minutes later, lights shined in through my windows and I heard a car door slam before an anxious knock came at my door. I tried my best to wipe my face, but my nose was congested, and I knew my face was puffy. The door opened and he came in immediately wrapping his arms around me of which I sunk into.

He caught my weight and brought me over to the couch before he went back to close and lock the door. On his way over, he kicked the bottle and held it up to see how much was left. Only a corner.

"You drank this whole bottle? What were you thinking?"

"I know. I shouldn't have drank so much. I feel like shit."

"I bet you do." he said, pulling me in close to him.

Not many words were exchanged for a while as I laid on his chest and cried while he stroked my hair gently trying to comfort me. That's all I really needed and slowly, the tears stopped flowing. I sat up and looked at his shirt.

"I'm sorry." I said quietly.

"Don't even worry about it. Sit up, let me get something for your face."

I did as he asked, and he returned with some tissue that he used to gently soak up the tears and dry my face with. My head was spinning, and everything seemed to be a blur. The nausea began to set in and I could slowly feel the contents in my stomach come up to my esophagus. I sprang to my feet and wearily but hurriedly ran to the bathroom and threw up.

The light in the bathroom came on and I yelled at him to turn it off. I felt his hands on my shoulder massaging me before my hair was pulled back gently. Just in time too, cuz more came up and it burned like hell which caused me to cry some more.

"It's alright Cay, you gotta get that shit out. Are you done?"

"Uhn uhn." I whined with my face still buried in the toilet. I gagged a few times, and the rest came up.

I spit the nasty taste out of my mouth before I flushed and laid out on the floor. He didn't let me stay there long before he scooped me up in his arms and carried me to my bed. He left and came back with some water and a cool washcloth to lay over my face.

A few kisses were placed on my forehead, and he began to walk away. "Where are you going?" I called him back.

"I'm just going in the living room so you can get some rest."

"Can you come lay with me?"

There was a bit of a hesitation before he came back to my side. "Are you sure?"

"Yes. Come lay with me."

In the darkness, I felt him lay on the bed on the other side. It seemed as though he didn't know what I wanted from him so he kept his distance. I rolled over to face him and rested my head on his chest. My actions seemed to have startled him for he jumped a little before nervously resting his arms around me.

The next morning, my alarm went off and I slowly opened my eyes to find myself laying on Jamal's chest. I had no recollection of how we got here, but I rolled over and turned the alarm off. My movement caused him to wake up and he stared at me for a while before speaking.

"How are you feeling?"

"Like shit. What the fuck happened last night? Why are you in my bed?"

He looked at me confused. "You really don't remember what happened last night?"

I shook my head. "Did we fuck?"

He laughed. "No, we didn't do anything. You seriously don't remember?"

I shook my head again before he told me in excruciating detail about what happened last night. My hands came up to my face in embarrassment as I sat on the edge of the bed.

"Oh my God. I can't believe you saw me like that."

He got out of the bed and stretched. "No worries Love. Shit happens."

"Thanks for being here for me. I really appreciate it."

"You know I gotchyu. What time do you have work today?"

"I'm thinking about calling out."

"I think that would be a good idea. You want some water?"

"Yes, please."

As he went to get the water, I tried my best to pull my hair back some sort of way. I know I was looking crazy, and I don't know how he put up with my hot, vomit breath. So fucking embarrassing.

I pulled out my phone and called my job up and let them know I wouldn't be coming in today. They told me to take the rest of the week off and more if needed. That was a relief.

The cup of water was handed to me, and I gulped it down before he took it and placed it on the table. "Feeling any better?"

I shook my head. "Not really."

"Go back to sleep then. You had a long night."

"How did rehearsal go?" I asked ignoring his request.

"It went well. I ran through the lighting and the stage placement and let the assholes go. They were acting so stupid and unprofessional, and it made me look bad. So they had to go."

My eyes grew wide with disbelief. "You actually did it?"

124

"I did and ran through the rest of rehearsal on my own and it wasn't that bad."

"Well good for you. You ready for the show?"

"Yea, I am. Super excited to know what the fans think of the new songs. Now that I know I'm doing it, I'm gonna release my videos the same night."

"You shot videos?"

"Last week I did."

"That sounds exciting. I'm so happy for you."

"Thank you Love."

"What do you have planned for the rest of the day?"

"I'll be super busy later on with last rehearsals and wardrobe, then the show… What are you doing today besides sleeping?"

"Working on your designs and copyrighting your songs. Check your accounts to make sure everything is going where it needs to be and make adjustments to them. Just stuff to keep my mind busy."

"I completely understand. Did you want some company? Or you need some alone time."

"I would like some company. I just have to get a shower and put something fresh on."

"Yea, me too. I'll come back in an hour. Sound good?"

"That sounds good."

I walked him to the door and before he left, he wrapped me up in a hug. "See you later Cadence."

The liquor was still in my system, and I still felt drunk as I went to take a shower. As I looked around the house, it seemed as if nothing had happened. The bathroom was clean, dishes put away. Even the blanket I was wrapped up in was neatly folded and laid on the couch. A warm smile spread on my face.

When I was dressed, I headed into the dining room with my computer in my hands and began working on a few new designs. They were posted on my website in his own collection. I just hoped he would like them.

More than an hour had passed, and he still hadn't returned yet. My stomach growled at me, and I made my way into the kitchen, looked inside the fridge but had no desire to cook in the slightest.

A knock came at my door, and I gleefully went to open it. Jamal was standing there with groceries in his hands as he looked down at me. "You hungry?"

"I literally just looked in the fridge to cook something." I said, stepping aside and letting him in. "What did you bring?"

"Some eggs, sausage, bread and stuff so I can make you something."

"You're gonna cook for me again?"

"Yea, why not. I know you're not feeling the best."

"Thank you, cuz I'm definitely starving."

He got quiet for a minute, not sure if he wanted to ask me this question or not, but he did. "Did you tell your friends what happened?"

I looked down sadly. "No. They're still being standoffish."

"Even Lil?"

"I kinda yelled at him the other day, so I doubt he will respond."

"I still think you should tell them. You're gonna need their support."

"I'll think about it."

"That's all I ask." He glanced at my computer. "What are you working on?"

"Your designs. I created a few and posted them on the site. Wanna see?"

"Yea, let me see what you got so far." He set the bags down on the counter and peered over my shoulder. "Damn Cadence, those look nice as hell."

"Thank you. You have your own collection called Mally's World. Cuz Cay City... Mally's World..."

"Ha. I like that. A nice play on the terms."

"I want you to help me though. Create a few designs you specifically want. And I need a picture of your logo in png format."

"We can do that later. Let me make breakfast first."

"You know, I've never had anyone cook in my kitchen and here you are cooking twice in it."

"You want me to not cook breakfast?" he said searching for what he needed.

"I didn't say that. I'm just pointing it out. I appreciate it."

"Any time."

As he cooked, I continued with the designs. Everything was still groggy and foggy, and my stomach still wasn't right. But I worked through the pain of it all.

A few more designs were created and posted, and breakfast was served to me soon after. We sat and ate in the silence before I went to work again with his assistance. The logo was sent over and added to the collection. He also told me what colors he liked and the look he was going for and of course ya girl made it happen for him.

The next thing I did was check his accounts to make sure the amounts were going to the correct accounts when I noticed something odd.

"Hey, when did you go to AC?"

"Atlantic City? I haven't been down there in years."

"Uhh, it shows that a transaction was made last night in the amount of three grand."

"What?"

"Look." I said pointing.

"I was in Philly all night."

"I know. Does anyone have a card or have access to your accounts?"

"Not that I know of. I used that card just now to buy groceries."

"Did you maybe buy something online?"

"Nah."

"You need to call the bank now and figure out what this charge is."

His phone was pulled out and he called the bank as I continued to search for anything suspicious on the account. There wasn't anything else I could find thank goodness.

"They said it was a transfer directly from my card to someone named Roscoe..." He got quiet and I turned to look at him. He was furious.

"What's wrong? You know who that is?"

"Hell yea I know who that is. I'll be right back Babe." he said walking away.

"Wait, Jamal, where are you going?"

"I have to go handle some shit. I'll be right back."

"Don't do anything stupid." I yelled as he jumped in his car and sped out my driveway.

What the fuck? Who the hell was Roscoe? And how did they get his card in the first place?

I impatiently sat in the living room finishing up with his accounts then moving back to creating more shirt designs. I glanced down at my phone when it lit up and started vibrating from a call from Khalil.

"Hello?"

"Hey. What's wrong with you?"

There was a brief pause on my end before I told him the news. "My grandmother passed away Lil."

"What? Grandma Elsie?"

"Yea..."

"When?"

"Yesterday."

"Why didn't you tell me sooner?"

"The last time we spoke, wasn't the best."

"Nah Cay. Something like that happens, you fuckin tell me. How are you holding up?"

"I'm doing better this morning but last night, I was a mess."

"Did you tell Char and Nelle?"

"No. For whatever reason, they still aren't talking to me. I'm tired of reaching out."

"You want me to call and tell them?"

"If you want. I don't care. But what's up? Why'd you call?"

"No reason really, just checkin in to see how you were doing."

"I've been better, but I'm alright. How about you?"

"I've been alright too. Imma about to hit up Janelle and Char. They better fuckin call you."

"I wouldn't hold my breath for it, but ok. Thanks Lil."

"No problem."

The phone disconnected and my mind was still off in another dimension. I could really care less if they reached out or not. My main concern was Jamal and what the hell was going on and what was he about to do?

I called him and he picked up.

"Hey. What are you doing?"

"Cadence, I can't really talk right now."

"What the hell is going on? What's all that noise in the background?"

"Nothing. It's nothing. You need anything?"

"No…"

"Then I'll call you back."

The line disconnected. What the fuck was going on? I decided to call Nia. Maybe she knew something that I didn't.

"Hey you! How are you feeling?"

"I'm doing alright. I have a question for you though."

"Sure, what's up?"

"Do you know who Roscoe is?"

"Yea, that's one of the guys that performs with Mally. Why?"

"I think your brother is about to do something stupid."

"What happened?"

"Last night, he let him go and I think they stole money from him. He left and he's pissed. And when I called him, there was a lot of commotion in the background."

"Oh gees. This isn't the first time this has happened."

"It's not?"

"No. About two months ago, he stole jewelry from him and they got into a big fight. But Mally doesn't carry cash on him. How much was taken?"

"Three grand. They transferred it off his card."

"God. He's gonna lose his shit. Do you know where he went?"

"I have no idea Nia."

"Damn it. Let me see if I can get in contact with him. I'll call you right back."

She hung up and a few minutes later, Jamal called me back. "You told my fuckin sister?" he yelled.

"I didn't know what else to do. I didn't want you to do something crazy."

"Well, I didn't. I couldn't find him. He's fuckin lucky but if I catch his ass, it's a wrap."

"Where are you?"

"I'm heading back to you now."

"I'll see you when you get here. Try to relax. I'm sure you can get the money back from the bank."

"For his sake, I fuckin better. I don't have time for this shit. I try to be nice to muthafuckas and this is how they do me? Gave him an opportunity to be on stage with me and he fucked it up and now, he wants to steal from me?" he ranted.

"I thought he came from Tom?"

"Not Roscoe. He was my boy. I gave his stupid ass another chance and he still did the same bullshit. I'm fuckin done."

"Relax Jamal."

"I'm trying to Cadence. I'm really trying to, but this shit makes my blood boil."

"I understand how it would, but you don't need to go out and do something stupid that could jeopardize your future. Honestly, I'm glad you didn't find him. I hope you never do."

"It's about respect and the principle of it all. You know?"

"Yes, I understand. Just come back so I can give you some love and hugs."

"I'll be there in ten."

Not long after he hung up, Nia called.

"Hello?"

"He didn't answer."

"He was talking to me and coming back."

"Thank God. Wait. He's calling me now. Talk to you later."

I sat back on the couch trying to calm down from all this crazy shit that was going on. I heard a deep voice yelling and coming closer then, the door swung open.

"Ok Nia, but what, I'm supposed to let this shit rock?" "I'm not saying that…" "Fine. Whatever." "I just walked into the house." "Love you too."

I stared at him from my seat as he closed the door and paced for a minute. I wasn't sure what to do, so I stood up and held him from behind hoping to pass some of my calm energy to him. He let me hold him for a while before facing me and holding me back.

"I'm sorry."

"For what?"

"Yelling at you on the phone. For all this. I know it's the last thing you need right now."

"I understand why, but like I said, he's not worth your future or your career."

"I know." He sat down on the couch.

"Call the bank and let them know what happened. See if they can give the money back. And also, get a new card."

"I will, I just gotta calm my nerves."

He sat back on the couch, and I joined him resting my head on his chest. He looked down at me a bit confused but soon rested his arms around me in a warm embrace. Before I knew it, I was passed out sleep on him and he let me.

You Will Be Mentioned

The sound of his voice woke me from my brief nap, but I didn't move from the comfort of his chest and warm embrace. He was on the phone with the bank trying to work something out and let them know what had happened. I spoke when he got off the phone.

"Any progress?"

"They said they could give me half back because it was done directly from the card and they're gonna send a new card out today." He sighed. "My bad, didn't mean to wake you."

"It's alright. We have work to do anyway."

"Your phone rang a few times."

"Where is it?"

"On the counter."

I made my way over to it and looked to see who had called. There were two calls along with a few texts from Charmaine and Janelle. I sucked my teeth and rolled my eyes.

"What's the problem?" he asked as I read the messages.

"Charmaine and Janelle hit me up."

"So what's the problem?"

"I don't feel like responding."

"Man, if you don't call them back. They're your friends."

"Sure as shit don't act like it."

"Just hit them back up and see what they want Love."

I scrunched my face up at him before I picked up the phone and texted the girls back in a group chat. They mainly just wanted to know how I was holding up and if I was going to be alright. I let the know I was fine and not to worry, but they insisted on coming over. This was going to be awkward.

"Are they coming today?"

"Yea, later on this afternoon." I said solemnly.

He nodded his head in approval. "Everything will be fine."

I shrugged. "Are you feeling better? More relaxed?"

"I am. How are you feeling?"

"I'm doing alright for the most part. We need to get your songs copyrighted though. Where's your computer?"

"At the house. Let me go get it right quick."

He was back in no time, and we got all his stuff together to get the songs copyrighted under his name and his label's name. I walked him through the process of how easy it actually was and made sure he used his business card to pay for the expense.

"So that's it"

"That's it. Easy right?"

"Yea. Thanks for showing me."

"Were you ever able to get the receipts from the gigs you did under Tom?"

"Still working on it. I got a few of them and he definitely did rip me off. A couple of hundred each show."

"That shit really pisses me off."

"It's cool. It will all get handled in court. But anyway, are you going to be able to make it one of my shows?"

"I would love to see you perform, but I'm not sure how I'm going to feel."

"I feel you. No pressure. I just feel like I perform harder when you're in the audience."

"You think so?"

"Yea. I wanna impress you."

"I'll try to make it to at least one. I wanna see these new songs you put out."

"I think you're gonna like them."

"You still haven't figured out what you're going to do with the slow jams have you?"

"Not yet."

"Well, that's what we're going to be working on next."

The both of us put our heads together to try and figure out how to put this new music out there under a different name. At least to see how people liked it and reacted to it. In all honesty, I thought he should put it under his name. The music was so nice and the beats were so dope, I think people would love it regardless.

So after not really coming up with anything he liked or felt comfortable doing, I decided to bring it up and see what he thought about it.

"I don't understand why you just don't put it out there as your name. You already have a following and people already like your music. I don't see what the problem is."

"It's not really a problem per say. I'm just afraid they're not gonna like it. They are so used to me playing this type of music, how am I gonna just switch up to slow jams?"

"It would just be a slow integration. Put a few out there, see what they say. You never know, you may reach different audiences that haven't heard you before."

"Imma think about it. If I did, I would want to post the one we recorded together to be the first."

"Which one?"

"The second one. Would you be cool with that?"

"I don't mind. It's your music. Just don't say who the female singer is." I laughed.

"Oh you will be mentioned."

"Are you serious?"

"I'm dead ass."

"Mal." I whined.

"Nope. If I put the music out under Mally Boy, I'm mentioning you in the song."

"Are you going to perform it or just post it up?"

"Post it on social media, then see where it goes from there."

"Oh my God. Fine. When are your other videos going live?"

"Tonight before the show."

Just as he spoke, his phone rang, and he answered. He stepped away for a minute before coming back to me.

"Sorry Love. I have to step out. They want me to go over a few things for tonight. Catch up on some rest alright?"

"I'll try."

A soft kiss was placed on my forehead, but I kind of wanted it to be somewhere else. In due time I suppose. I walked him to the door and watched as he pulled away.

I sat in silence on the couch for a minute and the thoughts of my grandmother began to consume me. I didn't want to think about it so I decided to make a few more shirt designs. Some were for my own shop and some for his collection. My eyes started to burn from looking at the screen, so I decided to take a break. Before I could get comfortable in the couch, I got an unexpected phone call.

Catching up to do

"Hello" I answered with Charmaine on the line.

"Hey. How are you feeling?"

"I'm doing alright. How about yourself?"

"I'm doing good. What time did you want us to come over today? We have a lot of catching up to do."

"We do?"

"Yes."

"Can we start off with why y'all have been acting so shady lately?"

"We wanted to give you space after the incident at the restaurant. We know how you get when you get pissed off. You tend to hold grudges."

"But if I'm hitting y'all up, how is that holding a grudge? Or is there more to it than you're not telling me?"

There was a brief pause. "What time do you want us to come over?"

"Whenever you're free I guess. I'm here."

"Wait. You're at home? You called out?"

"I was off for most of the week, maybe longer."

"I'll call Janelle then. We'll be on our way shortly. Did you eat yet? Are you hungry?"

"No, not yet, and yea I am."

"I'll pick up your favorite. See you when we get there."

"See you."

Half of me didn't want to see them, while the other half was curious as hell to find out why they were acting so strange lately. And it wasn't because they wanted to give me peace and space. I guess I would find out soon enough. My living room was straightened up a bit in preparation for the company. The tv turned on and I began to watch my show but only for a little while until I heard a knock on my door.

Seeing them actually made me feel a little better and their faces lit up like mine did. I didn't realize how much I actually missed them.

"Hey!" they both said as they came in and gave me a hug. "We brought you your favorite! Chinese food"

"Thank you. Come on and sit down so we can catch up a bit."

As we sat down, I noticed Janelle had a bit of disdain on her face. "What's wrong with you? How are you and Khalil doing?"

"I don't think it's going to work out. Which is actually why I've been kind of distant from you."

"Why? What happened? You guys seemed to hit it off."

"…About that." Charmaine interrupted.

"About what?"

The both of them exhaled before Janelle spoke. "I kinda broke up with him… because of you."

"Why because of me?"

"We think he may like you. More than just a friend."

"What makes you think that?"

"The way he talks about you. We have our private conversations of course cuz we were trying to talk, but every time we would talk, he would bring you up like, 'Oh, Cay does this' or,

'Cay does it this way'. It started annoying me and kind of made me resent you."

"Why didn't you tell me this before? Why would you... the both of you stop talking to me because of that?"

"I was kind of mad at you. And I know it wasn't your fault. I know, but it just made me feel some type of way."

I glanced at Charmaine waiting for her explanation. "I was kind of pissed at you too because of it. Janelle was so upset, and I felt I needed to be there for her. You had Jamal and Lil for support. We just have each other for the most part."

"Us being friends... you guys should have told me this. I had no idea this was going on. I thought y'all hated me and had no idea why. You both know I don't have feelings for Lil. Not like that anyway."

"We know you don't. We're really sorry Cay. We should have come to you earlier about it."

"Are we good now? Nothing else you want to tell me?"

"We're cool. We should have never let this come between us in the first place"

"What did Lil say when you broke up with him?"

"I mean, he wasn't thrilled about it."

"Did you tell him why?"

"Not really. Just said I was too busy with school and work and couldn't juggle it all."

"Damn Nelle. I'm sorry. I know you really liked him." I said eating more of my food.

"Ehh, it was alright. He was always in the studio anyway. It wasn't what I thought it would be."

"But how are you doing Hun?" Charmaine interrupted.

"I'm doing better. I really don't want to talk about it."

"We understand. We don't have to."

"So... what's going on with you and Jamal? Are y'all still close?"

As I finished off my food, I told them everything that had been going on between us. Even the embarrassing part of what happened the other night and the feelings we had towards one another.

"See, I told you there was something there."

"Yea, yea. Y'all were right. We just didn't see it yet."

"Are you going to his show tonight?"

"I was thinking about going. Would you guys want to go with me?"

"That would be fun. It's been a minute since we hung out."

"Where is it going to be?"

"I'm actually not sure. He didn't give me the details, but when I find out, I'll let you guys know."

"So are you guys going to be together?"

"I'm not sure yet. We're just taking it day by day, you know." I giggled.

They stood up and began walking to the door. "Let us know when you find something out."

"I will definitely do that. I'll see you soon."

I hadn't even realized how late it had gotten or realized the missed calls and messages sent from Jamal and from Khalil. Khalil. What was I to do with him? I had no clue he felt this way about me. He concealed it so well. In front of me at least. I guess it kind of made sense why Janelle stopped calling me. I could understand but it sucked, nonetheless.

"Hello?"

"Hey Babe. What's up? Did he girls come over?"

"Yea, they just left. We talked about what was going on and why they were standoffish."

"What was the reason?"

"Some umm… miscommunication and feelings I guess you could say" I kinda lied. I didn't know how to tell him the truth about why they were mad. I knew Jamal and Khalil were cool and worked together in the studio and didn't want to come in between that.

"I feel you. How are you going though? Did you eat?"

"Yea, they brought me something. How is your day going?"

"It's alright a bit busy, but nothing I can't handle."

"You never told me where you were performing tonight."

"In South Philly at a place called Lennox. Why? You coming?"

"I'm still thinking about it. How do you feel about the performance? Are you ready"?

"I'm ready. I just hope I see you in the crowd."

"Oh stop it. You'll do fine even if I'm not there."

"Not the point Cadence."

"I'm just saying is all."

"I have to get back so I will call you later or text you."

"Sounds good."

The time read seven-ten before I started to get ready. I tried to focus my thoughts on enjoying my evening and not on everything else that was going on all around me. I had already texted the girls and let them know the time and location and they were going to be here in an hour to pregame before heading out to the club.

I was excited to see what new material he would perform and how the crowd would react to it. I knew he would do a good job, so I wasn't worried about that.

Tonight, I was wearing my hair in loose curls and because it had been a while since I did this style, it took me quite some time to do. But it got done, I got dressed and the girls came over with a few bottles in their hands.

We chatted some and drank some before we piled into the car and drove to the club like we used to.

Exposed

When we got there, the place was crowded and unfortunately, we had to wait in line because we didn't know anyone at this spot. I'm sure we would have gotten in for free and without the line with Jamal's assistance, but I kind of wanted to surprise him. Good thing we arrived early and good thing the entrance fee wasn't that expensive.

Of course our first stop was the bar where we ordered our drinks and someone else paid. At least that hadn't changed for us. The girls danced with a few guys and although a few guys wanted to dance with me, I declined. Instead, I was just there dancing alone next to my friends.

The announcer finally came on and introduced Mally Boy and he came out just as hyped up as normal even though he was alone on the stage.

The crowd roared as he performed one of his older songs, and they got even more hyped when he performed his new songs. He told them to go watch the video on his social media, and also where they could find his gear on my website or his. He hinted about the new release of his own line and made sure to tell about the details.

As he talked his eyes scanned the audience, but I don't think he saw me in the vast sea of people. His face did fall a bit, but he kept up appearances.

When he was done, Khalil came on stage and gave him dap. Janelle's face scrunched up before she headed to the restroom with us close on her heels.

She cried in the stall, and I felt terrible for her as Charmaine and I tried to console her. In her drunken slumber, she shoved me away from her and Charmaine dismissed me fully. I guess she wasn't over it completely after all and, I must admit, it made me feel some type of way because I had no control over Khalil's emotions. Why was she taking it out on me?

Needless to say, I sat at the bar alone watching Mal take pictures with his fans. A few women tried to feel up on him and dance with him but he declined their advances. I guess he was trying to change.

As I watched him and had drinks sent my way by thirstys, I did notice his morale was a bit off but he tried to put up a good front. Poor guy.

When his fans dispersed some, I slowly made my way over to him. As soon as his eyes met mine, he instantly lit up and ran to me. I was lifted off my feet in a hug before I was held in his arms.

"I'm so glad you came. You surprised me!"

I smiled and ran my fingers through his beard. "You know I couldn't miss it."

"Did you come by yourself?"

My face changed. "No. Charmaine and Janelle are here somewhere. But they really don't want to be bothered by me."

"Why not?"

"Hey Ma. How you feeling?"

"I'm doing alright. How are you?" I asked giving Lil a hug. It did feel a bit different on my end knowing what I knew now, but I wasn't going to treat him any differently about it.

"I'm doing alright. How did you enjoy the show?"

"It was great as usual."

"Yea, he's been putting that work in man."

"So I've noticed."

"Did you come by yourself?"

"No umm, Charmaine and Janelle are here somewhere."

He made a face. "Oh iight. Glad y'all made up."

"Yea, somewhat."

As I spoke, Jamal looked at me oddly and knew something was up too, but he didn't speak on it. Not yet anyway. He just led me to the bar where both guys argued about who was going to buy me a drink briefly before ultimately, Jamal won.

My drink was handed to me as Jamal sat in a chair at the bar with me standing, posted up next to him. Khalil kept giving us looks and I had seen those looks before but never paid it any mind. He had liked me for a long time now and I had no clue and was oblivious about it.

About twenty minutes later, I spotted Charmaine and Janelle headed towards us. Janelle still had her face scrunched up as she approached Jamal. She was even drunker than before and was now getting sloppy. Fuck.

"You did a good job, Mally Boy." she flirted.

He looked at her sideways before responding. "Thank you. You look nice tonight."

"As do you." she said, rubbing her hand on his chest.

"Janelle, what the fuck are you doing?" I blurted.

"What do you mean? We're all friends here."

"But why you gotta touch him like that?" I fully stood up and was about to approach her before Jamal intervened.

"Baby, chill. Chill. She's drunk."

"Baby? Y'all together now?" Khalil asked.

"I don't give a fuck if she's drunk. She better come correct."

"Cadence. Relax." Charmaine intervened.

"Get your girl then Char. I'm not beat for the bullshit tonight."

"I should have never come out here with you tonight. I should have known his ass was going to be here. Did you set this up?"

Janelle yelled. "No. You wouldn't do something like that. He tagged along with Mally Boy cuz he knew you would be here."

"What is she talking about?" Jamal asked.

"You took him away from me Cadence. And you act like you didn't know how he felt about you."

"I didn't know Janelle. We shouldn't do this here."

"Fuck it, why not?"

"Because you're fuckin drunk and you're about to air out all our business in front of everyone." I looked at Char with pleading eyes to get her out of here.

"Jamal deserves to know."

"To know what? There's nothing to tell."

"He deserves to know his best friend is in love with his girl."

Everyone looked at her in shock then over at Khalil who really couldn't say or do too much.

"Char, please get her drunk ass out of here."

"Why do you get to be happy with both and I sit here miserably and watch the two of you flirt in my face?"

"Come on Janelle." Charmaine said, pulling her away.

"You can't have them both Cadence. You have to pick one." she yelled through the crowd.

I looked back at Jamal who was glaring at Khalil. "This true bro?" he asked, getting in his face.

"Jamal, relax." I said, trying to push him away. I could see his anger and frustration building up. Then he turned to me. "You like him like that too? You knew about this and you ain't say shit?"

"This is not the time and place for this, and I just found out."

Khalil was quiet before Jamal poke to him. "You want my girl bro?"

"It's not like that Mally Boy."

"You sure about that? I did peep how you looked at her earlier, but I ain't say shit."

"Jamal, this is not the place and time for this." I said pushing him away.

144

When we got to a secluded place, he went off. "What the fuck Cadence. You knew he was feeling you and you ain't tell me shit? You like him too? What's up?"

"I just found out earlier today when they came over. I didn't want any bullshit between y'all, so I left it be. I didn't know it was going to escalate to this."

"So you wanna be with him? Cuz y'all are mighty close. Y'all ever fucked?"

"I don't see him that way and no, we never did anything. I didn't even know he liked me. He's never come onto me or anything."

The alcohol in his system was making this process much harder than it really needed to be. He was not listening at all to my words and not realizing that Khalil never made any advances towards me.

As he paced back and forth in the garage I realized the girls probably left me here all alone, without a phone and without transportation home.

All of this was too much for me as I leaned up against the wall and heaved trying to get myself to relax at the thought of being abandoned by my so-called friends. On top of the ranting and raving Jamal. On top of the loss of my grandmother.

My eyes teared up and I tried my hardest to hold back the tears, but they began to fall. Noticing my crying, Jamal changed his attitude and came over to me for a hug.

"Why are you crying?"

"They fuckin abandoned me. All my stuff is in their car and I rode with them."

"You're not abandoned. I'll take you home."

"But my stuff… my phone, wallet, everything is in there."

"I'm sure once shit cools off they'll give you everything back."

"Why did she have to do that to me? I didn't do anything to her. She fucking hates me and for what? Some shit I can't control? She's supposed to be my friend. Mine and she's mad at me."

My hands were grabbed, and I was led to the other side of the parking lot where Jamal unlocked his car door and sat me down."

"Stay here. I have to go get my stuff."

"I don't want to stay here by myself." I cried.

He made a face at me as he thought. "Come on then." he said, grabbing my hand and escorting me along.

Back in the club it was as if nothing had happened. Everyone was still drinking and partying all except one person that sat at the bar alone. I spotted him but he hadn't spotted me and I prayed Jamal wouldn't spot him either.

I had to wait on the side for Jamal to get his things together backstage for I wasn't allowed back there. As I waited, I heard a very familiar voice behind me.

"Cay."

I turned around and was met by Khalil. "Not right now Lil."

"Can I please talk to you?"

"We will talk, just not right now?"

"Yes, right now." he said, grabbing my arm and pulling me away. I found myself out in the alleyway behind the club.

"What did you want to talk about?"

"How long have you known?"

"They told me today."

"How did they know?"

"Janelle said it was the way you talked about me. That's why she broke up with you. That's why they were so distant from me. Why didn't you ever tell me?"

He shrugged his shoulders. "Figured I wasn't your type. I see the type of guys you pull, and they are nothing like me. I was scared to shoot my shot."

I shook my head. "You still should have said something."

"Well now you know. How do you feel about it?"

"I still see you as a friend and want to keep it that way. And I don't want no beef between you and Mal. Is that Ok?"

Before he could answer, the back door swung open and a very pissed off Jamal came out. He pushed me back behind him and glared at Khalil.

"What are you doing back here with her?"

"Mal, we were just talking, it's ok." I said, rubbing his shoulder gently.

"Y'all don't need to talk anymore. Not tonight anyway." he growled.

"Look Mally, I didn't want it to come to this. She didn't know I had feelings for her, I never approached her or anything."

"We'll talk about it later bro. I should have paid attention to the signs. I knew what was up and I should have asked more about it."

He turned and looked at me. "You ready to go? You alright?"

"Yea, I'm ready and I'm fine." I said, wiping my face. I walked up to Khalil and put my hand on his shoulder. "We'll talk later. Are you good getting home?"

"Yea I'm good. Have a good night Cadence."

"You too."

The walk back to the car was a quiet one as we walked hand in hand. I was trying to read his emotions, but I couldn't. I couldn't even analyze mine fully.

The car door opened for me, and I got in as he went to the other side and sat down. The engine turned over and we pulled away. A few minutes later I broke the silence.

"What's on your mind?"

"I don't even know right now to be honest. What's on yours?"

"I don't know either. It's just too much. I wanna go home and go to bed."

"You and me both Love."

"No one said anything backstage about the disturbance right?"

"No. They didn't say anything."

There was an awkward silence the rest of the car ride home. He pulled into his driveway and walked me over to my house.

As we walked up, I noticed a trail of items strewn out on my driveway leading up to my ripped up bag and shattered phone. Anger filled my body and his as we began to pick up everything off the ground.

I looked at my phone and began to tear up again thinking of all the memories I had just lost along with some personal things saved on the internal data. He held me tight trying to comfort me and I knew he meant well, but I shoved him away, simply fed up with the night. Fed up with them and fed up trying to be the nice guy.

I stormed into the house leaving the door open for him and plopped down on the couch in defeat. He sat next to me and took my shoes off placing them by the door before returning. He rested back on the couch and my head soon rested on his chest while we sat there with our own thoughts for a while.

"Cadence, I think you should get some rest Love."

"I'm not all that tired. My mind is wired right now."

"What can I do to relax it and take your stress away?"

"Nothing at the moment." I said gently rubbing his chest. His strong, muscular chest.

I pulled away and sat up before my hands got me into more trouble that I didn't need.

He chuckled because he knew why I moved. "You sure there's nothing I can do?"

His voice got deeper as he spoke, sending chills down my spine. "Stop messing with me." I whined, but deep down I was a bit curious to see what he felt like.

I shook the thought from my mind and stood up to go to the kitchen. To get what? I don't know but I had to move away from him and his tantalizing scent.

Funny cuz I had never thought about doing anything sexual with him until tonight. I think it was the way he protected me and stood up for me in front of Khalil. That, and the fact that I hadn't had any in a very long time. And there he sat. Perfectly willing to please me even though he never brought it up himself.

"Cadence, what's wrong with you?"

"Nothing, just fighting inner demons over here."

He came to where I was and got dangerously close and whispered in my ear. "And what are they telling you to do?"

"Something I shouldn't do and something you're not helping with. Get out of here." I said pushing him away and moving. His laughter could be heard from behind me.

"I'm ready when you are."

His words caught me off guard and I turned to look at him. His eyes were glued to me as he licked his sexy, juicy lips. Slowly, I moved closer to him. One taste couldn't hurt. Right?

One Taste

My hands ran sensually down his torso allowing me to see with my hands what I've never seen with my eyes. Holding him close to me from behind, I inhaled his scent and lavished in it for a while. It only made me want him more.

I licked my lips before I bit and licked his neck softly. He quivered but didn't move. As I made my way to the front, my hands wouldn't leave his body. I bit my lip again as I moved slowly up his neck letting him feel my breath but not allowing him to feel the pleasure.

His breathing intensified and I knew if I kept this up he would act on his impulses to take what he already knew was his. Maybe that's what I wanted him to do. Or maybe I wanted to see how long he could hold out before the urge to touch became too great.

He said nothing as I brought my lips to his but didn't kiss them. Said nothing as my hands gently rolled over his body then gripped his shirt tight as if to say take me. He only grinned and inhaled deeply before leaning in for our lips to touch.

When they touched, it was like something I had never experienced before. My breath, gone. My heart rate increased. I wanted nothing more in that moment than for him inside me.

Finally, he couldn't hold out any longer and his hands began to wander on my curves. They began to explore places very few had ventured to. But he stopped and pulled away.

Staring deep in my eyes he said, "You're not ready for me yet."

He stepped aside and adjusted himself as he walked away, leaving me in puddles and a sense of yearning and curiosity.

"Are you going to be alright by yourself tonight?" he asked like this moment hadn't just happened.

"You're leaving?"

"Yes. I think that would be best for the both of us."

I sighed. "I'll be alright."

He kissed my lips one last time. "Good night Cadence."

My heart sank as he disappeared out the door, closing it being him gently. There was nothing left for me to do but go to sleep, but what a beautiful ending to this treacherous day.

Back to the Usual

My eyes opened as the sun kissed my skin from outside. I reached for my phone and remembered I no longer had one. A shower was taken before I got dressed and headed out the door. Just as I stepped out, a familiar face was staring back at me. He smiled.

"Good morning."

I couldn't help but to smile back and blush a little. "Good morning to you too."

"I called you earlier, but I forgot... you know. So I came by just to see how you were before heading out."

"I'm actually on my way to get a new one, so if you want, later, you can call or text...whichever." Was I really fumbling over my words because of him? Oh gees. I hadn't been this way in years.

"I will most definitely hit you up when I have a chance."

"Where are you on your way to?"

"Gonna look at a few spots to record some videos, then head to rehearsal."

"OK. I guess I'll see you later then."

"You absolutely will."

I half expected a hug, but one never came. I got into my car and headed to the store to get a new phone.

So many different styles and types. I wasn't all that mad that my phone was damaged minus the lost memories. I needed a new one anyway. The last one was from four years ago, but nothing was wrong with it, so there was no need to replace it.

I made my selection and got it activated before heading back home. Super excited to play around with the new features and customize it with new apps and wallpapers.

A text was sent to Mal that I was up and running again, but he didn't respond. Err. A message from an unwanted sender was there instead.

It was Charmaine apologizing for what happened last night between the three of us. She said it wasn't right what Janelle did to my stuff and she offered to buy me a new phone. I didn't respond. Infuriated at her for letting that bitch do that to my things in the first place.

That put me in a shitty mood, and I no longer wanted to play with my new toy. Before I could put it down, a new message appeared with my grandmother's funeral arrangements attached to it. I sighed and wanted to cry, but I held it together and gently placed the phone down.

To help distract my mind, I went to my vice and turned it on. The current show I had been binge watching started, and I sank down to watch it. I really wish I had some wine, but I really didn't feel like going out again to get any. I wish I could just call someone to get some for me but... I didn't have anyone.

Hours passed as I watched the show, and it didn't even bother me that the entire day was almost gone and was spent doing absolutely nothing. I was content in my quiet bubble for the time being. Spent watching tv all day. My eyes burned and I felt them getting heavier, but I wasn't quite ready for bed yet. And where the hell was Jamal? I hadn't heard from him all day basically.

With nothing left to do, I eventually made my way into the bedroom and turned on some nature sounds to help me relax. What I really needed was a damn vacation. Lay stretched out on the beach somewhere and enjoy the ocean and smell the salt water. I could envision it all now. In the meantime, I would just have to settle for the recreated sounds.

An hour after I had fallen asleep, I finally got a call from the one person I wanted to hear from.

"Hello?"

"Gees Babe, were you sleep?"

"Yea, I was. What's up though? How are you?"

"I'm doing alright about to head back into the club. Sorry I wasn't able to hit you up more. I was super busy."

"It's alright. I know how your weekends are."

"I'm assuming you won't be here tonight?"

"Not tonight Hun. I'm so tired."

"That's fine. At least you came to my first show."

"I wish I would have come on my own though."

"That's in the past, you'll be alright. But go back to sleep, I'll talk to you in the morning."

"Can I see you when you get home?"

"You want me to wake you up so we can see each other for five minutes?"

"I didn't see you damn near all day. I need a hug."

"Cadence, go to sleep. I'll call you in the morning."

"Err, fine."

"Did you just growl at me?"

"Yea, I did."

"Don't do that when we're in person. That shit is sexy. Good night Love."

"Good night."

In my mind, I wanted to be there to show my support, but my body was singing a whole different tune. I relaxed back once more and tried to fall back to sleep. Eventually, it came.

She's Busy Bro

Around mid-day, my phone rang causing me to wake up. The new ringtone that was assigned made my heart sing as I went to answer the call.

"Hello?"

"Well someone's in a good mood today. Hello gorgeous."

"Hey, how are you today? How was the performance?"

"It was great! I looked at the view of my new videos and they are the highest I've ever gotten."

"That's exciting."

"Have you checked the shirt sales recently?"

"No, I haven't. I need to get an app or something cuz I keep forgetting."

"Check it out for me when you get a chance. A few people in the crowd were rockin your shit Babe."

"Are you serious?"

"I took pictures for you and posted them on social media. I was gonna tag you, but I couldn't find your shop."

"I don't have social media for my shop."

"You kidding me? That's top priority for today. You want me to come over or you coming here? I wanna see you."

"We can change it up, I'll come over there today."

"Hurry up and get dressed then and bring yo ass."

I giggled. "I'm coming, I'm coming."

"Hurry up cuz I'm making lunch."

"What's for lunch?"

"You'll see when you get here." he said, hanging up the phone.

I laid there for another ten minutes trying to fully wake up and went and got in the shower. I didn't feel like putting anything fancy on so I opted in for my trusty leggings and a loose fitting shirt. My teeth were brushed, my hair was did and I was on the way out the door with my computer in my hands.

"What's up Cay?" Khalil's voice came out of nowhere. I looked up and found him standing in front of me, but something was off.

"Hey, what are you doing here?"

"I just wanted to check in on you and see how you were doing?"

"Why didn't you just call?"

"Charmaine told me what happened to your phone, and I know you procrastinate sometimes with things, so I figured you didn't get one yet."

"Yea, I bought one yesterday morning."

"Good, good. Listen, can we talk?" he slurred.

"Lil, I'm on my way somewhere."

"Where? Next door?" he joked I didn't find it that amusing. He cleared his throat. "Please. It will only take a second."

"Fine. I said walking back into the house and he followed. "What did you want to…" Before I could finish my sentence, his tongue was practically down my throat. I had to forcefully push him away. "What the hell are you doing?" I yelled angrily.

"Cay, I really wanna be with you. I've been thinking a lot ever since that night and I want to be something more with you."

"Lil. I told you we're just friends. Plus, Jamal and I are kind of talking. You know that."

"If you knew some of the shit I knew about him, you would rethink that."

"What?"

"My boy saw him leave with a chick last night. I'm assuming he didn't come see you after the show?"

"I'm not trying to hear this right now Khalil."

"Are you afraid it's true?" I paused for a minute, but he continued. "He's no good for you Cay and even you know that. I want you to take a chance with me."

"I don't see you that way. I see you as a friend. Maybe if you had approached me about it a while back… but now? I can't see that happening."

He approached me and each advance he made, pushed me further back into the room until my back was pressed up against the wall, and he kept coming.

"You need to back the fuck up. What the hell is wrong with you? You smell like straight liquor." I said, mushing him in the face and moving away.

"Give me a chance. We already know each other, so I don't see what the problem is?"

"You need to leave."

"You're really kicking me out right now?"

"Yes. You're over stepping your boundaries and you need to get the fuck out. Now."

"Why, so you can be with that womanizer next door?"

"It doesn't matter who I'm with, it won't be with you, and you need to get the fuck out."

My phone began to ring with Jamal's ringtone and the both of us looked at it. He began to laugh. "Really Cay? A fucking love song for him? Are you really that stupid and blind?"

The phone rang again and this time, Khalil answered it and put it on speaker. "Yo bro."

"Who the fuck is this?"

"Khalil, give me the phone." I yelled and tried to reach for it, but he shoved me hard in my chest out the way.

"Yea, bro, she's a bit busy at the moment. She'll have to call you back." he said and hung up.

I looked at him so confused and didn't even recognize the person standing in front of me. As I looked at him, I noticed his eyes were dilated and he had to be on some shit besides just alcohol. My heart raced in my chest. The phone that was still in Khalil's hands rang again.

"I told you she's busy bro."

"Put her on the damn phone."

"Jamal!!" I tried to yell, but his hand covered my face.

"She'll get back to you when I'm done." The phone was slammed on the floor and shattered before his giant foot stepped on it causing it to break further.

My eyes darted between the door and him and I decided to make a run for it. Of course he blocked my path and I began to run for the back. It was almost open to the point where I could get out and I could see my freedom before I was snatched up and pulled back inside. He held my arm tight as he forcefully slung me to the floor.

"Khalil. What are you doing?" I asked as he hovered over me.

"You're gonna be mine whether you want to be or not."

"Have you lost your fucking mind? Are you taking drugs again?"

My words only infuriated him more and his face changed to something I had seen before. This time, it was I that needed the help. Banging came from the front door and the door tried to be opened, but it was locked. The noise at the front of the house caused just enough distraction for me to make a run for it to the back, but not enough for me to escape.

He grabbed me by my hair and pulled me back causing me to fall, but not before I grabbed a knife and cut his leg as I went down.

"You stupid bitch, what the fuck!" he wallowed in pain as I stepped over him to get to the door, but my foot was grabbed, and I fell hard to the cold tile. I kicked as hard as I could for him to release me from his grasp, but this fucker wouldn't let go.

"Jamal!" I screeched and a window was broken out before I felt arms on my shirt pull me up and out of harm's way.

I heard his footsteps right behind me before I heard a loud thud. Khalil grabbed his ankle which caused him to fall. I went back to help him but he pushed me away.

"Get out of here Cadence. Go!" he said before turning his attention back to Khalil where he kicked him until he let him go. But he didn't stop there for he jumped on him and began punching him relentlessly.

"Jamal, stop it." I hollered. "Baby stop it!"

Khalil was now unconscious as Jamal looked up at me and stopped. His hands were still balled up and were covered in blood and rage was written on his face. Slowly, he stood up and looked around at what he had done before he made his way over to me and held me tight to his chest. Flashing lights appeared in what seemed to be nowhere, and cops came barging in.

Immediately they began to arrest Jamal. "No. What are you doing? He saved me. Stop."

"Ma'am, please step to the side and let us do our job."

"You're arresting the wrong person!" I yelled. "He saved me."

"Take him out of here please."

"No!" I roared and tried to get to him, but they wouldn't let me move.

Jamal was calm as they put him in cuffs and walked him out the door. "Relax Baby. It's going to be alright."

"No it's not."

"Relax and stay calm." he said as they walked him past me.

The EMT came in and assessed Khalil while an officer assisted me out the house as well. Neighbors surrounded us and tried to tell the officers what was going on and that Jamal had nothing to do with anything. Only then, did the officers turn to me calmly and asked me what happened.

I explained in full detail about the events that took place moments before. How Khalil was a friend that wanted more and attacked. How I tried to escape but failed. How Jamal broke through my window to help me once he heard me screaming from inside.

My story coincided with the neighbor's stories, but they still took us both to the hospital to get examined. As we were escorted to the ambulance, neighbors were recording the whole incident. Out the ambulance window, I could see Khalil being taken out on a stretcher. This was also recorded.

I sat huddled up in Jamal's arms looking at his swollen hands while the EMT took care of the wounds on his forehead. No physical wounds were inflicted upon me, but they wanted to examine me for head trauma from my falls. I cried softly, not sure of what to make of it all.

Original Destination

"No charges are being pressed against you or Mr. King and when you're done here, you're both free to go. If you have any questions, feel free to call us." The officer said handing me a card and leaving.

I glanced over at Jamal who looked at me pissed and worried at the same time. "Thank you." I uttered out trying not to relive what happened.

"You don't have to thank me. I'm just mad I couldn't get to you sooner." He sat up from the bed and wiped my face. "I was so worried about you. Why was he even there in the first place?"

"He wanted me to be with him and not you. He told me..."

"He told you what?"

I inhaled deeply. "He told me not to be with you because you hadn't changed. He said he saw you leaving last night with a female and that you were no good for me. That he was a better option. Is that true? Did you leave with someone else last night?"

"No I didn't. It's not true. Sounded like he was trying to push your buttons."

"What did you do after the show?"

"I went home and went to bed."

"Alone?"

"Really Cadence? Yes, alone. Why was he in your house?"

"He asked to talk to me right quick, so I let him in thinking it was going to be a friendly conversation. When I turned around, he kissed me and tried to come on to me. He had a look in his eyes I had seen one other time. I think he was on drugs."

As I spoke, a breaking news story came on the screen showing my house as the reporter spoke:

Breaking news this afternoon involving the popular local Mally Boy and his girlfriend Cadence Smith when an intruder came in and attacked Ms. Smith. Screams could be heard coming from inside her home before boyfriend, Jamal King, came to her rescue breaking a window to save her.

The attacker, Khalil Johnson, is in custody and is seeking medical help at this time. It has been confirmed there were large doses of cocaine and alcohol in his system at the time of the attack. Here's what neighbors had to say.

"He was standing on her porch when she came outside, and she let him in. A few minutes later, we heard her screaming and called the police."

"He was trying to get into her house as she was screaming, but the door I guess was locked so he broke the window to save her."

Both victims are being treated at Jackson hospital and are said to be doing fine. No charges are being pressed at this time.

The both of us looked at each other shocked that we had actually made the local news. I sulked down in my chair for a while before the nurse came in and told us we were cleared to leave. What little we had was gathered up and we made our way to the front entrance where we waited for a cab to pick us up.

"Mally Boy!" someone yelled in the emergency room, and it rippled back to everyone that was there. People began to flock to him as cameras danced in his face. I could tell he didn't want to be bothered, but still waved to everyone and even signed a few autographs before our cab arrived. My hand was held tightly in his before he opened the door for me to get in and he followed.

As we sat in the cab, he began to chuckle a bit to himself. "What's so funny?" I asked.

"They said you were my girlfriend. I guess we're official now."

I don't know why I expected to just go home and be at peace. Both of our houses were surrounded by people and newscasters as we pulled up. Jamal paid for the cab before we got out and headed to his house. My original destination for the day. We tried our best to ignore the people as we walked into the house and sat down on the couch.

"I need to take a shower." he said out of nowhere.

"So do I, but I'm scared to go back over there."

"Why?" he asked, checking his phone.

"I don't want to relive it all again."

"You're gonna have to go over there at some point."

"At some point, but not now. Plus, all those people are there. My window is messed up…"

"You wanna stay here for a while then?"

I paused. "I was thinking about a hotel but… how would that work?"

He chuckled. "What do you mean how would it work? I have spare bedrooms you can stay in."

I nodded my head. "Would you mind if I stayed for a few days? At least until I get everything cleaned up."

"I wouldn't have offered if I didn't mind."

There was a lot of action coming from outside the house. People were screaming and chanting his name which was disrupting the peace we were so accustomed to. I started getting agitated and he noticed.

"You wanna stay in a hotel for a few days while this shit settles down?"

"I really do. I really want to go to the beach though."

"Let's go to the beach for the week then."

"Are you serious?"

"Yea, why not?"

"What about your shows?"

"I don't have any gigs right now. Maybe I can set something up down there. I'd get more exposure…" his voice trailed off.

"What's wrong?"

"Nothing, my sister called." He dialed her number and put it on speaker.

"What the fuck is going on? Are you alright? How's Cadence? I can't get a hold of her."

"She's right here. You're on speaker phone."

"Oh my God Baby, are you alright?"

"Yes, I'm fine thanks to your brother."

"I saw it on the news and got so scared."

"All the way in Neptune?" he asked.

"Yes, are you guys alright?"

"We're fine sis. Relax."

"Don't tell me to fucking relax. What took you so long to call me back."

"I left my phone here. We've been at the hospital all day."

"You guys are going viral. You're everywhere."

"Nia, stop lying…"

"I'm so serious. Look at your social media."

"Imma check. I'll call you back."

The phone hung up and he looked on his social media platforms and she was right. Up and down his timeline were various pictures and videos of us with millions of likes and the captions were nothing but positive. His music videos had also reached a few million views and his followings reached one-hundred k as well.

He sat back in his chair in complete shock as his dream was slowly coming true. His dream to get noticed and to leave an impact on people's lives. Who knew that me losing almost everything would give him so much in return?

Baecation

I stepped out of the shower and into an unfamiliar room. The clothes I had been given to wear were twice my size and hung loosely off my body. Even though I so desperately wanted to get my own clothes right next door. I was terrified to do so.

The shorts kept falling off my ass, so I finally just took them off as I made my way to the living room in nothing but his shirt. And I mean NOTHING but his shirt.

When he heard my footsteps come closer, he turned and admired me like I figured he would. "Well damn. You look nice in my clothes."

"Oh hush." I said sitting down on the couch miserably.

"What's wrong?"

"I need my clothes and those people outside are noisy as hell."

"Want me to grab you some?"

"Yes and no. Yes, cuz I want them, no cuz I don't want you digging through my drawls." I joked. Kinda.

"Cadence, I'll go get you your stuff. It's fine."

"Are you sure?"

"I'm sure. Is it locked?"

"I don't know. There's a key under my mat in the backyard."

"I'll go out the back then. Anything you want besides clothes?"

"My laptop, charger and my phone. I at least need the sim card from it. And my keys."

He kissed the top of my head before he left out the back. It felt so weird to be here. Especially alone. I familiarized myself with the downstairs surroundings for a while until he came back with a few bags of what I had requested.

"Thank you so much." I said and stood up to get dressed.

"Wait."

"What?"

"Before you change I wanna…" his eyes wandered over my body as he licked his lips.

"Really?"

"No, I just got sidetracked is all. Gah damn. I wanted to record a video with you."

"Saying what?"

"That we're alright and thanks for the support."

"That can't wait until I change?"

"No. You look so adorable how you are now."

I scrunched up my face and sat down next to him. The camera began to roll and I covered my face out of shyness. He laughed and spoke.

"Hey everybody, just wanted to let you know we're alright and doing fine." He stopped and looked down at me before nudging me shoulder. "Babe, stop acting so shy. Say something."

"Hi. We're doing alright and we wanted to thank you for the support."

"Yea, what she said. We appreciate you so check us out on the next one. You know where to find me."

I bumped into him and looked in his eyes. "Us." I focused on the camera. "You know where to find us."

He smiled. "What she said. Holla!"

"I can't believe you made me do that." He played it back and we both watched it together and actually, we looked cute together.

"You like it? I'm about to post it and tag you in it."

"I like it, go ahead. Can I get changed now?"

"Yes, yes, go get changed and then we can leave."

"Leave? And go where?"

"To a hotel on the beach."

"Wait, are you serious?"

"Yea. I don't want to be surrounded by people. I'm about to go pack some shit while you change."

He finished what he was doing on his phone and stood up. That was my queue to get up and get shit moving. I was too ecstatic as I put my clothes on and headed back to the living room where he was waiting. All his things were in his hands, and we were ready to head out. The only obstacle in our way was the large crowd that surrounded the house and blocked the car.

"You think my car and my house will be alright until we get back?"

"Yea. I checked everything when I was there. Everything is locked up and that board isn't going anywhere."

The door opened and the people that were outside erupted with cheers. Their cheers soon turned to boos when they saw us with our things in our hands and packing the car. He opened my door for me to get in before getting in himself and turning the engine on. I couldn't believe we were doing this. It wasn't as if the beach was super far away, but it was definitely not home. Slowly, he pulled out of the driveway, and we pulled off to our next destination.

My hand was in his hands most of the way there. Excitement coursed through my body as we drove. We were headed to my favorite beach, Seaside Heights and I couldn't wait to get there. Thoughts of spending time at the beach with my grandmother began to flash through my mind and brought my morale down a bit. I let his hand go to wipe a few tears away. All the chaos from the day had caused a good distraction from it for the most part, but then there were times like this where it hit me hard.

"What's wrong Babe?"

"Nothing, just thinking about my grandmother is all."

He rubbed my leg before grabbing my hand and pulling it to his lips where a kiss was placed on it. "Do you think she would want you to be sad for losing her?"

I shook my head. "No."

"Keep that in mind. I want you to enjoy yourself. I don't want you to be sad or upset. Don't think about anything negative during this past week."

"I'll try not to."

He kissed my hand again before there was silence. "We're almost there, then you can relax, kick your feet up. We can go to the beach tomorrow, walk the boardwalk, ride the rides. Whatever you want to do."

"I appreciate it. I need to get a phone first though."

"We'll do that first thing in the morning."

"Wait, weren't we supposed to do something important today?" I asked just now realizing we already had made plans before they were interrupted.

"Uhh… we were supposed to create social media profiles for Cay City. You up to doing it tonight?"

"I don't see why not. The day isn't over yet."

Another half hour passed, and we finally arrived at Seaside. The hotel we chose to stay at wasn't anything lavish, but it was close to the beach and the boardwalk and the rooms were nice and cozy.

Our bags were brought upstairs, and we both sat down on our respective beds to take a load off. Eventually, I went and opened the balcony door and stepped outside to hear the calming sounds of the ocean and smell the fresh air. I closed my eyes to take it all in and to calm my mind. I was soon joined by a warm embrace from behind which I held on to me making this moment even better.

"You wanna work out here?" he asked, pulling away.

"I wouldn't mind doing that."

"It shouldn't take long to set up. Add a business page, make a few connections and upload a few pictures."

"All my pictures are gone. They were destroyed on the first phone."

"No worries. I'll download them and send them to your... phone."

"... Yea."

"We can set it up on my phone if you want. Share access to it so I can upload stuff as well."

"That's fine." I replied and sat down on one of the chairs outside.

He sat down too as he worked away on setting up the business profiles on various platforms. He wasn't lying when he said it wouldn't take long and in less than a half hour, Cay City was now on social media. The phone was handed to me as I looked through everything. It looked so professional even down to my logo being the profile pictures and my brand name.

I handed the phone back to him with a big smile on my face, but he kept working. "What are you doing?"

"I'm going back to my posts and tagging Cay City in them. I wish you started this a while ago. It looks so bare."

"We all have to start somewhere."

Even though he didn't look up, he smiled. A few minutes later, he handed me the phone back and there were a lot more pictures posted on the platforms. Most of them were of him for now, but I didn't mind. I was thankful he had helped me with it all.

"It's linked to your website, and I shouted it out so hopefully, you'll be getting more orders and followers and what not. When you get your phone, be sure to add the links on your personal pages to your business ones."

"I already did that."

"You did?" He began to search for me. "It's sad, I'm not even following your personal accounts. What's your name on here?"

"Cadence_Ximora."

He looked up from his phone and glanced at me curiously. "Where did Ximora come from?"

"It's my middle name."

"That's beautiful and exotic. I like that." His face was buried back in his phone before he spoke again. "I found you. Gees, you have a decent size following." he said, scrolling through my pictures. "Babe, your pictures are beautiful."

"Thank you. And one-thousand followers is not a lot."

"Umm… you're up to ten thousand."

"What?" the phone was taken from his hands. "Holy shit."

"I guess the viral video rubbed off on you too. I'm tagging you in the video I posted earlier. You better follow me back too." he teased.

"I will. I promise. I can't believe I have to buy another phone. That one wasn't even a day old."

"No negative thoughts. It's gonna be alright."

"You're right."

"Alright. I think I'm done for the day. Had enough excitement. Time to relax. What do you want to do?"

"I just wanna lay down. I'm so tired."

"Me too. Wanna watch tv or something?"

"Or something." I flirted and went inside.

He cracked a smile before he followed me in and sat down on the other bed. My eyes glanced over at him. Watching his actions as he turned the tv on before glancing over at me.

"What?"

"Nothing."

"You want me to come lay with you don't you?"

"I mean, it would be nice, but you don't have to."

He shook his head and made his way over. He got comfortable and I rested my head on his chest while his arm wrapped snugly around me. I don't even remember the rest for I passed out shortly after.

171

Beach Day

The next morning, I awoke to an empty spot next to me and to his strong voice on the balcony. After using the restroom, I stepped out and held him from behind as he continued his conversation. I inhaled his scent as he rubbed my arm with his free hand. Once I realized he was talking business and making arrangements, I headed back inside.

When he was done with his phone call, he came back in and closed the door behind him. "Good morning, gorgeous."

"Good morning handsome."

"I have some good news."

"And what might that be?"

"I got a few gigs this weekend in AC."

"Are you serious? How? Don't they usually book early in advance?"

"Usually, but with the recent news and viral videos, they were more than willing to accommodate."

"Where will you be performing?"

"Harrah's Pool on Friday night and the Tropicana in one of the clubs on Saturday night. It won't be my own show but they're gonna let me perform a few songs."

"Oh my goodness, that's exciting!"

"One more thing, we get a complimentary suite at Harrah's."

I squealed with excitement as I jumped up and down in his arms. "Are you serious right now?"

"Yes! So, are you ready to start your day? We should be able to get you a phone somewhere and we can just relax and do whatever."

"I'm ready. Let me go get dressed right quick."

"Then you're not ready."

I gave him a look before digging in my bags trying to find something to wear. Everything was everywhere and I was having a difficult time. Finally, I found something and disappeared in the bathroom to get changed. When I came out, we didn't hesitate to be on our way.

The drive to town wasn't long and neither was our stay at the phone store. Basically, the same phone was bought at a discount thanks to the news story and the insurance I had on the device. Everything was transferred over to it, it was activated and as soon as it turned on it began to hum and sing from all the notifications I had missed in the last 24 plus hours.

In the car, I began to scan through some of them and while most of them made me smile, there were quite a few I could have lived without. I guess the emotions transferred to my face.

"What's wrong?"

"I got a few messages from Janelle and Charmaine."

"Janelle? Are you kidding me?"

"Shh." I shushed and listened to the voice message. I rolled my eyes and played it on speaker phone.

"Cadence, it's Janelle. I know you probably won't get this for a while, but I wanted to tell you how truly sorry I am for what I did to your things. When you get this message, call me so I can replace everything I destroyed."

"Message marked for deletion. Next message."

"Cay, it's Char. Just wanted to know if you got my text. Give me a call when you can."

"Message marked for deletion. Next message."

"Cadence, you sorry sack of shit. How could you do that to Lil. I hope you eat shit and die. I'm coming for that ass for what you did. Mark my fuckin words. I better not catch you in these fuckin streets bitch. I will merk your stupid ass. Word up."

"What the fuck yo? Are you kidding me?"

"I'm keeping that shit in case something happens. There's more…"

"Iight, iight, that's enough. Just save them and… I don't know man. That shit is wild. Crazy thing is, he attacked you."

I shook my head. "I know. There's text messages, emails… and for what? A man that she dumped? This is going way too far."

"We'll handle it when we get home. But for now, let's relax. Let's go get something to eat and hit the water. Sound good?"

"Sounds good."

Before we reached the hotel, we stopped to eat at a really nice restaurant. As we waited for our food to be served, I added all my apps and signed in to everything. Even the ones that Mal had access to which had a few thousand followers already right along with some flirtatious messages to the both of us.

"Have you looked at Cay City messages today?"

"No. Why?"

"There's some wild, personal messages in there."

"Don't pay it no mind. If it's business related, respond. If not, ignore it."

It kind of made me worry about the amount of females that were hitting him up on MY business page. I could only imagine what was being sent to his personal accounts and if he was even entertaining that bullshit. I hoped not, but something deep down told me he was to some level or degree.

"What's wrong now?"

"Eww, stop reading my face."

"I can't help it. All your emotions are on your face. You suck at hiding them. So what's bothering you now?"

174

"Nothing Mal. Nothing at all."

"Are you reading those messages from the females?"

"…No."

He laughed, "You're such a fuckin liar Cay."

"Are you responding to any of them?"

"Does it look like I responded to any of them?"

"Do you respond to any other messages?"

He shook his head in disbelief. "No. I don't. And if I do, I thank them for their support."

I stared at him trying to read him but got little to nothing in response. Maybe I was overthinking shit. But then again, if I hadn't seen it with my own eyes, I wouldn't think twice about it. And yet again, again, I saw with my own eyes him turn females down even when he thought I wasn't there. Fuck. What did I get myself into?

"Stop staring at me like that. I'm not doing shit."

"Get out of my head Jamal." I teased.

"Once again, it's written on your face. I would love to play you in poker. I'd win every time."

The food was served and we ate happily together. Shared a few jokes, had some good laughs and tried to plan out our day. Our first stop would definitely have to be getting bathing suits. Neither one of us had one. The second thing on our list would be the beach and that's pretty much where we left off at. We would just see how the day panned out.

When we were done eating and on the way to go shopping for bathing suits, a few thoughts ran through my mind, so I decided to bring it to his attention. "Did you let your fans know you would be performing in AC?"

"I put it on one of my pages, that's about it. Why?"

"I was just wondering if you got the word out. Did you make a video for it?"

"No. Just a flyer type post. You think I should make a video?"

"It wouldn't hurt would it?"

"No. But I have an idea. I'll hold off for now."

"Uhh. Ok. Care to share this idea?"

"I gotta work it out in my head, but I'll let you know."

We arrived at the store and began to shop around. He went one way, and I went another, browsing through the aisles for a bathing suit. The one I picked wasn't anything special or fancy but it was a nice two piece suit that would do the job. I grabbed it off the rack and headed towards Jamal who was actually heading towards me. I held up my suit and smiled and when he showed me his, we burst out into laughter. Our bathing suits matched.

"How the hell did we manage to do that?"

"I don't know. Are you ready to head out?"

I glanced around the store one last time and grabbed two beach towels with the words 'Seaside Heights' on them and a beach umbrella while he grabbed two chairs and headed to the register. Everything was paid for, and we headed back to the hotel. When we got there, we changed clothes and headed directly to the beach with our gear in our hands.

The beach was only a good block away and we set up our stuff getting ready to go in the water. I took my shirt off and tossed it to the side before glancing over at Mal who was also taking his off. My eyes were glued to his sexy body that I had only seen with my hands. And they did not lie. His abs and chest were just as impeccable as I thought they would be.

His eyes met mine when his shirt was tossed to the side too and he smiled. "Why are you staring at me?"

"Nothing... No reason I just uhh... never saw you... Like that." I cleared my throat and turned away. I had lost my train of thought and struggled to remember what I was doing. Taking my clothes off to go swimming. Right.

"You like what you see? Cuz I'm lovin what I see." His voice was low and sexy as he approached me with a hug from behind. Our bare skin touched, and it was a new and amazing feeling. I turned to face him.

"Yea, I'm liking what I see too. Wasn't expecting all… that." I said gesturing with my hands. And oh how they wanted a taste of his caramel skin.

His only reaction was to laugh as he grabbed my hand and we headed down to the water. At first, it was cold but after a full body dip in, it was fine. We stayed in for a few hours before going to lay on the beach for some sun. Well, I did anyway and was able to get a beautiful tan out of it.

"Cadence, come here right quick."

I made my way over to him who had his phone in his hands. "What's up?"

"I wanna make a promo video with you right quick?"

"Why do you need me to make one with you?"

"Just come here woman and make the video."

"What do you need me to say?"

"Just go with the flow. It's letting people know we're going to be in AC for a few shows this weekend."

I sat on his lap with my arm around his shoulder and the camera began recording.

"Hey, what's up, it's ya boy Mally Boy down at Seaside with the lovely Cadence."

"Hi." I said shyly.

"We chillin at the beach right now, but this weekend, we'll be in Atlantic City to perform a few live shows. Check out my site, Mally Boy dot com for the details and we'll see you there."

"Don't miss the turn up, down in AC! Whoooo!" I added and he laughed, kissing my cheek.

"That was good! Imma send it to you so you can post it on ya page too."

"That was good." I responded, and soon I got a message with the video attached to it. I watched it a few times and smiled at how happy the both of us looked. I posted it and went back on my towel to finish sunbathing, but not for long.

"Cay, you wanna walk the boardwalk? I'm getting hungry."

"Yea, I don't mind. Let me go take a dip right quick to cool off and we can go."

Down at the water's edge, I dipped a toe in before fully walking in and immersing myself. The water felt so refreshing after laying in the hot sun for a while. I made my way back up and looked at Jamal who was holding his phone out for me to take. I looked at the screen and scrolled through the pictures he had just taken of me in the water.

"They look nice."

"They look nice? They're stunning. Whatchu mean? I'm bout to post these up."

"Are you serious Mal?"

"Dead ass Cay. I'm tagging you."

"You're posting it on your page?"

"Yup. Along with some selfies of myself. You'll see."

I shook my head and began getting our things together and packing it away. When he was done, he took down the umbrella and we both headed back to the room to drop everything off before making our way to the boardwalk.

We stopped at a few shops, got a few souvenirs and things we liked, took pictures with a few fans and sat down to eat in an air-conditioned restaurant.

"Do you ride rides?" he asked as he finished his last bite.

"I do. I'm assuming you do as well since you're asking me about it?"

"Absolutely. Wanna go to the pier next?"

"We can do that."

"What's wrong?"

"Nothing, just a little tired. It's been a long day."

"Better wake that ass up cuz it's not over yet."

I giggled. "Where do you get all this energy from?"

He shrugged his shoulders. "I wish I could give some of it to you."

"I'll be fine. I'll get my second wind when we ride the rides."

Our table was cleared off and we headed to the pier and, just like I said, I got my second wind as we rode several rides into the late evening. We stayed until the place closed and made our way back to the room.

When we got there, he was changing into his swimming trunks, and I collapsed on the bed. "What are you doing?" I muffled.

"I'm going to the pool. You wanna come?"

"No. I wanna go to sleep somewhere."

"I'll be back then." he said, kissing my forehead and walking out the door.

I laid there for a while battling myself on whether or not to go down and join him. Finally, I mustered up the energy to put my suit on and headed downstairs to the pool. When I got there, he wasn't alone. A few female fans were down there with him, and they were all taking pictures.

My jaw clenched and I went to turn around to leave but his words stopped me. "Babe, come and take some pics with me."

"Oh my goodness, is that Cadence too?" one of the girls squealed.

"Please can we take pictures of the both of you?"

"You guys are too cute together!"

I guess I overreacted in my head. My mood lightened up as I headed over to where they were all sitting. A few poses later, they were caught up in their phones giggling amongst one another and Jamal and I were in our own little world.

"So glad you decided to join me." he said, swimming up to me.

My arms wrapped around his neck as I brought him closer for a hug. "Just wanted to spend some time with you is all."

"All day wasn't enough?" he asked laughing.

"Nope."

He pulled away and stared in my eyes before pulling me in for a kiss. A long, seductive kiss that made my lady parts tingle. The only thing that snapped me out of his trance were the squealing girls behind us as they watched. More pictures were taken, and I'm sure they would be posted sooner or later.

I pushed him back and dove under the water to cool myself off, thanks to him making me hot and bothered. I was curious to know when he would give me the full taste, but I didn't ask him about it.

On the edge of the pool, I sat with my feet in the water and admired him as he swam a few laps. How he had so much energy was beyond me, but I loved the view, nonetheless.

Finally, he wore himself out and we headed back to the room hand in hand. My shower was taken first, and my bathing suit and towel were hung to dry. As I waited for him to finish his shower, I began to drift off to sleep.

When he came out, he wrapped the blanket around me before going to lay in his bed. I wanted to cuddle up with him but had no energy to even ask. I wondered why he never wanted to lay with me without being prompted to do so.

In Due Time

For the rest of our stay at Seaside, it was pretty much the same. Relaxing and enjoying the beach. Pictures with fans. Rides. And dips in the pool. Each night, yet and still, he laid in his own bed, and I didn't bother him about it, but it was still on my mind.

We had been here for four days, and it was time for us to head down the coast to Atlantic City. All of our things were packed and loaded into the car, and we made our way down the road.

The trip was only about an hour but with our conversation and jokes, it seemed like a lot less.

As the hotel came into view, I took several pictures of it hoping to get at least one good pic to post later. We pulled into the parking garage and, with a few of our bags in hand, we headed to the front of Harrah's to check in.

"Good afternoon Mr. King and Ms. Smith! We are delighted to have you here. You're going to be staying in the Waterfront tower, room 3617. Enjoy!"

"Thank you." he said before we headed to the elevators.

"I'm so excited!" I exclaimed, bouncing around in the elevator. All he could do was smile at my enthusiasm. The door to our room swung open and it was absolutely beautiful.

We placed our things down and began examining the space. My eyes met with his as he stared at me from a short distance with a grin on his face.

"What?"

"Nothing, just seeing you happy makes me happy. I don't know how much time I'll have to spend with you over these next few days though."

"Rehearsals and all that?"

"Yea. But Imma make the best out of today. Wanna grab something to eat and look around?"

"Yes! I'm so hungry and I have to go shopping for a few outfits for your performances."

"What I grabbed wasn't good enough?" he teased.

"You didn't grab any club wear, jewelry or heels but it's cool."

"My bad." he laughed. "Next time, I'll make sure to do that."

The room door opened once again, and we made our way to the main floor where we found a nice restaurant to eat in. Food and drinks were ordered, and before we could start our conversation, he was discovered.

Everyone in the restaurant seemed to flock over to our table to take pictures or get autographs. After a few minutes, he seemed to get a bit upset at the frustrated look on my face.

"Thank you everyone, but I would really like to enjoy lunch with my girlfriend. We will be here for a while, and I will be sure to take pictures and sign autographs at a later date."

The crowd slowly dispersed with slight attitudes until we were semi alone once again. Cameras were still held in people's hands as he grabbed mine in comfort.

"You alright?"

"I'm fine, it can just be a bit overwhelming at times."

"Tell me about it." The waiter came over with our drinks and I chugged mine down. "Babe, slow down, we haven't had drinks in days."

"I know. It's just my nerves."

"We're fine. Relax."

"I'm trying to." I giggled, then pointed something out. "So…"

"Oh God."

"I'm your girlfriend now?"

"According to them you are."

"According to you?"

"I would like you to be, but you never said anything about it. Are you ready to be? Officially?"

"Maybe."

He laughed and he shook his head. "Maybe ain't an option. I'm not gonna rush you though."

"Would you leave if I took too long to give you an answer?"

"I don't see myself going anywhere even if you wanted to remain friends or business partners."

A smile spread on my face before I asked my next question. "Why don't you ever lay with me at night?"

"I have a different respect for you, and I honestly don't think you're ready. I know how my hands can get and you turn me on, so I stay away."

"Who says I'm not ready?"

He smiled, leaned in closer and whispered softly, "You're not ready Cadence." A kiss was passionately placed on my lips before he sat back in his seat with a smirk.

I cleared my throat and adjusted myself in my seat before taking another sip from my cup. Thank goodness our food arrived to district my mind from the wild thoughts that were running rampant inside.

As we ate, the both of us threw flirtatious glances at one another that caused me to blush the entire time. In my mind, his words were on repeat causing me to smile.

"What are you thinking about?"

"Nothing. When do you have rehearsals?"

"We're having a meeting tomorrow at ten. I'm assuming we'll be going over it then."

I nodded my head in understanding. "Are you ready to head out? I wanna see what clothes I can get."

"Yea, we can head out." he said standing up before helping me.

As we strolled along, we tried to stay as low key as possible so we wouldn't draw any attention to us. A few stores were browsed for a bit, but there wasn't anything in them that really caught our eye. Until that one came. Both of us were able to find things that we liked, and we got enough for a few nights.

On our way back to the room, he stopped and looked at a few items in a jewelry store. I browsed a bit, but the things in here were a bit out of my price range. Everything inside was for a different class of people and I wasn't a part of that.

"Whatchyu think of this?" he asked, pointing to a piece under the glass case.

My eyes scanned it. "It's nice. I like it."

"Excuse me, can I see this right quick?" he asked the worker.

"What are you doing?"

"I want to see it right quick."

"Do you know how much that thing costs?"

"Nothing to get a closer look at it."

"Smart ass."

The large gold and silver, diamond encrusted chain was handed to him as he looked at it more carefully. I stood to the side and shook my head and watched as he held it up to himself in the mirror.

"It looks nice right?"

My eyes focused on him. "It looks very nice on you."

"It would be perfect for tomorrow."

"Are you really thinking about getting it?"

"It does look very nice on you sir. It matches your style." the worker chimed in. I glared at her.

"I think I might get it Babe."

"As your accountant, I advise against it." I said trying to use some authority. He only laughed at me.

"I'm not getting it. I was just messing with you. One day I will though. I'll get you one to match."

I shook my head again and smiled. "Good." I simply responded.

"Thank you miss." he said, giving the chain back and grabbing my hand to leave. "Why are you against me getting it? It's not like I can't afford it."

"I'm not worried if you can afford it or not. I just know what the bigger goal is and buying a fifteen-thousand-dollar chain isn't part of that goal."

"It's just for appearances."

"Appearances my ass." I joked. I felt his eyes on me and I looked his way. It was as if he was admiring me in a new light. "What?"

"Nothing. I just really appreciate you. Miss accountant." he said and burst out laughing. "I can't believe you pulled that on me."

"I had to do something shit." I laughed back as we stepped into the elevator. "I really thought you were gonna get it."

"I was thinking about it on some real shit, but the look on your face... I couldn't. And you were right. I have bigger goals that need to be achieved before I can get that kind of stuff. In due time, right?"

"In due time."

"So what do you want to do tonight? Wanna hit the casino?" he asked as we walked into the room.

"I'm not a gambler. I don't know how to play half of those games."

"Well, we know you can't play poker..." I gave him a side eye and nudged him gently with a smile. He was such an ass, but I liked him for it.

"Wanna check out the club you'll be performing at? Or the pool"

"That's not a half bad idea."

"Of course it's not. I came up with it." I said sarcastically.

"Damn with your smart ass mouth."

"What?"

"It's gonna get you in trouble."

"By who?" I snapped back.

He smirked and came closer, gently pushing me up against the wall with my hands held above my head. In his eyes was lust as he spoke. "By me." He bit his lip before kissing mine. "I'm trynna be a good boy here but Baby, you are making it hard." He bit my neck and I moaned softly before he backed away.

This was driving me insane with this teasing shit. I was so ready to pounce on him, he just didn't know. And I couldn't resist the urge anymore. I walked up to him while he sat on the bed and pushed him back, taking him completely by surprise. I laid on top of him and kissed him passionately before moving my attention to his neck. He let me for a while before he sat up taking me with him.

"Cadence!" he yelled, and I looked at him so confused.

"What? I can't take it anymore, I want you." I whined.

He exhaled deeply before gripping me up and flipping me on my back. My hands were held above my head as he hovered over me and put his weight on me. Our eyes locked before he kissed my neck slowly and softly, then bit it causing me to moan once again. His lips slowly moved from my neck to my chest before he started sucking on the exposed part of my breast then back up my neck.

He looked down at me. "You can't have me yet." he whispered tantalizingly and got up.

I laid there still mesmerized by the feeling he had just given me before I sat up angrily. "Why don't you want me?" I barked. "Is something wrong with me? Am I not attractive to you? What? What is it?"

"It's not that at all. I told you what it is already, but you don't want to listen." he said with a slight smirk. "I want you like crazy, but Imma take my time with you. Make you wait like you're making me wait."

It all dawned on me, and I sucked my teeth. "Are you fucking serious Jamal?"

"Dead ass Baby. So take your time."

"You're a fuckin jerk." I yelled and threw a pillow at him. He laughed at my hostility.

"Imma remember this and take it out on you. So keep going with that attitude."

"Ahh." I yelled out in frustration. "I need some dick now! Come and fuck me."

He shrugged his shoulders. "Sucks. I'm out of commission at the moment. But Imma do more than fuck you."

"What are you going to?"

He smirked again showing his beautiful, white smile and dimples. "Wouldn't you like to know."

"Yes. Come show me." I pouted.

"No. So get dressed so we can go to the pool and check it out."

"But I'm all wet and ready for you." I teased hoping it would change his mind.

"Go clean up then."

"Come clean it up for me."

"Cadence!"

"Ugg, fine. I don't like you right now." I said and stormed over to my bags.

"Love you too."

"No you don't."

"Gah, you're so adorable when you get mad."

"I'm not mad. I'm frustrated. Very, very frustrated. Only you can make it better."

"Damn. Wish I could help."

I had one last resort. Something I knew would almost be impossible for him to resist. First my shirt came off and was tossed to the side. Next my jeans were taken off and tossed to the side leaving me in nothing but my lace underwear and bra. I had gotten his attention and his eyes were on me and watching every move I made.

I went over to my bags again and bent over to go through them, not that I was looking for anything in particular, but it worked. His strong hands rolled over my ass and down my thighs as he pressed up against me giving me a feel of his hard dick that was ready for me.

"Gah damn Babe." he said, smacking my ass. But then he stepped back. "But two can play that game."

I turned around to see what he was talking about just as his shirt went over his head exposing his beautiful muscles. His chest, abs and obliques were chiseled to perfection, and I wanted him even more than before. He flexed his pecs one at a time, putting on a show.

I couldn't let him one up me like that. I was trying to prove a point here. My hands went behind my back and unhooked my bra. My eyes stared at him the entire time the piece of garment came off and was dropped to the floor until his eyes wandered down to my now naked breasts.

His eyes lowered and he bit his lip and he sexed me down with his eyes before he looked into mine again. I tilted my head and set my jaw as if telling him it was his move.

He nodded and smirked before he slowly undid his jeans and dropped them to the floor allowing me to see his large and hefty package under his boxer briefs. Speechless. There were no words for how amazing his body looked in the soft glow of the sunset emanating from the window.

With nothing left to lose, I played with the band of my lace underwear for a minute before I turned around and slid them off bending over to make sure they went down all the way. I looked back at him, and his face was priceless as he stared at my lady parts that wanted him inside so badly. I turned back around and posed. Waiting for him to make his next move. Was he as bold as I?

Before he could make his next move, I made mine. My fingers slid down slowly to my hole where they played with my button before I brought the juice back up to my mouth and licked it off. One finger at a time. His eyes got lower as he made his way over to me and dipped a finger in my cookie just as I had done but more. It went all the way inside. In and out and around and to places I didn't even know were accessible.

My knees grew weak, and I used him as support to keep me standing as he pleasured me. Right before I came he stopped, pulled his finger out and licked it before giving me a taste.

"Please keep going." I begged in his ear. "Please."

"I gotchyu." he whispered back and slipped his finger back inside to continue to pleasure me until I came. I came hard. Harder than I had ever cum, and he let me pulsate on him as my juice ran down his fingers before he licked it all off.

I collapsed into his arms, and he carried me over and gently put me down on the bed. He chuckled at the state I was in. "I win." he said with such confidence and kissed my forehead.

"No!" I cried with my face buried in the pillow. "What did you do to me?"

He laughed. "I made you tap out. What did you expect? Are you done fuckin with me now?"

"I want more."

"So do I."

I held my head up and glared at him before smiling and shaking my head. "I can't with you."

"Mmm, but you want to."

My jaw dropped as he got up to put his clothes on. It dropped even further, if that was possible, as I watched him walk away in his half naked glory. I buried my face again and screamed and it amused him.

"Come on so we can head out."

"Are you going to give me more when we get back?"

"Cadence!"

"Ugg. Fine!" I shouted and got up covering myself up as I walked to the bathroom.

"Don't cover up now. I done seen all of its magnificence."

"Leave me be Jamal." I said closing the door and starting the shower.

After I had washed up, I came out with my towel wrapped around my body and actually went through my things to get clothes this time. What I wanted to wear was already out, I just needed to get my underwear. When I found them, I quickly slipped them on before putting my dress and jewelry on.

Jamal was now in his jeans, but his shirt was still off, and I couldn't help myself. As he dug around for a shirt, my hands slowly caressed his back which caused him to stop what he was doing and take a few deep breaths.

He turned to face me. "You know I do want you right? I don't want you thinking I don't."

I nodded my head meekly. "I want you too."

"Ha, yes. You've made that very clear."

I giggled. "What gave it away?"

"Whenever you're ready, I'm yours." he replied and slid his shirt over his head. "And I promise, I won't disappoint." He kissed my lips before moving away to finish getting ready. I smiled a giddy smile before I continued getting ready too.

Kiss Kiss

We held hands as we made our way down to the pool only to find that it was closed for the after-hours party. The both of us laughed before heading to the car to go to the Tropicana. Hopefully, we would have more luck there.

We parked in the garage and took the elevators to the floor where all the action was. Hand in hand we made our way to the club that he would be performing at on Saturday night. Kiss Kiss. By the time we got there, there was a short line and we waited patiently even though we probably didn't have to.

We tried to lay low so that we wouldn't be bothered and so far, it was working. In the club, the DJ was playing some good music, but we made our way to the bar. He assisted me on the chair and ordered me my favorite drink along with his. We sat there for a while watching the crowd, enjoying the music and sipping our drinks.

One of my favorite songs came on after I ordered my second drink and I dragged Mal to the dance floor to dance with me. I don't think we had ever danced together like this. Yea, we had our moment, but it wasn't how I was about to put it down on him. I turned around and started whining and grinding on him. He held my waist as I worked my ass in a way I don't think he knew I could.

"Oh shit Babe, wait." he said, putting his drink down and readjusting himself. "Iight, let me see what you got."

I smirked and began to whine harder on him and he kept up. People around us realized who we were and began to scream and take pictures of us. My only focus was on him. I had to redeem myself from earlier this evening, but of course, he couldn't let me. He turned me to face him before picking me up and dancing with me like a mad man.

"Mally Boy! Mally Boy! Mally Boy!" the crowd chanted as we danced.

The way he had me up like that turned me on and when he put me down I attacked him. Kissing him lustfully. Our hands began to explore each other's bodies and we didn't care who saw our affection towards one another. Our actions ignited the crowd until I pulled away from him and led him back to the bar for another drink.

"Yo, I thought you were gonna fuck me on the floor." he said taking a sip from his cup.

"I thought you were going to do the same."

Before long, people started gathering around us and taking pictures. Asking us to kiss and pose together and we did. Happily I might add. He signed autographs and we took wild selfies with everyone that was around. I must admit, it was an exhilarating feeling.

"Yo yo what's up? I just got word that Mally Boy and Cadence were in the house. Let's make some noise!" the DJ announced over the speaker. "If y'all don't already know, he'll be performing here Saturday night so make sure you get your tickets and be here to see his live performance. At Kiss Kiss AC."

The crowd roared and I cheered and clapped for him too while he ate up all the attention. His arms wrapped around me and gave me a hug. I think he was just happy that he was being recognized.

As the night went on, we danced more in the crowded club. A few girls danced on his side, but I still had all his attention. A guy tried to grab me up and I shoved him hard in his chest. Jamal was on him and backed him down before he grabbed my hand and pulled me back to the bar. He was heated.

"You good Babe?"

"I'm good."

"You want another drink?"

"I'll take one more. Are you drinking with me?"

"Take a shot with me."

I shrugged my shoulders and he ordered us both a drink and a shot. I took a deep breath before I took my shot, and it burned all the way down. My face scrunched up and he laughed as he chased his shot with his drink. I followed suit and I was done in.

"Can we go back and dance Baby?" I asked and he looked at me twice. "What?"

"You just called me... Never mind. Come on with your drunk ass." he said, pulling me along past the crowd and back on the floor where we danced some more.

My feet hurt, but I didn't care for I was enjoying my little self with my best friend. Nothing else seemed to matter at that point in time. Females tried to dance with him, but he declined. Guys tried to dance and push up on me, they got rejected. By not only me, but the look Jamal made at them as well. For the rest of the night, no one else dared to try to come between us.

The music stopped and the lights slowly began to come on. People slowly began to make their exit and on their way out, wanted to take a few more pictures with us and we allowed it. Before we did, Jamal made sure I looked alright and that I wasn't going to be looking crazy in any of these photos. We stayed there for another half hour pleasing the fans before we made our exit towards the car.

When we got to the garage, my car door was opened, I got in and it closed before he got in the driver's side. The car started up and we drove the short distance away to our hotel.

When we got back, I damn near stumbled out of the car but good thing he was there and caught me.

"Come on Babe, what the hell are you doing?"

"I'm sorry Mal. I drank too much."

"Pull it together for ten minutes until we get back to the room." he said, holding me up. "Cadence!"

I straightened up at the sound of his stern voice and we walked back to the room without incident. I face planted on the bed and he laughed hysterically before taking my shoes off.

"Do you wanna take a shower? You feel sticky."

"I'm scared I'm gonna buss my ass if I go in there."

"I won't let you fall. Come on." he said, tapping my leg.

I slowly rolled over and got to my feet before being assisted into the bathroom where I got undressed. The water was turned on for me as I stood there naked covering myself up. He started taking his clothes off too.

"What are you doing?" I slurred.

"I'm taking a shower with you. Don't try nothing." He continued undressing and my eyes danced over him as sexual thoughts came into my mind.

"I can't make any promises." I uttered.

He laughed before taking his last article of clothing off leaving him in the nude just like me. My eyes grew wide as I stared at what he was working with.

"Aye, keep your eyes to yourself." he remarked before turning me around and helping me in the shower. My wandering hands though. "What are you doing?"

"You didn't say anything about keeping my hands to myself."

He laughed, "I can't with you. Eyes and hands to yourself."

The water touched my skin giving me instant relief from the sweat that had accumulated on it. A washcloth was lathered with soap before it was gently applied to my skin at Jamal's hands. Gently, he washed my body from head to toe ensuring that my entire body was clean before he rinsed me off.

I grabbed his washcloth when he was under the water and lathered it before I started washing his back. He flinched a bit at the unexpected touch and turned around and stared at me with gentle eyes.

He smiled. "You still got soap on you Babe." His hand came up and wiped the suds off my face before he allowed me to continue washing him.

My balance was shit and he laughed slightly at my clumsiness, but it was enough to get the job done. He rinsed off before pulling me under the water with him and wrapping me up in a hug.

"I hope you remember this in the morning." he whispered in my ear before he kissed it.

"You can always remind me of it again." I whispered back.

My head rested on his chest for a while as we embraced each other as the water and the energy flowed between us. I really did hope I remembered this moment for it was a beautiful one.

"Come on, let's get you in the bed."

The shower went off and he stepped out before lifting me out and wrapping a towel around my body before his. The towel he had was wrapped around his waist while he dried me off and wrapped me back up until he could dry off. Once he was done, we headed back into the room where I headed for my bed.

"Are you going to put some clothes on?"

I shook my head before laying on top of the covers. Soon, I felt his hands working to put me under the covers before he sat down next to me. Of course I wanted him to snuggle up with me at least but I already knew the answer to that. Especially now that I was naked. That would be a hard no. And that hard no was contingent upon me making it official between the both of us.

I twisted and turned trying to get comfortable. Eventually, I rolled over and looked up at him who was on the phone.

"What are you doing?"

"Looking at the tagged pictures of us from tonight."

"Let me see?"

The phone was placed in my hand, and I scrolled through. There were so many of them it took me by surprise. In almost every shot, the both of us looked so happy and… I handed the phone back before turning my back to him.

"What's wrong?"

"Just looking at the pictures we took. The way that we look at each other scares me."

"It scares you? Why?"

"It looks like we're in love."

"You think so?"

"Yea."

"Maybe we are and just can't see it yet. Why does that scare you though?" I didn't respond. "Cay."

"Cuz when I'm in love, I love hard and I don't want to get hurt."

"Is that why you won't commit to me? You're afraid I'm going to hurt you?"

"Yes."

"I'm not gonna hurt you."

"You promise?"

"I promise."

"So you're my man now?"

"Yes."

"All mine?" My voice began to trail off.

He chuckled. "I'm all yours. Now get some rest ok?"

"K." I simply said, and I was gone for the night.

All Mine

The next day, it was back to business again. For him at least. Me on the other hand was suffering from a terrible hangover. I woke up late to being naked in the bed and alone in the room. There was a bag from a bagel shop on the dresser and a message from Jamal on my phone saying he went to the meeting.

I rubbed my head trying to remember what happened last night. As I scanned through my blurred memories, slowly, some of it came to me. Did we take a shower together? The thought of that lit up my heart for I think it was a great moment we shared together. I don't know why he let me drink that much and why I allowed myself to do it as well.

My lounge clothes were put on before I lounged around in the room for a while trying to recover. My feet were still sore so they were propped up with pillows as I scrolled through my social media timelines eating a bagel. So many pictures and videos. Hundreds of thousands of likes and comments and most of them were positive. Looked like we had a great time last night and were received warmly by the fans. Were they his fans? My fans? Or both?

I went to Jamal's page to see what he had posted lately. Most of the pictures were of us and most of them, I had seen on my feed for I was tagged in them. There was one video, however, that was posted this morning that I hadn't seen before. It was a collaboration of our trip at Seaside, and it was paired with a new fast paced, yet mellow beat. As I watched, it melted my heart. At first the pictures of us together started slowly, then increased in speed. At the end there was text saying, "Untouchable, Unstoppable, Unbreakable" with a heart attached and yesterday's date.

Under the post, there were mixed reviews about it ranging from resentment and jealousy to kind words to our happiness to people asking who the artist of the song was. As I sat there with the video on repeat, the room door opened, and he came in. Immediately, I sprang to my feet and grabbed him up in a hug.

"Good morning to you too."

"I saw the post. It's beautiful."

"I'm glad you like it! How did you sleep my sleepy head?"

"I slept well, I just have a hangover. How was the meeting?"

"Good, good, they're excited to work with me. I have a quick run through at one, then at six I have to go down again to help set up and get ready. Then tomorrow, I have to be at the Tropicana to do the same thing basically."

"Are you ready? Are you excited?"

"I'm hyped up. I can't wait. Also, a Philly artist reached out to me on my way back and wanted to know if we could do a collab. You familiar with Young Kam?"

"Oh yea, I've heard some of his music before. He's on the radio right?"

"Yea, yea. I'm going to be meeting up with him on Monday."

"Have you ever done a collab before?"

"This will be my first, so it's going to be something new. Did you eat? I left some bagels for you."

"Yea, I saw them, thank you."

"You remember anything from last night?"

"A little here and there. Did we take a shower together last night?"

He chuckled. "Yea, we did. Do you remember what happened?"

"We shared a nice little moment together right?"

"Wow, you actually remembered? You remember what else happened last night after the shower?"

"I remember laying in the covers. And talking to you... I was talking about not being hurt? And you said you wouldn't... And... you said you're all mine."

He smiled. "Yup. And you're all mine. Officially."

"I need to stop drinking so much."

"Yea, you do. It's partially my fault cuz I keep buying them for you and asking if you want more. I ain't doing that shit no more. You get a three-drink limit... make that two. And you're capped. At least while we're out."

I nodded my head as I looked at the time. "What do you wanna do? You wanna relax? Walk around? Go to the beach?"

"We can walk around if you're up to it. I wanted to check out another hotel that's close by. They have a deck that overlooks the ocean."

"But we can see the ocean from here." I said pointing.

"I know we can, but that's not the point. It's not that far."

"I'll go with you. Let me throw something on."

"What's wrong with what you have?"

"This is alright?"

"Yea, you look cute just like that."

"It's just leggings and a shirt."

"And you look fine. Come on, we're running out of time."

He took my hand in his and we headed to the garage and got in the car headed towards the other casino. When we got there and up to the deck, the view was absolutely stunning. Much better than what we could see from the room. The smell of the ocean hit me and took me to a place of serenity. I could have stayed up there all day.

A few selfies of us together were taken and some just us alone before we headed down to see what the rest of the casino had to offer. Some shops and restaurants. But the main thing I wanted to do was go to the spa.

"Please will you come with me?"

"I can't. I won't have time. We can go after the meeting. Or you can go by yourself."

"No. I wanna do it with you."

He laughed. "Why?"

"I wanna experience it with you. That's why. If that's alright with you."

He threw his hands up. "Whatever floats your boat Cay."

"I wanna float your boat Jay." I flirted.

"Oh no worries. I gotchyu."

We walked around some more taking in all the scenic views and then stopped to grab a bite to eat. We couldn't stay too long because he had to go to the run through, so we had to head back. He walked me up to the room, gave me a hug and a kiss before heading back downstairs.

That was enough walking for me. I stayed in the room working on his accounts and shirt designs and trying to figure out how to get a social media feed on the website. Finally, I found an app that did that and linked it to my business account. The pictures popped up and there were new pictures that Cay City was tagged in from people wearing and loving my designs. I was absolutely thrilled about it.

My order status was checked as well, and I had over two-thousand shirt sales. The room door opened and in he came.

"Please don't tell me you stayed in here all that time."

"I was working."

"On?"

"Your accounts and the website. I made a few designs and put them up. I even linked my social media on the site."

"Oh shit, you did that by yourself?"

"You say it like it was impossible for me to do. It was easy though."

"Let me see your new designs."

I pulled up the screen and showed him. "They look nice!"

"Thank you. So how was the run through?"

"It was good. They just showed me where I was going to be standing and where the crowd was going to be and what not." He yawned. "I think it's gonna go well."

"I know it is. Are you tired?"

"Yea I am. I was up extra early this morning."

"Why?"

"Just excited about the day. I might have to take a nap."

"Go ahead and get some rest. What time do you have to be up?"

"Wake me up at five-fifteen."

"Ok."

"What are you going to do?"

"Same thing I'm doing now."

"Alright."

He stretched out across the bed that I was sitting on which took me by surprise. I half expected him to lay in his own bed, but he didn't. I rubbed his back and soon he was out cold. I continued on with adding pictures to my site and updating the homepage with the new designs. Even added some sale items on there for a limited time only and posted that on my social media site.

I glanced over at Jamal who was sleeping so peacefully. My phone came out and I took a picture of his handsome face and posted it to my now twenty-thousand followers. The phone began vibrating instantly from all the comments and likes and then from a call from an unknown number.

"Hello?"

"Cay?" I was not expecting to hear the voice on the other line.

"Khalil?"

"Yea, it's me."

Anger consumed me. "What the hell do you want? Why the fuck are you calling me?"

"I just wanted to apologize for what I did to you."

"I'm not accepting your apology. Are you fucking kidding me? I almost died because of you."

"I wasn't going to kill you…"

"Yea, whatever. Why are you even calling me?"

The commotion caused Jamal to wake up and he took the phone from my hands. "Don't you ever call this fuckin number again bro." He hung up and looked at me. "Why you even answer?"

"I didn't know it was him."

"What did he want?"

"To apologize."

"He can take that apology and shove it up his ass."

He stretched and tried to relax. "I'm sorry I woke you up."

"It's alright. What time is it?"

"Four-forty-five."

"That's not too bad." He sat down next to me and rubbed my back seeing that I was now in a shitty mood. "You alright?"

"Just hearing his voice pisses me off. He was a really good friend, and I still can't believe he did that. We came out here to get away from the bullshit, but there's no escaping it is there?"

"Not at all. We just have to work through it and focus on the positive. Don't think about it too hard. You were enjoying yourself."

I nodded my head. "You feel rested now?"

"I do. I'm ready to get this show on the road! I'm performing in fuckin AC!"

I smiled at his enthusiasm. "Indeed you are. How does it make you feel to know that you'll be performing at Harrah's Pool in only a few hours?" I pretended to be a newscaster and held the 'mic' to his face.

"It feels damn good. Been one of my dreams for a long time."

"Do you think that, after the show, you will give your girlfriend some dick?"

He burst out laughing. "Only if she behaves during the night."

I wrapped my arms around him and kissed his lips slowly before letting him get ready for his performance.

Better

The both of us were dressed and we headed down to The Pool. I sat leisurely by it, taking in the beautiful scenery and watching him help set up. A small rehearsal was done where he made sure the music was right and did a run through of the song. By the time they were done with everything, it was already seven and people were lined up at the door to get in.

The DJ started playing music and I was accompanied by Jamal soon after. We talked a bit about his performance and how he was excited which was nothing new. I loved seeing him happy this way. It made my heart smile to know he was following his passion.

The place filled up quickly with party goers and anxious people that were awaiting the performance. As the night went on, we headed to the bar and got a drink each. This time I paced myself not wanting another recap of what happened last night.

Of course people wanted to stop and take pictures with us. Some females only wanted pictures with him and to my surprise, a few guys only wanted pictures with me. Although he didn't say anything, I could tell it didn't sit too well with him. His eyes were steady on the guys' hands making sure they didn't wander to places they need not be.

When the both of us had had enough, we went to the dance floor and began to dance for a while. Same thing applied. Females wanted to dance with him, guys wanted to dance with me. All of them were denied. While the guys had no problem with it and had respect, the girls on the other hand-held grudges which I paid no heed to.

Jamal was called to the back, and I made my way to a nice viewing spot almost directly in the front. The DJ announced his name, and the crowd went wild as he came out. Including his biggest fan. Myself.

He performed a total of three songs and at the end, he made an announcement.

"I wanna thank everybody that came out and showed their support. I wouldn't be here without y'all. I wanna give another shout out to my biggest supporter, my girlfriend who pushes me to push myself harder to achieve my dreams. On that note, I wanna dedicate this next song to her."

My face flushed as the music played. It was a fast-paced song that was similar to the ones he just performed, but the lyrics were different. Now that I listened to it, it was the song from his post from this morning.

The crowd went wild as he performed with the exception of a few females, of course, who stared at me with hatred in their eyes. But my focus was on him, and every so often, he would rap the lyrics directly to me before acknowledging the rest of the crowd.

The song ended all too soon and he closed out his performance. "Thank you for having me tonight. Y'all know where to find me."

As he exited the stage, I felt a strong pull on my hair causing me to fall on my back. Chaos and screams came from all around me as a girl attempted to jump on me and punch me in the face. All I could do was kick at her before she followed through. My kicks landed on her chest and face before a few people pulled her away.

I stood to my feet ready for anything and ready to finish what this bitch had started. Another female approached from my side and pulled my hair trying to bring me down, but she got a two piece in her jaw before she was pulled away. Yet another girl tried to attack but I swung. My fists landing on her lip. Someone else from another side tried to get me, but they were pulled away before she could throw a punch.

Someone from the crowd moved me away from the situation and asked if I was alright.

"I'm good, I'm fine." I replied, fixing myself, but not letting my guard down.

Jamal came from out of nowhere and was in attack and protection mode. "What the fuck just happened?"

"Some stupid ass bitches tried to jump me."

He looked me over. "Are you alright? Are you good?"

"I'm fine. Motha fuckas better learn how to fight before they step to me. Bitch. Didn't even land a hit. Come see me one on one outside and square the fuck up." I yelled into the crowd.

Some that were close came to ask if I was alright, but Jamal gently nudged them away, saying I was good and needed space.

My hand was grabbed, and we started walking to the door. I stopped. "Where are we going?"

"Outta here so you can cool off."

"I'm not ready to leave yet. I wanna enjoy the rest of my night. I'm not gonna let some hoes fuck it up."

He shook his head before taking me to the bar for my second drink. "You sure you good?"

"I'm fine Babe. I'm ok." I replied, finally starting to calm down. "I loved your performance by the way!" I said trying to change the subject.

"Thank you. I'm glad you enjoyed it. I wrote the last song this morning."

"This morning? And you performed it that well?"

He laughed. "Yea. I got skills Babe."

"Well I already knew that, but damn. I think you pissed off some of your fans though."

"Like you said, I probably gained a few more." I smiled and gave him a hug.

For the rest of the night, we stayed by the bar. Yea I wanted to dance some more, but Mal didn't want something else to happen. In exchange, he bought me an extra drink. My final drink for the night and it was just under my limit.

Although we didn't dance on the floor, we still danced from where we were. As he sat in his chair, I grinded on him a bit and he seemed to enjoy it. A lot. The more I danced, the harder he got and I just hoped I would get my first taste of him tonight.

The night finally came to an end, and people started leaving. On their way past, they wanted to take more pictures with us and we agreed. We made our way out and to the room where I sat on the bed.

He approached me and helped take my heels off before getting relaxed himself. I ran my shower and got in. Soon after, I heard the bathroom door open, and he got in behind me.

I stared at him as he stared at me before I began washing him up with his washcloth. He reciprocated the actions before the both of us got out.

Before I could get some clothes to put on, he led me over to the bed and laid me down. Soft kisses were placed on my lips before they moved down my neck and then to my beasts. Soft whimpers were released from my lips as he sucked on my nipples, down my abs, my thighs and then between them.

His tongue swirled, sending surges of ecstasy through my body. A tight grip was around my waist to hold me still and keep me from running away. Before I came, he stopped and wiped his face from my juice he caused to be released.

"Damn Babe. You get mad wet."

"Damn yourself, you feel mad good."

His weight came on me as he began to kiss me softly. Both our hands wandered, exploring each other for the first time in new ways.

"Can I have you now?" I whispered in his ear.

"Yes Love, you can have me. Are you ready?"

"I've been ready. I'm waiting on you."

Our lips touched and the pressure came as he slowly eased his way inside. My nails dug into his back as my teeth gently bit down on his shoulder.

"Fuck. You mad tight."

"You're just too big." I moaned.

"That smart ass mouth."

"But you love it." I whispered before I yelled out from the pain. He stopped and pulled back. "What are you doing?"

"I don't want to hurt you."

"You're fine, keep going." I replied.

He came closer to me and the pressure continued. I let out soft whimpers but this time he didn't stop. Finally he was in and I could feel the full experience of him. We slowly rocked and kissed each other as we both pleased one another.

Before long, he pulled out and came. "Wait. No!" I yelled out in frustration because I was about to cum myself.

"My bad. It's been a minute. Give me a sec. I'll finish you off."

A kiss was placed on my forehead before he got up and disappeared in the bathroom. I laid there yearning for more and before long, he came back and gave it to me.

His strokes were long and intense. My body was in shock at how good he made her feel. Not only with his dick but with his fingers that played with my clit as he stroked.

Our bodies intertwined as they became one. We rocked simultaneously and I felt myself cum.

He smirked and slowed down before kissing my shoulder. "Did you just cum?"

"Yea. I just came all on that dick." I remarked.

"You like this dick huh?"

"I love it."

"Want me to keep going?" he asked as he began to stroke again.

"Yes." I moaned.

"I can't hear you."

"Yes." I moaned louder. "Keep going."

"You gonna cum on me again?"

"As long as you keep fuckin me like this."

I bit his shoulder again and dug my nails in his skin and he went deeper. Harder. My spot was discovered which made me run and my actions only made him want to hit it again.

"Where you going?" he chuckled and stopped.

"It feels too good."

"So you run from the good feeling? Come here." he demanded and moved me to a new position where he began again. This time, I couldn't move and had to take it all and enjoy it.

"Fuck!" I yelled as I came again. He finished shortly after before collapsing on top of me. "Babe, you're too heavy." I said laughing and trying to push him off, but at no prevail.

He smothered me in kisses before shifting his body. "Better?"

"Better. Fuck that was amazing."

"As good as you thought it would be?"

"Better."

He kissed my check and gripped my breast firmly. "You felt amazing too. I was scared I was gonna hurt you."

"But you did the opposite so stop it."

"Ayo."

"Don't ayo me."

"Or else what?" I got up and sat on his lap and glared at him. "What's that supposed to do? Intimidate me?" he laughed and flipped me over before I knew what had happened. "Now what?"

His kisses rained down on me again and I laughed, pushing him away and trying to dodge them. For a minute, he tried to fight my hands away, but he gripped them up and pulled them over my head.

"Now what?" he repeated.

All I could do was look in his eyes, then they wandered down and back up before I but my lip. He smirked before inserting himself again and giving me another long round.

If You Want

The morning came and I woke up so sore and swollen. I had actually woken up before he did and made my way to the bathroom before getting dressed. I sat uncomfortably at the desk and looked through some of our social media pages.

My following had grown another twenty k in the span of one night. Up and down the timelines were videos of the song that was dedicated to me and his performance. It was either that or the fight I had gotten into.

I slammed my computer shut and the sound of it woke him up.

"What's wrong?"

"Nothing, just that the fight is all on social media."

"So? It's not like you got ya ass beat. What are people saying about it?"

"I don't know, I didn't read them."

He laughed and pulled out his phone to see what I was referring to. After some silence, he responded. "They were cheering you on. You worrying about nothing." He rested his head back on the pillow. "Fuck, I gotta get up soon."

"What time is the meeting?"

"Same time."

"At the Tropicana?"

"Yup."

"Will you have time for breakfast?"

"Maybe something quick. Babe, it's already nine fifteen. You asking me questions you already know."

"I wasn't talking about food."

A smile came over his face. "I'll get you later on tonight. I wanna take my time to enjoy that meal."

I blushed and smiled away. "But for real, you have to eat something."

"I'll get something on the way. No worries." he said standing up and kissing my cheek before disappearing into the bathroom.

The shower turned on and I opened my computer back up to do what? I didn't know. Just stared at the login screen for some time trying to figure out something to do.

Jamal came out in nothing but his towel which caused me to redirect my attention his way. Water still dripped down his body as he stood over his bags to get his clothes.

"Are you intentionally trying to tease me?"

He chuckled and turned around. "What? I'm trying to get dressed so I can leave. Ain't nobody worried about you." he joked.

Every nerve in my body told me to go touch and I tried to resist but failed miserably. My hands rolled down his back followed by my lips that kissed his marks I made last night.

He tensed up and tried to ignore the feeling I was giving him before he gave in and turned to face me once more. Our lips connected and the lust flowed causing a chain reaction to our bodies to want to do more.

He pulled back. "Babe, I can't, I gotta go."

I sighed. "I know, I know. I'm sorry." I said, trying to catch my breath. "I'll be ready for you when you get back."

"You fuckin better be."

I backed away slowly even though I didn't want to and sat down uncomfortably in the chair once again.

"What's wrong with you?" he asked, noticing my weird movements.

"You! I'm sore as shit cuz of you."

"Aww. I'm sorry. And don't even try to blame it all on me. You said to keep going."

"I know what I said. Doesn't mean I'm not sore cuz of you."

He shook his head and put on his shirt. "I'm sorry."

"It's ok. Do you know how long you'll be?"

"I'm not sure, but can you do me a favor and not stay in the room all day? Go to the spa, go to the boardwalk or another hotel and walk around."

"I can do that."

"Good." He came up to me and cupped my face in his hands and stared in my eyes for a while before he smiled warmly. "I'll see you later Love." he said, kissing me, grabbing his things and walking out the door.

A sense of sadness rolled over me as I stood there alone in the room once again. Taking his words into consideration, I decided to get out a bit and explore some. A shower was taken, I got dressed and headed to a destination unknown. Maybe the spa would be the perfect starting place.

As I made my way down, a few people recognized me and wanted to take pictures. Two people turned into twenty and I took pictures with them all. It felt weird, I must say, that even without him by my side people still knew who I was and even wanted selfies with me.

In the spa, I was treated warmly and decided to get a full treatment of pampering. Body scrubs, massages and hot stone massages as well. It all ended too soon though, but when I exited, my stomach roared at me.

I found a nice restaurant to sit in and eat and ordered myself a small drink. I finished my delicious food and headed out to the boardwalk to walk around.

The day was hot, and I wanted to swim in the ocean, but there was only one beach I felt comfortable swimming in and that was Seaside.

My phone rang with Jamal on the other line and my heart sang. "Hello?"

"Hey beautiful, what are you up to?"

"Walking on the boardwalk. How is everything going?"

"Everything is going smoothly. I'm hoping to be done soon so I can see your beautiful face."

"Me too. I miss you."

"Aww, you miss me?"

"I actually do."

"Actually? What is that supposed to mean?"

"Uh…"

"I'm just messin with you. I miss you too. I'll call you when I'm done, and we can figure out what to do before the show."

"Alright then. See you soon."

I hung up and kept walking, stopping in any shops I thought I would find interesting things in. A few souvenirs were bought here and there, but nothing too crazy. My feet began to hurt after a while and this heat was kicking my ass, so I decided to make my way back.

In the room, I sat and watched some basic cable. More or less, flipped through the channels and found something that was semi-interesting. Something more interesting, however, walked in through the door.

My face lit up as I ran over to him and practically jumped on him. "Hey!" I simply said after he let me go.

"Hey yourself. I see you're in a good mood."

"Of course, you're here. Everything went well?"

"Yea, everything went well." His voice sounded a bit off.

"Are you alright?"

"I'm just tired." he said, scratching his head. "I'm ready to lay in my own bed."

"I feel you. We only have one more night left and we can head back home. Are you ready?"

"I'm ready. How I'm feeling though, I just wanna perform and come back."

"No partying?"

"Nah. I'm good for a while. You're coming right?"

"Why wouldn't I?" He shrugged his shoulders. "Go take a nap if you're tired. I'll wake you up."

He nodded and agreed before laying down in the bed I was initially sitting on. I sat on the other bed, before I heard him say, "Why are you over there?"

"I didn't want to disturb you."

"Come lay with me. If you want."

I smiled and agreed and made my way to lay next to him. My alarm was set just in case I ended up falling asleep, which I did and we both took a nap, happily in each other's arms.

No alarm went off, but I woke up to soft kisses. Jamal had gotten a phone call from his lawyer about the upcoming court date and he was up after that, but let me sleep. The both of us got dressed and headed to the Tropicana a bit early so he could help set up and do a run through one last before the performance.

It was the same as last night, just in a different environment. Plus, we had partied here a few nights before. I sat in the cut quietly watching him work, making sure the music was just right and knowing where to stand to entertain the crowd. He was definitely in his element with this type of thing and, as usual, it made me happy.

The DJ started playing the music and people started coming in. By my side, Jamal stood and had a drink with me but we didn't do much dancing. Too worn out from the previous nights. Pictures of us were taken along with selfies from fans. Nothing out of the ordinary and I was actually getting used to it.

A few hours into the night, he headed backstage to get ready for his performance leaving me alone in the crowd. I didn't mind it, I just hope we didn't have a repeat from last night. His name was called, and he performed the same four songs as yesterday and the crowd ate it up. Thankfully, there wasn't any hostility towards me tonight, even though a few shady glances were thrown my way.

When he was finished, he came back to my side, we had another drink and made our way back to the room. The both of us were exhausted. We took a shower together, admired each other, and got out. I wanted to do a little more. We both did actually, but in the middle of being affectionate, we both passed out. Me on top of him.

Trust Issues

I woke up the next morning and found myself naked. Still laying on him in the same position I was in when I fell asleep. I couldn't help but to giggle before I started kissing on his chest, making my way up to his lips. Soon enough a smile spread on his face as he felt me showing him affection.

"Good morning gorgeous." he said without opening his eyes.

"Good morning my handsome. Did you sleep well?"

"Slept better than most nights. Had a beautiful goddess laying on me all night."

I blushed and tugged on his beard before resting my head on his chest. "Are you ready to go home?"

"Yea man. I got mad shit to do when I get back."

"You and me both. I'm not looking forward to it."

"Like what? What do you have to do?"

"I have to clean up my house and get the window fixed. I still don't really want to go back and see everything."

"You're welcome to stay with me as long as you need."

"I appreciate it, but I wanna lay in my own bed just like you. Lounge around and relax on my couch and watch tv."

" I'll help you get situated, but my schedule is stacked."

"Doing what?"

"I gotta get ready for this court date coming up. Make sure I get all my papers in order. I have to go into the studio... find a new one first. Make a few music videos, Meet with Young Kam and he wants me to help him with auditions..."

"Auditions? For what?"

"Some music video he has coming up for the song he wants to work on with me."

"Umm... What kind of auditions?"

He sighed. "He emailed me his lyrics and the song is about... getting bitches."

"Getting what now?"

"Yea... So he wanted me to help out and pick some female dancers since I'll be in it."

I tried to keep my calm and not let my jealousy take over. "Ok." I simply said and got up. He completely blew my vibe with that one.

"Babe." he said, trying to grab my hand, but I snatched it away and went into the bathroom slamming the door behind me.

The door swung open, and I was met by his face. "What?"

"Are you mad?"

"I'm not thrilled about it, but I get it."

"Do you not want me to do it?"

"Do what you're gonna do. Just don't do some dumb shit. Can I use the bathroom now?"

The door closed and I was at peace to do what I needed to do. Another quick shower was taken while I was in there and I stepped out in my towel to get dressed. His eyes were on me as I put my clothes on, but neither one of us said anything. As he took his shower, I began to pack my things up to get ready to leave. I really did enjoy myself, but our little baecation was over and it was time to go back to reality.

I sat quietly on my bed scrolling through the channels as he began to get his clothes. Even though I was in a mood, my eyes couldn't help but to stare at him who was in nothing but a towel wrapped around his waist. Several urges came and went to go up and touch, but I didn't act on them.

When he was dressed and packed up, he came close and gave me a kiss on the top of my head. "You ready? It's almost check out time."

"Yea, I'm ready." I went to stand up but was grabbed by my arm.

"Babe."

"Yes?"

"I'm not gonna do it."

"Why not? Do what you feel is necessary for your career."

"I don't want you to be pissed at me."

"I'm not pissed at you. I'm just not thrilled about it, but I have to get over it. That's your career so I'm not gonna tell you not to do it. I'm sure they'll be other times when you have to do it, but like I said, I just hope you don't do anything stupid."

"What does that even mean? 'Anything stupid.' You think I'm gonna fuck one of those hoes?" I gave him a look. "Are you really that insecure?"

"I'm not insecure, I just know how you used to get down."

"Have I not shown you that I just wanna be with you? All the restraint I had, even towards you? That wasn't enough? I'm not gonna hurt you Cay. I know how to keep my dick in my pants. Damn." He stood up angrily, grabbed his things and left the room.

I stood up too and double checked to make sure we had grabbed everything before leaving as well. The only thing was, I had no idea where he went. My only assumption was to the front desk, so that's where I went. But he wasn't there. What the fuck? Where did he go?

"Hi, I wanted to know if room 3617 was checked out of." I asked the woman at the front.

"Yes, it was checked out a few minutes ago."

"Thank you."

I stepped off to the side and sat in a chair in the lobby fumbling with my phone to call him. Before I could dial, I heard him call me.

"Babe."

I looked up and he was walking towards me with flowers and food in his hands. Honestly, I thought it should have been the other way around for how I reacted to what he told me. A smile appeared on my face as I hugged him.

"I don't want you to be upset with me man." he said, handing me the flowers.

"I'm not upset, just scared, but thank you."

He grabbed a few of my bags and we began walking to the garage. "What are you scared of?"

"I told you before, I just don't wanna get hurt."

"And I told you before I'm not gonna hurt you. Why would I want to fuck up something good?"

"It may not be intentional... Simply put, I have trust issues. Ok?" I finally admitted.

"Clearly. But why? Who hurt you?"

We packed our things in the car, and he opened the door for me to get in. Once he was in as well, he looked at me waiting for a response to his question. I looked down and took a deep breath and exhaled slowly, not wanting to relive that moment of my life.

"The last relationship I had, he cheated on me non-stop and for some reason, I kept going back to him. It was always something. Always new messages, new bitches, new excuses. My gut was telling me to leave, but my heart was telling me that he would change. That he would change because he loved me. But he never did."

"How did you get out of it?"

"He got some chick pregnant and left me to be with her."

He rubbed my leg gently. I could feel the tears building up inside so I turned my head so he couldn't see.

"Don't cry. He's a dick to not see what a great and loving person you are. He didn't deserve your love and loyalty. Don't you dare cry over an asshole like that."

"I'm not crying because of him, just the feeling and the pain of not ever being good enough for someone. In almost all of my relationships or whatever you wanna call it, I've been cheated on, lied to and whatever. I stay down and give my all and in the end, I'm shitted on and left for the next chick."

"Not every man you date is going to be like that. I mean, yea I was loose, but that was because I was single. I'm not gonna do that to you Cay."

"I hope not."

The car started and we made our way out of the parking lot and to the road headed home.

Home Sweet Home

The street was quiet as we pulled into his driveway. Nothing like it was when we left. I glanced over at my house that still had a board up to my window and sighed. Jamal was already unpacking the car by the time I came out to help. His things were taken out first, then he helped with mine. But I didn't know where to put them. Didn't know if I was ready to walk back into my house.

"Can you come with me?"

"Oh, that wasn't even a question. I wasn't gonna let you carry all this stuff over there or send you over there alone. Are you ready?"

"Yes and no. I just wanna walk in and have everything be normal."

"It will be like that soon. No worries."

I grabbed the few bags that were left and followed him next door to my house. I took a deep breath as I unlocked the door and stepped in. Immediately, I was hit with the overwhelming feeling I had felt when this chaos in my house was created. Glass was scattered everywhere, and my things were too. There were dry blood stains on my white tiles and of course, there was the broken window and the horrible smell. He walked past me putting my things down.

"Let's get to work."

"You don't have to help me."

He completely ignored my sentence and began picking up the things that had been misplaced. I watched him for a while before joining him. He left my side after a while and the smell of bleach came from the kitchen. I looked over to see what he was doing and found him cleaning the mess off my floor.

Honestly, it made me feel relieved that he was here and was willing to help me. As time went on and things started looking normal, it made me feel better being here. The terrified feelings I had slowly diminished, and I began to look at it as my home again.

A few hours had passed, and everything was cleaned up and put back in its original spots.

"Did you want to stay here, or do you want to come back to my crib?"

"I think I can stay here. I should be alright. I'm about to take a shower and go lay in my bed though."

He smiled. "I'm about to do the same. My bed is calling my name."

"I guess I'll see you later then?"

"You absolutely will. If you need anything I'm right next door or a phone call away."

"Thanks for helping me." I said, giving him a hug.

"You're welcome. I'll see you later Babe." He kissed my forehead and walked out the door closing it behind him.

I looked around at my space and a sense of peace came over me. I would have someone fix my window soon and it will all be back to normal. A few incense and candles were lit before I went around the entire house with sage to cleanse the space of any negative energy that was left. My Himalayan salt lamp was also turned on before I began to unpack my things.

A load of laundry was started before I got in the shower to wash the sweat away from the day. As I was in there, I heard a noise which caused me to turn the shower off to get a better listen. I heard it again and I went to look around. Nothing was there. Was I hearing shit?

I finished drying off and got dressed. Switched the laundry and added another load in and it started. I began laughing to myself when I realized the noise I must have heard was the machine. That helped me relax a bit as I made my way to the living room to watch my tv shows. It felt great to be back and doing what I usually did on the weekends. Being a hermit and staying in the house. I was still getting accustomed to swarming crowds that always wanted pictures. But little did I know, it was just the beginning.

We're Good Now

My bed was so nice and cozy, and I didn't want to get out of it the next morning. Especially not to go to work. But, I had taken enough days off and the bills weren't going to pay themselves. Even though I was making a substantial amount of money with the shirt business and the accounting, I wasn't all too sure on how long it would last. Needed something solid, you know.

There was a message on my phone from Jamal asking if I was up. I guess after getting no response, he figured I wasn't and went ahead and told me good night. I wish I could see his handsome face before I went to work. So, I texted him good morning to see if he was up but got nothing in response. I guess that was my answer too.

I unwillingly got dressed after my shower and headed off to work not knowing what bullshit to expect when I got there. Surprisingly, everyone welcomed me warmly and I got right to work as usual. For a while anyway, until my boss called me into his office. What now?

"Good morning Cadence."

"Good morning, how are you doing today?"

"I'm doing quite well. I see you have been a bit busy lately, being in the news and being all over social media."

"It's been an interesting week."

"Interesting indeed. How are you feeling though? We haven't spoken for some time."

"I've been alright for the most part." Would he just get to the point already?

"That's good. I brought you in here today to say that some of your online activity goes against our policies. The fights and the hardcore partying being displayed nationwide isn't the best look for our company. And, I hate to do this Cadence given the recent circumstances of a family loss, and that you are a great worker but we're going to have to let you go."

I sat there shocked not knowing to be relieved or to be upset. Pissed off or happy that I didn't have to come to this place anymore. "There's nothing I can do to keep my job?"

"Unfortunately no. I tried to get the upper ups to keep you because we need you, but they weren't having it."

"But no one knows where I work. And the fight wasn't even my fault."

"We understand that but we're afraid that the new life you are going down could pose issues in your work. And people in corporate don't want their name tarnished by your actions."

"But I'm only doing what a normal twenty-five-year-old is doing. It's not like they've never went out to clubs and partied or lived their lives. Probably did worse than I have."

"The only difference here is that it is being broadcasted everywhere."

I shook my head and stood up. Without saying a word, I headed to my desk, grabbed a few of my belongings and headed out the door. In my car, I broke down a little bit, but then a smile appeared on my face knowing I didn't have to deal with their bullshit anymore.

I pulled up in my driveway just as Jamal was coming out slinging a bag over his shoulders. "Hey Babe, I thought you had work today. You taking another day off?"

"I got fired."

"What? Why?"

"For partying and being on social media about it." I sighed. "What the fuck ever."

"I'm about to go get breakfast, you wanna come?"

"Sure. I guess. Get in."

He opened the door and sat in the passenger's seat. "Don't be upset, you didn't like that place anyway."

"But my bills did."

He chuckled. "Aren't you making money with the shirts?"

"I am and I have enough to hold me down for months but who knows how long that will last."

"You'll be able to find something else. No worries. Are you open to running the books for other artists?"

"I hadn't thought about that."

"I know a few people that could use your help. Even the guy that does my videos and stuff complains about the shit all the time. I'll give him your number and tell him to reach out."

"I appreciate that. So where are we going for breakfast?"

"Ihop. I have a taste for pancakes."

"Then Pancakes it is." I said pulling out of the driveway. "So what else do you have planned for today?"

"Going to meet Young Kam today to record. I already wrote my part last night. I'm excited to get back into the studio."

"I bet after taking more than a week off."

"He invited you too, but I figured you'd be at work. You wanna come?"

"Are you sure you want me there?"

"Why not?"

"What time?"

"Eleven-thirty."

"Ehh, are y'all holding auditions today or…?"

"Just recording Babe."

"I don't mind going with you. As long as I don't have to sing or anything." I teased.

"Sit there and look cute and enjoy the experience."

"I think I can do that."

We pulled up to the restaurant and when we got seated, we ordered our food. While I was excited to go to the studio with him, I was still a bit nervous as well because that wasn't my territory. But it never hurts to try new things and experience new experiences. Plus, I liked the fact that I could watch the growth and progress of Jamal.

After eating, we headed directly to the studio. This one was bigger than the other one.

"I want something like this." he said quietly in my ear.

"You'll have something better." I replied with a smile as he opened the door for me and we both stepped in.

We were greeted kindly by a woman in the front. "Hi, you must be Cadence and Mally Boy. How are you guys this morning?"

"We're doing good thanks."

"Young Kam is running a little behind, but he's on his way. Please follow me." The woman led us to a conference room down the hall a ways. "There's water and refreshments in the fridge. I know it's a bit early, but there's liquor in there as well and you're welcome to have some. He should be here shortly."

"Thank you." we replied.

When she left, we looked around at the space. "It's nice in here." I said to him, then looked at his face, who seemed a bit down. "What's wrong?"

"Just thinking is all. I want my own studio like this."

"One step at a time Love. You will get there. I have no doubt about that. Look at how far you've gotten now."

"You right. I appreciate it." He stood up and looked in the fridge. "You want some water? There's juice in here too."

"I'll take some water."

The bottle was handed to me, and we sat in silence, anxiousness and nervousness in the room for a half hour before the doors opened and Young Kam and a few other guys walked in.

"Mally Boy! What's up brotha? How's life treating you?" he said, giving dap to Jamal.

"Life is good man. Life is good. How you doing? It's good to meet you."

"I'm good, I'm good. This is Cadence I'm assuming? Lookin all good in the business attire. What's up shawty." he said, shaking my hand.

"Hi, it's nice to meet you."

"This is my boy J-Rock, B-Easy, and Sykes. They help make shit happen in the studio. So what you got for us Mally Boy?"

They all took a seat around the table as Jamal pulled out his laptop and played what he had recorded for his part of the song. Although I liked it, it was a different flow than he usually recorded but everyone else seemed to vibe to it.

"Damn, that shit was hard. I like it. It matches what I have already. You ready to hit the recording studio?"

"Yea, let's do it."

"I have a question." I intervened.

"What's up Shawty?"

"In regards to royalties and rights to the song. How does that go?"

Everyone in the room looked at me like I was crazy. All except Jamal who knew I only had his best interests for him.

"We would own the copyright."

"Even to his part of the song? There's no paperwork he has to sign? You just want him to work for free?"

"It's mainly for exposure…"

"Is that exposure guaranteed?"

Young Kam looked at Jamal. "Where you find shawty at?"

"She's my neighbor."

He looked back at me. "This song is gonna be pushed to get on the radio. Exposure is guaranteed."

"So he won't be compensated for the time in the studio, nor any percentage of the royalties you'll be earning from being on the radio?" I asked sternly.

He sat back in his chair and pointed. "J-Rock, get something in writing for Mally Boy. Twenty percent ownership and royalties from the song and the video." He sat up and looked me square in the eyes. "We good now?"

"We're good now." I said standing my ground.

His eyes shifted over to Jamal. "I like her. While he's getting that together, wanna walk around the studio?"

"That would be great."

We all stood up and took a tour of the building. It was remarkable I must say, but come to find out, he didn't own it. He just recorded in it. But it didn't seem to change the fact that Jamal wanted something like this of his own. I couldn't blame him for it. When the tour was over, we headed back into the conference room and a few papers were in front of Jamal's chair.

He sat down and began to read it and asked a few questions. "What's the two grand price for?"

"Recording time. Onetime fee to use the facilities, use our equipment, produce the video and your portion to help master and promote the song." J-Rock responded.

I grabbed the paper and scanned through it and everything seemed to be alright and exactly what we had agreed upon. It was slid back to him along with a pen.

"Is Shawty your manager?"

"No. She's just smart. She's my accountant though. Does a great job if you need one or know someone who does."

"Oh word? I could use one and know a few people who could too. Write ya number down. We'll be in contact." he said, sliding a pen and notebook over to me where I jotted my information down.

Jamal and Young Kam signed the contract, each got a copy and everything was set in play. The next thing to do was to record the song so we all went to the studio. Young Kam went into the booth first and recorded his part. It took a couple of takes and he sounded nothing like what he sounded like on the radio. Ok, maybe a little bit, but his voice was definitely altered.

Next was Jamal's turn and it only took him a few takes to get his part done. He had the hook, the chorus and a verse. Watching do his thing was worth the world to me at that moment in time. When the song was recorded fully, we headed into the conference room.

"Yo Mally Boy, you did ya thing in there. I like your energy! This shit is gonna be a hit!"

"Thank you, thank you. I like your energy too. Can't wait to see where this goes."

"So look, we gonna be holding the auditions for the video tomorrow. Here's a few pictures of the girls that are coming." A few pictures of half-naked women were laid out on the table in front of us. My throat got tight, but I didn't say a word.

"Yo Cadence, you trynna be a dancer?"

Jamal cut his eyes sharply at Young Kam. "That's not an option for this type of video."

He threw his hands up. "My fault, my fault. I feel you."

Both of our eyes scanned over the pictures in front of us. These ladies were drop dead gorgeous. Even I had to admit that. But this only made me more nervous about him being around them and having them grind up on him and whatever else they had planned for this video. Why couldn't he just do the damn verse and chorus by himself damnit.

"Cadence, you have any thoughts on who we should go with for a preliminary? We need about five."

"Business is what I'm good at. I'll leave the creativity to y'all."

"No doubt. You see anyone you would like Mally Boy?"

"I like these two, but I'd have to see them in person. Check out their dancing skills and make sure it's strictly business."

"All they gonna do is be shakin they ass on you. If you want more than just business, then you can have that too."

"I'm not interested in that. I don't do that shit any more. My girl is sitting right next to me." He sounded a little pissed and offended.

"Wait... y'all are together?"

"Yea."

"My bad bro. Didn't know y'all was a serious thing." He looked at me. "My bad shawty."

"It's all good." I replied.

"Like I said, I have to see 'em in person to check their skills and to be sure they're professional."

"Iight, bet. Just wanted you to see 'em in advance so you could get an idea of what you wanted."

"Thanks bro. What time are the auditions tomorrow?"

"Twelve. It will be here. Cadence is welcome to come too."

All of us stood up and shook hands. "I'll be here then. Thanks for having us."

"No problem at all. Yo Cadence." I turned to look at him. "I'll be hitting you up about the accounting jawn."

"I will be looking forward to hearing from you."

Jamal opened the door for me, and we walked out the room then to the car. We both sat down and looked at each other smiling.

"I'm so hyped about this shit. I think it's gonna be a hit"

"I think so too! Ahh, I'm so excited. You did so good in there!"

"You too. Good look with that shit. I was about to just record and be happy to work with him. My heart raced when you said something, I ain't gon' lie."

"You thought I was gonna fuck it up didn't you?"

"Just didn't know how he was gonna react to it."

"He obviously wanted you there for a reason. He's not gonna get work from you for free."

"Damn Babe. I'm hype right now."

"Let me take your hype ass home."

More Than I Could Chew

We pulled into my driveway, and both got out. He came around and embraced me in a hug after helping me out of the car.

"What you bout to get into for the day?" he asked, looking down at me.

"I have to call around to get this window fixed, then after that, my usual. Just lounge around and watch tv."

"What the hell you be watchin?"

"I watch different shit and binge watch long shows. Is that a problem with you?"

"No. Just wondering."

"What are you getting into?"

"Gotta look around for new studios to get into and start recording new shit. Probably write some songs, record 'em and put them on social media. Market myself a bit."

"Good."

"Did you wanna go to the auditions tomorrow?"

I shook my head. "Nope. You do what you gotta do. I don't want to be a distraction."

"How would you be a distraction?"

"You wouldn't do what needs to be done so as to not upset me."

"That's gonna happen regardless. I would like you to go."

"Why?"

"Be my support. Watch the process."

"Babe. Do what you gotta do. Imma support you even if I'm not there."

"Fine. You want to come over? Or want me to stay?"

"I thought you were going to write and record?"

"I can do that with you around."

"I'll come over. Just let me change and grab my stuff."

"The door will be unlocked. Just come in." he said walking away.

I shook my head and went inside to change. It only took me longer than expected because all of my clothes were still in the baskets from when I washed them. I hated having to dig through the baskets. This would be done asap when I got home. My things were grabbed, and I headed to the door and walked outside. There was a new car parked in his driveway. One that I had seen a few times before.

Slowly, I made my way over and opened the door to find him talking to a female in the living room. More or less, they were arguing.

"Shantice, you need to get the fuck out. I don't even know why you're here."

"Because I saw you with some new bitch on social media. I thought we were building something."

"Where did you get that impression from? I never said I wanted to build something with you. I told you I wasn't looking for anything serious."

"You said that, but now you and that bitch are mighty fuckin close. Why would you want something new when you can have me? We already have chemistry."

"Look at how you comin at me now. You think I wanna wife someone up like you? With the attitude and the bullshit and something negative to always say? Hell nah. You were just a good fuck and I told you that from rip."

"Fuck you Jamal." she said and started hitting him. He didn't hit her back, but I sure as hell was.

"Get the fuck off him." I yelled deckin her in her face.

Her hand came to where my blow landed as she looked up at me from the floor before getting up. "You his new bitch right?"

"Yea, I am. So what the fuck you gonna do?" Usually, I'm not the type of person to fight over a man, but this situation was different. She was attacking him knowing he wouldn't hit her back.

"Babe, chill." he said, putting himself between us.

"Babe? This is your girlfriend now? You wanna be serious with her? Are you fucking kidding me?"

"You saw the posts. Yea she's my girl. You need to leave!"

"You were supposed to be with me. I'm supposed to be the one you're writing songs about, and the one in front of the cameras. Not this ugly, skank ass bitch."

"I could neva wife a hoe like you up. You need to go. Now! Lose my numba and neva come back here."

Her eyes darted past him and were glued on me as her fury began to rise. I stood there waiting for her. What's up bitch, let's rock. She made her move around Jamal and came at me swinging. A few punches landed, but my one blow sent her wailing on the floor holding her face.

Jamal looked at me shocked before he went over to her. "You need to get the fuck out of my house before I call the police."

"Fuck you Jamal. Fuck you." she said in between her cries.

He pushed me away from her as she slowly stood to her feet and staggered to the door. "He's gonna be back. I know he is. He always comes back to me. We've been doing this for three years and you're not the first. Don't call me anymore Jamal when this shit falls through too." she said, slamming the door after leaving.

He tried to give me a hug, but I pushed him back. "What the hell is that supposed to mean?" I yelled angrily. "What the fuck was she even doing here? You called her over?"

"No I ain't call her over here. Why the hell would I call her if I knew you were coming? I blocked her when we had our discussion. Hell, I blocked everybody. I guess she showed up when I never responded."

"So what was the rest of that bullshit? Y'all been talking for three years?"

"More or less fuck buddies…" I held my hand up. I didn't want to hear anymore. I grabbed my things and headed to the door. "Where are you going?"

"Home."

"Why?" he asked, following me out.

"I'm pissed off and just need to calm down before I talk to you."

He continued to follow me in the house. "Talk to me now. Ask me what you wanna know?"

"I need a minute Jamal. Get out."

"Babe."

"Get out. I don't wanna say something ignorant so give me a minute to cool off."

He set his jaw and gave up. "Fine." He walked out the door.

I yelled out in frustration. Was it going to be like this all the time? Me having to literally fight these bitches for him? Yea I knew how to fight, but all that was behind me now, and dealing with him, I've had to fight twice in less than a week. What the FUCK.

Was she going to come back? Would he actually sneak behind my back to be with this chick? What happened if we got into a bad argument? Would he run back to her? So many questions swirling around in my head. I wanted to know the answers but didn't want to at the same time. I plopped down on my couch and a few tears of anger fell. I didn't know what to think and honestly, I think I bit off more than I could chew.

New Client

A few hours had gone by and in that time, all my clothes had been folded and put away, the house was straightened up- not that there was much left to do- and an appointment to have my window fixed was made. I had just sat down when my phone rang with my favorite ringtone.

"Hello?"

"Are you calm now?"

"Yes."

"Can we talk now?"

"Yes."

"Come open the door then."

I looked at my door as the phone disconnected and went and opened it. There he was in all his handsomeness standing right in front of me. As I looked at him with his sad eyes, it seemed as though all my anger left out the door when I opened it. I stepped aside and he came in and sat on the couch putting his book bag down beside him.

"Let's hear it cuz I know you have a shit load of questions."

"I did, but I'm not going to ask them. We both know what we have to lose so I hope choices will be made wisely."

He looked at me sideways. "That's all you have to say?"

"That's all I'm going to say."

"I was expecting a full-blown attack."

"I know you were, and I was gonna give it to you, but I'm not. But you heard what I said."

"I heard you, and I know but… what do you have to lose?"

"You. I don't want to lose you and spending time with you and your affection for me."

"So the money don't mean shit to you?"

"Never has. I had my own money before we met, so no."

"The attention from other people and being on social media?"

"Never was my thing in the first place."

"So you really do like me for me and not what I have or what I can give you?"

"I like you for you. Wouldn't be with you if I didn't."

"Glad we got that settled." He exhaled all the stress out. "So, on another note, I wrote a few songs."

"A few?"

"Three actually. Two hype songs and a slow jam. I didn't put them to a beat yet. Just wrote the lyrics."

"Well let's hear it then." I said before he dug in his bag for his computer. "What are you going to do with the slow jams anyway?"

He smirked but didn't respond. Instead, he showed me his computer screen and pressed play. The second song we had recorded played from his social media account with his logo on a spinning record as the video.

"When did you post this?"

"This morning before I left my house. Look at the views."

"Seventy-five thousand?"

"Not bad for only being up for a few hours. They love it Babe. Love your voice, love the chemistry we have."

"This is the first slow song you posted, right?"

"Yea."

"That means all your fears were for nothing. They love it."

"They really do." It sounded like he was still in disbelief that they would.

"So when are you releasing an album?"

"I was thinking about next year…"

"Next year? Why? Next year is seven months away. You need to jump on it."

He began to laugh. "Ok, ok. I'll jump on it. Maybe I'll throw like a release party or something."

"That's a good idea. Make sure you market it on your social media."

"Oh absolutely, that's a given. I'm thinking of putting slow songs and hype songs on there."

"I think you should. Put the album on your website and people can download it from there."

"But what about physical copies?"

"No one buys physical copies any more, but if you think…"

"Nah, you right. I think at least for now, downloads are the best."

"Is your music on any other platform like Spotify, iTunes…?"

"Not yet, I'm working on that. Someone else brought that to my attention. I gave so much power to that damn manager and he wasn't doin shit."

"When's the court date again?"

"Friday."

"Want me to go?"

"I would love for you to go. Iight, so bet, I'm about to work on putting this album together."

"Need any help?"

"Not yet my Love." he said, kissing my cheek and going right to work.

He put his headphones on so I could listen to my show. My legs rested comfortably on the part of his that wasn't preoccupied by a laptop. The both of us were content.

"Baby, I'm hungry." I whined a few hours later.

"You wanna go out to eat?"

"Not really, I wanna stay in but I didn't go food shopping yet."

"You wanna order something then? I can go pick it up."

"Are you sure?"

"I don't mind. I wanna get a bottle anyway. What do you have a taste for?"

"That Spanish place we ordered from before. I want oxtails."

Without hesitation, he pulled out his phone and placed our orders. He tapped my legs to move them before he stood up. "Imma go now and stop at the liquor store before getting the food. You want rum or Moscato?"

"Both."

"You can't mix those. Eww."

"I want it for later."

"Oh. I'll get your pineapple juice too." He kissed my forehead. "I'll be right back."

"Drive safe." I yelled before the door closed.

I pressed play on my show before my phone rang causing me to pause it again. There was an unfamiliar number on the caller id.

"Hello?"

"Hey, can I speak to Cadence?"

"This is her."

"What's up Shawty, it's Young Kam."

"Hey, how are you doing?"

"I'm good, I'm good. I was calling to find out more about your accounting jawn. What do you do? What do you offer?"

"I do bookkeeping. Essentially, I'll set up your accounts and connect your banking information to your accounts. And if you would like, I will make sure your bills are paid and that your invoices are received and applied to the correct accounts and reconcile them monthly. Make sure everything is ready for your taxes when you go to file. I also can file your taxes and get the best deductions for you and your business."

"Damn. I don't know much about that shit. You could help me budget too?"

"Yes. I can do that as well."

"I'm glad you came along cuz I keep getting hit with late fees and shit cuz I keep forgetting to pay the bills on time."

"There's no need to worry about that anymore. If you want, I can write up an estimate for you."

"Yea, yea, that would be great. Much appreciated. Any other service you offer?" he said with a different meaning behind it.

"Strictly accounting sir." I replied coldly.

He chuckled. "Iight Shawty. I'll send you my email. Is it alright if I pass your number to mah boy? I know he's slackin on it as well."

"Absolutely. Thank you. I'll have the estimate over to you by the morning."

"No doubt, good look."

"Have a good night."

"You as well Shawty."

Soon after we hung up, he sent his email over to me. My heart skipped about in my chest as I went to get my computer and write up this estimate. Could I really be getting a new client? Holy shit!

As I worked, Jamal came in the door with our food and drinks. He looked at my beaming face and smiled. "What has you in a good mood?"

"Young Kam just called asking about keeping his books. He wants an estimate."

"That's what you're working on now?"

"Yes! He said he knew someone else that could use my services too. He's gonna give them my number." I walked over to him and gave him a hug before taking a few of the bags out of his hands.

"That's good Babe. I hope he accepts your proposal."

"Me too. Fingers crossed right?"

"Fingers are crossed."

"Oh my God, this food smells amazing. You want me to pay you back?" He gave me a look before the words fully left my mouth. "Or not."

"I told you I gotchyu Babe." he said picking me up in a hug. "I got you with something else if you want it." He bit my neck.

"Ooo. You know I want that." I flirted.

"Make sure you clear your schedule for tomorrow cuz Imma wear that thang out. Put you right to sleep with a big ol smile ."

"Alladat though?"

"Alladat and then some."

"Damn Baby." I giggled rubbing my nose against his. "Alright, but for now, I'm hungry, so let's eat."

Everything was so good as we ate. I even had a bit of his food which was curry goat that I had never tried and fell in love with. He had some of mine and afterwards, we poured our drinks and went right back to work. I loved doing this with him and I wouldn't trade the time we spent together for nothing in the world.

His headphones came off and I looked up from my computer. "Wanna hear the lineup?"

"Yea, let's see what you came up with."

Only a few seconds of the songs were played so I could get the feel of what the album would sound like. I bobbed my head to each and every note that played.

"I like it! It all flows together so well!"

"Forreal. Got the slow jams that lead into the fast songs… I think it's gonna be good."

"I think so too. Can't wait to blast it in the car. People gonna be like 'who dat?' and Imma be like, 'my boyfriend Mally Boy'."

"You silly Babe." he said and the look in his eyes changed. They got lower as he looked me up and down and bit his lip.

I couldn't resist. I moved closer so he could taste my lips. Before we knew it, we were stripped down naked, making love on the couch, then the floor and finally the bed before we both passed out.

Do You Mean That

I woke up to the sound of my alarm and quickly turned it off. Jamal was still passed out lying next to me and I was definitely sore again from the passionate and intense session we had last night. Soft and loving kisses were placed on his cheek before my fingers ran through his beard as I watched him sleep. He looked so peaceful as I took a picture of him and saved it as my wallpaper. I couldn't resist myself.

To pass the time, I scrolled through our social media accounts to see what was being said about our content. Most of it was positive, but for some reason, only the negative ones stood out to me. Jealousy and negative words about our pictures, videos and his songs. If they didn't like the shit, why the hell were they following us and why not just keep scrolling? I never understood that shit.

I laid there for a few more minutes before going to the bathroom and heading into the living room. His phone was placed on the charger before I sat down and relaxed on the couch. A close eye was kept on the time because I knew he had to get up for the auditions today. I wanted to make him some breakfast, but I still needed to go grocery shopping. I guess that would be on my list of things to do today. So instead of cooking, I ordered us something. My treat. I just hoped he liked it.

His deep voice came from behind me as I got off the phone from ordering the food. "Good morning Babe." he said in a groggy voice.

I turned around and saw him in nothing but his boxer briefs. I swear if I wasn't feeling how I was feeling, I would have attacked him and started something else up.

"Good morning my handsome."

"How long you been up?" he asked, sitting next to me.

"About an hour, maybe more. I ordered us something to eat. I hope you like omelets."

"What kind?"

"One with some vegetables. Onions, peppers, and tomatoes."

"That sounds good. Need me to pay for it?"

"I got it, it's fine. You sleep good?"

"Hell yea I did. How you feeling this morning?"

"Sore again."

"I'm sorry Babe."

"Tuh, don't be. Shit was amazing."

"Is it gonna be like that every time?"

"I don't think so? I don't know. I've never been with someone with a dick that big."

He started laughing. "My shit ain't that big."

"Keep telling yourself that. It's long, and hefty. Mmm."

"Oh stop it. It's average."

"Ain't nothing average about that monster."

"Oh my God." He laughed again.

"Anyway. You ready for the day?"

"Yes and no. Excited for the opportunity, not so much the events leading up to it? Any other time I'd be like, yea, bring the bitches, but now, not at all. It's played out. I found my person."

"Aww. You trynna butter me up?"

"I'm dead ass." He sat back in his seat and twirled my hair in his fingers. "You sure you don't wanna go?"

"I'm sure. You'll be fine."

"What are you gonna do when I'm gone?"

"Create some promos for the shirt. Finalize and send the estimate over to Young Kam. Recuperate." I teased.

He chuckled once more. "You think you'll be good by tonight? Cuz I want more?"

"You so greedy. I should be fine so you can do whatever you want to me."

"Mmm. Don't say that. I love it when you talk dirty to me."

"I'll talk dirty to you all. Day. Long."

He cleared his throat and adjusted himself. "How long ago did you order the food?"

"Right before you walked in."

"Do I need to get it?"

"Delivery."

"Can you do me a favor if you have time? Can you help me get the papers ready for court?"

"Did you get all the receipts yet?"

"No."

"Why not?"

"Been busy Babe."

"Work on getting that today. I'll work on getting what you were actually paid. And I need a list of all the songs you asked that dick to copyright. Maybe I could just pull it up in the database by his name."

"I'll give you a list just in case. Let me do that now." He stood up and my eyes followed.

"Can you put some damn clothes on? You're turning me on with your sexy ass."

"Sucks for you. I'm comfortable."

I rolled my eyes as he sat down next to me with his computer. Before he could open it, I straddled over him. Since how he wanted to be a tease, I could be one too.

"What are you doing?" I said nothing as I ran my hands down his chest, then came closer and licked his neck. "Why?" he asked, but I didn't stop. "Baby."

"Are you gonna put some clothes on now?"

"No."

I shrugged my shoulders and kept going. My hands ran down his entire body before they grabbed his dick. They fumbled around on the outside of his briefs before going inside to get a real feel. I pulled it out and got lower until my lips touched him. My tongue swirled around his head before I fully engulfed his hard dick in my mouth. The only thing he could do was rest his head back and enjoy the feelings of pleasure.

"Iight yo chill. Chill before I take you down."

"Take it, it's yours." I teased and kept sucking.

"Fuck, I'm about to cum." he said before I felt his warm juice explode in my mouth. I swallowed and kept going. "Babe, stop." he whined and tried to run, but my lips followed. "Oh mah God."

I kissed up his abs softly and each time a kiss landed, he flinched and quivered. "You want more?" I whispered in his ear as I straddled him again.

"I don't know what the fuck you did, but I don't want more of that. That felt too damn good."

"Oh, so now you know how I feel when I say it." I giggled.

"Give me a kiss woman and go away."

I did as he asked and got up. "Wait, you swallowed my shit?"

"Every drop."

"Ooo, you nasty."

"Only for you."

There was a knock at the door, and I opened it. Our food was handed to me, and I closed the door before putting everything on the table.

"Are you gonna come and eat?"

"Yea, just... Give me a minute. I need to regroup."

I giggled and began taking the food out. I was soon joined by him, and we sat and ate quietly. Every so often, we would exchange flirtatious glances at each other, then shy away.

"I don't know what it is about you that makes me feel like a kid with a crush. You're just so sweet and adorable."

"I try. I feel the same. I get all giddy inside."

"You truly are like my best friend, and I love you for that."

"I love you too." I paused as the words left my mouth.

He looked at me stunned before he spoke. "Do you mean that?"

I quickly stood up from the table and walked away but he was on me before I could get too far. He gently forced my head up to look at him. We stared at each other for a while before he quietly and gently said, "I love you too Cadence." and kissed me.

No other words needed to be spoken and we left it as is for the time being. The dining room was cleaned up and he looked at the time sadly before putting his clothes on that were scattered in the living room. "I gotta head out. I gotta go get ready. You still not coming?"

I shook my head. "I'm only one call away."

His forehead came to mine and inhaled before he placed a kiss on it. "I'll see you later then Love."

"I'll see you later."

I was still in shock at myself for what I had said to him. Was it just because I was caught up in the moment or did I really mean it? Did he mean what he said back?

No Need to Guess

The time passed quickly, and I did what was asked of me. Of course the proposal was sent over and I had pulled up everything I thought Jamal would need for his case. Afterwards, I decided to create a few promos to post on my business page. The one I did before was alright, but I felt it definitely could be better and generate more leads.

My phone lit up and my favorite ringtone played.

"Hi Baby!" I said with much excitement in my voice."

"Hey Babe, just checkin in to see how you're doing."

"I'm doing alright. How's the auditions?"

"It's uhh… interesting. I'll tell you more when I get back."

"Interesting? Interesting how?"

"We'll talk. I'm about to head over and see if I can get the rest of the receipts. It may take a while cuz I performed at a few different spots."

"Did you eat yet?"

"I'll get something on the way. I want dessert when I get to you."

"I think that can be arranged. I'll see you when you get back? I guess?"

"No need to guess. I'll see you when I get there. Later."

Ugg. This feeling in my heart. This wonderful feeling, I didn't want to let it go. I had been here before on false pretenses. I just hope it wasn't going to be the same as before. I absolutely loved this feeling. This high. And I never wanted to come down from it. And it seemed I wasn't the only one feeling it this time.

As I sat there in bliss, I got a call from an unknown number, and I answered it. "Hello?"

"Hey, is this Cadence?" the woman on the other line asked.

"This is her."

"Hi, this is Camila, I believe we met yesterday at the studio."

"Yes, I remember, how are you?"

"I'm doing well. Young Kam wanted to set up a meeting to sign the contract. He wants you to be his accountant. When will you be available tomorrow?"

My heart skipped two beats y'all, I swear. "How does ten sound?"

"Ten works. I will see you then."

"Thank you!"

I was even higher than a few minutes ago and dialed Jamal up right away. Unfortunately, he didn't answer. Didn't even call back for another hour and a half. The worst began to sink in my mind.

"Hello?"

"Hey Babe."

"What's up?"

"What's up yourself?"

"On my way to the last club I performed at. The last guy wanted to talk my head off, but I got him to host the release party. So the location is set for that. How's your day? You seem frustrated, you good?"

"I'm doing alright." I said changing my tone. "I have some news for you."

"What's up?"

"I'm going to meet with Young Kam tomorrow to discuss the terms of a contract."

"For what? Music?"

"What? No. To be his accountant."

"Oh shit, my bad. That's good. I'm glad to hear that. He was talking about it with me today. I gave you some good reviews."

"Aww, thank you! But I won't hold you up and I have to work on a final contract."

He chuckled. "Ok my Love. You want me to bring anything while I'm out?"

"Some food! I don't care what it is."

"Iight, I gotchyu. See you soon. Oh, and check the stats of the song." he said and hung up.

One million views is what I saw when I pulled up our song. One million. My head began spinning before I had to sit down and catch my breath. This was unreal and unbelievable. I scrolled through the comments and a lot of people were trying to guess who the female singer was. Most guesses were me, but then others were for other artists. Big name artists. Did my voice really compared to theirs?

After a while, I had to put the phone down. It was all too overwhelming. I started working on the new contract and had to leave spaces to be filled in by hand for I didn't know the full details of what I was getting myself into. I was still excited, nonetheless.

There was a soft knock at the door and the person standing there looked exhausted, tired and was holding a few bags of food. I grabbed a few bags and we put them in the kitchen.

"Gees, are you ok?"

"I'm fine, just had a long ass day. How are you? Did you look at the song?"

"Yea, I did! I'm still in shock." He plopped down in the chair and sank down. "What's wrong?"

"Nothing. I'm just tired."

"Did you get all the payment documents?"

"Yea. I got em. I gotta send them to the lawyer."

"What did you get? Want me to make your plate?"

"Please."

"So how were the auditions?"

"They were alright. Most of them were thotties and thought too highly of themselves. It was frustrating as hell. They are the type of bitches that wanna sleep around to get up in the world. I'm glad you ain't go. There would have been some fights."

"Why do you say that?"

"Cuz man. They were doing the most during the auditions. All they were supposed to fuckin do was dance and grind a lil bit so we could see… ya mean, what it would look like. These bitches wanna grab dick, try n get my number. The fuckin most. Young Kam, I know he bagged about three of 'em. If not more. Shit is sickening. I got fuckin molested the entire time."

"Did you pick anyone?"

"I picked one chick. The most professional one. I guess if you wanna call it that. In all honesty, I'd prefer to do my part on my own. Or with you, but I don't want you to be a part of this song. It's all about sex and hoes and money and stuff."

"Your part isn't. You talk about coming from nowhere and being something greater."

"I know. It's a great opportunity though, but this ain't really my style."

"Well, follow through with it and next time, you know what you will or won't do."

"You right, Baby. Come here. I missed you." he said, pulling me by the hand and sitting me in his lap. His arms wrapped around me for a bear hug.

"I missed you too. But come on and eat. I already made your plate. You got my favorite too."

"Iight, come on then."

"So when are you thinking of having the release party?" I asked setting his plate down in front of him before sitting down in front of mine and eating as we talked.

"I scheduled it for Friday."

"Wait, this Friday? Coming up?"

"Yea, why not? I don't have any gigs scheduled this weekend and next weekend, we'll be shooting the video."

"Where's it at?"

"Club Secret. It was the first place I performed at when I came up here. The place is always poppin. The owner is mad cool too."

"Will that be enough time to advertise?"

"Plenty. My following is going through the roof now."

"Yea, I saw." I said taking another bite.

"You stalkin my page Babe?"

"Not stalking per say. Just checkin for new material. I am a fan too you know and sometimes you leave little surprises up there."

"You like my little surprises?"

"Very much so. Who knows, you might find some on my page."

"Is that so? I'll keep looking in anticipation."

"Wait, you look on my page too?"

"Absolutely. I love scrolling down and looking at all your pictures and the videos of us. Always cheers me up."

I blushed. "Aww, I didn't know that."

"Well now you do." He stood up and stretched. "You need help cleaning up? I'm about to head home."

"You're not staying over?"

"Not tonight. I need to stretch out across the bed."

"Fine. No, I got it. Go ahead and get some rest. I'll see you tomorrow. And thanks for dinner."

"Any time Baby." He gave me one last kiss before heading out the door. "I still want that desert." he yelled back.

"It will be here when you're ready."

The house was cleaned up, food put away, shower taken and in the bed I laid. I had a big day tomorrow and I was excited to see how it would turn out. Hopefully for the better.

I'll Be in Touch

My alarm went off again because I had forgotten to turn the damn thing off. It was no longer needed. At least not after today. As I laid there trying to fully wake up, I turned my phone on and was greeted by text.

"Good morning gorgeous"

"Good morning my handsome"

"Are you ready for the day?"

"Absolutely. A bit nervous tho"

"No need to be. I have something that might cheer you up"

"And what might that be?"

I got no response back. I half expected to hear a knock at my door but got nothing back in return. Err.

I scrolled through our social media pages and found what he was referring to. An entire song dedicated to me. As I listened, I damn near cried at how beautiful it was. And it was all for me? It already had over one-hundred thousand views and it was still rising. I called him quick, fast and in a hurry after I listened to the song at least five times.

"Babe?"

"Hey. Wait, why are you crying?"

"The song was so beautiful. Thank you."

"It wasn't supposed to make you cry though."

"It's happy tears, I promise. It has so many views, so many people like it."

"I know… Babe, stop crying."

"I'm sorry. I just really appreciate it. It really does mean a lot."

"You're welcome my Love. Now go get cleaned up, I know you look like a hot mess."

"Eww, stay on your side of the phone." He chuckled. "Fine, fine. Did you want me to come with you today?"

"No, it's alright. I can go by myself."

"You sure?"

"I'm sure."

"Let me know how it goes then. I want all the details."

"I'll be sure to tell you everything. Are you going back to sleep?"

"Maybe. I was up damn near all night making that song. I thought it would make you smile, not bring you to tears."

"Well, it managed to do both." I teased. "But go back to sleep. I'll talk to you later."

"Talk to you later."

I laid in bed for another twenty minutes listening to the song before getting up and starting my day. The contract was printed, and I was dressed in my business attire and ready to go. My nerves wouldn't allow me to eat anything, so my stomach roared at me the entire way there.

I arrived fifteen minutes early, sat in the car for about five and had to wait in the conference room for another ten. As I waited, I fidgeted about but when the door opened and he came in, it was a different level of confidence that showed through. I stood up and shook his hand.

"Good morning."

"Good morning Miss Cadence. Lookin nice today. Where's your other half?"

"You just get me today."

"Shiiit, I'll take that any day. You know Mally Boy talks about you a lot. He must really be feelin you."

"He does?"

"Yea, he does and his face lights up when he does. What you doin to ol' boy?"

I laughed slightly. "Nothing. Our energy just matches well. He's my best friend but better."

"Mmm hmm. Look, your face is lighting up too. It's cute though, I can dig it. So what you got for me Baby?" he said sitting across from me.

"I have a few different offers for you that could meet your needs depending on what you need. The first one, I can help set your books up and get them ready and you manage them. The second, I set them up and manage them on a monthly basis making sure they reconcile up to three accounts. The third option, I do everything for you. Invoicing bill payments, budgeting, reconciliation and at the end of the year, you get a large percentage off for tax filing if you choose to file with me. It also includes payroll if you need it."

"Damn Shawty, you ain't no joke. How long you been in accounting?"

"Three years. I graduated with a bachelor's degree double majoring in business and accounting."

He nodded his head. "If I wanted the last one, the works, how much would it be?"

"There is an initial, one-time setup fee starting at seven hundred, then a monthly fee of three fifty which includes up to five bank accounts either personal, business or a mix of both. Each additional account adds another fifty to the total."

"Your prices are kinda low Shawty. You know that?"

"These are discounted prices designed specifically for you."

"Why?"

"Because you're working with Jamal. And I believe once you see my work, I will be referred."

He chuckled. "Damn. I like you man. So what would you need from me in order to set everything up?"

"I would need access to your bank information, receipts, payroll if you have it, assets, liabilities and tax documents."

"What kind of access?"

"View only."

"So how can you help me budget?"

"When I go through your accounts, I can give suggestions on how you can save money and, if I see any, some alternatives to what you use."

He nodded his head and thought for a minute. "Let me see the contract?"

I slid the paper over to let him view the documents and he began to read over it. "We can fill in the blanks when you have decided on what service you would need from me."

"I want the full service." he said, sliding the paper back over to me. "Sign me up Shawty, I'm sold."

A slight smile fell over my face, but it was nowhere near how I truly felt on the inside. The blank spaces were filled in with the numbers I told him, and he signed. My signature was signed afterwards, and copies were made.

The both of us stood up and shook each other's hand. "It's my pleasure doing business with you. I will need the information listed as soon as possible so I can get you up and running."

"No doubt, I'll be in touch Shawty. If all goes well, I'll definitely send my peoples your way."

"I have no doubts that you won't be pleased."

He walked me to the door and opened it for me and I got in my car and drove off. Before I could hit the road, Jamal was on the line.

"Babe! I did it! He signed!"

"Good shit. I'm proud of you."

"Aww, did I wake you up? I'm sorry."

"You're good, you're good. I had to get up anyway. You think you can grab breakfast on your way in?"

"What do you have a taste for?"

"That omelet thing you got before."

"Anything else?"

"That's it."

"Ok. I'll see you in a bit."

"Love you." I looked at the phone in shock before responding.

"I love you too."

On the way home, I stopped and got us breakfast as promised and pulled up into my driveway. I didn't even go into my house, just went straight over to his and knocked on the door.

"What are you knocking for? I'm right here?" his voice said from on the porch causing me to jump back.

"What the fuck Jamal? You scared the shit out of me."

"How you not see me?" he asked, standing up and walking to me.

"I was spaced out. What are you doing out here? How was your morning?" I asked before receiving a kiss.

"It was iight. I'm still tired though. And I wanted fresh air if that's cool with you. I'm working on a few songs." He looked me up and down. "Damn Baby, you look hella good."

I smiled. "Thank you. Now are we going to eat or what? I'm hungry."

"You ain't eat before you left this morning?" The door opened and we walked in.

"No. My nerves wouldn't let me. But I'm hungry now."

The bags in my hands were taken from me and placed on the dining room table. The contents were removed before we sat down and ate. Of course I was asked about all the details of what went on in the meeting and I was too happy to tell him.

Just as I finished, he got a call.

"Yo bro, what's good? Ain't heard from you in a minute." "Nothing, having breakfast with my girl." "Yea, I got a girl now. Her name is Cadence." "Word? You coming down here?" "Iight, bet. We can definitely link up. There's this spot called Fantasy Lounge, you wanna meet there at ten?" "Iight man, see you then."

I stared at him with curious eyes to know who he was talking to. "My friend from high school. He went to college in New York and he's coming down to visit for a week."

"How did you know I was gonna ask you that?"

"It's written all over your non-poker playing face."

"But it's nice that he's coming and wants to meet up with you."

"You feel like going to Fantasy Lounge tonight?"

"I don't mind it. What else do you have to do today? I know earlier you said you had to get up."

"Gotta go talk to my lawyer, make sure everything is straight and give him the receipts."

"What time?"

He looked at his watch. "I got a good hour. But I need some dessert first." I was scooped up and tossed over his shoulder and carried upstairs. He must have enjoyed the desert cuz he devoured it and still, it wasn't enough.

Let's Rock

"Babe, please tell me you're ready."

"I'm ready, I just have to put my shoes on and my jewelry."

"Then you're not ready."

"I'm almost ready. Will you relax? I can move faster if you weren't hovering over me." I said nudging him out my room. "What's the rush anyway?"

"I'm not trynna stand in line."

I looked in the mirror one last time and made some final adjustments. "Ok, I'm ready, let's go. If I'm forgetting something, it's your fault."

I closed my door behind me and walked down the driveway. I was about to walk through the grass when he picked me up and carried me over to his driveway. I absolutely loved the way he catered to me. My door was opened and when I got in, it closed. He went to his side and got in and we drove off as he started complaining again.

"How is you forgetting something my fault? You had plenty of time to get ready."

"Half the day was spent recovering from you."

"We ain't even have sex."

"My legs were still weak."

"You're so full of shit. I swear." He laughed.

"So what's your friend's name?"

"Xavier. I don't know if his wife will be there too or if it's just him."

"You didn't care to ask?"

"It slipped my mind."

As he drove, I grabbed his hand and held it the entire way there. The car was parked, and he let me out before we walked to the entrance of the lounge and stood in line.

"Yo Mally Boy." the guard at the front yelled and waved us over. Phones came out instantly and the screams began.

"What's up bro, how you feelin tonight?" Jamal said, giving the guard dap.

"I'm good, I'm good. How you doin? You trynna get in tonight? You performin?"

"Just meeting up with a good friend and enjoying the night."

"Word, what's their name? I'll make sure they get in."

"Xavier."

"No doubt, let them know to come straight to the front."

"Word, thanks man."

"No problem. Y'all have a good time. Hi Cadence."

"Hi." I said shyly as we walked through and to the entrance.

"I was not expecting that."

"See, you rushed me for no reason." I said, nudging his shoulder from behind.

"Yea, yea, blah."

"Gah, you're so mean." I pouted.

He stopped walking and took my face in his hands. "Aww Babe, did I hurt your feelings?"

"Yes." I whined.

"Well get over it." My jaw dropped and he began laughing before kissing my forehead and leading me to the bar.

My favorite drink was ordered along with his and we people watched from our seats.

"Oh shit, let me text him and let him know to go to the front." He said pulling out his phone.

"It's so quiet in here today." I noted.

"It's still early and it's the weekday. I'm sure it will fill up. Why? You trynna find a man tonight?"

I cupped his chin in my hands. "Nope. I'm happily off the market."

His beautiful white teeth showed when he smiled, and his adorable dimples appeared as he blushed. He leaned forward and I met him in the middle for a kiss. My arms wrapped around his shoulders, and I held him tight for a hug.

"You alright Babe?" he asked, noticing my extra affection.

"Just appreciating you is all. Plus, you smell mad good."

"Wish I could say the same about you." he teased, and my jaw dropped. "I'm just playin Babe, I'm just playin." he laughed, holding me back in his arms.

"Yo Mally Boy, can we get a pic of you two?" a fan yelled.

"Absolutely." The both of us posed and the picture was taken. Along with others from people that realized who we were.

"Cadence, was that you singing?"

"That song was absolutely beautiful."

"It had to be her."

The chatter began. Neither one of us responded, just shrugged our shoulders and smiled to keep them guessing.

"Jamally boy, what's goodie bro." a man said from behind us.

We both turned around and the two men hugged. "What's up Xavi Baby, long time man, long time. This is my girlfriend Cadence."

"Damn my boy. How you doing Cadence, it's nice to meet you." he said, shaking my hand.

"Is your wife coming?"

"Nah, she wasn't feeling too well tonight. We're expecting."

"Oh word? That's what's up."

"Congratulations." I chimed in.

We all took a seat and they started talking. About any and everything. Mainly just catching up. Then about sports and so on and so forth. They talked for at least a good hour and I sat there and stayed in my own lane before ordering myself another drink and another one for him. Even though he was caught up in his conversation, every now and then, he would reach his hand over and grab my leg to make sure I was alright. Eventually, I just held his hand, so he didn't have to worry.

The place started to fill up just like he said it would and I watched the people go from standing on the wall to grinding half drunk on the floor. Is this really what I looked like when I was dancing?

There was one person, however, that caught my attention, and I could feel the anger burning up inside me. It was actually two people that, just by simply seeing their faces made me see red. In my anger and trying to hold myself together, I subconsciously squoze Jamal's hand and he looked over to see what was wrong. His eyes glanced over to where mine were glued.

"Don't worry about it Babe. Let it go."

"I'm trying to." I replied through gritted teeth.

He moved my attention off of what I saw and back to him by turning my face and kissing me passionately. That worked for the time being, but we couldn't stay like this forever. And when he let me go, my focus was back on those two people.

"I'll be right back."

"Babe, don't do nothing crazy please." he said as I hastily made my way to the bathroom to try and cool myself off.

Who knew that of all the places, they would be here at this one. How the fuck did they even get in here? Why on this fuckin day? Oh the fuckin irony of it all. As long as they stayed away and didn't notice me, we would be good. Right?

A few deep breaths were taken trying to allow me to clear my mind and that seemed to work. When I came out of the bathroom, Jamal was standing by the door waiting for me.

"Are you alright?"

"I just had to clear my head and relax. I'm fine. As long as they don't bother me, I'll be cool." I tried to reason with him. And myself.

"Mally Boy! Can you take a few pictures with us?" a group of people asked, which only caused more people and more to come and soon, we were surrounded.

I started getting flustered and I squoze his hand basically asking him to do something. He came to my rescue. "We would be happy to take pictures with you all at a later time, for now, we just need some space."

Although the crowd was a little upset, most of them understood except for two people. One of which was just as pissed to see me as I was to see her.

"I told you bitch, the next time I see you, Imma fuck you up."

"For what though Janelle? You think I'm scared of your stupid ass?"

"Cuz of what you did to Lil."

"Bitch, he fuckin attacked me you mad for what? That he didn't want ya goofy ass and wanted me?"

"Babe."

"Nah, she wanna rock, let's rock but she know she don't want no parts. I used to fight off her bullies. She know she don't wanna square up. Just talkin shit to hear herself talk." I said standing with my hands down, fists balled up.

"Just cuz you got a lil fame now you think you all big and bad Cadence?"

"I been big and bad. And? Ain't nothing changed but the time, so what's up?"

"Janelle, she's our friend. She's been there for us through some shit, we are not about to do this." Charmaine tried to intervene, but her words fell upon deaf ears.

261

"You're a piece of shit Cadence. You nasty hoe. You going around thinkin ya shit don't stink but it does. I know you liked Lil on the low, he told me how you sucked him off one night when you were drunk. You were probably too sloppy drunk to remember the shit."

"Yet you still wanted my sloppy seconds. Just like Byron right? I'm tired of talkin, you gon square the fuck up or what?"

Jamal tried to hold me back as I tried to approach Janelle after she tried to swing on me. "What's up bitch!" she yelled and swung again, missing and hitting Charmaine.

I tried to lunge at her, but Jamal held me back, until a man's voice spoke out. "Janelle, what the hell is going on?"

Jamal let me go and ran up on the man and started yelling. "What's up Bro, you gon try and steal shit from me and think I ain't know it was you? Pussy ass bitch." he yelled, and the man swung trying to push him back. This only pissed Jamal off, and he started wailing on the man.

"Baby!" Janelle yelled then turned to attack me. "You ruin fuckin everything!"

"What's up!" I yelled as she approached and hit her in the ribs and on her way down, hit her in the jaw knocking her down. She dared not get back up as she held her face and looked at me horrified.

"Cadence, why you do that?"

"Whatchu mean? She been threatening me for a minute now. Don't act so innocent, I know you had parts. You wanna run up, you can get some too."

"I'm not fighting you Cay." she said calmly and went to assist Janelle.

My next move was over to Jamal who was fuckin the man up. He easily overpowered me so there wasn't much I could do but yell. "Babe, enough." I hollered. "Enough!" Hearing my voice, he stopped and looked at me. Security came and escorted the both of us out. The only thing we could do was make our way to the car.

"What the fuck Babe? Who the hell was that?"

"Roscoe." he simply replied. "What the fuck to you too. What the hell was that bitch talking about? You gave Khalil head?"

"I never gave him head. He probably just told her that shit boasting."

"I don't know, you do be blackin out."

"Are you serious right now?"

"I'm just sayin."

"I never did that shit."

There was a brief pause before he glanced at me. His eyebrows were furrowed. "Are you alright? Did she hit you?"

"She didn't touch me. I'm fine. Are you?"

"My hand is fucked up, but I'm alright. FUCK!" he yelled and slammed his hands down on the steering wheel.

"What?"

"I hope this shit doesn't affect what I got going on."

"It was self-defense. He swung on you first."

"But what are people gonna say? Especially about you. Y'all aired out some shit."

"The only thing we can do is wait." I grabbed for his hand but he moved it. I thought he was pissed at me and I was about to catch an attitude, but he grabbed mine instead, brought it to his lips and kissed it.

"You're so badass, you know that? 'So what's up?' 'She wanna rock, let's rock'." he mimicked. "I fuckin love it, I'm not gon lie. No fear whatsoever."

"She ain't shit and she knows it. Like, why would you run up on me when you already know how I get down. Fucking dumb ass."

"Iight Babe, chill. You bouta chew my head off. Shit."

His phone rang with Xavier on the other line and he answered the call through his car.

"Yo bro."

"Yo, what the fuck happened? Are y'all iight?"

"Yea, we're good. Sorry about that man. It was some old beef that we both ran into."

"Y'all are fuckin wild. I'm glad y'all are iight though. We'll just have to catch up another time."

"Most definitely."

"One."

"One."

I sank down in my chair. "Ugh, what a fuckin day." I sighed.

"It's almost over and a new one will be here."

"I wonder what shit it will bring us."

When we got back to his house, I helped him clean his cut up, swollen hands. I could only imagine the damage that was done to the other guy's face. I put some ice on it and we sat down on the couch and tried to watch a movie to relax our minds. Well, I got a bit too relaxed and fell asleep on his shoulder.

Soon after, I felt movement and was picked up and carried upstairs to his bed. He undressed me and wrapped me up in the covers before he cuddled up behind me. Hs strong hands played in my hair and I felt soft kisses on my neck, shoulder, cheek and ear. All too soon, it stopped, and he passed out behind me.

Down With The Blues

"Babe." he whispered in my ear. "My gorgeous."

A smile spread across my face as I felt his strong hands caress the side of my face. "Yes Babe?"

"I have to get ready to go, but you can stay here and sleep."

"Where are you going?"

"I have to go meet with the new studio director. He's gonna give me a tour to see if I like it."

"Ok."

"Go back to sleep my Love. I shouldn't be long."

He kissed my forehead then disappeared out of the room. It wasn't until I heard the door close downstairs that I fully woke up. It was like a dream. Like, I could hear him, but I wasn't fully there with him. It was weird. But what was also weird was me laying in his bed without him being here. Being in his house period, while he was gone.

I ran through my usual 'just waking up' routine and scrolled through our social media pages. I was kind of upset that he didn't post anything new today but, just as I thought, up and down my timeline were videos of the fight. There was even a meme that I thought was hilarious circulating of me saying, "She wanna rock, let's rock". There were homemade, put together skits of the two of us fighting our opponents. I found it fucking hilarious. What a way to start my morning. The only thing that would have made it better was some morning sex.

I walked over to gather my things that were neatly folded and placed in a chair on the other side of the room. My dress was thrown over my head and I wandered through the house a bit. Everything was so beautifully decorated, I could never get over that. Much better than my simple decorations that I thought were something special.

I made my way downstairs and out the door headed to my house with my things in my hand, barefoot and all. I was almost there when one of our neighbors came out and giggled before waving at me. I waved back in embarrassment and headed to my house. Only thing was, I didn't have my keys. Must have left them in his car.

At the back of the house, I found my spare key and let myself in that way. I felt so relieved. My things were tossed on my bed before I started my shower and got in. After getting out, I did my usual until the window replacement guy came. As he worked, I retreated back to my room.

Young Kam had sent over everything I needed to start his books, so that's what I was working on until I heard a familiar voice at the door. Or through the open space in my house I should say. Footsteps came towards my closed door before it swung open.

"Why aren't you sleep? You scared me when you weren't at the house."

"Well where else would I be?"

"I don't know. I just didn't know where you were."

"I'm here, I'm safe. Hi. How was your tour?"

"It was alright. Not quite what I'm looking for and they're a bit on the expensive side."

"What ever happened to getting your own equipment for your own studio?"

"I'm still saving up for it. You see my accounts, I'm not there yet."

"You have to buy it all at once? Why not just buy the basics and as you get more money, start getting the rest?"

"That may be an option. I don't know man. I don't know."

"But why do you seem down?"

"I just want shit to be there already. You know? Be making money the way I want to. Have my studio in place. Traveling and performing. I feel like I'm stagnant right now."

"You've come a long way. Don't think of it that way. And it's gonna take time. Enjoy the process now, that way you can look back and be like damn, I came a far ass way."

"Thanks Babe. You always know the right things to say."

"I try."

"I got us breakfast though. Come and eat." he said, tapping my leg. "What are you working on anyway?"

I stood up and followed him to the dining room. Before I said anything, I looked at the lighting in the house and it was so much brighter, just how it used to be. I fuckin loved it and couldn't wait for him to be done installing the window.

"I'm working on Young Kam's books. Getting all the accounts set up for it. He has a lot of different expenses, so it's just taking longer than expected."

"Expenses like what?"

"I can't tell you that my Love. Sorry. It's all confidential."

"Iight, I feel you. I didn't know what you wanted, so I got a few different things."

"You could have called or texted."

"I thought you were sleep. There's bagels, muffins, croissants."

"Thank you Babe. Eating out is something we're gonna have to cut back on so we can get your studio. Also drinking when we're out. That shit is really adding up."

"I'm not the only one getting drinks."

"Hence why I said WE. I'll go food shopping and we can start eating in more."

"Anywhere else I can cut back at?"

"That's the main thing. You cut back on everything already. Mostly what's left are bills."

"Any of those I can get rid of?"

"I have to look again." I said stuffing my face.

He burst out laughing and pinched my cheeks. "My little chipmunk."

"Leave me be. Oh. Have you seen the memes of us?"

"Ha. Yea. I saw them earlier today."

"I fuckin can't. I cracked the hell up when I saw it."

He came closer to me and brushed my hair out of my face. "Babe."

I swallowed hard not knowing what to expect as I looked up into his sad looking eyes. "Yea?" I said quietly.

"I wanna make another song with you."

"What kind of song?"

"A love song."

"Why you look so sad about it?"

"I'm not sad about that. Just thinking of other shit. But I wanna make another song with you and a video to go along with it. I wanna try and get it on the radio or something."

"Did you ever create accounts for other music platforms?"

"I did. They're getting traction."

"Why do you want to make one with me though? There's other qualified and popular singers out there you could collab with."

"The chemistry won't be the same."

"But you'll get their fans as well."

He shushed me. "Please just say yes."

I exhaled and kissed the finger that was on my lips. "Yes. I'll make a song and a video with you."

"Perfect. Cuz I already wrote it. Wanna hear the beat for it?"

I nodded my head and he led me over to the computer and played the music. I instantly fell in love with it. It was so slow and melodic with a nice vibe.

"I love it. What's the song about?"

"Basically falling in love with your best friend. I left a verse open if you wanted to write it."

"I don't know how to write like you do. Or rhyme."

"Then write down how you feel, and I'll write the rest for you. Or you can tell me."

"I'll write it down. I'm not the best at expressing feelings like that."

"Not even to me about me?"

"I'm shy Baby." I bashed away.

"Fine. Let me know when you're finished."

"I will. What else do you have planned today?"

"Look up more studios I guess."

"Aww, don't sound so down about it."

"I can't help it. I have at least ten songs that need to be recorded and no studio. I don't wanna talk about it anymore. I'm jut gonna look the shit up. You want me to stay or what you wanna do?"

"I was in my room cuz of the window. You mind sitting back there?"

"I don't mind."

After grabbing his stuff, he headed to my room with me and sat on a chair and continued with his search. Me on the other hand, I felt terrible and wanted to make him feel better, so I did some research of my own. I tried my best to conceal my smile as I ordered a few things off line that I knew he would absolutely love. I couldn't wait to see his face when I gave it to him.

"I found another spot Imma go check out."

"You want me to come with you?"

He stood up and started gathering his things. "Not today Babe. I might just head home after. I don't want to bring your positive energy down."

"I'm trying to rub my positive energy off to you. But I understand. At least tell me how the studio tour went."

"I will do that. Love you Gorgeous."

"Love you too."

After he left, I continued working on Young Kam's books. When that was finally completed and all set up, I looked to see if there were any other expenses the both of us could cut back on. There were some subscriptions for his business account I thought he could do without, but they weren't anything substantial. I sighed before getting to work on my verse for the song.

This would be my first time writing a verse. I had no idea what I was doing or where I needed to start. As I stared down at the blank piece of paper, nothing in that moment came to mind. But I had an idea. I texted Jamal to see if he could send the music to me as well a his part of the song. In a matter of minutes, I had received an email with both of my requests attached.

Before I could really dive in, the window tech yelled out for me and told me the window was done. He was paid and then he left before I went back to my task.

The music played as I read his beautiful lyrics about me and it absolutely warmed my heart. This feeling that I had now, was exactly what I wanted to describe. But how? I just wrote it all out and that led to a chain reaction of the words just flowing. Before I knew it, I had a whole front and back page of how I felt about him and what he truly meant to me.

I picked up the phone and dialed.

"Hello?"

"Hey, are you home yet?"

"Yea, I'm home. What's up?"

"I finished. Want me to bring it over?"

"Yea, you can. You coming now?" his voice seemed to brighten up.

"Yea, I'll come over now. See you in a few."

I grabbed my notebook and headed next door where he was waiting for me. His face lit up when he saw how excited and happy I was. Not just for the song, but just to see him in general. I handed him the notebook as we stepped inside.

"Well damn. You were only supposed to write a verse."

"I know. I got carried away. But let me know what you think."

His eyes scanned the page, and began to tear up a bit as they did. He looked up at me. "This is how you really feel about me?"

"Yea."

"God you're so sweet. I can write you another song if you want, plus the verse. Would you want to do a song by yourself?"

"I hadn't thought about it."

"I'll write it and you let me know. I already know what it's gonna be and the beat I want to make for it. Damn though. You really feel like that?"

I giggled. "Yes!"

"I wish I could hear that come from your mouth."

"I'm warming up to it. And hey!" I said, nudging him, "You were supposed to tell me how the tour went."

"My bad. It was ok, but it was still expensive. But they master songs so maybe I'll record and have them master it for me."

"What else is going on? Why are you so sad? I don't like seeing you like this." I asked, running my fingers through his beard.

"I know. But I'll snap out of it soon enough."

"Anything I can do to help?"

A slight smile fell on his face before it disappeared again. "No Babe, there's nothing you can do. I appreciate it though."

"Well, I'll give you your space then. I just wanted to bring that over to you."

"Thank you."

He walked me to the door and gave me a hug on the way out. Damn I hated seeing him like that. He was so down, and I had no idea how to cheer him up. When I got inside, I called Nia for some ideas hoping she would be able to help a sista out.

271

"Hello?"

"Hey Nia, how are you? It's Cadence."

She laughed. "I know who it is. How are you doing?"

"I'm doing fine, it's just Jamal that I'm worried about."

"What's going on?"

"He's just been really down all day and I don't know how to cheer him up. I hate seeing him like this."

"Did he tell you what today is?"

"Uhh. No. What's today?"

"Today is the fifth-year anniversary of our mother's death."

"Oh my God. I didn't know."

"He doesn't like to talk about it, but he'll work through it. Just give him some space."

"How are you holding up?"

"I'm doing alright. A little down as usual, but I'll be fine."

"Aww. I wish I could give you a hug."

"Me too. I could really use one."

"I have a suggestion, do you want to come up to visit? Maybe it will cheer the both of you up."

"I do, but I have to work in a little bit. Maybe I can come up this weekend."

"Yea, that would work. I miss you!"

"I miss you guys too."

"Well, let me know what your schedule is like and maybe we can surprise him."

"He would love that. He has his release party coming up right?"

"Yea. On Friday."

"Maybe I can make it to that. But I'll let you know."

"Most definitely. I'll talk to you later."

"Bye."

It all made sense now but that didn't change the fact that I felt terrible for him feeling that way. Another idea sprang into my head to have seafood night which was his favorite. I grabbed my things and went to the store to go shopping.

Come Join Me

Everything was almost done and the last thing I had to do was take a quick shower and call him over. Once I got out of the shower, I put on something really nice, lit some candles and made it like a romantic dinner. I picked up my phone.

"Hello?"

"Babe, I need your help with something. Can you come over?"

"I'm about to go to bed. Can it wait?"

"No. Please can you help me? I can't figure it out."

"I'm on my way Cadence. Give me a minute."

I sat patiently on the couch until a knock came at my door. The door opened and he walked in.

"Why is it so dark in here?"

I ignored his questions and led him by the hand to the dining room. "Care to join me for dinner?"

His eyes danced over everything, and a smile finally appeared on my Baby's face. "You cooked all this?"

"Yes. I thought it would cheer you up. I know it's your favorite. Will you eat with me?"

He gave me a hug. "Yes, my Love. I will eat with you." My chair was pulled out and I sat down before he did. He still looked shocked at the meal that was prepared before him but he didn't hesitate to dive right in. Mussels, clams, crab legs, shrimp and fish were all on the table for us to enjoy.

"Babe, I have something to tell you."

"What… Did you wanna tell me?"

"The reason I've been down a little bit is because today is the fifth anniversary of my mother's death."

"I'm sorry to hear that. Why didn't you say something earlier?"

"I don't really like talking about it but, we used to do stuff like this all the time, and it reminds me of the good times we shared. Thank you for doing this for me."

"I would do anything for you. I just hated seeing you so upset."

"I should have told you sooner, but I had to get through it."

"I understand. I'm glad you told me. Maybe we could do this every year in her memory. Invite Nia."

"I would like that." A smirk came over his face. "So you trynna be with me for a while huh?"

"Uhh, yea. I don't see myself going anywhere. What. You wanted something temporary?"

"I never said that. Just pointing out what you said."

"Hush and eat. Mind ya business."

"You are my business."

I made a face at him but didn't say anything back. Dinner was peaceful as we ate under the ambiance of the flickering candles. When we had finished and were stuffed, he helped me clean the kitchen and put the food away. A kiss was placed on my forehead before he headed back home.

For a while, I sat on my couch watching tv as usual. What I had gotten him was coming tomorrow and I couldn't wait to see his face. The only problem was, how was I going to set it up? There was a whole plan in my mind of how that moment would be, but leading up to that moment, I was drawing a blank. I'm sure I would figure out something by then, but for now, it was time for me to go to sleep.

Dismissed

"I'm so nervous."

"Don't be nervous. You'll do fine. Just let your lawyer do most of the talking. He knows what he's doing."

He sat back in his seat and fumbled around with my fingers. A nervous wreck was the least that he was. I hadn't even seen him like this. Not even when he was about to perform his music in front of hundreds of people. The best I could do at this moment was to try my best to calm his nerves and conceal mine so he wouldn't see.

The judge called his name, and he went to the podium beside his lawyer. He was sworn in and they began.

"Mr. Rosenbaum, to my understanding, your client hired the defendant to be his manager for his musical career. Correct?"

"That's correct your honor."

"And while he was the manager, he was in charge of what exactly?"

"He was hired by my client to help build his musical career. He was in charge of setting up recording sessions, booking gigs, getting my client's name in front of producers, managing finances as well as ensuring his work was protected by the law."

"Mr. King, do you believe your manager did any of that?"

"No your honor. I believe my manager fell short on those tasks."

"Why is that?"

"Most of the shows and performances I booked myself even when I was told nothing was available in the area. I marketed my shows on my own as well. Also, the copyrights to my music were placed under his name."

"We'll get to that in a minute. Mr. Brown, do you have anything to say against these allegations?"

"Yes I do. When I called around to different places I thought were suitable for Mr. King's work, they all turned me down."

"How is that possible when Mr. King was performing at the times you told him weren't available?"

"The places he booked weren't places I thought he should be. I had a higher expectation of where he should perform."

"So after realizing the places you expected him to perform in declined him, what did you do?"

"I spoke to my client who advised me not to keep looking, he had found something."

"And how long did this go on? Where the places you called declined him and he told you to stop looking?"

"A few months. Then he decided to move closer to the city."

"Were you able to find him jobs there?"

"A few here and there, but he was a new artist. Most places wanted someone who had a strong following."

"Mr. King. Did you have any trouble finding places to perform when you first moved?"

"Mr. Jones told me there weren't many places willing to let me perform but when I called those same places, they were eager to work with me."

"Do you have any proof of that?"

"Yes, your honor. I've submitted exhibit G which are text messages from the defendant to my client about not being able to find him work. Exhibit I is a receipt of payment to my client for doing work in that same time frame."

"Thank you Mr. Rosenbaum." The judge took a minute to look at the documents that were submitted then looked up. "Are there more documents like this?"

"Yes your honor. At least four different scenarios where my client was told there wasn't work, but still performed the same weekend at the same places he was told there wasn't any."

The judge nodded. "In that matter, I'm voiding the contract between Mr. King and Mr. Brown. On the next matter, Mr. King is suing Mr. Brown for being underpaid for the performances he worked. A total of three thousand, four hundred and seventeen dollars."

"Yes, your honor. Mr. Brown was in charge of my client's finances as well as signing the payment receipts for the jobs he booked. My client was supposed to get full payment for those jobs but was only paid a small portion of what was owed. We are suing for the remainder of the money."

"If he was booking the jobs, why didn't he sign the paperwork himself?"

"He was under the guise that the defendant was legally supposed to handle that for him. It is also what he was paid and hired to do."

"Do you have proof that money was withheld after the payout?"

"Yes your Honor. "Exhibit A shows the deposited amounts from the defendant and exhibit B shows the receipts with the amounts that were actually paid for the service."

The judge again looked over the documents as my heart skipped about in my chest. He made some calculations before he spoke.

"I'm granting you the total amount of three thousand, four hundred and seventeen dollars."

"Your honor. We had a separate agreement for that." Thomas interrupted.

The judge looked up. "Do you have that agreement with you?"

"It was a verbal agreement."

"Under what pretenses?"

"That I would pay for his studio time. It was like a cash advance."

"And did you pay for his studio time?"

"No your honor I…"

"Then I'm granting Mr. King three thousand, four hundred and seventeen dollars. In the matter of the copyrights. I see that the songs were copywritten in the federal database under a Thomas Brown. Is that correct?"

"Yes, your honor."

"And I'm assuming it is the defendant, correct?"

"Yes, your honor. He was in charge of copyrighting Mr. King's music under Mr. King's name. Instead, he filed them under his. Therefore, this is infringement, and we are suing for another five thousand, nine hundred and eighty three dollars for the money he made off the songs."

"Do you have proof showing that's how much he made off the songs?"

"Yes, your honor. Exhibit D."

The judge read through the document that I didn't even know was available. He nodded his head. "Do you have proof that the original works belong to your client?"

"Yes your honor. Exhibits K through P. Those are screenshots and pictures of where the beats and the vocal audio were put together in his musical program and where the lyrics were written by hand."

"How many songs were there in total?"

"Twenty-two."

There was a long pause before the judge spoke again. "I'm granting the plaintiff five thousand, nine hundred and eighty-three dollars that the defendant made off the songs. Plus twenty-two thousand dollars in fines. I see you are suing for two thousand in court and legal fees. I'm granting you that. I'm also granting full rights and ownership to the songs listed on this page. You will have to get them changed. I assume you know how?"

"Yes, your honor. I do."

"Case dismissed."

I damn near yelled in excitement from my seat, but I did run up to him for a hug once he left the podium.

"Thank you so much Mr. Rosenbaum." he said, shaking the lawyer's hand.

"My pleasure. The songs will be changed to your name today and I wish you both the best of luck."

Pure elation and relief were on both of our faces and filled the space of the car. The outcome was unbelievable, but we both knew it was possible. He kissed the back of my hand over and over again on the ride home and I couldn't have been happier for him that he got what he rightfully deserved.

Nothing is Wrong

After court, the whole day seemed to fly by. Jamal was busy getting everything ready for his release party while I was plotting on how to make my vision come true. What I had ordered had arrived but getting it to its final location was going to prove tedious. I came up with an idea and it better fuckin work.

I had gotten ready to go to the party early and made my way over to his house. He was quite surprised that I was actually ready to go before him and on time. I watched as he got ready and made my way over to the back door unlocking it when he wasn't paying me much attention. Just before we were about to leave, I pretended to have an emergency call.

"What do you mean there's something wrong with the books?" I fussed on the phone with no one on the other line. "No, I double checked everything." "I will have to look at it in the morning. I'm on my way out." "Fine." "Yes, I understand. I'll look into it now if it's causing such a problem."

"What's going on?"

"I have to fix something with Young Kam's books."

"That can't wait til tomorrow? We're literally on the way out the door. We're already running late."

"It can't wait my Love. Go ahead and I'll meet you there."

"Nah, I'll wait for you."

"Babe, please just go. I'm not sure how long I'll be and you can't miss your own party."

"You can't miss it either. Babe, this is big."

"I know. Go ahead, I'll be there. I promise."

He wasn't the happiest about the situation, but he finally agreed to go on without me. "You call me when you leave and when you park. I'll meet you at your car."

"Ok. Now go."

He kissed my cheek at my door step before getting in his car and driving off. Finally, one by one I had to drag the three heavy ass boxes over to his house and down to the basement. The items in them had already been assembled while I was at home, so the only thing I had to do was set it up and plug everything in.

Thank God it didn't take too long to do so, cuz he was already on my line asking where I was and only forty-five minutes had passed.

"I'm leaving now. I'm on my way." I replied, throwing my shoes on and hopping into the car.

"Call me when you get here. I don't want you walking the streets alone."

"I will, I promise. Bye."

The entire ride there was spent trying to calm myself down from the race of trying to get everything set up and the excitement for multiple, obvious reasons.

As I pulled into the garage, I called him and waited for him to show up. Once I saw his handsome face, I got out of the car and ran up to him.

"How did it go?"

"How did what go?"

"The books Babe. Were you able to fix them?"

"Oh, yea, they're fine."

"What was wrong with them?"

"Uhh… I mixed up the accounts and it threw some shit off. It's fixed, no need to worry."

He looked at me like I was crazy and like I was hiding something. I was, but probably not what he thought it was.

The place was crowded, and everyone cheered when the both of us walked in. His music was playing on the speakers, and everyone was drinking, dancing and having a great time. This turnout was great, but there was one more surprise I had up my sleeve. I kept looking at my phone and his eyes kept wandering over to see what I was looking at. Finally, he couldn't take it anymore and pulled me over to the side.

"What the hell is wrong with you? You've been acting weird all night."

"Nothing is wrong. I don't know what you're talking about."

"You don't know what I'm talking about. Who are you expecting a call from? You've been looking at the damn thing in anticipation for an hour."

"No one. I'm not expecting a call from anyone."

"Bullshit. What the hell is going on yo?"

"Nothing. Come on, you're missing the party." I said grabbing his hand and leading him away, back to where everyone was.

My phone vibrated shortly after and I pretended to have to use the bathroom and dismissed myself. Instead, I headed towards the front and had a security guard escort me out to the garage. I just didn't know Jamal had followed.

"Babe, what the fuck? Are you leaving with him?"

"What are you doing out here?"

"Are you about to hook up with him?" His eyes darted to the guard. "You trynna fuck my girl bro?"

"What? Babe, it's not like that." I said pushing him back.

"So what the hell?" His eyes were brimming and had so much hurt in them. I felt awful but I was saved by a voice from behind us.

"Mally!"

He looked up and ran up to Nia giving her a hug. "I didn't know you were coming!"

"Me and Cadence wanted to surprise you. What's going on? Why are you out here?"

Out of nowhere, he started laughing at how foolish he was being. "This is why you were acting weird?"

"Yes." I could see the relief fly off his shoulders.

He turned to the guard, "Ayo, my bad bro. I didn't know what the hell was going on."

"It's all good man." he replied and left.

"I really thought you were sneakin around with ol boy."

"Really?" I said sarcastically and gave Nia a hug. "I'm so glad you made it safe. It's so good to see you."

"It's good to see you too."

"Come on, let's go back and enjoy the rest of the evening."

Nia and I were escorted back into the club where we did indeed enjoy the rest of our evening. The countdown to his release was being live streamed over his social media platforms and thousands of his fans were watching. As soon as the album was released, the sales ticker started flying. By the end of the night, he had sold over ten thousand records and the numbers were still climbing. It was an epic night.

"So how do you feel? Still think you should have waited til next year to do this?"

"Hell no. I'm so glad we did it tonight."

"I'm so proud of you big brother!"

"Thank you, thank you. God, I feel amazing right now."

Nia and I both giggled. Unfortunately, we all had to ride back in separate cars and couldn't fully enjoy our night cap, but we were sure to finish it off when we got back to his house. With one more thing to conversate about.

Two cars pulled into his driveway as I pulled into mine. When I got out, I was met by two beaming faces who walked me back to his house. A few cups were poured and the after party continued.

"Baby."

"Yes my Love."

"I want to show you something."

"What's up?"

I grabbed his hand and led him to the basement. Nia followed just as curious as he was. At first, he was a little skeptical, but he followed me down anyway. The light came on and showed what I had gotten for him. He looked at it a bit confused, but once he realized what it was, he lost his mind.

"Babe are you fucking kidding me? What the hell? When did you get this stuff?"

As he went over to check everything out like a kid at Christmas, Nia walked up beside me. "What is all this?"

"He's been stressing about not being able to go to the studio and how he wanted his own. So I got him a mini studio to record in."

"Oh my God Cadence. That's so sweet. Look how happy he is."

"I know. I may never see him again." I teased.

He ran up to me picking me up off my feet. "I fuckin love you Babe. Thank you! When did you do all this?"

"Before the party. There wasn't anything wrong with Young Kam's books."

"Wait a minute, how did I not notice that with your non-poker face?"

"I have a poker face when it's needed. You might want to check the connections though cuz I was being rushed."

"I will, I will. I can't wait to record. In my own fucking studio!"

Shock and disbelief still consumed him as we headed back to the main floor. Nia headed up to her room and Jamal and I sat in the living room.

"This has been a great fuckin day." he blurted resting back.

"It really has. Very productive."

"Are you staying here tonight or going home?"

"You trynna get rid of me already?"

"No. I'm just tired and want to go to bed."

"I'll head home then." I stood up and stretched and made my way to the door.

Of course I was walked home, and a long and passionate kiss was placed on my lips.

"Good night Babe. I love you so much."

"I love you too. Get some rest."

"Oh I definitely will."

My shoes and dress were taken off along with my other accessories before I sat on the couch and watched some tv to help unwind. Well, I ended up unwinding too much and fell asleep on the couch.

Heartbroken

Today, I really felt like doing absolutely nothing, but Jamal and Nia had a lot planned. They wanted to go shopping, well… Nia did, and wanted to go explore the city. I tagged along but mainly stayed behind them so they could enjoy their sibling time together. Even though I didn't want to come out in the first place, walking around was quite nice.

There weren't any performances scheduled for this weekend, which was rare, so he had all this free time on his hands and I don't think he quite knew what to do with it. And of course, most of the places we went, even walking on the sidewalk, people stopped us to take pictures, sign autographs and even took pictures and videos from afar. Nia was taken aback from it all, but nonetheless enjoyed the attention.

My feet hurt and I was ready to go home, but they wanted to stop and eat before we headed back. I said nothing as we sat and ate. Even on the car ride home, I barely spoke. Not that I felt some type of way or had an attitude, I was just purely exhausted.

"Mally, can we go to that club we went to when I came the last time?" she asked as we pulled up into the driveway.

"Uhh, we might be able to go back there for a little while."

"Why not?"

"We sorta got into a fight. A big fight."

"Like an argument or something?"

"Nah sis, like a fight, fight. Security threw us out and all."

"What the hell?"

"Long story, but we can go somewhere else if you'd like."

"Yea, I wouldn't mind going somewhere new. Cadence you up to going out tonight?"

"Not really. I'm super tired and need to go to sleep somewhere."

"You feelin alright Babe? You been quiet like all day."

"I'm alright, just tired. But go and enjoy yourselves."

"Iight. Let me walk you home then, hold up."

Before coming to me, he walked his sister in the house, then me to mine. "You sure you're alright? You don't look too good."

"I'm fine Babe, really. Enjoy yourself. It's just been so much excitement, I'm still getting used to it all."

"Well that's bullshit. We've been doing this for weeks."

"Exactly. I usually use my weekends to sleep and do nothing. We've been on the move for weeks."

"Ahh. I got you. Well I won't bother you tomorrow so you can get some rest."

"That's not… I don't mind your company, or hers."

"Baby, I understand. Just call me when you're ready to see my handsome face."

"Well that's cocky of you." I giggled.

"Go and get some rest then. I'll talk to you later."

"I hope you guys enjoy yourselves."

"Not as much as I would with you being there. Good night my Love."

"Good night my handsome."

My fingers ran through his beard, and he disappeared into his house. I really did want to go out with them, but I was definitely going to listen to my body tonight and she needed rest. So I gave it to her.

About three in the morning I was awakened by loud noises and laughing. I recognized two of the voices, but not the other female voice. I sat up and listened and the voices diminished into the house next door. What the hell?

I looked at my phone and it was bone ass dry. I laid back down and tried to go back to sleep but my wandering mind wouldn't let me. I called Jamal, he didn't pick up. Err. I tried to go back to sleep, but nothing.

Letting my curiosity lead the way, I rolled out of bed, threw some clothes on and went next door. Music was playing and it sounded like a mini party was going on. I knocked on the door, and when I got no response, I banged on it. The music was turned down and when the door opened, Jamal was met with a very agitated and irritated Cadence.

"Hey. What are you doing here? I thought you were sleep."

"Having an after party I see?"

"It's nothing like that. Go back to bed." he stepped outside and started walking me home.

I walked past him and burst in through the door. The unknown woman in club attire looked at me shocked. Quickly I turned around and shoved him out of my way glaring at him with hateful eyes as I damn near ran to my house heart broken.

"Cadence!" I heard him yell from behind me, but I had no desire whatsoever to respond. Actually, I did respond. With my middle finger high in the air before I slammed my door closed.

I didn't even make it to the couch before my knees buckled from under me causing me to collapse on the floor in sadness. Knocks could be heard outside, but I had no desire to answer the door. My phone rang and it also went unanswered. I knew this was going to happen eventually, I just didn't realize eventually would be this painful.

Emotional

Face swollen, nose congested, I woke up on the floor to banging on the door. I didn't want to open it and slowly stood up and started heading towards my room. Before I could make it there, my back door burst open, and Jamal came in along with Nia.

"What are you doing in here Jamal?" I yelled.

"Babe, listen to me."

"Please listen to us."

"I don't wanna hear shit you have to say. You said you wouldn't do this shit and you fuckin did it anyway. Get out!"

"Babe."

"Get out!"

"She was my company." Nia interrupted. My eyes darted at her. "She was there for me. He was actually on his way to your house to stay the night with you."

"I don't get it."

She exhaled. "I like girls. I picked her up at the club."

"So why were you actin shady?" I asked Jamal.

"How was I acting shady?"

"Tried to get me to leave all fast and shit."

"I didn't want you to know. I didn't know what you would think about me when you found out about it. He was trying to protect me but when I saw how you reacted, he had to let you know."

"So you weren't going to…"

"Hell no. Seriously?"

"There's no way in hell I would let that go down in the first place and second, he really does love you Cay. He's changed even though I thought he wouldn't."

"Gee thanks Nia."

"I'm sorry, I'm just pointing out the facts. At the club, he sat at the bar all night. Wouldn't dance with anyone. He's really changed."

"I had to listen to them two do whatever the fuck they was doin cuz you were mad. I wanted to cuddle up with you maybe… ya mean."

"Mally."

"Oh stop, I heard that shit all night. Ehh."

"Nia, I don't think of you any differently. You like who you like, but you're still the same sweet person. Why were you scared to tell me?"

"Not many people know. I've gotten a lot of backlash from it even from those who were close to me. I was scared."

I walked over to her and gave her a hug. "I still love you and you can tell me anything."

"Do I get a hug too?"

I scrunched my face up at him before giving him a hug. "I'm sorry for overreacting. I just saw that girl in that little ass dress and assumed…"

"Always assuming shit. This is the last time Imma tell you. I'm not gonna hurt you. We good now, we cool?"

"Yea, we're cool. I don't appreciate you bursting through my back door like that though." I teased.

"Oh I'm coming through every time for you Baby." he said approaching me once more.

Nia threw her hands up. "I'm gone. Y'all make me sick. I'm just glad we got it all cleared up. I'm sorry."

"Don't be sorry. I'm glad you enjoyed your night."

"Thank you. Bye y'all."

We both stared at each other for a while and when we were alone, he spoke. "You gotta stop that shit Babe. You were all upset for nothing. Look at your face."

"I know. I know. I really am sorry. You were just acting weird, and I heard voices. I didn't know what to think."

"Did you get enough rest at least?"

"No. I was up damn near all night."

He shook his head. "You hungry?"

"Yes."

"Want me to order you something?"

"How about we cook something instead."

A smile appeared on his face and stayed there along with mine as we cooked a simple breakfast of french toast, eggs and sausage.

"Did you get a chance to record in the studio yet?"

"No. I was too worried about you. But I do want to show you something though."

He pulled his phone out and showed me how many downloads he had gotten. "You're up to fifty thousand sales? That's unreal."

"I'm about to start looking for studios to rent out."

"Rent or buy?"

"Do you know how much it is to buy a studio?"

"So don't buy a studio. Buy a building, fix it up and turn into one. It could even be a house and you turn it into what you want."

"That's what I'm gonna do then. With all this money rolling in right now, the sky's the limit."

I giggled. "Don't be wasteful now. Always think of your next investment to grow your money. Don't blow it on dumb shit."

"Too late, I already have three luxury cars on the way and I'm about to buy this big ass house across town."

I stopped eating and looked at him. "What?"

"Yea, I figured, why not. I got it to spend." I still looked at him in disbelief until he started laughing. "I'm just playin Babe. Gees."

"Not even fuckin funny. I was about to go off like, we're not gonna be neighbors no more?"

"Nah, when I do that, we're gonna be roommates." His voice was stern.

"You mean that?"

"I mean that. You helped me get to where I'm at now. I upgrade, you upgrade."

"I didn't help you do shit. You did this on your own."

"You've helped me in so many ways I can't mention them all."

"You had it in you this whole time." I tried to one up him.

"And you helped bring it out."

"You would have figured it out eventually."

"When it would have been too late."

I sat and thought for a minute trying to come up with something, but nothing came. I admitted defeat. "I almost had you."

"Good, cuz I was runnin outta shit." he laughed.

As I sat there looking at him sitting across from me, I broke down and started to cry.

"Baby, why you crying?" he asked, coming around to my side.

"I didn't think I would find someone like you. I don't know what I would do if I lost you. And it's like, even though we haven't been dating that long, I feel this strong ass connection with you and this bond, and I don't want it to go away. We've been through so much already."

"I'm not going anywhere. I feel the same thing, stop crying." He held me in his arms before he pulled me to my feet. "Come on."

"Where are we going?"

"To record."

"Now?"

"Right now." My door opened and we headed to his house.

"But I don't want to sing now. I don't even know what I'm singing."

"I do. I'll show you when we get there. You're full of emotions right now and I want you to sing it and let it out."

His door opened and we passed the living room where Nia was still hugged up with the girl from last night. "What's going on?" she yelled as we passed her.

"Tell you later Nia."

Down in the basement, he gave me a piece of paper with lyrics to read while he finished setting up the studio. His computer was plugged in, headphones were on my head and I was placed in front of a mic.

"Just listen to the beat and read the lyrics. Feel the lyrics. They're all your words."

My heart skipped around in my chest as the music played in my head. I was so nervous and shy to sing in front of him but he waited patiently for me to start. Finally, I did. My voice was raspy from the crying, but soon it cleared up. As I familiarized myself with the lyrics by singing them over and over again, I began to relax and let loose and sing the song for my Love. Almost like my second nature, I let all the emotions go onto the track and at the end, I cried some more.

He clapped his hands and I heard footsteps at the top of the stairs. "Holy shit. That was Cadence?" Nia said, peering around the corner.

"That was fucking amazing." the girl added.

He stood up and held me tight in his arms. "That was fuckin great." He hooked the speakers up to his computer and played it back while making adjustments. Even I was shocked when I heard it and I teared up again.

"Aww, why are you crying? You're gonna make me cry too." Nia said, giving me a hug.

"I'm sorry. I was having a moment and this guy brought me down here to record." I said through my tears.

"Are you glad I did?" I nodded my head and buried my face in his chest. "Babe, oh my God stop it before I give you something else to sing. I gotta sing my part, wanna listen?"

"No cuz Imma cry some more." He started laughing.

"Well too bad, cuz this is for you."

I stepped to the side as he approached the mic with his headphones on. Nia was at the computer and pressed play and soon his voice rang out singing the song of how he felt about me. All three of the women were in tears by the time he got done.

"Oh what the hell y'all."

"Was that for her?" the girl asked.

"Yea, I wrote it for her."

"And her part was to you?" Jamal nodded. "Oh my God. That's too cute." she cried. "Y'all are going to have everyone crying with this one."

"Alright, alright. Nia Bye." he said, shooing them away and they left.

I wiped my tears and he helped. "It's gonna be good when it's done."

"It's gonna be perfect. I have a few more for you…"

"No, no, I'm done for the day. Damn it. My face is going to get puffy again." I tried to shake my emotions away, but they came back when he played the song again for his own enjoyment.

"Can you imagine if this gets on the radio?"

"When. When it gets on the radio."

"Iight, I'm done with you for now."

My jaw dropped. "Damn Mal, it's like that."

"I'm just playing. But this setup is really nice. You did a good job Babe."

"Thank you. I'm glad you like it."

"You calm now, you're relaxed?"

"I'm good now. I just have to go clean up the kitchen."

"Come on then."

Back up the steps we went and back to my house where the both of us cleaned everything up.

"When are you trying to look for spaces for your studio?"

He scratched his head. "I don't know yet. Soon though. I have a lot of catching up to do. I've missed weeks in the studio, so Imma be down there a lot. Plus that, and the music video coming up. Plus our music video."

"One step at a time."

"You right. One step at a time. Iight Baby, I'm out though."

"Wait, where are you going?"

"To edit the song."

"Can I come?"

"Nope. Gotta wait til it's done."

"Err."

He stopped in his tracks and came back to me. "Do it again."

"Err." I repeated which led to a gentle bite on my neck.

"That shit is sexy."

"How?"

"I don't know, you're growling at me. I think it's sexy as fuck."

"Sexy enough for you to want dessert?"

"I want the appetizer. The main course and the desert." He replied taking my top off and sexing me down with his eyes.

The look he gave me got me every time and made me very impatient. I pounced on him and well, you know what happened next.

What do You Think

While Jamal was busy editing our song, I was busy working on my clients' books. As I was working, I got a call from an unknown number.

"Hello?"

"Hi, is this Cadence?"

"This is her."

"Hey, this is J-Rock. Young Kam said you could help with my bills n shit?"

"Yes, I can help. What do you need help with?"

"Mainly paying my bills on time. How much would that be?"

"Seven fifty initial start-up fee and the monthly fee depends on how many accounts you want me to manage as well as how often."

"What you mean?"

I gave him the rundown of everything I offered and he ended up wanting the whole package less the payroll. We agreed to meet at the studio to finalize everything and for me to get his receipts and financial information.

"One last thing tho. You help with copyright? Mally Boy was telling me about that."

"I helped him with his, I'm sure I can help with yours."

"Iight cool, let me know how much you charge for that shit too."

"I will do that and have it for you by tomorrow."

"Good look Sis. You mind if I pass your number to my cousin?"

"Not at all. It would be greatly appreciated."

"Iight. See you tomorrow."

"Have a good day."

It seems like Jamal wasn't the only one going through a rise in his career. Two new clients? I was hyped. A knock came at my door with Jamal standing there.

"Hey, I tried to call but the line was busy."

"I was on the phone. I just got a new client."

"Who?"

"J-Rock. I'm going to meet him tomorrow to finalize everything. What's up? What's going on?"

"I'm excited for you. I finished the song! I was about to post it up, but I wanted you to hear the final cut first."

"Let's hear it then."

"It's at the house, come on."

My hand was grabbed, and I was led to his house and down to the basement and he played the song. I was trying my hardest to fight back the damn tears and this time managed, but the song was absolutely beautiful.

"You like it?"

"Of course I like it. Where are you posting it to?"

"Our social media platforms of course and on the other music platforms I have."

"Go ahead. I'm anxious to know what they think."

"I've been getting really positive reviews about the album too which is only causing more and more people to buy it."

"I guess you need to start working on new ones then."

"Already on that." His face was planted in the phone as he began posting the song. "I just need to figure out what we're gonna do for the video."

"That's all on you. I have no idea."

"Well, just think about it. We can bounce ideas back and forth later." I sat on his lap as he worked. "You alright?"

"I'm fine. Just… happy all around."

"I'm gonna get more stuff for down here and decorate so you can have a place to sit and do your work while I work."

"You wanna be around me that much?" I teased.

"Absolutely. You bring so much positive energy how could I not want to be around that."

"When does the music video start shooting?"

"Initially it was for this weekend, but they want to start Wednesday, so I'll be busy for most of the week."

I nodded my head. "Ok. It's gonna be great."

"I have no doubts about that. How are your shirt sales?"

"Steady, but they did dip a little bit."

"Are you marketing and adding new designs?"

"Yes, I just need to come up with more marketing techniques."

"We'll work on that Babe. No worries. Have you thought about selling more than shirts?"

"Like what?"

"Hoodies, long sleeves. Even like, fitness apparel and leggings. You always wear them, you could be a walking advertisement. Or you could even sell like dresses and stuff and people can buy the Cadence look. You can sell jewelry, all that."

"I hadn't thought about that. I'll have to look into it. You gonna have the 'shop the Mally Boy look' too?" I giggled.

"If you want me to, I could do that. You take such amazing pictures, you should be modeling your own shit."

"I'll definitely look into that. Thanks Babe. It will be like my own clothing line."

"Exactly. Another thing, I wanted to know if you wanted to share my account with me. Make it like a couple's account or create a new one together."

"And post what on it?"

"Pictures and videos of us. Different events we go to, be like our own brand. Just another way to get out there."

"I don't have a problem with that."

"Better not."

"Mal." I nudged. "Where's Nia?"

"Boo'd up somewhere. She really likes ol' girl."

"Aww that's too cute."

"We might be seeing more of her on the weekends."

"That's cool."

"The hell it is. I don't want my sister around me that much. Especially what they be doin. I don't need to hear all that shit."

I laughed. "You are more than welcome to stay with me then."

"I'll definitely take you up on that offer."

"I gotta get back though and work on that proposal. You wanna come with?" I asked standing up and heading to the steps.

"I think I'm gonna record a few songs before the rush of this week comes. You comin back when you're done?"

"I don't want to distract you."

"You're not a distraction. I'll set up a temporary space so you can relax until I get more shit."

"Don't go crazy."

"I won't. But I'll make it perfect for you."

He walked me to my house and kissed me before walking back to his. I went right to work on finishing the proposal as well as doing research for my own clothing brand. As I searched, I couldn't wait to get started. Yet another adventure to embark on.

Your Space

The meeting with J-Rock went exceptionally well. He signed the contract for the accounting services as well as the one I created for helping him with his copyrights. All his financial information and receipts were handed over and when I got home, I got straight to work.

Jamal had been down in his studio working on his new recordings and editing them, so I pretty much left him to work his magic. I couldn't wait to hear what he had come up with. In between that time, he had also created our couple profile and added several pictures to it. Even though the pictures were older, they still filed out the blank space and still got new traction from fans. Our following was already at twenty thousand the last time I looked.

"Hello?"

"Are you free? How did the meeting go?"

"It went well. I'm working on his stuff now. How's your music coming along?"

"I took a quick break. Can you come over?"

"Yea, give me a sec. I'll be there in a minute."

I did something quick with my hair and made my way to his house where he greeted me at the door.

"Took you long enough." he said, pulling me inside and to the basement door. "Close your eyes." he demanded.

"Wait. Why?"

"Babe, please."

"Fine." I agreed and my eyes closed as he led me carefully down the steps.

"Ready? Open."

My eyes opened and I looked at the completely transformed space. There was new lighting, couches and tables. He basically created a living room that connected to the studio. A much larger and more equipped studio.

"When did you do all of this?"

"I can't tell you all my secrets now. There's a space where you can sit down and do your work or just relax. I got more equipment."

"Yea, I see that. It looks so nice in here. It's like a mini lounge."

"Wait, there's more." he said, leading me to another area. "I got the stuff to do photoshoots, but I didn't get a chance to set it up yet."

"This is so dope."

"Thank you. Come and try the couch out. See if you like it."

I was led again over to the couch where the both of us sat down on it. More or less sank down in it. It was even more comfortable than the one I had at home. I snuggled up next to him and he wrapped his arm around me, kissing my forehead gently.

"Now, if you want, you have room to sit and relax. Watch some TV. And I can work and still be around you."

"You're too sweet. There's a nice vibe in here too."

"That's what I was going for."

"So what are your other plans for it?"

"For now, just record in it until I get another studio."

"Have you thought about what I said in regards to getting a building?"

"Yea. I think I'm gonna do that. Just haven't had the chance to look around and see what's on the market."

"Ok. Well, let me go get my stuff and I'll be right back."

"Want me to walk you?"

"No. I'll be fine."

I stood up and headed upstairs and out the house. My things were quickly gathered from my house before I made my way back to where he was. He was already hard at work when I came back and set up my things in my new area.

It was quite comfortable to work with him there in the same room as me. I hadn't realized that he enjoyed my company all the time just like I enjoyed his. It was a great feeling to know that the feelings were mutual and, even though we didn't communicate that much, it was good to feel his energy there with me.

While he worked on his music, I worked on finishing setting up and syncing the accounts. Once all that was completed, I continued my research for starting my own clothing line. There were a few vendors that had stuff that I would be really interested in buying from so I decided to call them up.

Each one I called was surprised that it was me calling and wanting to work with them. I was excited too, the only thing I wasn't excited about was the profit margin. I could understand if I was paying for the manufacturing of the items, fine. But they wanted to keep seventy-five percent after that.

I sat back in defeat and Jamal noticed. He stopped what he was doing and came and sat next to me bringing me in for comfort.

"What's wrong my Love?"

"Just talkin to these vendors pissed me off."

"Why? What happened?"

"They wanted me to pay for the cost of making the item, which is fine. But they also wanted to keep seventy-five percent profit."

"So just charge more to get a higher profit."

"That's not the point. I would be bringing them business and they make the most profit from it. It doesn't feel right."

"Well keep looking. I'm sure they aren't the only ones out there that do what you need. Don't give up Babe. Don't be upset."

"I won't, but it's still frustrating. How's your music coming along?"

"Good. I almost have enough tracks for a new album. Some of the songs are older but they don't know that."

"Well go ahead and finish. I'll keep looking shit up."

"Alright. You'll find something. I know you will."

"Thanks Babe."

He left my side and went back to his computer while I focused back on mine. Most of the vendors I found had the same "scheme". Was this the norm? I continued my search until I discovered drop shipping. Sources from other countries that I could choose my clothes from and have them fulfill my orders. It was perfect and I clapped in elation.

"I take it you found something?"

"Yes! Drop shipping."

"I've heard of that."

I cut my eyes over at him. "So why didn't you tell me about it?"

"It slipped my mind. My bad."

I exhaled deeply and tried to add apps to my store that would support the site that I had. A few things were ordered and added to my shop. The only issue was the time it took to ship. I sat back in dismay again and his eyes glanced over at me.

"What's wrong now?"

"Shipping takes two to three weeks."

"Alright. You know what." he said, taking off his headphones and pulling me to my feet. "Let's take a break. I'm hungry anyway."

"What do you want to eat?"

"Not food." he smirked and carried me up to his room.

With some of my stress relieved, we cooked an actual meal before getting back to work. My mind felt clearer, and I was in such a better mood.

I back tracked my thoughts and decided to search for printing companies that offered a wider range of products. When I found the one I felt was a good fit, I transferred my designs and added the app. I ordered a few of my favorite products and that was that.

I yawned and rubbed my eyes as I got more comfortable on the couch. Jamal, I swear, was the energizer bunny and he kept working.

Being down in the basement, I couldn't tell if it was day or night, but my body put me to sleep anyway. I was soon carried upstairs once again and laid in the bed joined by my Love.

Out of My Element

The next two days were pretty much the same. Work, eat, make love and go back to work. Our song had over 5 million views across all platforms, and we were more than ecstatic at the outcome.

We had planned on making another song together, but unfortunately, he had to start the recording of the song he made with Young Kam. Although he was excited to shoot a professional video, he still wasn't too keen on having to shoot with other females.

My packages came with my new designs, and I tried the outfit on and loved it. I took a few pictures in them and created a short video clip of the pictures trying to advertise that I sold more than shirts. It was posted to my personal accounts as well as Cay City and after about ten minutes, the orders for what I posted started rolling in. I couldn't believe it actually worked.

More designs were created and bought for future pics and posts. I even created a few couple's outfits. I hoped he would take a mini shoot with me to advertise. Caught up in lala land, I almost missed a call from Jamal.

"Hi Baby! How are you?"

"I'm iight. Just checkin in on you."

"Are you ok? You sound… off"

"Just frustrated man. How you doing? What you up to?"

"Umm, you're not gonna say why you're frustrated?"

He took a deep breath. "Young Kam wants the girls to be all up on me and wants me to interact with them and I'm like nah. That's not my speed and you know I got a girl. He's like it's show biz... so we been going back and forth about it."

"Do what you gotta do Babe. It's just a video."

"It just feels fuckin weird."

"Hold on, someone's calling on the other line." I clicked over. "Hello?"

"What's up shawty, it's Young Kam."

"Hi, how are you?"

"I'm iight. Look ya boy don't wanna dance with the girls so I'm trynna find out if you'll dance with him."

"Me? Why me?"

"We need this shit to work and can't do it without Mally Boy. You think you could come down?"

"I have to check with him."

"No doubt."

I clicked back over. "Uhh Babe?"

"Yes?"

"Young Kam wants me to do your part with you."

"That's who called you?"

"Yea. I know how you feel about it though so I wanted to ask you first."

There was brief silence on the other end. "What do you think?"

"I wasn't expecting him to ask me that. Seems like he's trying to work with you. Said he couldn't do the video without you. I'm here to support you so I don't mind."

"It's gonna be something new and I don't want you be out of your element."

"Everything going on in my life right now is new and out of my element."

There was more silence on his end. "I guess come on, see how you like it. If anyone gets outta hand you let me know asap."

"I will. I promise."

"I'll text you the address."

"What do I need to bring?"

"Just you, they have clothes n shit here."

"See you soon then."

"Iight."

He didn't sound too thrilled, but the address was sent over and I texted Young Kam letting him know I was on the way.

Yet again, my heart raced in my chest in anticipation of what to expect. As long as Mal was there, I definitely felt safe. I quickly got my things together and headed down to the set right across the bridge. The ride was short, and I pulled up next to the familiar car and was greeted by a familiar face who walked me into the building.

"Hey Babe, you ready?"

"Umm, what exactly will I be doing again?"

"Grinding on me. Just like we're in the club."

"What's up Shawty? Glad you could make it."

"No problem."

"So, Imma need you to change and head over to hair and makeup." Young Kam said and nudged me in the right direction. I felt Jamal's eyes on me as I left.

I walked into the dressing room only to find the other females in there. As soon as I walked in, it was all eyes on me and some were excited to see me while most... Not so much.

"Right this way Cadence, you're late." the hair stylist snapped, pulling me to her chair.

"Late? I was called in at the last minute."

"Are you and Mally Boy really together?" a random girl asked.

"Yea. That's my boyfriend."

"He surely doesn't act like it."

"Not at all." another girl chimed in.

"Whatever you say."

307

"He be asking for our numbers, takin us on dates."

"Tierra said she fucked him."

"If that's the case, why isn't Tierra dancing with him? Why am I here in the first place? Get a fuckin life and stop worrying about mine and where my man dick goes. Half y'all hoes wouldn't even be here if you ain't suck dick and sling pussy to get here." I snapped. I saw the game they were trying to play and I sure as shit wasn't about to let them get to me.

The stylist doing my hair burst out laughing and so did the clothing designer.

"Oh shit. You hatin ass hoes got called the fuck out."

"Ok Cadence, we see you."

"What the fuck ever bitch, we'll see you in the streets."

"You don't wanna meet me there either, but you're more than welcome to wait."

The designers started laughing again. "Girl, give it up."

"Yes honey. You know Mally Boy ain't do none of that. You just mad cuz his fine ass ain't want you."

Laughter erupted again and the girls stormed off. I most definitely had to keep my eye on them. Another girl came up to me while my hair was getting done.

"Don't pay them any mind. They're just mad because he's taken and won't give them the time of day. My name is Nicole. It's nice to meet you." she said, holding her hand out.

"Nice to meet you. I'm Cadence."

"Girl, everyone knows who you are. The man won't stop talkin about your ass. Plus, we're all big fans of yours." the hair stylist chimed in.

"You are?" I was a bit taken aback.

"Yes. That song y'all sang together, really touched my heart."

"Mine too. It was beautiful. We didn't know either of you could sing that well."

"And the chemistry. Are y'all gonna be putting out more shit cuz if so, take my money now."

I giggled. We're planning on it. Just don't know when yet."

"Ooh, girl, if you need a clothing stylist, give me a call."

"Call me if you need ya hair and makeup done too. This shit is beautiful."

"Do you guys have cards?"

"Chardonnay, can you give her my card please?"

"I got you boo. Here you go mama. Please call us."

"I will be sure to. Thank you."

"We heard you run books n shit, is that true? You working Kam's books?"

"I'm an accountant. Yes."

"Can you take on more clients?"

"Yes, I can. I will be in contact you today about what I offer."

"Call me too cuz I need help girl."

"I will call you both." I smiled.

"Chardonnay, come work your magic." the hair stylist said and I was spun around in the chair and makeup was applied.

"Yes Hunty, work." Chardonnay said when I got up from the chair. "Yas! You better work it."

"Go on cuz I know they're waiting."

"Uhh, where am I going?"

"I'll show you. Come on."

The hairstylist grabbed my hand and walked me to the set. Jamal's jaw damn near dropped when he saw me and all the guys around tried their hardest not to stare. The other females were less than impressed, but their opinions didn't matter.

"God Damn Babe." he said, eyeing me up and down.

"God damn yourself." I said rubbing on him.

"Alright, alright. Save it for the camera." Young Kam shouted.

Directions of what I needed to do were given to me and my heart began to race for all of this was too real. I looked at all the cameras around and then at Jamal with worried eyes.

"It's ok Babe. Just pretend it's me and you. Every now and then, look at the lit camera flirtatiously. Don't be nervous."

A kiss was placed on my forehead before the music started. I was stiff as a board moving on him and they were forced to cut. The other females started laughing and cracking jokes which only made me more self-conscious.

Jamal turned to me again. "Don't pay them no mind. Remember the time when we were at Kiss Kiss and we were dancing on me like nothing else mattered?" I nodded my head. "Do that. Show these hoes what you're really made of. Make love to me with dance."

I took a deep breath and cleared my mind before remembering that night. That night, I was trying to prove a point and show him what I was really working with. Today, I was trying to prove a point to everyone in the room and make a great scene to showcase my man. I couldn't let him down. I wouldn't let him down and I damn for sure wasn't about to look stupid in front of everyone.

The music played again, and I began to grind and whine on him. Every now and then, my eyes would glance at the camera before focusing back on him and they were full of lust and love. I even added a few hand motions in to go along with the lyrics and pointed at him like he was the shit.

"Cut!"

"That's a wrap, we got it! Good shit."

"That's it?"

"That's all Baby. You did great."

I glanced at the hatin ass females on the side with a smirk on my face before Young Kam approached us.

"Yo man, that take was dope bro. That chemistry y'all have was exactly what we were looking for. Shit, if shawty wasn't already wifed up…"

"Aye man." Jamal cut him off.

"My bad but that shit was hot. We most definitely need to do another collab together."

"Most definitely. Just hit my jack and keep me in mind."

"If she's up to it, we could all do a track together. You and I rap and she sings the chorus."

"Hell yea. I'm game. Just let me know."

"Iight brotha. Y'all can go, we just gotta wrap up here. I'll email you the final cut before we post it."

"No doubt."

We began to walk back to the dressing room when I heard someone yell my name. I turned around and saw the stylists waving me over excitedly. I walked over.

"Girl. I'm so proud of you, you did your thing. Make sure to call us about the books and if you need hair and makeup."

"Thank you. I definitely will be hitting you up."

"Now go fuck that man good cuz he lookin at you like a whole snack right now."

I blushed and turned to Jamal who was definitely giving me that look that I knew all too well. They pushed me away towards him as I waved bye. I was even nice enough to wave to the other hatin ass girls. Only two waved back.

In the dressing room, we took a few selfies for our social media pages. I was about to get changed when he interrupted. "Babe, wait. Shoot a video with me right quick."

I stood in front of him, and the camera rolled. "What's up, it's Mally Boy and Cadence on the set shootin somethin real nice for y'all. Keep a heads up for the upcoming song. You know where to find us. We out." A kiss was placed on my cheek before the camera stopped rolling.

"Why you don't ever say nothing"

"You seem like you got it under control."

"Let's take another one for your pages. I'm not gonna say shit. Here." he said, handing me the phone.

"Uhh, I don't know what to say."

"Make shit up. Have fun with it."

"Ok, ready?" I pressed record. "What's up, it's ya girl Cadence with the handsome and fabulous Mally Boy. We're on the set making some hot shit we know you're gonna like. Be sure to follow us for more details. You know where to find us. We out."

"Yea. There you go. One more with us both talking. Ready?"

"Babe, really?"

"Hell yea really. Let's go."

The camera rolled one more time.

"What's up, it's Mally Boy."

"And Cadence."

"We on the set right now recording some new shit."

"Some hot shit. We know y'all gonna like it."

"Be sure to follow us for more details of when the song hits."

"You know where to find us."

"We out."

He kissed my lips sensually this time before the camera stopped recording.

"Hell, yea, that's what the fuck I'm talkin bout."

I couldn't help but to laugh. "Babe, you so extra."

"No, you so extra. Extra fine. Damn. You made my dick hard when you came out."

"Oh gah. Shut up."

'You already know what I'm gon' do to you"

"You gonna take good care of me?" I said lustfully, bringing him closer to me.

"You already know Baby."

"Gonna make me feel real good."

"Make you feel like a new woman."

"Gonna wear my lil ass out?"

"Night night comatose."

I bit my lip. "Mmm. I love you Baby."

"I love you more." I kissed him before moving away to get dressed. The entire time, he kept his eyes on me. The entire time, I gave him a nice show to enjoy. After the both of us were fully dressed, we stepped out of the dressing room and headed to our cars. Of course he opened my door and let me in first before he got in his and we both headed home.

Biggest Around

"Babe, did you record us in the dressing room?"

We had been home for about an hour now, had our quick session and I was lounging on the couch scrolling through our social media pages and posting our pictures. When, out of nowhere, a video of us being affectionate towards one another appeared on my timeline with all three of the accounts tagged.

"No. Why would I record that? I was too caught up in you and plus, that was our little moment."

"Look." I said, showing him the video. And just as it ended, another picture video appeared showing him opening the door for me and of us getting in the car.

"What the hell? Let me see." He took the phone so he could get a better view of it. "Someone was definitely spying on us. I just better not fuckin see you strip teasing pop up on here. Who the hell is… Show_Me_More?"

"The hell if I know. That shit is creepy as hell."

"I know. We look cute though."

"Give me my phone back." I said snatching it from him. He started laughing. I finished posting the pictures and videos and went to call the two stylists about running their books. They both agreed and we decided to meet and finalize everything on Friday morning.

"You're getting a lot of clients. Are you gonna be able to manage them all?"

"Yea, it's fine. The program does most of the work. I just make sure everything is working and that all the connections are still good."

"Iight. Don't want you to overwork yourself."

"It's all good. I appreciate your concern."

"Oh absolutely. We had a good day today. Did anybody bother you?"

"Besides some hatin ass bitches trying to instigate shit, everyone was cool. I even have a stylist and hair stylist to call if I need one." I said with a smile.

"What hatin ass bitches tho. Did you handle it? Why you ain't tell me?"

"Yes, I handled it. It's nothing to worry about. Relax."

"Iight then. You posted the videos and stuff?"

"Yes. I just did."

"Cool. I posted mine already. It's getting a lot of views." Just as the words left his mouth his phone rang. "Hello?" he listened for a while before putting the phone on speaker.

"…Would that be something you are interested in?"

"I'm sorry, can you repeat that?"

"I'm calling from Black Heart Record Label. I wanted to know if you wanted to schedule an appointment to meet with our executives to work out, possibly signing you with our label."

"Sure. When are you available?"

"We have an opening at one o'clock tomorrow. Will that work?"

"Yea. That will work."

"Great. We will send over a confirmation of the meeting as well as our location. We look forward to speaking with you."

"Thank you." He looked up at me with beaming eyes after he hung up. "Holy shit Babe. That's one of the biggest record labels in this area."

"Are you serious?"

"Hell yea Babe. You have to go with me tomorrow."

"Of course I'll go with you, but what about your own label?"

"It won't hurt to at least see what they're talking about. I've been dreaming of this day for years."

I smiled brightly. "That call came out of nowhere. It wouldn't hurt to see what they're talking about."

"You don't seem too happy about it."

"It's not that I'm not happy about it. I'm just skeptical. I don't want anyone to take advantage of you or shorting you in any way."

"That's why I need you with me."

I giggled. "I told you I'm coming. I got you like you got me."

"What if more call?"

"I assume they would. You're blowin up on social media and all these other platforms. They would be foolish not to call."

"You right." He sat back on the couch with me and snuggled up while I messed around on my phone. Before I knew it, I heard deep breathing and I knew he had passed out. I giggled to myself, but he heard me.

"What's so funny?"

"You fell asleep. Go to bed."

"Only if you come with me."

"I'll lay down with you. I know you had a long day."

"Indeed I did. Come on my Love." he said standing up and stretching.

He led the way to the room where he helped me get in the bed before getting in himself. His strong arms wrapped gently around me as he held me from behind. He fell asleep first and it took me a while, but I fell asleep after him.

Built Off a Lie

The sun was up, and he was wide awake in anticipation for what this new day brought us. So excited, that he decided to cook us a full course breakfast and served me breakfast in bed. I swear it was the sweetest thing ever as he fed me bite by bite until I had had my fill.

The time ticked by slowly as we waited for it to go by so we could go to the appointment. Eventually, I made my way home so I could take a shower and get dressed. According to him, I took too long. This was nothing out of the usual.

"Babe, you look fine. We have to go."

"Why are you always rushing me sir?"

"Why are you always running late?"

"We're going to be on time. Relax." I said buttoning up my suit jacket.

"Are you ready now?"

"Damn it man! I'm ready. Gees."

We made our way to the car, got in and pulled off. I swear he was speeding and acting a fool the entire way there. I was so happy when we pulled up to the building and he finally parked. Next time something like this came up. I was driving. And he did all that and we were still a half hour early.

I made the suggestion that we wait at least fifteen minutes to go in so he wouldn't look desperate. It always seemed as though desperate people were always dealt a shitty hand. And being as though I was already skeptical, I didn't want to take that chance.

He opened the grand doors for me, and we proceeded into the lobby where the receptionist greeted us. "Good afternoon. You must be Mr. King. How are you today?"

"I'm doing well. How about yourself?" I turned and looked at him shocked at his professional manner in his professional attire. It made me smile on the inside.

"I'm doing well. It's nice to meet you. You must be Ms. Smith."

"Yes."

"Nice to meet you as well. You can follow me to the conference room." She led the way down a long and naturally lit hallway into a conference room. "Mr. Novak will be with you shortly."

"Thank you." we said before taking our seats.

"I'm so nervous Babe." he said once we were alone.

"There's no need to be nervous. Everything will be alright."

About ten minute later a tall, well-dressed man walked in through the door holding a few papers in his hands. "Good afternoon Mr. King. I see you brought company. I'm assuming this is Ms. Smith."

"Yes. Hi. How are you?" I asked as he shook both of our hands.

"I'm doing well. It's good to meet you both. You guys are taking the nation and possibly the world by storm these days."

"It's nice to meet you as well."

"If you don't know, my name is James Novak, and I am one of the owners of Black Heart Records. We were reaching out to you to discuss a few things that could benefit the both of us in the near future. How does that sound?"

"It sounds interesting. You've piqued our interest."

"Good, good. I'm glad. We have worked with some of the most renowned artists in the industry such as Ambrosia, Kyle Rittenhouse as well as Lil Mere. Are you familiar with them?"

"Yes we are."

"Good, good. We brought you here to see where you wanted to take your career. Do you see yourself being just a local artist? Or do you see yourself traveling the nation or the world? Entertaining millions of people on tour."

"I do see myself traveling the world eventually."

"It takes a lot of hard work and dedication to be able to book worldwide events, get large stage performances ready and to reach the right and professional people to do so. With our team, I believe we can make that happen for you. Would you be interested in learning more about how?"

I could see Jamal's face lighting up. I just hoped that he didn't get suckered into the glitz and glam of it all and not realize what he could possibly be giving up. Of course he wouldn't. I was here to help with that.

"Yea, I would love to learn more."

We sat there for about a half hour as this man, Mr. Novak, gave a whole shpeal on what needed to be done in order to be great. In order to achieve higher levels in his career. Bragged about more artists he helped and about all the places he got them into. Went on about booking world tours and painted pictures of selling out stadiums, being on superior guest lists and being part of the elite. I watched as my Baby fell deeper and deeper into this rabbit hole. This man was selling him his dream but what was the cost of it all? What was the cost of doing business with them?

"So are you ready to get started?"

"Yea, it all sounds great. What do I have to do?"

"We will start you off with a five-year contract with us and if all goes well, we will move on to a seven year contract. We will put you on the radio, in front of more faces that haven't heard you yet. We will be in charge of booking your gigs at large scale events and making sure you put out high quality music. We also will set you up with one of our world-renowned choreographers in order to make your performances come to life. So, once you're ready, we can have you sign the contract, and you will be on your way to the fame you deserve."

"Do you have the contract?"

"Yes I do. We created one specifically for you and your needs."

"And what are his needs?" I asked coldly.

Mr. Novak's eyes cut sharply at me as a nervous grin stretched across his face. "To be international. To have his voice heard by millions of people and to be front and center of those people with live entertainment. Talk shows, radio shows. You name it."

The man pulled out the contract and flipped it to the end and handed Jamal a pen. I could see it in his eyes that he was ready to sign on the dotted line. The man that sat across from us was eager for him to do so too. But. He stopped and flipped to the front and began scanning the pages.

"Oh, that's just saying what I've already gone over. How we will build your success and the terms and conditions we must abide by. Now I must tell you, this is a once in a lifetime deal and opportunity. Once you leave out those doors, we won't be able to offer this again."

"And why not?" I asked.

"There are so many artists that are willing to work with us. We get thousands of letters from them, but we only have but so many spaces to fill. I'm afraid that if this opportunity isn't taken advantage of today, we will have to pass it on to someone who is willing to work hard. Just as hard as we are."

This man was fucking good. I had to give it to him, but Jamal kept reading through the pages of the contract that he so desperately wanted to sign.

"So, if we wanted to take this to a lawyer?"

"This contract was written on the merit that he signed today Ms. Smith. If he needed more time to look it over, a new one would need to be created with our basic services. Here, we are willing to go above and beyond for you."

Jamal pointed to a section of the contract for me to look over. My eyebrows furrowed when I read it. "Any songs made under your name belong to you in perpetuity?"

"Yes, that is correct. We need the full rights in order to give to radio stations and even television commercials for them to use since he will be working for us."

Another section was pointed out to me, and I spoke on it. "He only gets fifteen percent of the royalties? Why?"

"That's actually higher than industry standards. We will be, of course, using our resources to book performances, get the stage ready and also market for the events. And that's just the basics."

Jamal looked at me again with his teeth clenched. He looked a little defeated and I read what was written. I got upset too. "You have the right to alter his image and tell him what he puts out and what he can't?"

"Yes. Certain artists must meet our listener's needs. In some cases, our artists fall short, and need a little guidance to get them back on track."

The rest of the contract wasn't even read. The papers were slid back to Mr. Novak untouched. "I'm good man. I appreciate you reaching out to us, but I can't agree with some of those terms." he said standing up.

"Mr. King. What could we do to make you sign today? We are indeed one of the biggest record labels in the area and we would consider you an asset to this company."

"The only way I'm signing that is if I keep the rights to my music, I get to stay original and I receive at least eighty percent of the royalties."

"That's absurd…"

"And so is the contract. Like I said, we appreciate you taking the time to speak with us today, and we're sorry to have wasted your time. This is just not a good fit for us."

"Thank you Mr. King. Ms. Smith. I will have Melina walk you out."

"Thank you."

He sat back down with his face buried in his hands when we were alone once again. "What did I just do? That's everything I've been begging for, and I just gave it away." Tears welled up in his eyes as he looked at me.

"Wait til we get to the car, and we will talk. Don't you let them see you like this."

He took a few breaths to help him relax and soon after, Melina walked in the door. "I heard you declined our offer. What if we revised it for you to give you fifty percent ownership of your songs and thirty percent of your royalties. Would you reconsider then? We only want you to be happy with everything while still being fair."

I looked over at him as he fought with himself. He stood up and I stood up after him. "I appreciate that, but I want full ownership of what I create."

"No problem. If you change your mind, you are welcome to contact us again, but I can't guarantee the conditions will be the same."

"I understand that."

"Then we won't hold you up any longer. You can follow me."

We followed the woman back to the front door where she opened it for us, and we made our way back to the car. He was getting worked up and I offered to drive, and he gave me the keys. The engine started, but we didn't go anywhere. He broke down right in front of me and I held him for comfort.

"Can we just go home Babe. I'm ready to get the fuck outta here."

I put the car in reverse, pulled out and headed home. He stared blankly out the window and I held his hand tightly in mine. The drive seemed abnormally long, but we pulled into his driveway. He got out and slammed the car door and headed into the house leaving the door open for me to follow. When I got inside, he was upstairs with the room door closed and locked. Soft sobs could be heard from the other side.

I knocked on the door and spoke gently. "Baby?" "Babe, please open the door."

"I just need a minute."

I sat down on the floor and leaned up against the door and listened to him cry. Knowing that he was in pain made me suffer. Could I be partly to blame for this? So caught up in him getting the best that he deserved? Could I have cost him the chance of a lifetime?

My knees were at my chest with my face buried in my arms when the door flew open, and I fell flat on my back. He looked down at me looking up at him before he helped me to my feet.

"Why are you crying?"

"Because you're crying, and I think it's partly my fault."

"Why do you think it's your fault?"

"If I wasn't there, you would have signed and fulfilled your dreams. You wouldn't have listened to me, and you could be on tour and selling out stadiums…"

"My dreams were built off a lie."

"What?"

"That's not what I imagined for myself. To be restricted from being me? To give up my hard work and have someone else profit off it? That's not my fucking dreams. You saved me from five years of hell. I'm just pissed off that it wasn't what I expected it to be. He had my hyped up and for what? I can do half of that shit on my own."

"You already have. Your videos are getting millions of views. You're getting steady income from your music and it's all yours. You don't have to split the royalties or any profit. It's all yours."

"You right. I didn't need a label to get me this far and I don't need one now. I'll just figure this shit out on my own. Come here woman. I fuckin love you yo. Stop crying."

"I love you more."

"You hungry? You wanna eat something?"

"Yea, I'm hungry." I replied wiping my face dry. Somewhat.

"Let's go see what we can cook for lunch."

Unread Invitations

After making and eating a healthy lunch, we went on and went back to work. Some items I had previously ordered had arrived and I tried them on while Jamal set up the photo booth and background for me. I absolutely loved the design. It was a nice printed, tight-fitting shirt with a matching design on the leggings and they were so comfortable. I headed back to his house, and he adored them too. I surprised him with the matching set for men.

He put them on before we both gave each other a mini photoshoot in front of his new setup. Each of us took individual pictures, then took couple selfies showcasing that they were a matching set. The pictures were posted to the website, as well to our social media accounts. Soon after, the sales started rolling in. Both men and women were buying either single pieces or sets.

"You're doing one hell of a job."

"Why thank you. It's all about business Baby."

"You have more designs like these? This shit is tough."

"I have a few and I'm working on more."

"Well, order me more when you order yours… Hold on." We were interrupted by a phone call. "Hello?" He listened on the phone for a while, then put it on speaker.

"This is him."

"Hi, my name is Kevin and I wanted to invite you to talk on my podcast, Broken Records Hip Hop. Would you and Cadence be interested in talking about a few things? Like your background, how y'all got together, what inspired you and what's your process? Things along that manner."

He glanced at me, and I had a big smile on my face as I nodded. "Yea, we would love to. When did you want us to come? Where are you located?"

"We're located on Broad Street in Camden. Are you familiar with that area?"

"Not really, but my girl is."

"No worries, we'll send you over the address. Does this Saturday work for you? Around three?"

"Yea, that works."

"Awesome man. We look forward to seeing you. This isn't just a podcast though. We also stream the live video and post it on our platform where our millions of loyal listeners can watch it. So be sure to dress to impress."

"We will. Thank you for reaching out."

"No problem. We'll see you then."

The both of us looked at each other stunned and excited. When we looked up the podcast, they did indeed have a few million subscribers on, not only their podcast, but also they're social media platforms. Being on this show could definitely prove very beneficial to his career.

Just as we were celebrating this podcast, another phone call came through. He answered it and put it on speaker. "Hello?"

"Hi, my name is Taylor Mclean and I work for the Voice It Live Show with Andre Garcia. We wanted to reach out to you to see if you and Cadence were available to meet and talk about your song."

"Is this for a podcast?"

"No. We are a radio station located in New York. We talk about upcoming artists and allow them to have a voice and just let the audience get to know them better. We fell in love with the song and had to reach out."

I nodded my head in excitement again. "Sure. We would love to come up and meet with you. What day and time is good?"

"Our show comes on weekday mornings. How does… Monday at seven sound?"

"Sounds good."

'Great. We will send over the confirmation email shortly. Can't wait to have you."

"Thanks for inviting us."

The phone hung up and the both of us jumped for joy.

"Go check your emails!"

While I sat in his lap, he opened up his email and there were several invitations to different podcasts and social media shows that he had been invited to along with the current ones.

"When was the last time you checked this thing out? You don't get notifications on your phone?"

"It's been at least a week. And I used to, I don't know what happened."

"You have to go through these. See if you can get on some."

"I've never even heard of half of these. It's gonna take a while to get through them."

"What else are you doing today?"

He chuckled. "Nothing much. I have two more songs to record and then my next album will be ready to be put together. But…"

"But what?"

"I need your voice to be on them."

"Oh here you go."

"Come on Babe, please. I'm also waiting for Young Kam's song to come over too. But I really need you to sing on these tracks."

"Fine. What are they about?"

"One is about hustling hard to get where you need to be in life. You would just sing the chorus on it. The other is about being in love with someone you can't live without." "Are you gonna write my parts?"

"The one is already written. The first one. The second one, I can just use the rest of what you wrote and turn it into something."

"You know, you should be a ghost writer. Maybe that can be one thing your label offers."

"It can also offer services like yours. Accounting, copyright." The gears in his brain started ticking. "Website design..."

"Website design? I don't do that."

"But I know someone who does. I can get them to freelance for me. Babe!"

"What?"

"We need to get this shit rollin."

I giggled. "It's not rolling enough for you?"

"I need to do some work. At least find a building and start a site for the label. I also wanna see if I can book a few events in New York while we're up there."

"One step at a time my Love. We can look at buildings tomorrow and reach out to different venues that are close by to where we will be. For now, get through these emails."

"Can you do it for me? I was in the middle of a song. Just respond to the ones you like."

"But it's not about me. It's about you."

"They want both of us. I trust your judgment."

I sighed and held my hand out for his phone, and it was given to me. While I went through the hundreds of emails responding to the ones I thought would be beneficial while also letting the others know we wouldn't be joining them, he recorded his last solo song.

My eyes began to burn trying to get through everything. I responded to quite a few emails that I had done the research on and felt like they would be a good fit for us. Most of them were invitations to different podcasts and there were also a few to little known radio stations. I actually wanted to book them all, but there was no way we would have the time to. And, some of them offered no benefit to us.

I put the phone down and closed my eyes. "Baby, I'm tired." I complained.

"Go to bed then. You know where it is."

My eyes cut over at him. "Really? That's how you gon do me?"

"Babe hush and go to bed. I'll be up in a little while when I'm done editing this song."

"I have to get some clothes from my house though."

"Wear something of mine." he replied, barely acknowledging me.

"Babe!"

"Yes Babe?"

"Will you look at me?"

His eyes glanced up briefly before going back to the screen. "What's up?"

I sighed. "Never mind. I'll see you when you come up I guess."

I made my way upstairs, took a brief shower and laid in the bed all alone. It felt weird without him holding me and it took me a while to go to sleep.

Booked

The next morning, I woke up alone with a cold spot next to me. He really didn't come to bed last night. One of his shirts was thrown over my head and I headed downstairs. To my surprise, breakfast had been ordered and was sitting on the counter, but he was nowhere to be found. There was only one guess.

On my way down, I grabbed a bagel and followed the sound of the music. He was hard at work doing who knows what and I startled him when I spoke.

"Did you stay down here all night?"

The music went off. "Yea, I did. I was working on the final masters for the album. How did you sleep?"

"Bad. I needed you there with me."

"I'll lay with you tonight. I promise. I just got so caught up with it. I also looked up some places I could perform at in NY. I just have to call them and see what they say."

"That's not healthy staying up like this all night. You need to take a break."

"I will Babe. Soon." His eyes focused back on the screen as I sighed and walked over to the couch with his phone. Only after I sat down did I realize I needed his password.

"What's your password?"

"Your birthday."

I giggled and blushed. "Really? Mine is your birthday."

He smiled. "What you bout to do?"

"Check your emails to see if anyone responded to me. Well, you."

"You my little secretary now?" he joked.

"I will be whatever you need me to be."

"Mmm. I like the sound of that." His eyes finally peered at me over the computer screen.

"Oh, I got your attention now huh?"

He dropped his shoulders. "You always have my attention Love. I'm just trynna jump on shit while I'm still relevant."

"I understand that, but you're gonna burn yourself out that way. You've been at it at least for twelve hours. You need some rest. I'm here to help."

Soon, his computer closed, and he stood up. "You right. I'm gonna take a shower and take it down for a while. Before I do though, I wanna call those spots to see if they have anything either this weekend or next weekend."

I handed the phone back and he called the numbers one by one. There was a club that wanted him to perform next weekend, and this was yet another huge step for him.

"I'm booked for next Friday, and Saturday night at a club in Brooklyn."

"Good shit. Are you ready for that scene? It's a lot different than Philly."

"I'm most definitely ready. This is just the beginning!"

"Good. Now go take your shower and get some rest. I'll be going through emails. If I see some I like, want me to schedule a few?"

"Yea. You could do that. I don't think we really have anything else planned."

"I'll figure something out. Go ahead now."

"Wait, are you coming?"

"Yes, yes. I'll be up in a few."

"Iight." He kissed my forehead and went upstairs as I looked through the emails.

Quite a few people had responded, and I needed to get my schedule set up so we wouldn't overlap times. I tried to keep everything local for the most part and scheduled a few New York interviews since we would be going up there anyway.

Everyone I got in contact with couldn't wait to meet us and I couldn't wait to tell him the good news. Basically, our whole week leading up to his performances were packed with interviews. I knew he would be thrilled.

Upstairs in the bedroom, he was already knocked out. I wasn't all that tired, so I sat on the chair in the room and worked on the books and of course, created more designs. It never ceased to amaze me at how many sales I had gotten and still was getting. Even all the positive reviews filled me with joy.

All of our social media accounts were through the roof with hundreds of thousands of followers. And they interacted well with one another. Even when I would add comments in and join their discussions, they ate it up. It truly was a great feeling.

Broken Record Hip Hop

The rest of Friday and most of Saturday seemed to drag, but, before we knew it, it was time for our interview on the podcast. The first of many. During the day, however, more record labels called looking to sign Mally Boy and each one had the same ol' gimmick. Sign over everything to us and we'll give you the world with little pay. He wasn't buying it and every company that called was declined.

His new album was finished, and he even set a release date that was posted on his site as well as social media. He planned on having a big release party like he did last time, but we thought it would be best to wait until after our trip to New York. Even searching for buildings was on hold until after that time. Instead, we focused on doing research on the shows we would be on as well as creating a business plan that would work out in both of our favor. Basically, I would handle the business end of things while he handled the creative end of things. It was perfect.

I sat downstairs in his living room waiting for him to come on so we could leave. For once, I wasn't the one that was late and I made sure of it this time so I wouldn't have to hear his mouth. But today, he got to hear mine.

"Babe, come on. We gotta go. What's taking so long. You look fine." I mimicked how he usually sounded towards me.

"Gees, that's annoying."

"Tell me about it."

"Yet you still don't make the effort to hurry up."

"What do you call this?"

"Iight, I'm ready. You sure you know where we're going?"

"If I don't, the GPS will."

The trip to the studio wasn't long, and twenty minutes later, we were at our destination. We walked in through the doors and were greeted by a man in the front holding a camera.

"Hey, what's going on Mally Boy. My name is Kevin, how are you today? What's up Cadence?"

"Hey, what's going on?"

The man introduced us to the camera, and we were shooting live straight from the gate. This would have been a big surprise, but we had watched a few of his shows and knew this was to be expected. So we came prepared.

"What's up Broken Records of Hip Hop, Mally Boy and Cadence just walked in the door. Check them out in their matching outfits. If someone wanted to get these, where would they go?"

The mic was placed in between the both of us and I spoke. "You can get these at Cay City dot com. We have so many different designs to choose from. You can buy single sets like mine or his, or you can get a matching pair."

"You can also check 'em out on Mally Boy dot com. We always have some exclusive shit poppin on there. You know where to find us."

"Nice, nice, you ready to get this show on the road?"

"Absolutely."

"Iight then, let's head to the back."

The main camera cut off and the host, Kevin, relaxed a little bit. Other cameras still rolled to get extra material needed for the show.

"Hi, how you doing lady and gent? Sorry about all that, we just like to get the first impression, you know."

"We get it, we did our research on y'all."

"Ohh, that's what's up. So we got Bryn and Bryan over here recording at all times. Mason is in charge of audio when we get in the booth and Tyler is our other camera man. There's also going to be cameras mounted so we can get close ups of when y'all speak. Y'all ready?"

"Yea, let's get it done."

Everyone headed to the back where the podcast studio was, and it looked so nice and professional. We all sat around, and drinks were passed out to help loosen up our nerves and get relaxed.

"So basically, as mentioned before, we just want our viewers to get a sense of who y'all are as individuals and a couple. We'll just be asking simple questions about you, and we want it to be a convo."

The both of us nodded our heads. "Y'all ready?"

"Let's go."

"What's up and welcome to the Broken Records of Hip Hop. If you don't know by now, I'm Kevin and today we have the highly requested and up and coming hip hop artist in the building Mally Boy along with his lovely accomplice Cadence in the building. What's up y'all?"

"Hi." I said shyly.

"What up, what up."

"So Mally Boy, where you from?"

"I'm from Newark originally but lived in Neptune for most of my life."

"So what made you decide to move out this way?"

"To be closer to the city so I could make more moves."

"You already had a pretty big following when you came out here, how did you manage to grow from there?"

"Just promoting myself. Just trynna make a name for myself. Get people to know what my music is all about. Let people hear my voice. And they ended up liking what I had to offer."

"Nice, nice. Cadence, what about you?"

"I actually grew up in Camden."

"Aye! That's what's up."

"Aye. But I wanted to live in a more relaxed area so I moved to the suburbs and I've been there ever since."

"Iight, iight. I get asked a lot about this from the listeners and there's a lot of gossip out there. How did y'all meet and how in the hell did you get that man to settle down? We heard how he got down."

I started giggling a little bit. "We're actually neighbors. When he moved, he moved into the house next to me. It's actually funny cuz he was loud with his truck outside, and I was pissed that he woke me up early. But somehow, after that, we kept bumping into each other like it was meant to be."

"So tell us, how did you first start talking? Like, when did the connection start? Cuz y'all have some amazing chemistry."

"She was sitting on her back porch. And we had talked briefly before, but she was sitting out there and I asked her if the music I was playing was too loud. Cuz she barked at me about the truck. Well, when I went over there, the company that I had didn't like that too much."

"Oh, you had female company?"

"Yea, yea. So the girl called her all types of names and Cadence kept her cool about the shit. But I couldn't have that and the girl was dismissed. I brought her a bottle of Moscato to apologize."

"A big ass bottle."

"And we basically started talking from there. She's business minded and I needed her assistance."

"At first, it was literally just on some friend type shit and all about the business talk, but somewhere, I fell for him, and we realized it at the same time."

"Damn, that's deep. So you help out with his songs and stuff?"

"No. That's all him. I just do his accounting and make sure his bills are paid on time."

"Nah, she does more than that. She helped me get my copyrights back and helped me get out of a shitty contract."

"We heard about that, what was that about?"

"Long story short man, the manager I had wasn't the best and he put my songs under his name. I didn't even realize it until she looked it up."

"Did y'all get that situated?"

"Oh absolutely."

"So where do you get your inspiration from? Cuz your music is a lot different than what we're hearing now. Got that eighty's vibe with the new day twist on it."

"Just things I go through in my life. What goals I set out for myself. What I see on a day to day and my perspective of it all."

"So do you write all your lyrics?"

"Every single one. I create the beats too. I was going to a studio and recording there, but shit fell through, so I've been recording in my basement and mastering my songs myself."

"Wow man. You do it all. Very talented."

"Thank you. Thank you."

"So, do you plan on signing with any labels? Have any of them reached out to you yet?"

"I've had a few reach out to me and I appreciate it, but I think I'm gonna do my own thing."

"Do you know how many people would kill for that? And you just gave it up? Why?"

"Me and my Baby got a few tricks up our sleeves. But we can't disclose that yet."

"When can we expect to hear this news? Can we get a hint?"

"We don't know yet, but visit our site frequently, cuz it might be up there sooner than you know. And nah, no hints yet. We still working out the details."

"Ok. Ok. I feel you. So, one burning question my listeners are dying to get the answer to. What inspired that song the both of you made together? That song man. Right now, it has over ten million views. Everyone is loving it. What inspired it?"

"Just the love and affection we have for each other. I don't think I'd be in the spot I am now without her. She's my rock and we both gonna make it to the top. We neva stop. Neva gonna drop. Always gonna make it hot. And if fuckas wanna pop I'll have to take em to the chop shop. Cuz I ride for my Baby. Cuz I'll die for my baby and even when we're eighty I'll spread the thighs of my lady."

"Whoooo! Had to showcase a few bars."

"A little something. But nah, I love her with my everything and it's the best feeling to know that someone genuinely loves you and wants only what's best for you." I blushed a bit at his words.

"Hold on, hold on. Did y'all see her face when he just said that? Look at her. Blushing over here. I know y'all see that." I blushed harder. "I wish y'all could feel the chemistry in this room right now. The love is real. No doubt. Cadence, did he know you could sing like that?"

"I didn't know I could sing like that. I was crying right before I recorded the track."

"Why were you crying?"

"I just had a moment where I realized I loved him so much and I broke down. He damn near forced me into the studio to sing my emotions and that's what y'all hear. My true emotions for him and his for me."

"I definitely think that's why it has touched the hearts of so many people. So many of us can relate to that and we feel it when we listen to that song. Can we expect more songs with the two of you together?"

"We're working on it. She's a bit shy but we workin on that too."

"We have a few questions that our audience wanted to ask you guys. Here's the first one. 'What is your favorite feature about each other?'"

"For me, it's definitely her smile if we're gonna keep it PG here. Even if I had the worst day, just seeing that smile melts away all the stress of the day."

"Cadence. What's your favorite feature?"

"Well damn, he took mine." Everyone laughed. "Umm. Imma keep it PG here too. But I would definitely say his dimples. They don't always show when he smiles but I know he's really enjoying himself when those cute little dimples appear."

"Ahh. Y'all gotta stop with the mushy stuff. Ok. Next question. 'Do y'all see yourself getting married anytime soon?'"

"Whoa. That came from nowhere. I think it's a bit too soon for us to get married, but I definitely don't see myself with anyone else in my life."

"Mally Boy, what's your response?"

"Who knows, I may already have something in the works."

"Whoa, whoa, whoa. Hold up, rewind. What?"

"You never know. I can't see myself with no one but her either. Might have to lock it down soon."

"Don't say that cuz now I'm gonna be anticipating something." I whined.

"Don't spoil it. Don't spoil it."

"I'm not saying a word."

"Last question. 'What is the most romantic thing each of you have done for each other?' Again with the mushy shit. Let's hear it. Cadence. The most romantic thing Mally Boy has done for you."

"Uhh. There's so many to choose from. He's always the perfect gentleman. I think the most romantic thing he's done for me was cook me breakfast in bed and fed it to me."

"Was there a special occasion?"

"No. Just decided to do it. It was actually earlier this week."

"Mally Boy. Most romantic thing Cadence has done for you."

"Can I say two?"

"Sure, why not."

"Well, the first one isn't romantic, but it really spoke to my heart. I was looking around for studios and wasn't having any luck. She ordered some equipment and set it up for me as a surprise. The second was on the fifth anniversary of my mother's death. She cooked my favorite meal and we had dinner by candle light. She didn't even know why I was upset, she just wanted to make me feel better."

"Damn bro. Sorry to hear that. That's really sweet. On that note, we will close out for the day. Any last words for the listeners?"

"Just stay tuned for what we have going on next. We're always trying new things. And be sure to check out our sites for the latest updates."

"We really appreciate the love and support we get from you. It means the world to us, and we wouldn't be here without you guys!" I added and Kevin ended the show.

"Yo, I'm really sorry to hear about your mom bro."

"It's all good. I appreciate it."

"You guys did a great job. Love the chemistry. We should definitely do it again. The fans love y'all."

"We'll be in contact. We appreciate you having us here."

"No doubt. Catch y'all on the flip side."

And just like that, we were done and headed home hand in hand. Smiles beaming on our faces. My phone kept going off and when I went to check what the hell was going on, I realized it was all the new followers we were getting from simply being on the show. It almost doubled just from the new exposure. I wonder what the New York trip had to offer.

New York New York

Instead of driving, we decided to take public transportation up to New York. It had been such a long time since I had been there and the same with Jamal. We made the decision to head up there a day early so we wouldn't have to do a mad dash of trying to get up there and find the place. After a few train rides, however, we realized we should have driven, for everywhere we went, cameras danced in our faces and people wanted to take pictures and videos with us.

All of that would have been fine if we weren't lugging around our heavy ass bags with our belongings for this week's trip. Finally, we made it to the hotel that was pretty close to the studio and made it up to our room where our bags dropped to the floor and we collapsed on the bed.

"I wanted to go sightseeing but I'm so exhausted." I muffled from his chest.

"I did too, but that was crazy. Next time, we're driving. We can always go later this evening after we rest up a bit."

"Not this evening. We need to be well rested for tomorrow. We have to be there by five. But we have the rest of the day and the week to do things."

"Not really. You have us booked for the rest of the week and I have to go to rehearsals later on so I'm gonna be busy."

"We will find the time my Love. No worries."

I walked over to the window and looked down at the hustle and bustle of the city. Although I enjoyed visiting, living here would stress me out. Too much going on. Too much noise. I could never get used to it all.

"What are you thinking about?"

"Just looking at how busy it is down there. Everyone meeting up in one place for a brief moment before going on about their day, never to see those people again."

"Damn Babe, that's deep."

"I wonder how many times you pass someone, and you never realize it."

"Ok. Alright. Come have a seat Love." My hips were grabbed, and I was guided to sit on his lap. "Hey gorgeous."

"Hey my handsome! Are you ready for tomorrow?"

"I imagine it will be the same as yesterday just with different people and a different vibe. We'll be fine."

My forehead rested up against his and I just enjoyed the moment of being here with him. "I'm hungry."

"Of course you are. There's a restaurant in the hotel. Want to check it out?"

"Yes."

"You sound tired."

"I am. Lugging all those bags and being swarmed by people took a lot of energy from me."

"I know. I wanted to get the experience of New York and take the trains and stuff, but not when everywhere you go, you're surrounded. And the people up here give zero fucks about your personal space."

"But think about it, people in fuckin New York know who you are!"

"Know who we are. You got a few fans out there too Babe. It's not all me."

"I still can't believe it."

"Me either." He tapped my leg for me to get up. "Come on. Let's go feed your greedy ass."

"Leave me be." I said standing up. "You haven't fed me all day."

"Neither have you." he replied with a different meaning.

"I'll fill you up later."

"Nah, that's my job."

I giggled. "Babe, you so nasty."

"But you love it."

Inside the restaurant, we were seated, and our food was ordered. As we waited a few people noticed us and cameras came out and the crowd flocked over. We smiled and posed a bit before our food came out and people left us be. For the most part. The food was delicious and soon I had my fill. I waited for Jamal to finish, and we headed out to the streets of New York.

I could never get used to the smell, but we walked around for a few blocks seeing what New York had to offer. We stopped in a few stores and went shopping before heading back to the room. That was more than I could take for one day and rested back on the chair and flipped through the channels.

"It seems as though the couple that has taken the nation by storm has arrived in New York City today. They were spotted at a hotel restaurant where they posed to take a few pictures with their fans. Mally Boy, who is an up-and-coming artist and girlfriend, Cadence, caused a big stir when they arrived."

"Do we know what they have come for Jill?"

"They're supposed to be doing a few radio interviews this week and performing at one of Brooklyn's hot spots. They are becoming the new power couple. I would expect to see them doing more interviews in the near future."

"Maybe we'll have them on the show next week. But now, let's pass it over to Jim. Jim…"

The both of us sat there in shock for a moment before he spoke. "Holy shit."

"Holy shit is right. What show is that?"

"I don't know. I was just flipping through." I looked at the guide. "It's called The Afternoon Five."

A smile appeared on his face which caused one to appear on mine. "We're actually getting noticed. It's finally happening."

"I'm sure it will only get better as time passes."

"Iight. I'm ready for my desert now to top off this day."

"Do you mean that literally?"

"Yes. Come here my Love."

The Pay Off

My alarm went off and I did not want to get up. Jamal on the other hand was cheery like it was the middle of the day. Showers were taken, clothes were put on, words of encouragement were spoken, and we were headed out the door. On our way, we stopped and grabbed something to eat, caught a cab and rode a few blocks away to the studio, which was something we hadn't experienced before.

The building was at least fifty stories high, and we walked in where we were greeted warmly.

"Good morning, how are you today?"

"Good morning. We're doing alright. We're here for Voice It Live."

She gave us visitor passes and said, "You'll be going to the twenty fifth floor to the right. You'll see a big sign. Just walk in."

"Thank you." we both said before making our way to the elevators.

On our way up, he was shifting about nervously and I looked at him surprised. "What's wrong?"

"I'm nervous."

"Why? Don't be nervous. You'll be fine. Take a few deep breaths to help you relax."

He took a few deep breaths. "It didn't work Babe."

I stepped in front of him, grabbed his face in my hands and brought his lips to mine for a passionate kiss. "Did that help?"

"A little, yea. Now I have another problem."

I giggled. "You'll be alright. It will be like Saturday's show."

The elevator doors opened, and we headed to the right where a big sign was for the show. We entered through the doors where we were greeted before heading to the back. He held my hand tightly.

"Hi. My name is Angela. I'm one of the hosts for the show. Andre will be out soon. We are so pleased to have you here. Would you like any coffee, tea or water?"

"No, thank you. And thank you for having us."

"Any time. It will be a simple interview just asking you a few questions about who you are, your background, your music and of course, your relationship."

"Hi. I see you've already met my cohost Angela. I'm Andre. Great morning and welcome."

"Good morning." We replied back.

"I know it's early. Are you guys ready to get set up?"

"Yes, we're ready to get this started."

"Great, follow us." They said leading the way.

We all took a seat around the table and put our headphones on. The crew did mic checks and the show started.

More or less, the show was the same as our first and they asked us simple questions about our background, family life and where his inspiration came from. We were also asked about how we met and how we have helped each other grow and where we see ourselves in the next five years business wise and relationship wise.

Jamal was itching to tell about the release party and getting his own studio and what we had planned, but he held back. If he did disclose anything, I had his back regardless.

The interview lasted about forty-five minutes and afterwards, they played our song on the radio. The both of us teared up as it was broadcasted over the entire north eastern area of the US.

"We noticed you getting emotional, are you guys alright?" Angela asked while we were still live."

"It's been a dream of his to have his music play on the radio and you guys made it happen. I'm just happy that he's happy."

"I think we'll be hearing a lot more of this song along with other songs. It speaks in ways that very few songs nowadays do."

"That would mean the world to us. We really appreciate that." he said.

"That's all the time we have for now. We hope you enjoyed the interview with Mally Boy and Cadence. We'll be right back."

"You guys did great." Andre said when we were off the air. "We're going to let you speak to the producers and see if we can get more of your songs to play. Would you be interested?"

"Most definitely."

"Come this way."

We followed Andre to another floor and to another office space and were seated in a conference room. "Michelle will be out shortly. It was a pleasure having you on the show. We wish the both of you the best." he said before leaving us alone in the room.

"Are you ok Babe?"

"I'm just in shock right now, but I'm alright. How are you doing?"

"I'm excited. I wanna know what they're going to say. They played our song." I squealed quietly.

He chuckled. "I know. That's why I'm shocked. Do you know how many people just heard that?"

"Good morning, good morning. My name is Michelle, and I am one of the producers of this radio station. How are you today?"

"We're doing good. How about yourself?"

"I'm doing fabulous. You guys did great on the show. How did you like it?"

"It was great. They welcomed us warmly and asked some really good questions that got us thinking."

"Good. Well, I have brought you in today to discuss having some of your songs played on our station. Usually, I would be having this discussion with your manager, but I see you've gone the solo route and want to congratulate you on coming this far and doing it alone."

"Thank you. It took a lot to get here, but I think it's worth it."

"Absolutely. So first, I want to start off by asking what are your goals? Why would you want your music to be played on air?"

"My number one goal is just for my story to be told. Everyone doubted that I would make it and I know that the ones that want their story to be told too have been told the same thing. I want them to know to never give up on their dreams, no matter what it is because if you put the hard work in, it pays off."

"Very nicely put. The way we work, we usually have artists pay an upfront fee and if we like the songs, they are played, and we monitor it. The royalties of the songs get paid to you of course and you will get forty cents per four plays.

However, we have had one of the highest-ranking shows in months because of you so I'm willing to waive that fee and put your songs on air. You will have to send in a list of songs for us to review and choose the ones that we think would do well. Is that alright?"

"Yes. How many do we need to send in?"

"At least ten radio ready songs."

"That's no problem at all. How many songs will be played at once?"

"Two at first and we'll monitor and see how well they do, but I don't think we'll have an issue with that. Every quarter, we will reach out to you to see if you have new material that you want to submit."

"Do we have to sign anything?"

"Yes. Just a statement of what I just explained to you. I can go get it if you would like."

"Please do. Yes!"

"Not a problem. Give me one minute." She left the room.

I glanced at Jamal with bright eyes as he glanced back at me. "We fuckin did it Babe!" he whispered grabbing my hand in excitement.

"You did it. You never gave up and you did it!"

Michelle came back with a few papers in her hand of which the both of us read and signed. There was no scheme, just a contact that would pay us out for the royalties. It would have only been him signing, but I owned part of the copyright for a few of the songs.

"I will send over the instructions on how to submit the music and the next steps." she said, handing each of us a copy. "Just follow the instructions and we will be good to go. We will be in touch on which songs we have opted for. Congratulations!"

We shook her hand. "Thank you so much."

"Right this way. I'll lead you out."

We followed her out the room, down the hall and to the elevators before she disappeared. In the elevator, both of us jumped and screamed in celebration of what had just happened.

"Hello?" I answered my phone once we got back to our room.

"Cadence?"

"Yes. Who is this?"

"You don't recognize my voice girl? It's Charmaine."

"Oh. Hi?"

"I'm just calling to check in on you. I heard you guys on the radio. It sounds amazing."

"Thank you."

There was a long, awkward pause before she spoke again. "So how are you doing? What's been going on?"

"Everything is fine. Just working. How are you?"

"I'm doing alright. Working as well. I miss you. Why didn't you tell me you were going to New York? That's been a plan of ours for years."

"Because you stopped talking to me out of nowhere for no apparent reason. Plus, we're here for business, not leisure."

"Well maybe next time we can take a leisure trip. Just the three of us like we planned."

"The three of who?"

"You, me and Janelle."

I burst out into laughter. "There's no way I'm going anywhere with her. Most likely not even with you."

"Maybe we could start off slow and work on things."

"I tried that already and it didn't work. Now out of nowhere you wanna be buddy, buddy. Why? Cuz you heard me on the radio?"

"That's not it all. I really do miss the friendship that we had."

"You didn't miss it enough a few weeks ago. Don't miss it now. Have a good day." I yelled and hung up the phone.

Jamal stared at me with a black face. "What the hell was that about?"

"Charmaine wanted to rekindle our friendship. What a sack of bull."

"Don't let that fuck up your day."

"I'm not, it's just. I know why she called, and it wasn't the reason she said she did."

"Maybe there was some truth to that."

"Ha. I highly fuckin doubt it."

"Alright Babe fine. Are you ready?"

"I just have to change my shoes and we can go."

One of things the both of us wanted to, if anything, was to visit Madison Square Garden and the Empire State building. If we had time, we would stroll through central park or walk the streets.

After I put my shoes on, we headed out, caught a cab and were on our way. During the ride, we chatted about this morning and it caught the attention of the cab driver.

"You two are the ones I heard on the radio this morning?"

"Yes, that's us."

"My wife loves that song and sings it to me almost every day. She would lose her mind if she knew I gave you a ride. Today."

"Can we talk to her?" I suggested.

"You would do that? That would make her day."

"We would love to." Jamal added.

"Yes, I will call her now." He dialed a number and let it ring while on speaker phone a woman's voice answered.

"Did you forget your lunch again?" Jamal and I chuckled.

"No. No. You wouldn't believe who I have in my cab." he said and handed us the phone.

"Who is in your cab?"

"Hello?" I said into the phone.

"Who is this? Why do you have my husband's phone?"

"This is Mally Boy and Cadence."

"Shut up. You're lying. Oh my God, I listen to your song all the time!"

"Yes, we heard. We just wanted to say hi. Your husband said it would mean a lot to you."

"Yes, yes. I can't believe I'm talking to you right now. Oh my God. Thank you for calling."

"You're welcome. What's your name?"

"Veronica. Oh my God."

"It was nice talking to you."

"Nice talking to you too. I can't wait to hear more."

"We appreciate it. Have a good day."

We handed the phone back. "I will call you right back." He looked at us through the mirror. "Thank you, thank you both."

"If you have a pen and paper, we'll sign it for her."

"Yes, yes please." he said, handing us the items just as we pulled up to our destination.

"How much do we owe you for the ride?"

"Nothing. It's on me for making my wife happy. Do you mind if I get a picture?"

"Yes, of course." We all stepped out and posed for a selfie.

"Thank you. I wish you both the best."

"You're welcome."

The driver got in the cab and drove away but we had already attracted the attention of other passerbyers. They stopped, pointed and stared as we walked into Madison Square Garden.

Madison Square Garden and the Empire State Building were amazing. I just wished we had more time to stay and see everything, but the both of us were exhausted. Not only from being up early that morning and walking around, but also being surrounded by so many people everywhere we went. It was mentally draining.

There was a new dream that he had, and I had no doubts that he would achieve it. He wanted to perform at Madison Square Garden and have a sold out show. I would give it another few months before that happened and would try my hardest to do what I could to make it happen.

Although the night was still young and the streets were still full of life and people, the both of us took a shower and relaxed for the rest of the evening. I sat back and checked our social media accounts and each one had gained another half a million followers. Easily. And our song was now up to twenty million views on each platform it was uploaded to.

He checked his emails and replied to the radio station with what they had requested. I could only imagine what the outcome would have been if he had tried to do this a few weeks ago without his copyrights. It would have been a disaster. All his royalties would have been given to someone else, he could have been sued and all his hard work and sleepless nights would have been for nothing. The same applied if he had signed with a record label.

I stared at him as he worked. A slight smile spread across my face as I watched him. He must have felt my eyes on him for he glanced up from his computer. He smiled.

"You ok Babe? Why are you staring at me?"

"No reason. Just watching you work is all. What you doing?"

"Just checking emails. Looking at the confirmations and what we need to bring or do. What are you doing besides burning hole in my face?"

"You say it like it's a problem. I won't look at you no more."

"Tuh, yea right. You can't keep your eyes off me like I can't keep mine off you."

"So what you complaining for?"

"I'm not complaining my Love. What do you want to eat? I'm hungry as hell."

"I'm hungry too, but I don't feel like going out."

"Me either. We can order room service I guess."

A menu was pulled out and handed to me. I glanced over it and made my selection before he made his and called to place the order. Now it was just a matter of waiting and while we waited he got an email from the club venue.

"What does it say?"

"They want me to go up there tomorrow and run through rehearsals and what not. Nothing out of the ordinary."

"What time do you have to be there?"

"Three in the afternoon."

"That's not bad. So what songs are you going to perform?"

"Some hype shit."

"What's wrong? You sound worried."

"I am a bit worried. It's a new city, a new place, I just don't want to fuck up or have something go wrong."

"You've done it before. When you moved and performed in Philly, you were new. So what's the difference now?"

"It's New York. It's like a different breed of people. Even how today went was new. They are more assertive."

"You'll be fine my Love. I'll be there with you." He gave me a look. "What's that look for?"

"Nothing. You ever party in New York?"

"No. I assume it would be the same as any other place. Plus, you'll be there with me. I'll have a personal bodyguard."

He chuckled. "You right. Maybe I'm just over analyzing shit."

"I think you are. I think you're tired and you need a break and some desert after your meal."

"Can I have dessert before my meal and another meal later?"

"I think that could work."

"Good, cuz I'm stressed and I'm about to release it out on you."

"I've never complained about it." I said walking closer to him and looking at him with low eyes. He bit his lip and took me down.

So caught up in having an intense intimate session, we hadn't even realized the food came. The door opened and he quickly grabbed the bag before anyone could notice his half naked body. We sat and ate peacefully while going over tomorrow's schedule. We had another interview at a different radio station and different hosts along with his rehearsal that I wouldn't be attending. I was a bit upset that I couldn't go and I couldn't tell if he was upset as well or relieved.

After that, we had another interview that literally came out of nowhere and we couldn't decline. It was with the same radio station, just on a different show. I was convinced that after our time here, New York would be tired of hearing from us. Like, how many times can we explain the same stories? But nonetheless they wanted us to appear, and we couldn't say no.

I yawned and stretched as I shut my computer down. "I think I'm gonna call it a night. You wore me out."

"I'll join you in a minute my Love."

"You better. Don't stay up all night on that computer. We have a long ass day tomorrow. Plus, I wanna snuggle up with you."

"Ten minutes."

"Fine." I said, wrapping myself up in the blanket and closing my eyes. But ten minutes turned into thirty which turned into an hour. "Babe!" I shouted and his computer instantly turned off. I was held from behind as we drifted off to sleep.

Brooklyn

The entire week leading up to his performance was a busy one. Our schedules were packed full of interviews from various radio stations as well as local podcasters that wanted us on their show. And at the end of those interviews, different songs of his were played and the radio stations also wanted to play his music on the air. Some were lenient and waved the initial fee, while others, not so much but we both felt the final result would be worth the couple of thousand dollars up front. At the end of the day, what needed to be sent, was sent and we were straight in the bed.

His rehearsals went well, and he realized he was stressing himself out for nothing. Most of the day was spent in the room resting up for tonight was his first performance in New York. It was about a half hour away and we decided to take the train.

I stood really close to him when we rode the crowded subway, and I definitely should have worn flats on the way cuz I knew my feet would be killing me by the end of the night with all this walking we had to do. But nonetheless, we made it and entered the large building. In front of us was a large dance floor as well as a stage. I couldn't wait to see him perform up there next to the DJ.

The night was just beginning and very few people were there. I went to the bar and ordered a much-needed drink. We both did and I sat down to rest my already hurting feet.

A kiss was placed on my forehead before his voice followed. "You alright Baby?"

"I'm fine. It's just my feet."

"I know my Love. Once that liquor kicks in you should be good."

"I hope so or you'll be carrying me." I joked, but half of me was dead serious.

We stayed in the cut as the night progressed trying to keep out of people's way. I danced in my seat and he danced with me to keep me company but I could tell he wanted to dance more than what we were doing.

"You wanna dance on the floor don't you?"

"I do, but I don't wanna leave you here alone."

"Come on, I'll dance with you Babe." I said jumping down off the stool and grabbing his hand, leading him to the middle of the floor.

One of my favorite songs was playing anyway and y'all know how I love to put it down on my man. Song after song played but there was one that really caught our attention. It was our song sped up and remixed and the shit was hot. It was interesting to watch how everyone reacted positively to it and we were in the mix of it all.

During the song, the DJ came on over the mic. "What's up what's up. Hope y'all are enjoying yourselves tonight. We have a few special guests coming to perform tonight. We got Mally Boy and Cadence in the house!"

The crowd roared. People that were near us started pointing us out now that they realized we were going to be there. Cameras came out and started snapping pictures and recording videos as Jamal and I danced to our remixed song. I must say, it was an absolute mind fuck to hear our voices over the speakers in a club and have people react so positively to it.

"Let's make some noise for Mally Boy and Cadence!"

My hand was grabbed, and I was led up to the stage by Jamal. My heart raced for I had no idea what this guy had up his sleeve. Thankfully, he let me go before we got to center stage and his song began to play. Before he started the performance, he got the crowd hyped up and ready for him. I felt like his little cheerleader on stage as I danced in the background. That is, until he brought me center stage with him.

There was no time to even react. The lights were on us and I knew exactly what he wanted me to do, so I did it. I danced on him like we were down on the floor with everyone else and the crowd loved it. I must admit, so did I.

Only three songs were performed before our time was up and we headed back into the raging crowd. For a while, we posed and let people take pictures of us and with us before we made our way back to the bar where I had to sit down.

"Why didn't you tell me you were going to do that?"

"I wasn't. It was the spur of the moment type of thing. You want your last drink of the evening?"

"Yes please."

As our drinks were being made, a fight erupted on the dance floor. A very large fight and we watched as it slowly began to ripple back our way. He grabbed my hand and quickly began leading me to the exit. Chaos came upon us when several gunshots were let off. Everyone began screaming. The music turned off and the lights came on fully.

More gunshots were shot aimlessly into the crowd. Jamal shoved me on the floor, and I felt his body weight come on top of me. Shot after shot sprang out and a few bodies dropped only a short distance away from us. As we all laid there on the floor terrified, we watched a man take his last breaths.

The gun ran out of bullets and I was hoisted to my feet and made a mad dash to the exit. Everyone was pushing and shoving to get out and I felt his hand slip out of mine. I searched frantically for him and more gunfire began to go off. Desperately, I tried to fight my way back into the building to get to him, but the crowd wouldn't let me.

Once outside, I frantically searched for my Love, but he was nowhere to be found. Someone grabbed my hand trying to pull me away but when I turned to see who it was, it wasn't a familiar face. They were shaken off as I continued to look at the people who were fleeing for their lives. Heart racing in my chest. Every nerve in my body told me to run away, but I couldn't.

Tears streamed down my face as the crowd slowly began to diminish. A huge weight on my shoulders was relieved when I finally saw his face searching for me too. I ran up to him, grabbing his hand and pulling him away from all the chaos. When we were a good distance away and couldn't run anymore. We stopped and held each other tight and cried for what could have been.

"Why didn't you run Babe?"

"I couldn't leave you behind. I couldn't do it." I cried. "Are you alright?"

"I'm fine. I was so worried about you."

"Me too. What took you so long to come out?" I asked as we began to walk in a direction unknown.

"The crowd. It was crazy." He stopped and looked around. "Where the fuck are we going?"

I looked around too and pointed. "The train station is that way."

"Come on then. Let's get the fuck outta here."

He tugged me along, but I couldn't walk as fast as he needed me to. I wanted to take my shoes off and walk barefoot but that was a big hell no in a big city like this. He eventually stopped and knelt down in front of me.

"Get on."

"What?"

"Get on my back Babe."

Awkwardly, I got on his back and he repositioned me to where we both were comfortable. Somewhat. And we made it to the train station safely where we boarded and headed to the hotel.

When we got back, the room door swung open, and I collapsed hard on the bed after kicking my shoes off. Never the fuck again. Both of us took a shower at the same time but little words were spoken between us for a while. When we got out, our night clothes were put on and I rested back on the bed. A nice foot massage was given to me as I flipped through the channels.

Of course, there was a news story about what had happened at the club. My eyes welled up before tears streamed down my face thinking about the events preceding.

"What's wrong?"

"That man died right in front of us Babe. I watched him die. I was so scared. I don't wanna lose you. And when your hand was snatched from mine." I couldn't even finish my sentence. He came up to where I was, and I buried my face in his chest and let it all out.

"It's ok. I'm right here. Both of us are fine."

"I know." I said in between sobs.

Not another word was spoken about it. I literally cried myself to sleep in his arms and he let me as he rubbed my back gently to help calm me down and settle my nerves.

You Ready?

Due to the fact that the club he was supposed to perform at on Saturday was closed, we decided to head back to the comfort of our homes early. Although I didn't want to get up that early, I was definitely ready to lay in my own bed and hear nothing but quiet and nature sounds outside my windows.

All of our things were packed and before we left for the train station, we stopped to have a bite to eat. The train ride was quiet and thankfully, not too many people bothered us on the way back. Hopefully, it would be the same when we got back to Jersey. I could really use a vacation. One that didn't involve people flocking around us at all times. Was this to be our new norm? No wonder celebrities bark at people. Shit can get aggravating.

Unfortunately, we were swarmed when we got to the New Jersey train station. It was as if they were awaiting our arrival and when we got there, they all cheered and took pictures and videos. There were so many people, the station's security guards had to escort us to our car.

Bags packed in the trunk, we pulled off finally heading home. My hand was held tightly in his the entire ride as I sat back and rested. Relieved that we were in silence again.

He glanced over at me. "How you feeling?"

"Exhausted, but I'm alright. How are you?"

"The same. You look stressed."

"I am a little bit. It's too many people. Too many different energies all at once. It can be overwhelming. I just need to recharge and be in the quiet for a while. All this doesn't bother you?"

"I've had more time to get adjusted to it and when it first started, there weren't this many people. I'm pretty much used to it now. But it can be overwhelming when it's all the time and I don't like that you're stressed about it."

"I'll get over it. Like I said, I just need time to recharge."

"I feel you. We're almost home. I'll give you some space."

"I don't need space from you."

"Oh. Ok." he chuckled.

The rest of the ride was quiet and finally, we pulled into his driveway. He helped me unpack my bags and bring them to my house before doing the same with his things. I stayed home and unpacked and enjoyed the peace of being there. He didn't bother me for the rest of the day as he knew I really did just need a moment to myself.

The rest of my day was filled with cleaning, lounging and watching my shows. Nothing out of the ordinary there. Soon, I found myself fast asleep on the couch.

The next morning I awoke from a phone call. "Hello?"

"Babe, are you up?"

I rubbed my eyes and yawned. "I am now. What's up?"

"I need you to get dressed. I'll be there in a half."

"What? Why?"

"Just get dressed. Love you."

I looked at my phone confused but I did as he requested. I wasn't even sure of what to wear. What was the occasion? A nice pair of jeans and a simple shirt was put on just as a knock on my door came.

"That was not a half hour."

"I know. I missed you tho. You look nice." He said giving me a hug.

"Thank you. I wasn't sure what to wear since you didn't give me details."

"What you have on is fine. You ready?"

"For?"

"You'll see. Come on."

I was escorted to his car, and we drove off to a destination unknown. Although the drive didn't seem long, it seemed a lot longer because I had no idea where we were going. A few times I asked, but he simply smiled and kept his eyes on the road. Occasionally, a soft kiss was placed on the back of my hand that was curled up in his.

We pulled up to a mid-sized house and got out where we were greeted by a woman in a suit. I looked over at him curiously before looking back at the woman.

"Good morning, so glad you could make it. Glad you were able to bring her as well. Are you ready to take a look inside?"

"Yes, please."

"Come on and follow me."

"Babe, what the hell is going on?" I whispered up to him as we made our way to the one-story house. He only responded after we had walked through the open door.

"I'm thinking of buying it to be our studio. It's on a busy road. We can make parking in the back. This part can be your office and back here can be the studio. Take a few walls out and build it how we want to... What do you think?"

I walked around and examined the space trying to envision what it would look like once it was done. It needed a lot of work done to it, but it definitely had potential.

"When did you find this place?"

"Yesterday. It was posted online, and I gave her a call. She has more to show us too. Two more and the prices are reasonable."

"I would assume so, it needs some work."

"Almost everything would have to be redone anyway to open up the floor plan and turn it into a studio."

"How do you both like it so far?"

"I like it, it just needs work."

"Yes, that's why it's on the market for ten thousand less than the original market value."

"Are you ready to see the next one?" he asked.

"Yea, let's go. Is it far?"

"Right around the corner."

"Ok. Let's see it then."

He wasn't lying when he said right around the corner. The door was opened for us to the two-story house and we walked in. As he talked to me, I tried to envision his sight, but I had my own thoughts. This one was in better shape than the other, but it still needed some help.

"What do you think?"

"I like this one better than the other one. It already has an open concept so we wouldn't have to tear walls down. What did you have planned for the upstairs?"

"Make it into a place where we can do photoshoots or video shoots if we want. It could serve as a meeting room or whatever really. Open up the walls…"

I giggled, "What is with you and open concepts? It would be a nice look though if it was open."

"See. Let's go look at the last one. It's much cheaper than all the other ones but it doesn't have an ideal location."

"What's that supposed to mean?"

"It's on a quieter street." he said, tugging me along to the front door."

The last house… Although it had a great layout, I couldn't stay in it for too long. It gave me the creeps but everything in it was new. I waited on the outside until they came back out.

"Is everything alright?" the woman asked.

"I don't like this one. It has bad energy. Something bad happened in there."

"Like what?"

"I don't know, but something dark is in there."

"It's not one of my favorites mainly due to the location, but we won't consider this one if you get a bad vibe from it."

"Ok. That's all of them?"

"Yea. That's all that caught my attention." He turned to the woman. "Thank you for showing us the houses. We'll be in touch when we decide what we're gonna do."

"No problem, you have my number."

She got in the car and drove off and so did we. "Which one did you like the best?"

"I really liked the second one. I could definitely see a studio in there as well as my office, a nice lounge area. Fix up the kitchen a bit. Set the photography studio up. It could be something really great. How much is it?"

"Thirty-two thousand."

"… That's it?"

"Yea. I could ask for thirty and pay it cash."

"It is definitely going to need work."

"So? You act like we don't have money for that either. I was going to put it in both our names."

"You were?"

"You sound surprised."

"A little bit. It's your studio."

"It's our business."

My face scrunched up at him before I smiled and grabbed his hand. "Did you see any others you liked?"

"Not really. Everything else was in a neighborhood or was a rowhome. I wanted something detached so we wouldn't have too many problems with the neighbors."

I nodded my head. "So when are we going to get it?" Realizing this was actually a possibility, I began to grow anxious and excited. "How much do you want me to chip in?"

"Nothing. I got it."

"You do know I have money too."

"I never said you didn't. I'm just saying I got it."

"Ugg. Fine. I'm so excited to get started!"

"I am too. So it's the second one then?"

"Yes!"

"I'll call her later on and we can get things rollin."

"Ahh!"

The Test

A few months had gone by and so many new and exciting things had happened in the short amount of time. We literally blew up. Almost all the songs Jamal submitted were played on every single hip hop and RnB station. They played each song at least twice an hour.

Our fan base was growing and really strong. A few upcoming artists used our songs as covers to get their name out there. Other creatives drew fanart of us, tagged us and still others created their own videos or to simulate ours.

Jamal had gotten me to sing and rap on a lot of his tracks. There were even a few that I was the main singer, and he just did the hook and chorus. Instead of it just being Mally Boy, it turned into Mally Boy and Ximora or Mally Mora as the fans liked to call us.

The song and video we did with Young Kam finally came out and it is currently at fifty million views and still rising. Funny enough, the views on our social media are higher than on his. Everyone loved it and loved the natural chemistry between me and Mal.

Every week we were invited to different podcasts and even had a few interviews on popular tv talk shows. They had reached out to us and how could we say no. We were flown to at least ten different states to do the interviews and we are scheduled to go out of the country to Australia, believe it or not, to do a few interviews there. Who knew our music had gone international?

In between interviews, we would perform at clubs that had invited us to perform at. Yes, I said we. I was basically forced on stage one night and ever since then, you couldn't get me off. The both of us love the adrenaline rush and it being all eyes on us for that time being. We were still working on getting a concert together, but the big-ticket venues were calling us and anxiously waiting for us to let them know when we could do it.

Most important of all, today was the big day we opened up our mini studio. All the construction was complete, and it was exactly what the both of us had envisioned. A nice and relaxed place where artists could come and record music, take head shots and photo ops and network.

We offered services from ghostwriting, beats production, website design, accounting and the legality of being an independent artist. It definitely was a niche market and we definitely capitalized on it. At the way things were growing, this building wouldn't be enough space to accommodate the people we would have to hire to help us run the place. But it would do for now.

I paced back and forth nervously as I waited. I really didn't know what to think or how to feel at this time. I was so nervous, not just for myself, but at what Jamal's reaction was going to be. Were we even ready for this next big step in our lives? Most importantly, was I?

"Are you ready yet?" his voice sprang out from behind the closed door.

"Almost. Give me a minute."

My hands were sweating, and my heart was racing. I hadn't felt this way since the first time I performed months ago. Time was up and I was afraid to look, but I picked up the test and read the results. Positive. Fuck. Yay! But fuck.

Another knock came at the door. "Babe. What the hell? What are you doing?" I slowly opened the door and looked at him with soft eyes. "What the hell?" he barked but changed his tone when he saw the expression on my face. "What's wrong my Love?"

I showed him the test I held in my hand, and he took it from mine. At first he looked at it confused and then his expression changed to pure elation. I was scooped up in his arms and kissed all over.

"You really bout to be my baby mom?"

"Ewl. Don't say it like that."

"I'm gonna be a dad though? Holy shit."

"I know. I'm going to be a mom." The both of us stood there in shock as it really dawned on us that our lives were about to change when we had just hit the peak of our success. At least that's what I thought, but he was elated, nonetheless.

I took a deep breath. "Come on, we still have shit to do. Today is a big day so let's get it done!"

We got in the car and headed over to our studio. When we got there, we could barely find parking. The place was mobbed with people even though we had told only a select few people about the grand opening. Cameras were everywhere snapping pictures and recording video as we walked up to our doors.

"Well, we weren't expecting this many people to arrive, but we do thank you for all your support. This has been a big dream of ours for some time and I'm glad to have it finally come true and now, here we are. I would like to officially announce the grand opening of Mally Mora Studios!" he said, and everyone cheered.

The few people that were actually invited came in and we showed them around. Showed them where they would be working and all the amenities we offered. They were in love with it just like we were, and we could already tell this was going to be a great new adventure. Or was it?

Author Bio

Leaza Norman is from South Carolina but moved to New Jersey and has been there ever since. As early as 2001 she has been writing short stories, poems and lyrics that have eventually led her to writing novels. The first of which is The Hunted: How It Started. Being a hopeless romantic herself, most of the novels and other works she has written have been around love and romance. Most of the characters are put into difficult and even non-traditional situations and must battle with their heart to prevail in the end.